The Kramski Case

James Ward

COOL MILLENNIUM BOOKS

Published in the United Kingdom. All rights reserved. No part of this publication may be reproduced, distributed or transmitted in any form or means, without written permission.

Copyright © James Ward 2012

James Ward has asserted his right to be identified as the author of this Work in accordance with the Copyright, Designs and Patents Act 1988.

This is a work of fiction. All names, characters, and events are the product of the author's imagination, or used fictitiously. All resemblance to actual events, places, events or persons, living or dead, is entirely coincidental.

First published in KDP 2012.
This edition published 2021.

A CIP catalogue record for this book is available from the British Library.

ISBN: 978-1-913851-21-7

Cover picture taken by the author on 5 April 2014: shows the view from Trafalgar Square towards Whitehall.

This book is sold subject to the condition that it shall not, by way of trade or otherwise, be lent, re-sold, hired out or otherwise circulated without the publisher's prior consent in any form of trading or cover other than that in which it is published and without a similar condition including the condition being imposed on the subsequent purchaser.

This novel was produced in the UK and uses British-English language conventions ('authorise' instead of 'authorize', 'The government are' instead of 'the government is', etc.)

To my wife

Chapter 1: Them Ol' Paparazzi Blues

Kendal, Cumbria.

Someone called Jilly's name, then the name of her band, Four Girls on Fire. At first, she thought she was dreaming – they'd just won the nation's biggest talent show all over again, and from now on, life was going to be *really amazing!* - then her stomach turned over.

She disengaged herself from Rob, got out of bed and went to the window. Bloody hell, yes, down in the narrow cobbled street that fronted the guest-house. Paparazzi, sixteen or seventeen of them, all men, full of last night's chip fat and strip-club testosterone, leering up at the net curtain like they could see through it. She swallowed.

The other girls had warned her about dating a member of a boy band, but only tongue in cheek. *Twice the publicity, babes, sure you can handle that?* She couldn't help herself, though. Two years ago he'd been her hero and she'd been a nobody. Now they were equals.

"They've found us," she told him.

Rob stretched and yawned. He discarded the bedclothes, picked up his boxer shorts and put his foot in one leg. "The press?"

"You don't seem very bothered."

"You were bloody brilliant last night, Jilly."

"How did they know we were here?"

"I mean it. Outstanding."

She realised she didn't even like him much. "Did you tell them?"

"Me?"

"Wake up, Rob! It's the press! I said the press have found us!"

He pulled on his boxers and put his arms round her. She disengaged herself, plonked herself at the dressing table and brushed her long brown hair, pulling halfway down as if it was full of knots. She was trying to stop herself shaking.

"Anyone could have told them," he said. "It definitely wasn't me, babe."

"Put your clothes on. We're leaving."

"Why? They can't get in here."

She fished her bra from the pile of clothes on the floor and put it on. "We're in the bloody Lake District, Rob. We're supposed to be miles from anywhere. How did they find us so quickly?"

She looked round the room: the plaid curtains, the beds with valances, the 1920s lampshades, all the varnished wooden surfaces, so unlike the places she always stayed when she was touring with the girls. She'd fallen in love with it at first sight. She'd been drunk, true, but she'd never wanted to leave.

Rob pulled his socks and T-shirt on then looked at her. "You're not frightened, are you?"

"They've probably got the place surrounded. And yes. Yes, I am frightened."

"We'll just call a taxi. We can be downstairs and in the car before anyone knows it."

"I'm not bothered about us, Rob. I'm bothered about them." Tights, tights, where were her bloody tights?

"'Them'?"

"Yeah, 'them'. The photographers, journalists, whatever they call themselves. Them!"

He laughed. "First time anyone's cared what happens to paparazzi. Anyway, what could happen to them?"

"Haven't you been watching the news recently? Are you really that self-obsessed?"

"Hey, now - "

"Four photographers shot dead in four weeks. Following Bobby Keynes, Zane Cruse, Mikey from Bad Lads Zero, Stallone Laine - "

"No such thing as bad publicity, from what I hear. Not that you need it, girl, but it won't hurt. Besides, they're all douche bags, right?"

She pulled her dress on and smoothed the waist. She'd had enough now. She wanted out. Of everything. "I misjudged you, Rob. They're still human beings."

"No, they ain't. Anyway, what are the chances?"

"I don't want to think about it."

He picked up the telephone. "Is that reception? Hi, yeah … Room …"

"Fourteen," Jilly said.

"Fourteen. Could you get a taxi pronto for me and the shorty? And fetch us the bill for the room? … Yeah, we're leaving … Yeah, all good things have to come to an end sooner or later … Yeah, we're disappointed too." He put his hand over the receiver. "She knows us," he told Jilly. "It'll be her that told the reporters."

"Bitch."

He put the phone down. "About fifteen minutes. Get your face on, gorgeous."

"I'm not waiting for her taxi to come, Rob. Not if she's with them. I'll get my own. There's a rank down the road. Come on."

"What about your make-up?"

She rammed a pair of sunglasses on and picked up her travel bag. He followed her downstairs. They didn't stop at reception. Rob reached into his wallet, pulled out four fifties and thrust them at Mrs whatever-she-was-called, the proprietress. "Keep the change."

Suddenly, they were out on the street. Paparazzi to their right, shouting Jilly. Jilly take off your shades, Jilly flick your hair, Jilly wave, Jilly smile, Jilly stop, who's that with Jilly, that's Rob from Simply Boyz, Rob give us a smile, Rob –

She took off her glasses, grabbed Rob's hand and turned left and accelerated. She almost changed direction. There was a loud crack and she jumped like she'd been hit.

Behind them, the paparazzi roared. One of them – a photographer, about twenty-five - lay prostrate and bloody. Four others photographed him, ten or twelve were in full flight, one was trying to get a signal on his mobile. No one was interested in Jilly and Rob any more.

Rob looked at them then at her. "Oh, my God. Oh, my God."

Jilly started screaming.

Solikamsk Prison, the Urals.

Colonel Orlov came in looking lean and muscular. Bald, sunken eyes, sinewy hands. Much as Deputy Commissioner Khrantsov had been told to expect: like a skull on the body of a statue. He was forty-three, but he looked older from the neck up, younger from the neck down. He wore the regulation prison outfit: coarse grey jacket and trousers, white vest, black boots.

He sat at the table, straightened his back and flattened his hands on the Formica surface. Above him a single strip light buzzed and flickered. The walls were grey plaster, never painted. A patch showed where the portrait of Brezhnev had once hung.

Commissioner Khrantsov, ten years younger than the convict, with a shelf of blond hair and hard Kamchatka eyes, removed his greatcoat and bearskin hat to reveal an expensive blue suit, and sat leisurely opposite him. He nodded for the guard to wait outside.

"I've read a lot about you," he said when they were alone.

"I haven't the inclination to play games with the FSB. Either tell me what you want or leave me alone."

Khrantsov lit a cigarette and leaned back. "I'm not in the FSB."

"I've no means of verifying who you are or aren't, so once again, why not just come to the point?"

"We've looked after you well while you've been in prison."

"'We'."

"And I'm here to tell you you'll soon be released."

"After I've done one year of a twenty-five year sentence."

"You've got a lot of friends in high places, Colonel Orlov, and they think your country needs you."

"I'm in here for treason, tell them."

Khrantsov smiled. "Thank you. Like I said a moment ago, I've read your files."

"These 'friends in high places', they wouldn't happen to have names, would they?"

Khrantsov ignored him. He took a small gift-wrapped box from his pocket and pushed it across the table. "This is for you."

Orlov looked at it then opened it. A chess set. His chess set. He slid back the lid and took the thirty-two pieces out, spacing them equally for a full minute till they were all accounted for. He looked at Khrantsov. "Where did you get it?"

"I understand it was stolen from you two days ago."

Orlov gathered the pieces and dropped them back in the box. "And how did it find its way into your hands?"

"As I said earlier, we're looking after you. The thief's being raped and beaten as we speak. It won't happen again."

Orlov's expression filled with contempt. He pushed the container back across the table.

"Joke, Colonel, relax. Can't you take a joke?"

It remained in the middle of the table. Khrantsov sighed. "If you ever hear of anyone being maltreated on behalf of your precious chess set then, yes, I'm with the FSB. Which I'm not."

Orlov hesitated then retrieved it.

Khrantsov smiled. "Every man has his weakness, Colonel. Yours is your intellect. If we were other than we are, we might wish for something a little more malleable. But we aren't."

"When are 'we' going to secure my release?"

"I'm only here to tell you to be ready when the call comes. It'll seem trivial. Don't despise it."

"Community service, you mean."

"Not exactly. You're going to England in the first instance."

"England?"

"That's right. We'd hardly send you to England if we were FSB now, would we?"

"What's in England?"

Khrantsov ground his cigarette into the floor and stood up. "It was a pleasure meeting you, Colonel."

2 Marsham Street, Westminster.

The Home Secretary's office epitomised tidiness, polished walnut and the cultural triumph of the desk. Three floors below, men in yellow jackets with drills dug the road and the traffic was at a standstill, but the soundproofing in here was so complete you could hardly hear it. The Metropolitan Police Commissioner, Sir Colin Bowker, came in holding his cap and waited to be asked to sit on the chair obviously reserved for him.

The Home Secretary, already seated, donned his glasses and leaned forward. His spiky hair, long eyes and hawk nose all seemed drawn to a point ready to poleaxe his visitor. Sir Colin was much slighter and in his retirement year. He guessed he didn't cut much of a retaliatory figure. But he had his stratagems. It was just a case of deploying them in the right order.

"Sit down, sit down," the Home Secretary said. "I take it you've seen the papers?"

"For what it's worth, yes. I have."

"'Serial killer'? 'Police apathy'? 'Amnesty International expresses concern'?"

Sir Colin brushed his right cuff. "We went through this a week ago. Up until Tuesday hardly anyone gave a damn. Because the fifth victim happens to be Harriet Johnson's nephew, all hell's been let loose. The truth is, I've got officers working on it flat out. Any 'apathy' has been the media's not ours."

"You've been lucky so far. The press has been itching to make more of this since day one, but they know they've got their work cut out drumming up public sympathy for gutter rats. Now Harriet's on board, though, they're on a roll. And *I* don't bloody deserve it."

Sir Colin chuckled. "Have you told the Secretary of State for Education you think her nephew's a gutter rat?"

"I didn't drag you here to bandy witticisms, Colin. I want to know how far you've got. If anywhere."

"We've made a lot of progress, actually."

"Amaze me."

"I've come up with a plan to take the heat off."

The Home Secretary sighed through his teeth. "Perhaps you'd be good enough to tell me what it is. I'm not in the mood for teasers."

"Firstly, we've been in contact with Interpol. I know what you're thinking. Whose bright idea was that? My reaction too. I'll come to that in a minute. Anyway, it turns out to have been very germane."

"You mean – what? - there have been similar crimes, elsewhere?"

"About a year ago. Four in the USA, within the space of about a month. And another five in Russia, of all places."

"So someone's been killing paparazzi in three countries."

"It seems so," Sir Colin said.

"A copycat, you mean … or copycats?"

"There's a ballistics match. The same make of weapon. None of that's public knowledge."

"You're saying it's the same culprit?"

"Or group of culprits."

The Home Secretary looked hard at his own reflection in the desk. "I can imagine a murderer operating in the USA, say, then coming to Britain to continue the slaughter when the net starts closing in. But Russia? Why Russia?"

"We don't know."

"I mean, did it begin in Russia? Is it a Russian weapon we're talking about?"

"I see where you're going. Russian murderer, starts domestic then branches out, goes international. But the first murder was in the USA, only a few hours before the Russian one. There wasn't time for a single murderer to get from one location to the other."

"So how? I'm a busy man, spell it out for me."

"Possibly some sort of internet cult. That's speculation, of course."

"Look, I'll be blunt, Colin. I've a cabinet meeting in fifteen minutes. Harriet Johnson's going to chase me down the corridor with a cricket bat if you haven't got something better than 'speculation'."

"We're creating a special unit."

"Details."

"Three persons. One British, one American, one Russian. We each put up a third of the cost."

"And the Americans and the Russians have agreed to that, yes?"

"The US Department of Justice has already named its man. We're waiting to hear from the Russians."

"Who's our man? I mean, rank? What's he do?"

"He's an Inspector. You might know him. Hartley-Brown."

"No relation, surely?"

"His son."

The Home Secretary laughed. "Sons, nephews, whatever next? Is he any good?"

"A bit wet by all accounts but exceptionally good at putting two and two together. A First in Computing and Electronics. Very good at searching information for patterns, that sort of thing."

The Home Secretary pinched his chin. "What my granddaughters would probably call a 'geek', I suppose."

"It'll get Harriet Johnson and the papers off our backs. Next time she decides to chase someone down the corridor, it'll be the Shadow Foreign Secretary. In any case, I don't expect there will be any more shootings. There were four in the USA and five in Russia. We've had our quota. If I'm right, and I usually am, the murderer's already looking to move on."

"Let's hope so. I'm not sure it's the point."

"These things tend to follow patterns."

"Who are the Americans sending? Just out of interest?"

"A 'Lieutenant Detective Commander' from the New York City Police Department, name of David Bronstein. Brilliant investigator, by all accounts."

The Home Secretary sighed. "Let's hope so, for your sake as well as mine. There's a very low limit to how stupid I'm prepared to look in public."

Yekaterinberg, the Urals.

Khranstov's office was carpeted and freshly painted, with a dado rail that ran the perimeter halfway up. In the middle of the wall, facing the desk, hung a picture of a woman, barely more than a teenager, with blonde hair and a long coat, presenting something to a much older man. Vera Gruchov. The man was Khrantsov himself.

Rostov entered with his cap under his arm and came to attention. Khrantsov swivelled on his chair and spread his hands. "Well?"

"It's just been confirmed."

"When?"

"A week today. Eleven hundred hours."

"Does Colonel Orlov know?"

"Excuse me, sir, but I understood you'd already informed him."

"I told him to expect it," Khrantsov said. "I mean, he needs to know when."

"I'll send word to the prison authorities."

"He needs to be prepared. Make sure he's got an Ots-33 and sufficient ammunition. And a light aircraft. If we can get him out of the country, we'll drop him in Minsk and he can proceed by commercial flight from there."

"'If'? You mean there's a chance he might not make it?"

"His enemies have been trying to get him released from prison for months. They know we've got him covered in there. Once he's free, he's entirely in the open. Do you really think we could have secured his release without their cooperation?"

"I hadn't thought about it."

Khrantsov shook his head. "You'll never get promoted if you don't learn to look ahead, Alexei."

"What do you think his chances are?"

"Of making it out of the country alive? Not even fifty per cent. But we can't keep him locked away for ever. We need him."

"Do the British know he's coming?"

"Not yet. It seems pointless telling them, given how precarious it all is."

"What will we do if he doesn't make it? Send someone else?"

"I don't know. All I know is that the situation over there's more complex than the British can possibly imagine. It's not remotely what they take it for."

Chapter 2: Air Rage

David Bronstein arrived at Heathrow carrying the wallet of papers he'd been instructed to read *en route* and a disordered copy of *The Independent*. He was thirty-two, stocky, clean-shaven, with heavy glasses and a skull-cap. A pair of unkempt eyebrows and scuffed shoes seemed to unite his upper and lower extremities, giving him the aura of a distressed scholar. He wore a black blazer.

Beneath an electronic billboard, just to the right of the benches, he caught sight of a young man in a bespoke suit with his hands folded behind his back. Definitely the guy in the photo he'd been given. Their eyes locked and they gripped hands.

"David Bronstein, Lieutenant Commander, NYPD."

"Jonathan Hartley-Brown, Metropolitan Police Inspector."

Hartley-Brown was a good two inches taller than most men, and according to Bronstein's notes, twenty-four. He had brown hair with a side parting, well-proportioned facial features and shiny brogues with grey socks.

They exchanged half-hearted quips about transatlantic flights, sent Bronstein's luggage ahead and installed themselves on the back seat of a pre-paid London cab. As per protocol, they spoke about the weather and the traffic till it reached Scotland Yard, where they disembarked in a drizzly mist. Hartley-Brown gave the driver a tip. Then they took the lift to an open-plan office to examine two forlorn-looking faux-pine desks with matching PCs and an inch-high midway fence to curb proliferating untidiness. Secretaries, photocopiers, and softly ringing telephones surrounded them as far as the eye could see.

"My apologies for the world's greatest anti-climax," Hartley-Brown said. "You can take either one. I'm not fussy."

"Any progress on the case?"

"Not yet. I was only informed I was being deployed last night and my brief today is to help you settle in. I believe we're simply supposed to spend time getting to know each other."

"Yeah, that's what *I* was told."

"I'll show you your flat next and we can eat a meal, then go to a bar or a West End musical or whatever you prefer. All expenses paid. Work begins in earnest tomorrow at eight am sharp, so I suppose we'd better not burn too much midnight oil."

Bronstein smiled. He could tell Hartley-Brown didn't buy the 'bonding' crap, either, and just wanted to get started. Which meant they were going to hit it off. "It's 'Johnny', yeah?"

"Jonathan. But you can call me that."

"'Hartley-Brown'. Your parents are divorced?"

"Not last time I checked. It's an old family name."

"Some kind of peers of the realm, then."

"Well, not in this generation but - "

"My dad's a Hasidic rabbi, incidentally. See this?" He twiddled a tassel sticking out from his belt. "This is in deference to him, although I'm not that heavily into it myself. You ever heard of a tallith?"

"A Jewish prayer shawl, yes. While we're on the subject of fathers, mine's the Shadow Foreign Secretary. Thought I'd better say early since you'd have found that out soon enough anyway. I've overheard people say I wouldn't be more than a sergeant now otherwise."

"Sheesh, you don't believe them, do you?"

"I don't beat myself up over it. Everyone's born with advantages. You've just got to do the best in the position you've been given. I do try hard. I am dedicated."

"Good enough for me. What side's your dad on, just out of interest?"

You probably haven't heard of the Conservative Party much in America - "

"The Republicans writ small, yeah?"

"I don't know about that. He's called Sir Anthony Hartley-Brown."

"Doesn't ring a bell. Still, a 'sir', eh? How long till the next election?"

"Nine weeks max."

"Impressed. You're son of the future king, then."

"My mother asked me to invite you to dinner, by the way."

Bronstein smiled. "So you told her about me, huh?" He ran his finger across the desk to check for dust.

"Not in any detail. I simply told her you were coming from America. She thought a traditional family meal might make you feel more welcome."

"That sure is good of her. I'm touched. I mean it."

"Is a week next Monday all right?"

He laughed. Jonathan certainly didn't believe in beating about the bush. "Apart from the little matter of the investigation, I'm free for the foreseeable. But what does one wear for a sir?"

"My parents are a little old fashioned. Maybe an evening suit?"

Bronstein raised his eyebrows. "A tux? I haven't brought one."

"I could lend you my spare."

"How tall are you?"

"Six foot two."

"Shame. I'm five-eleven."

"Actually, that's ... good. That's just fine. Stay here."

Hartley-Brown walked to the other end of the floor, weaving between yucca plants and desks with miniature teddy bears on, and disappeared behind a panel. He returned with a black-haired man of about his own age, in a brown suit. "This is the fellow you're replacing," he announced. "Nicholas Fleming of CID. Nicholas, this is David Bronstein from the NYPD. David, Nicholas has been looking forward to meeting you for obvious reasons."

Fleming looked considerably more rugged than Jonathan. He took Bronstein's hand in what felt like the first move of an arm-wrestle and shook it hard. "It's you I've to thank for my secondment to New York, then? I'm leaving tomorrow. I've always been a bit of an Americanophile so I'm really looking forward to it."

"Glad to be of service," Bronstein said. "You'd better not be much of a cop, mind, because I'd like them to miss me."

Fleming grinned. "I'm honoured they even consider it a fair swap. My best friend tells me you're in need of an evening suit, by the way, and we look about the same size. I'll drop mine off at his place before I go to the airport. Least I can do."

"Thanks."

"The chef's excellent, incidentally, and Jonathan's parents are charming. Watch his sister doesn't sweep you off your feet, though."

"Bit of a knockout, huh?"

He glanced at his watch. "You'll have to excuse me now, I'm afraid. I've a fair amount of work to catch up on before I leave. Good meeting you."

"Nicholas and I did two years on the beat together," Hartley-Brown said when Fleming had gone. "He was in the Coldstream Guards for three years before that. You mustn't mind what he says about Marcie. He was in love with her at one point."

"What happened? If that's not too personal a question?"

"I don't think he was her type. She calls him 'Mr Brown' because he's always wearing brown suits." He sighed. "I know. It's not much of a joke."

"Sorry to change the subject," Bronstein said, "but aren't we supposed to be a three-man unit? I was told to expect a Russian."

"They may be sending one. Nothing's been finalised. It's why the dinner invite's a week next Monday, sorry to harp on about that. Just in case we need to set another place at the table."

"Who's in charge? You, me or him?"

"It could be a 'her', for all we know. I don't think any of us is strictly 'in charge'. I'm supposed to coordinate the investigation."

"So if we both want to, say, take a certain detail, you get to decide who goes, yeah?"

"I suppose so."

Bronstein frowned. "That's all I need to know."

"I'd probably send you. It makes things easier to coordinate if you don't rub people up the wrong way."

He smiled. He'd forgotten, this was a nice guy. "From what I read on the plane over, the Met's identified a number of paparazzi who were at the scene of each crime. I've a list of twenty-three. You know about that, right?"

"It sounds as if we've both been given the same prep."

"Prep?"

"Homework. Background reading."

"Anyway, the cops will already have spoken to a lot of them, but it looks as good a place to start as any."

"We'll split the names tonight, if you like, then we can get straight onto it tomorrow morning."

"And meet back at the office seventeen hundred hours tomorrow, yeah? Swap tales?"

"Done. Shall I show you your flat now?"

Orlov left the prison two hours before schedule by a side entrance, bypassing the usual homily from the governor and the paperwork at reception. He went straight to an unmarked Mercedes. The driver took him across the river Kama and transferred him to a ZiL at Teterina. His new driver gave him a trench coat to change into and sped him to Efremy, where he changed cars and drivers again. Half an hour later, his car pulled to a stop on a straight road edged with pines and piles of chopped timber.

The driver opened and closed his door for him and walked in front. They passed through six or seven rows of trees and emerged onto a makeshift airstrip, surrounded on all sides by forest. A Technoavia crouched at the far end with its propeller roaring.

Khrantsov stood to one side with a group of soldiers who smoked and blew on their hands. From the look of the clouds above, a heavy snowfall was in the offing.

"Best of luck," Khrantsov said. "We've supplied you with a gun and several rounds of ammunition in case you meet with ... obstacles *en route*. If you give them to the pilot when you land we'll see you're reunited with them in England."

Orlov looked to the sky. There were two other light aircraft already airborne, several hundred feet overhead. SP-91s, apparently circling.

"Anything to worry about?" he asked.

"We don't think so. In any case, you should be able to outrun them."

"I understand I'm to be investigating the deaths of newspaper photographers," Orlov replied contemptuously.

"Beggars can't be choosers. The important thing is to get you out of Russia."

"And then?"

"We've devoted a lot of time and money to keeping you safe in prison. If the liberal cause is ever going to succeed in this country, organisations like ours need to utilise their resources more efficiently."

"I didn't need to be looked after. I'm quite capable of taking care of myself."

"We understand that. We didn't like to take any chances."

"I take it you expect me to defect once I'm in Britain?"

"That's an anachronistic term, but there are equivalents. It would solve an awful lot of problems."

"Forget it."

"You once wanted to do some good, as I recall. You can remain loyal to that, or you can be the quintessential pig-headed patriot with a death wish."

"If I defect, I'll look like a traitor. It'll play straight into their hands."

"Applying for asylum was what we were thinking."

Orlov laughed. "Britain's got more immigrants than it knows what to do with. Do you think for a moment they'll give me a second look?"

"You could be very useful to them."

"As a defector. That will be top of their terms and conditions."

"We're wasting time, Colonel. Go."

Orlov put his hat on and walked to the plane. He climbed into his seat and they took off, clearing the tops of the trees with inches to spare. They banked and headed West.

"I'm Cherepnev," the pilot said, turning to face him with his hand extended. A young man of about twenty-three, dark hair, thin, with a goatee. "If you feel like smoking, there are some cigarettes and a lighter under the dash."

Orlov shook hands. "I take it that means you want to."

"Not necessarily. It's against regulations."

"I was told there was a gun and some ammunition on board."

Cherepnev handed him a new Ots-33. "The bullets are on the rear seat."

Orlov removed his seat-belt and leaned over the back. The plane listed slightly.

"Don't do that!" Cherepnev said.

There was a curtain covering the ammunition. Orlov pulled it back to find a crate of vodka and a bundle of pornographic magazines. The ammunition was on the floor.

Cherepnev was blushing. "I'm not smuggling any of that, really. It's for my own personal use."

Suddenly, they saw something they weren't expecting. Eight or nine ad hoc airstrips in forest clearings almost identical to the one they had left, each giving birth to a plane in flight.

"I take it you weren't anticipating this," Orlov said.

"We're going to have to change direction."

There were six aircraft in the sky now, and no sooner had they turned about than they encountered a new contingent emerging from the miles of foliage below.

"You're going to have to try and land," Orlov said.

"How?"

"I doubt they'll try to kill me here. If they're who I think they are, they'll want to ensure I suffer."

"Who do you think they are?"

Orlov grinned. "FSB, KGB, Spetsnaz, what's the difference?"

"I thought the KGB didn't exist any more."

"Oh, we all thought that ... ten years ago."

Suddenly, gunfire. They felt the fuselage fill with punctures and Cherepnev took the plane into a dive. When it righted, they were fully surrounded. Orlov wondered if he could take the controls if Cherepnev was killed. He tried to remember what to do. He couldn't.

The air was full of the sound of shot now, like crackling in an oven. Four or five planes appeared heading straight at them. They went into a loop and started to descend.

"Call to ground," Orlov said. "See if you can get Khrantsov."

"He must know. He must be watching. What can he possibly do?"

Orlov grabbed the radio. "Khrantsov, can you hear me?"

"We've called for assistance," came Khrantsov's voice. "Try to stay airborne, Colonel. Don't land unless you absolutely have to. Repeat - "

Orlov wondered what Khrantsov thought 'assistance' was. A few conscripts firing in the air with training rifles, probably. The SP-91s had grouped now. Three broke off from the main body to spearhead the attack.

"Take us down as close to the trees as you can," Orlov said.

They dived and levelled out just above the pines. The three pursuers followed them. Orlov saw their planes weren't equipped with guns; instead, men leant out of the windows discharging pistols. It was the sort of thing someone might have dreamed up during a heavy drinking session. The way they were shooting, it was probably still going on. He reached for his ammunition feeling a lot less anxious. Then he turned the vodka crate upside-down, dispatching the bottles onto the floor.

"Hey, what are you doing?" Cherepnev yelled.

"Bring us up a bit."

"How much?"

"Enough to be able to fly with your nearside wing down thirty degrees for a bit. I need to see past the tail."

Orlov slid the passenger door open. He looked behind and tossed the crate high enough to clear their own tail. It hit the wing of the plane behind to their right, but hardly made it swerve. Meanwhile, they were rising. The three planes on their tail began to follow them.

"Bank it," Orlov said.

He loaded his pistol and leaned out. He could see between the vertical fin and the elevator now.

"Right a bit!" he shouted.

Suddenly, the middle of the three planes came into view. First the wing tips, then the landing gear and finally the cabin. He took aim and fired. He saw the pilot snap into inactivity. The plane veered and hit its neighbour and the two fell into the forest and fired a plume of flame into the air, way behind.

"See if you can get the third underneath us!" Orlov shouted.

Given what the other plane had just seen, he calculated the pilot would panic and try to take evasive action. With Orlov above him he'd descend without thinking. As soon Cherepnev had executed the manoeuvre, the third plane hit the trees. It somersaulted and burst into flames, narrowly missing the Technoavia. Cherepnev pulled into a sharp ascent.

"I may need a cigarette," he said.

Five other planes were arriving to resume the attack.

"Where's the fuel tank?" Orlov shouted.

"In the back."

"Have we got access to it?"

"Not unless you pull out the rear seats."

"How secure are they?"

"This is a new plane. Bloody hell."

"What's the matter?"

"You may *have* to access it now, if we're to stay afloat. It's been punctured. We're losing fuel."

"Problem solved. Your vodka, is it good?"

"What are you talking about?"

Orlov leaned out of the door again. He could see where the leak was. Perfect. Behind them, six planes fired erratically.

He thrust his gun in his pocket and scooped up a handful of bullets. Stones would have been preferable but if he remembered his Galileo aright, it wouldn't matter, providing he adjusted his pitch sufficiently. He threw the first and it didn't even clear the tail. The second went straight over the cabin of the pursuer. He could see the pilot laughing. The third hit his propeller.

He went back inside. When he emerged again, it was with a three-quarters full vodka bottle with a burning scroll in. He gauged its weight with a few gentle shakes then cast it.

"Accelerate," he told Cherepnev.

The bottle exploded on the propeller of the plane behind and the flames were sucked deep into its engine. The fuel Orlov's plane was losing and the fuel in the SP-91's own tank combined to create a fireball that engulfed all six pursuers almost simultaneously.

Orlov looked at the remains of the glossy magazine he'd just dismembered. 'Red Hot Women'. "How long before we have to land?"

"A couple of miles. How many more planes are there?"

Orlov scanned the skies. "Three, eleven o'clock."

But ahead of them, they could already see the forest producing new SP-91s. One … two, three, four …

They gave up counting at twelve.

Suddenly, a dark speck appeared close to the horizon, getting bigger as they watched, emitting an increasing growl. A squadron of fighter jets, Su-37s.

Cherepnev laughed hysterically. "They'd better be on our side."

Orlov picked up the receiver. "Khrantsov?"

"I told you you had friends in high places," Khrantsov said.

Suddenly, the SP-91s were in full retreat without a shot being fired. The jets shepherded them away, criss-crossing each other's paths until the sky was clear again. Then they regrouped and diminished until they were a dot on the horizon.

Below the Technoavia, the forest thinned and gave way to farmland.

"We're losing altitude," Cherepnev said.

"Proceed due northeast to Shchekino," Khranstsov said. "We'll patch you up there."

Sir Colin put his hat on the Home Secretary's coffee table again and sat down. The PA brought in two cups of Darjeeling on a tray.

"You sounded rather upset on the phone," the Home Secretary said. "I'd have ordered something stronger, but it's not the time of day. What's the problem?"

"We've had word from the Russians. They've chosen their man."

"Oh?"

"Colonel Sergei Orlov."

The Home Secretary stroked his chin and looked up. "Rings a bell. I've heard that name."

"The wrong man for the job on so many levels."

"Who is he?"

"A dissident ... of sorts. In prison for treason until a week ago. But he's obviously been given a second chance."

"You think he's here on an information gathering exercise?"

"I've been in contact with MI6. There's some sort of power struggle going on in the Kremlin. One of those periodic spats where the left hand doesn't know what the right's doing. Someone over there's telling us to put him in charge of the investigation, someone else is telling us to deliver him up to the embassy as soon as his feet touch the ground."

The Home Secretary smiled and sipped his tea. "These things have a habit of working themselves out. Can't we just wait to see which faction wins and deal with the matter accordingly? We don't want to put the Russians' backs up."

"He's been in intelligence. If he's here to spy on us, I'd rather not have the responsibility."

"You invited this, Colin. You proposed the idea of a Russian-American-British team. You should probably have anticipated it."

"That they'd try to exploit it? No, I didn't."

"Tell me who he is again."

"He was involved with the investigative journalist, Anna Politkovskaya. Remember Anna Politkovskaya? Assassinated in Moscow in 2006. She uncovered a host of systematic abuses in the army, and five and a half million square miles of regional and central government corruption."

"Involved romantically?"

"No, politically. Orlov worked in the Special Intelligence Regiment of the Ministry of Defence. He helped bring several of the worst offenders to trial, and he's supposed to have established a secret network of politicians, humanitarians and high-ranking military personnel pledged to bring the army under the control of the civilian executive."

"Sounds like a noble fellow."

"Apparently he prepared a dossier of hitherto unknown abuses that would have been dynamite had it found its way to the right authorities. He was arrested shortly before Politkovskaya's murder and it never came to light. And only he knows who's in the secret organisation."

"Don't they inject people with truth-drugs and that sort of thing once they've been arrested over there?"

"If they do, they didn't work."

"Well, I like the sound of him. I didn't get involved in politics to send men like him to their deaths. If he makes it here, he's staying, understand?"

"I wouldn't be too hasty."

"Sometimes I like to do things hastily. I do still have gut reactions. Believe it or not, Colin, I used to be an idealist."

"MI6 seems to think he might be a plant."

"Meaning?"

"That he might have realised the 'error' of his ways; that maybe he's reached an accord with his former enemies and they're offering him some sort of rehabilitation in return for favours."

"Spying on us, you mean."

"Treason's a fairly serious charge when you're as devoted to your country as he apparently is. You might do anything to clear your name. Especially after a year in Solikamsk prison with another twenty-four to go."

"Come on, Colin. It's Scotland Yard you're running. What's he going to spy on? UK crime statistics?"

"You know as well as I do that we've been working much more closely with the Secret Intelligence Service since 7/7."

The Home Secretary drained his cup. "Yes, yes, fair enough."

"What do you recommend?"

"Keep in touch with SIS. We'll give him the benefit of the doubt for now. And keep me informed."

Chapter 3: The Curse of Gnome

It was the Daily Express building that Bronstein wanted, and he was prepared to stand outside it all day if necessary. The honking traffic echoed between the London Rehearsal Rooms and the Britannia Hotel and on Lower Thames Street people scurried unseeingly to work with jackets draped over cuffs and Smartphones to ears.

He took the stairs and arrived on the fourth floor just in time. In a busy, parquet-floored corridor with fire doors leading left and right and phones bleeping and people shouting, Garvey Simpson stood before the elevator with his hands in his pockets. He wore a short sleeved shirt, chinos and trainers. He had a pair of sunglasses perched in his hair, although the sun wasn't shining outside. Bronstein waited for the lift to arrive and got in beside him.

"What floor?" Simpson asked.

"I need to ask you some questions."

"What do you mean?"

"You were there when Jerry Cauldwell was killed, yes? The photographer?"

Simpson scowled and pressed Ground. "Is this for a features article? Because I charge."

Bronstein showed his card.

"I've already spoken to the police," Simpson said.

"Speak again."

"I'm busy. Can't we do this another time?"

"You kept any pictures of that day?"

"Nope."

Bronstein followed him through the foyer and back into the city bustle. Commuters and shoppers brushed past, taxis and red double-deckers blared their horns, the air smelt of diesel and dust.

"You're the seventh photographer I've spoken to who was there at one of those murders," Bronstein said. He had to walk quickly to keep up with him. "Not one of you kept any pictures. To anyone else in my position, that might appear suspicious."

"So arrest me."

"Let's say, for the sake of argument, I was doing a features article. How much would you charge?"

Simpson smirked. "Two hundred thousand, up front."

"You must have some pretty decent information."

"Maybe I'm just a good poker player."

"A man who claims to have information of that quality is probably worth arresting."

"I've sued for wrongful arrest before. And won."

"My, another bluff?"

"That's for you to judge."

Bronstein removed a wad of stills from his pocket. "I've been doing a little photographing of my own. Have a look at these."

Simpson flicked through them. "Pictures of me at a bar with a hot chick," he said, pretending to yawn. "Boy, the features editors will be climbing over themselves to get hold of these."

"The girl you're talking to. Know her?"

"A girl."

Bronstein smiled. "Only, she's a reporter for *Private Eye*."

"So the hell what?"

"Let me join the dots for you, then. A: You've just come out of the Daily Express building. B: The Daily Express is owned by Richard Desmond. C: Richard Desmond's one of *Private Eye*'s most vilified targets, and someone keeps telling *Private Eye* all about him. Stuff that really shouldn't get out, embarrassing stuff. 'Dirty Des', they call him. D: If Mr Desmond were to see these photos of you talking to Miss - "

Simpson had turned pale. "He might draw the wrong conclusion."

"And you might find it difficult to get paid."

"Look, if I tell you what you want to know, will you promise to destroy them?"

"Better than that. I'll let you have the camera."

Half an hour later they sat in a bar on Gracechurch Street where a handful of early morning customers – mainly women - sat on padded benches against the wall with coffees and phones or copies of *Metro*, listening to Susan Boyle on the jukebox. Faded watercolours in gilt frames hung on maroon wallpaper. Bronstein ordered a Martini, shaken not stirred. Simpson tore open a packet of crisps and ate them singly in between gulps of Strongbow.

"Given that a man died," Simpson said, "no one wanted a still of Jilly Bestwick teetering away in a pair of Jimmy Choos trailing 'Rob from Simply Boyz'. It seemed disrespectful. Or at least it was thought that's how it would be perceived by the punters."

"So you simply trashed those pictures?"

"Deleted them, yeah."

"Even before the police had time to arrive?"

"I haven't time to get involved in a pig investigation. I've got work."

"And you all felt that way?"

"It wasn't a conspiracy, if that's what you're saying. More like great minds think alike."

Bronstein shook his head incredulously. "It didn't occur to you that by scrapping your pictures you'd be helping the murderer? Of your colleague?"

"I guess it might have. To some of us."

"Did it to you?"

Simpson grimaced as if he didn't like looking too hard at himself. "Look, you've got to remember that most of us are drunk most of the time. We don't always do the most ... sane thing."

"Were you drunk?"

"Sort of."

"Did you tell the police?"

"They didn't ask. What difference would it make? They're our pictures. If we're destroying evidence, we might conceivably be guilty of a crime. If we're destroying it under the influence of booze, we might just as conceivably be let off on the grounds of diminished responsibility. Unless it's a crime to be drunk at ten in the morning."

"Even so: your colleague?"

"I didn't know him. He was a rival."

"You're saying you were pleased by his death?"

Simpson shrugged. "I guess I'd have preferred it if he'd just been maimed or something like that. Something that meant he couldn't take photos any more."

Bronstein shook his head. "Hot diggity, now that's compassion."

"I happen to know that some of my 'colleagues', as you keep calling them, were pleased by his death."

"On the grounds that he's a rival."

"Nothing personal, that's correct. I'm hardly the worst of them."

"Hasn't it occurred to any of you that you might be next?"

"Like I said earlier, most of us are poker players. And the odds are pretty good. Say the murderer turns up at every twentieth photo-op. Individually, we only attend one in every three. Each time, there's roughly sixteen of us. That's odds of about a thousand to one against."

Bronstein's mobile rang. He picked up, as glad of the interruption as if he was coming up for air.

"Where are you?" Hartley-Brown said.

"I'm doing an interview. Garvey Simpson."

"Bring him in. I think I've found something. And his life might be in danger."

Bronstein ended the call and leaned over to Simpson. "If I buy you something nice to drink on the way, would you mind accompanying me to the police station?"

Bronstein left Simpson in the waiting room, with instructions to the WPC in charge not to allow him to leave. Hartley-Brown was stationed at his computer. Around him, a hundred men and women sat working at desks or carrying documents. Rain slapped against the tinted windows.

"Early this morning," he said, "I went round to James Docherty's flat in Islington. Initially, he was reluctant, but he decided to cooperate when I showed him the 'Lady from Lord Gnome' photos we mocked up. Even so, he didn't make an awful lot of sense. He'd drunk half a bottle of Courvoisier for breakfast and the other half for lunch, and he was about ready for bed. Ten minutes in, he went to the toilet and when, half an hour later, he still hadn't reappeared, I thought I'd better check on him. He'd fallen asleep in the bath. I tried, but I couldn't wake him."

"So what did you do? Call an ambulance?"

"Eventually, but not until I'd copied the contents of his hard drive."

"Attaboy. And?"

"Case solved, I think."

"Go on."

Hartley-Brown plugged a USB pen into his computer. "Docherty told me he'd deleted all his photos. Not true. And, from what I've been able to piece together so far, neither did any of his friends."

The phone on Hartley-Brown's desk buzzed. He looked at his watch and picked up. "Hello? ... Yes ... Thank you." He listened for another thirty seconds, said 'thank you' again and hung up.

"News?" Bronstein said.

"Our Russian is about to arrive. Name of Colonel Sergei Orlov. We're to meet him at Heathrow in just over an hour. I'll tell you the rest as we drive over."

"That wouldn't be *the* Colonel Sergei Orlov, would it?"

"You're ahead of me."

"Listen, Jonathan, you need to file a report on what you've found, pronto, before we set off. You wouldn't want a newbie taking credit, now, would you?"

Orlov sat in his window seat on commercial flight BA-1264X, next to a woman in a Greenday T-shirt and flip-flops with rubber flowers on. A representative from the British Embassy in Minsk had given him a briefcase containing yesterday's newspapers and an update on the case he was scheduled to work on. It was a thorough analysis, he had to give them credit. About Bronstein and Hartley-Brown, he reserved judgement. Their photographs showed them looking impassive.

As the plane entered German airspace, he turned to the newspapers. He read the headlines, the leaders and one or two features and turned to the chess page of *The Independent*. Checkmate in two. He looked at it for a long time. Bishop to c3, then black was forced to block, and Rook to a8.

But then – what if: Queen takes Rook? It was still checkmate for sure, but not in two. For some reason, he felt angry. He tore it out and thrust it in his pocket.

The plane landed at Heathrow in bright sunshine. He wondered if the Kremlin had sent someone to intercept him. He hoped not. He'd handed his Ots-33 in at Minsk.

He walked into Arrivals and put a trilby on by way of a disguise, pulling it down at the front. There was no one at all as far as he could tell. He sat down on a plastic seat and took out the chess puzzle.

"Bishop to c3," said an American voice above him. He got up and realised the two men grinning at him must be Bronstein and Hartley-Brown. They exchanged handshakes.

"Yes, then Rook to a8," he replied for want of anything better to say, "but what if Queen takes Rook?"

Bronstein took the puzzle. "I think it's c7 to c8, Queen. Or Rook."

Hartley-Brown wasn't paying any attention. He was intensely focussed on something beyond them. Suddenly, he grabbed both their arms and pulled them down, hard. The advertising hoarding behind them burst like someone had hit it with a halberd, and people started screaming.

The marksman was already on his way out. Dressed only in a T-shirt, shorts and trainers, with a man-bag strapped across his chest, he cleared two sets of plastic chairs like a professional hurdler and ran into the road outside.

"Where's our car?" Orlov said.

"It won't make any difference," Hartley-Brown said. "After that, there'll soon be a queue out there a mile long. If the airport staff are properly trained, they'll be ready. They'll stop him at one of the checkpoints on the way out."

"Better get going then," Bronstein said.

A round of gunfire came from outside the building. More screams.

"I think you'll find he's just been killed by security," Orlov said.

They looked at each other as if the seriousness of what had happened was only just sinking in. Hartley-Brown brushed himself down.

"Shit," Bronstein said.

"We think we may have solved the crime, sir," Hartley-Brown said. "Or crimes."

Bronstein turned to Hartley-Brown. "Wait a minute. You just called him 'sir'."

"That's right. He's in charge now."

"No one told me."

"I've only just found out myself. I received an email forty minutes ago."

Bronstein shrugged. "Although it is kind of a technicality, I suppose."

"Excuse me, gentlemen," Orlov said. "I believe you said you had something to tell me."

A group of policemen in flak jackets was on its way over slowly with guns trained on them at arm's length.

"Put your hands on your heads and lie down on the floor," a megaphone said. *"Repeat - "*

"Tell you another time," Bronstein said.

An hour later, they were on their way back to Scotland Yard in a London taxi. Orlov sat facing the rear. Hartley-Brown and Bronstein sat opposite him.

"I've been looking into a computer owned by one of the paparazzi," Hartley-Brown said.

"How did you get in there?" Orlov asked.

"Low-level subterfuge. He fell asleep and I copied its contents. We've interviewed seven photographers so far. All of them claimed to have no relevant pictures, including the fellow whose files I copied. It turns out they were lying. Look at these." He handed Orlov a set of photographs. "The first batch was taken at the shooting of a photographer following the *Britain's Got Talent* star, Bobby Keynes. The second comes from when the photographer following Zane Cruse was killed, the third Mikey from Bad Lads Zero, these Stallone Laine, and finally, these from Jilly Bestwick. I've produced a grid," he said, passing Orlov a new piece of paper. "In the first column, we have the celebrity who was being pursued, in the second, the photographer who was killed, and this last column lists the photographers who have been secretly sharing pictures of the killings. Some twenty-five names."

Orlov looked hard at the grid. There wasn't time to digest it, but it was obviously good work. "What's your theory?" he said.

"They think if they pool enough photos they can identify the killer. A big news story and when it breaks, the pictures will be worth their weight in gold."

"Have they?"

"Identified the killer? Yes."

"So why haven't they gone to the police?"

"They've discovered a face. I think they believe – given a little more time - they might be able to put a name to it."

"Why would they think that?"

Bronstein smiled. "Jonathan thinks, and it rings true, that they believe the murderer's a professional rival, another photographer out to eliminate the competition."

"That would surely be rather a drastic way of staying ahead."

"Not one of these guys is normal," Bronstein said. "You've got to meet them to appreciate that."

"The face of the supposed murderer," Orlov said: "presumably, you've isolated it."

"First thing I did," Hartley-Brown said. "It isn't too difficult. It's the common denominator to most of the pictures. A man, some way behind the celebrity, usually with his body partially obscured. We've no idea who he is yet. Here."

He handed Orlov a new batch of pictures and was surprised to see his expression change.

"What's up?" Bronstein said.

"This isn't a photographer," Orlov said. "It's a Russian secret serviceman. Dmitri Vassyli Kramski. He once interrogated me. I say 'interrogated'."

Bronstein let out a guffaw. "This wouldn't be your classic misinformation, would it?"

"I'm sure you'll find MI6 has a photo of Dmitri Kramski somewhere in its mainframe," Orlov replied.

"Yes, of course ... Apologies."

"What would a Russian secret serviceman be doing, killing paparazzi?" Hartley-Brown said.

"I've no idea," Orlov replied. "However, I do have a question for you two."

"Fire away, sir," Bronstein said.

"According to the briefing I received before I arrived here, you've been out interviewing newspaper photographers. John Boorman, Kevin Wiles, Sydney Cromberforth, Jake Cassidy."

"Add to that list James Docherty and Garvey Simpson," Hartley-Brown said.

"Do you know anything about what happened to them afterwards?"

Bronstein shrugged. "We haven't had them watched, if that's what you mean. There's only us two. We don't have extra manpower at our disposal."

"It may surprise you to know that Boorman, Wiles and Cromberforth are all dead."

Hartley-Brown sat up as if he'd been stung. "How?"

"Alcohol poisoning. Nothing remotely suspicious, given their medical histories. Unless you're aware of their common involvement in this, and you're looking for a pattern, you probably wouldn't notice anything untoward."

"Who the hell briefed you?" Bronstein said. "We sure knew nothing about it."

"What about that photographer you brought in earlier?" Hartley-Brown asked Bronstein.

Bronstein scowled. "Simpson? Hell, I forgot all about him. He's probably still there."

"You'd better find out," Orlov said.

Bronstein took out his mobile. "Reception? This is David Bronstein. I need you to confirm that you're still holding on to Garvey Simpson. ... What? But I specifically requested you – *what?*"

He listened for a few moments in silence like he couldn't believe his ears were still working, then he lowered his phone, pressed 'end call' and looked up.

"You're not going to believe this," he said. "They're clearing our desks. As of thirty minutes ago. We've been folded."

Chapter 4: Marcie Brown, Investigator

The three men filed into Sir Colin's office. The carpet smelt new, a landscape window overlooked the city and there was a reproduction Vermeer on each wall. Chairs had been laid out facing the glass-topped desk. Sir Colin sat with his shoulders dropped, idly twirling a ballpoint as if he was at peace with himself and the world.

"This shouldn't take long," he said. "You've produced an excellent report, Jonathan. Fertile enough for the rest to be considered loose ends. Now I understand how frustrating that must sound when you've come so far towards a solution, but that's the nature of police work. We're all aiming, in a sense, to make ourselves redundant. The fact that you've achieved it in double quick time ought to make you feel proud."

"You could at least have allowed us the dignity of clearing our own desks," Bronstein said.

Sir Colin folded his hands. "I must admit, Mr Bronstein, I was disappointed to discover you're a member of the US Central Intelligence Agency, not the New York City Police Department … as I was led to believe, and as it says in your application."

"What? No, I'm not."

"I resent being misled, Mr Bronstein."

"So that's what all this is about?"

Sir Colin clicked his tongue. "With respect, if I can't rely on you to tell the truth on your application form, when can I rely on you to tell the truth?"

"But I'm not a member of the CIA."

"In addition to which, I'm not running an intelligence outfit. This is police work, pure and simple. We can't be doing with an outfit in which intelligence officers outnumber policemen two to one."

Hartley-Brown leaned forward. "Surely, if we're getting results?"

"I'm not a member of the CIA," Bronstein insisted.

"Excuse me, sir," Orlov said. "Perhaps you could clarify something. Who led you to believe that Lieutenant Bronstein is a member of the CIA?"

"I have it on excellent authority from Her Majesty's Secret Intelligence Service."

Bronstein shook his head. "I'm a member of the New York City Police Department. I've never even been near the CIA. I wouldn't even know where to look for it."

"So what happens to us now?" Hartley-Brown asked.

"Jonathan, you'll go back to what you were doing before, but with a promotion in the pipeline. Mr Bronstein, you'll report to the US Embassy within twenty-four hours for further instructions. Colonel Orlov, I've been authorised by the Foreign Office to offer you indefinite protection in this country as a human intelligence source defector."

Orlov frowned. "How unexpected."

Hartley-Brown stood up. "Sir, this is disgraceful."

"Sit down, Jonathan."

"I don't know whether Mr Bronstein is or isn't a member of the CIA," Hartley-Brown said. "But it appears as if you cobbled this – this 'unit' together simply so MI6 could get its hands on Colonel Orlov. It looks like it was a sham from the beginning."

Sir Colin glowered. "If Colonel Orlov had remained in Russia, he'd be rotting in a prison. For him to return there would be suicide. We're not forcing him to accept our offer. And how dare you speak to me like that?"

"I resign."

"And I'm not a member of the CIA," Bronstein said. "You're going to be in diplomatic deep shit when I do report to the embassy - in about thirty minutes' time. We Americans don't like it when you call us liars. My application form was countersigned by Raymond Kelly, Commissioner of the NYPD himself, so eat that apple, wise guy."

Sir Colin flushed. He'd obviously forgotten the countersignature. "I – I can only go on what information I get, and if what I get from SIS - "

"Presumably, you'll cover my flight back to Moscow," Orlov said. "Meanwhile, since you brought me over here at considerable personal inconvenience, I'd be grateful if you could direct me to whatever safe house you've provided for me until my plane arrives. Put it this way: it would be an unexpected bonus for my enemies in Russia if they could both kill me and kick up a fuss about your ineptitude in protecting me. And it would send a very clear message to any future would-be defectors."

"Yes, yes, I'll arrange, yes, I'll arrange that now - "

"You mean you've arranged nothing?"

Bronstein shook his head. "Buddy, you're going to be the butt of every joke in town when this gets out."

"Please leave my office. You too, Hartley-Brown. You can pick up any personal effects you may have brought with you at reception, otherwise I expect you – no, not you, Colonel Orlov, I simply meant - "

Hartley-Brown waited till his colleagues were outside then followed them and slammed the door behind him. They marched down the corridor together.

"Where's the goddamn exit?" Bronstein said.

Hartley-Brown was blushing almost to the point of tears. "I can't say how very, very sorry I am. I've never felt so ashamed of my country as I feel at this precise moment."

Bronstein put his arm round his shoulder. "You were great in there, Jonathan. Don't feel bad. Hey, if it helps, there are slimy, backstabbing bastards in all countries."

"We didn't even get the chance to tell him about our new leads," Orlov said.

"You've nowhere to stay, Colonel," Hartley-Brown said.

Bronstein cleared his throat. "Er, you remember that dinner invite, Jonathan?"

Sir Anthony Hartley-Brown's constituency was in Hertfordshire. He lived there with his wife and two of his children, a seven-year-old adoptee from Darfur named Anya, and his grown-up daughter, Marciella. Mannersby was a Grade 1 listed Tudor building with wide gables, an imposing porch with steps to the front door and a turning circle for vehicles. It had ten bedrooms, a sulky look when it rained, and it sat in four acres of parkland looked after by gardeners.

They arrived by taxi, since they no longer had the use of an official car. All along the way, Orlov claimed they were being followed, and after a while, Bronstein agreed with him. It was a discreet tail, nothing aggressive: clearly those working it genuinely wanted to know where they were going rather than to menace them.

When they got onto the M25, Hartley-Brown rang ahead to let his parents know they were coming and ask them to make up three beds.

"That's right, Mother, I've resigned," he said sadly. There was a pause and he added, "There's no point, I've already handed my cards in … No … No, I don't think so."

"How did she take it?" Bronstein said, after he put the phone down.

He sighed. "She said I should talk to my father first."

"Sounds just like my mom. If it's anything important she can't pronounce because she's only a woman, and you wouldn't know because you're only a boy. It's either your dad or complete ignorance."

"And the problem is, mostly you both know what he's going to say before he even opens his mouth."

Bronstein laughed. "Tell me about it."

Forty-five minutes later, the car crossed onto the gravel of the driveway and slowed. It started to drizzle.

"I think we've lost our tail," Orlov said. "Or more likely they're satisfied as to our destination."

"Maybe we should stay here an hour and move on," Bronstein said. "If they're going to attack, we don't want them putting Jonathan's family in danger."

"I'll get my father to get another contingent of security guards in. He won't mind. He can charge it to expenses."

"Whoa, I've heard all about your famous expenses scandal," Bronstein said. "Last thing I want is Sir Anthony Hartley-Brown being pilloried by the Fourth Estate on our account."

"My father has very firm views on the expenses scandal. He thinks it was the result of an institutional failure to make clear where an MP's salary begins and ends. Of course, he never says that in public."

"Remind me, what's side's he on again?"

"Conservative."

"Ah."

"They all think it. They all think the same thing."

"Are you going to vote for him in the next election?"

"He's my father. Of course I am."

"What if he wasn't?"

"I've never considered it."

"Why not?"

Hartley-Brown took a deep breath. "Well, I know my mother sometimes votes for the other side. And some of their policies seem reasonably well thought-out. But it just wouldn't seem right."

"This little sister of yours. Is she good looking?"

"Not really, no."

Bronstein laughed. The car pulled up outside the front door and Hartley-Brown ran inside to get some money to pay the driver.

His parents stood on the front steps with Anya, looking grave. Mrs Hartley-Brown wore a skirt, a cardigan and pearls. Her grey hair was as round and smooth as an onion, and doubled the volume of her head. She wrung her hands. Her husband was a full eighteen inches taller than her, thin, balding with a moustache. He wore a tweed jacket and grey trousers. Anya stood erect in a smock and pigtails with her feet and hands together. She alone smiled, a picture-perfect child.

Orlov and Bronstein got out of the car. Hartley-Brown formally introduced the two couples and they exchanged handshakes. Mrs Hartley-Brown – Joy – had difficulty restraining her tears. She blew her nose. When they went into the house, father and son walked in front. Joy took up the rear with Orlov and Bronstein, clinging to Anya's hand as if it was all that remained to her of life or hope.

"Your mother tells me you've resigned," Sir Anthony said. "I've news for you, my boy. No, you damn well haven't."

"I'm twenty-four. I think I'm old enough to make my own decisions now, thank you."

"Come into the study. I want to talk to you."

"Fine, but you're wasting your time. I'm not going to change my mind."

"I don't know whether it's penetrated that pea-brain of yours, but there's a global recession going on. Even Oxbridge graduates have difficulty finding jobs nowadays."

"It was a matter of principle."

"Tripe. We're going to make a little phone call to Sir Colin Bowker and you're going to eat deep-pan humble pie, do you understand?"

"No. Sorry, absolutely not."

They turned left into the study and Sir Anthony slammed the door, leaving Orlov and Bronstein and Joy and Anya alone.

"I've – I've made a pot of tea," Joy said.

Orlov drew himself up and adjusted the angle of his body so he was directly facing her. "Mrs Hartley-Brown, you may or may not have heard of me. My name is Sergei Orlov. I'm Russian. Several years ago, I served in an elite tank regiment where I was decorated and promoted to the rank of colonel. Shortly afterwards, I transferred to Intelligence, then, thanks to an unanticipated combination of circumstances, I began to work behind the scenes to set the rule of law in my country on a firmer footing. But I was stopped and sent to prison. Two days ago, I was released at considerable risk to my own safety and brought here under false pretences to conduct a murder investigation. I was duped, Mrs Hartley-Brown, and, with less serious consequences, so was the man on my left. When I go back to Russia, as I will have to now for honour's sake, I will almost certainly be killed. In all the time I have been here, your son is the only British citizen who has stood up for me. He did so immediately and completely and in a way that hardly anyone else has ever done in my life before. Whatever happens to me now, I owe him a huge debt of gratitude. He has proved to me that there are still good men in the world."

"Er, I'd like the second that," Bronstein said, by way of cutting the silence.

Joy sat down at the telephone table and burst into tears. A few seconds later she stood up and threw the study door open. Hartley-Brown and his father were still locked in battle.

"It's all right, Anthony," she said. "Stop it, stop fighting. It's going to be all right." She put her arms round her son.

Hartley-Brown looked as humiliated as Bronstein had so far seen him, and after what Sir Colin Bowker had done that was saying something. He should sit him down sometime with a quadruple whiskey and tell him more about his own parents, particularly his mom when she'd had too much Shiraz and there was a half-eligible woman in the kitchen. Mortifying didn't even begin to do it justice.

The dining room was wainscoted and mounted with antique hunting trophies and prints of horses running at Epsom with four legs in the air. They ate beef consommé while a middle aged manservant called Geoffrey, wearing a red waistcoat and a bow tie, stood under a sconce. They would have eaten in silence, but for Joy's determination to keep the conversation going and Bronstein's usual garrulousness. After four glasses of wine, Sir Anthony smiled. He leaned over to his son and patted him affectionately on the shoulder.

"At least you're not a coward," he said. "I've never thought much of Sir Colin Bowker, anyway. Bloody pen-pushing nonentity. What's the country coming to when we've got farty-arse squirts like him in charge?"

"Where are Marcie and Anya?" Joy said. "We're about to start the main course."

"You're still young," Sir Anthony said. "There's always the armed forces. Your eyesight's still twenty-twenty, I trust?"

"I specifically told her," Joy went on, "seven o'clock sharp."

"Don't worry about a reference. Colin Bowker will write whatever I tell him."

"I think you'll be hard pressed to get him to write anything positive about me after today," Jonathan replied.

"Nonsense, it'll glow in the dark, it'll be that good. Then you can distinguish yourself in Afghanistan or Iraq. And when you get back we can get you onto the board of some company or other and you can spend your free time – of which there'll be bags, we'll see to that - managing the estate."

"It sounds like a living death," Hartley-Brown said.

There was a thick silence.

"So what's your plan?" Sir Anthony said frostily.

"Jonathan, will you go and get Marcie and Anya?" Joy said.

"I was thinking of becoming a social worker."

Sir Anthony rolled his eyes and expelled an exasperated flute of air through his nose. "That again."

"Shall *I* go and get them?" Joy said.

Jonathan wiped his mouth and stood up. "I'll go."

Joy turned to Bronstein and Orlov. "I'm terribly sorry, this always happens. We're sitting here eating dinner and Marcie's upstairs with Anya playing *Call of Duty* or *Grand Theft Auto*." She smiled. "Of course, you tend to lose track of the time when you're wasting prostitutes in the hood."

"Quite," Sir Anthony said.

Suddenly, the door opened and Marcie burst in with Anya. She had long black hair tied with a clip at the back, brown eyes, big lips and a small nose, and she looked sporty. She was dressed entirely in black – jumper, jeans and pumps – and her face was streaked with mud. She wrapped her arms round her brother and kissed him.

"Sorry I'm late, I've been out on a recce," she said. "You must be the Russian chappie," she said to Orlov, "and you must be the American. Is that a yarmulke?"

Bronstein grinned and removed it. "Would you like to try it on?"

She sat down. "I'll just eat my consommé first. I'm really sorry, Mummy, cross my heart and hope to die. Eat up, Anya, there's a good girl."

"I take it you were playing that horrible game again," Joy said.

"This is Colonel Sergei Orlov," Jonathan said. "And this is David Bronstein."

"Secret agents, yes?" Marcie replied. "That would explain a lot."

"I'm with the NYPD," Bronstein said. "I'm not with the CIA."

"Daddy, did you know the house is surrounded?"

"I beg your pardon?" Sir Anthony said.

Marcie sprinkled pepper on her soup. "Like I said, Anya and I have just been on a recce. I wasn't on the Nintendo, Mummy, honestly. Anya saw some men earlier out of her bedroom window and she came to get me because she was scared. I told her we'd wait till dark, then we'd go and investigate. You see, for some strange reason, Benjamin and Jolyon have disappeared into thin air."

"Who are Benjamin and Jolyon?" Bronstein asked.

"Our security experts," Jonathan replied.

Sir Anthony leaned forward. "They've gone missing?" He turned to the servant. "Geoffrey, would you mind going and confirming that?"

"I rang the police, of course," Marcie went on. "About an hour ago. But they haven't arrived. So I went out to investigate. There are about twenty-five of them. I can draw you a map of where they are, if you like. They don't seem to be moving."

"I wish you'd told me first," Sir Anthony said.

Orlov stood up. "I imagine they're here for me. It wasn't my intention in coming here to put anyone here in danger."

"Where are you going?" Bronstein said.

"To give myself up, of course."

"It's all right, Mr Orlov," Marcie said, "they're not Russian. They're English."

"How do you know?" Bronstein said.

"Because I asked one of them."

"I wish you wouldn't keep *doing* things like that," Joy said. "Mind your own business and you don't invite trouble. As you of all people should know."

"Mummy's referring to my Anti-Social Behaviour Order. Don't look at me like that, Mummy. It's public knowledge, it was in all the papers. I admit, I was slightly over the limit at the time. But I'd do it again."

"Marcie - "

"You can't just let people walk all over you like that," she said, as if the subject was closed.

The door opened and Geoffrey slid round it. "I can't find Benjamin and Jolyon anywhere, sir. And no one recalls seeing them leave."

"Have you tried phoning them?" Sir Anthony said. "Their number's in the book under Security. Home and mobile."

"That's the other thing, sir. It appears the phones have been cut off."

"What?"

"Let's get to the point," Jonathan said. "Marcie, what did you ask this fellow you spoke to?"

"What he thought he was doing in my back garden, of course. He apologised and said it was a matter of national security."

"My mobile isn't working," Bronstein said, looking at it.

"Nor mine," Hartley-Brown said.

"Geoffrey, would you mind serving the main course?" Marcie said. "I've finished my soup. Tell Kenneth it was very nice."

"Young lady, are you mad?" Sir Anthony burst out.

Marcie stood up. "Daddy, sit down. Mr Orlov, you too. There are twenty-five of them at least. If they were going to storm the building, they'd have done so by now: it's not exactly a fortress. My guess is the only reason they've cut the phones off is because you're in the Shadow Cabinet, and you might have influence above and beyond my petty 999 calls. They're probably here for our protection."

Everyone was stunned by this outburst of common sense. Orlov and Sir Anthony crept back to their seats and Geoffrey served the main course. Marcie sipped her wine.

After dinner, Joy went upstairs with Anya to put her to bed. Marcie and the men carried on talking for a while, then retired to the lounge. Sir Anthony settled down to read some papers, Hartley-Brown took up a crossword, Orlov and Bronstein found a chess set.

"Do you mind if I watch you play?" Marcie said. She pulled up a chair and put her elbows on her knees and cupped her chin in her hands.

After an hour, Bronstein looked up at Orlov, smiled and shook his hand.

"What are you doing?" Marcie said.

"I just resigned," Bronstein replied.

"But why? It's only nine-thirty. There's plenty of time yet. You're winning: look you've all these pieces left, and you've got a Queen."

"Checkmate in ten," Bronstein said. "Play on if you don't believe me."

"Okay, I will."

She swapped seats with him. Two moves later, she lost her Queen and Orlov boxed her king in. Then she lost a knight and Orlov converted a pawn.

She laughed. "Oh, I see. Yes, I can see it now. You two must be quite clever."

Bronstein sighed. "How come we ain't rich?"

At ten o'clock, they decided on a guard-duty rota and went to bed, leaving Bronstein the first on patrol.

Orlov fell asleep as soon as he got into bed. He knew he'd need it tomorrow. But at three o'clock the next morning, he awoke to the sound of the doorknob turning. He forced himself to remain perfectly still as someone slipped inside and closed the door.

"Mr Orlov? Are you awake?" Marcie.

He sat up. She was dressed exactly as she had been earlier. He rubbed his eyes, grabbed the dressing-gown he'd been given and pulled it on.

"Don't switch on the light," she said. "I've brought you a pair of field-glasses. It's a full moon. It was cloudy earlier but it's clear now. They're not making any secret of their presence, not any more. The weird thing is, they must know we know they're here."

"Thank you for your concern," he said. "But as you said earlier, I don't think they represent a threat. Otherwise they'd have carried it out."

She bobbed her shoulders. "But don't you want to at least *see* some of them? You might see someone you know. With your trained eye - "

He decided to humour her. He pulled the curtains to.

She pulled them back. "Don't do that! They're probably got night-vision binoculars. They'll see everything you're doing."

"I haven't got X-ray vision."

"I thought we might go to my room. I always sleep with the curtains open."

He smiled. "If your mother and father or brother were to catch me creeping to your room in the middle of the night, I doubt the people outside will be my first concern."

"I didn't come here just to give you the binoculars."

"Oh?"

"And sex is the furthest thing from my mind."

He let out a flute of air. "That is a relief."

"Anyway, don't flatter yourself. And you seem to have forgotten that I sneaked into your room. Mummy or Daddy or Jonathan could have seen that - "

"Maybe we should continue this conversation downstairs."

"But they didn't. Mummy and Daddy are fast asleep and so is Jonathan."

"What is it you want to talk about?"

"I might be able to help you. I know the local vicar. I can fetch him tomorrow morning and we can be married in the estate chapel. Obviously, you wouldn't get to hump me. I'm talking about a marriage of convenience, just to keep you from getting deported and killed. Because that's what's going to happen if you go back, isn't it?"

"You would do that for me?"

"Not for you as a person – I don't know you well enough yet - but because I want to make the world better. God knows, it's boring enough here. I'm not achieving a thing. Since the ASBO Mummy and Daddy have kept me stuck in the house, and I can't leave because I saw how much that upset them last time. I'm in limbo."

"You mean, we can help each other."

"That's right. And who knows, I quite like you and you probably quite like me. We could work together for human rights and stuff and after a few years we might even fall in love and we'd be flying."

He smiled. "I'm afraid I'm going to pass. Although you make it sound very tempting."

"But why?"

"Because I'd have to become a British citizen."

"So? What's wrong with that?"

"The one thing that's kept me going these last few years is that I'm a better Russian than the men and women who have been trying to frustrate me and kill me. I can't let go of that."

She hmm-ed. "I see where you're coming from. A bit. But you're going to get killed, aren't you?"

"Nothing's ever completely certain. But either way, life isn't worth holding on to on any terms. Not for anyone."

"Plan B, then. The priest-hole."

"The …?"

"We used to be Roman Catholics, our family. In the olden days, priests came to Mannersby to administer communion, but it was illegal, so they needed a secret passageway. It takes you right outside the grounds."

He drew a sharp breath. "Where is it?"

Chapter 5: The Priest Hole

According to what the rest of her family thought, Marcie explained, the tunnel could only be reached by a trapdoor beneath the entrance carpet. But she'd discovered a book about it in the library and there was a much earlier entrance off a blocked-up staircase in the east wing. She handed Orlov a torch, took one for herself and grabbed a key from her wardrobe. They crossed the gallery in their socks. Thirty seconds later they emerged into another passageway and took a left-hand door to an oaken staircase.

He could see she was excited. Equally obviously, she didn't want him to notice. What was she up to? Could she be leading him into a trap? That wouldn't make sense. They'd already agreed their besiegers, whoever they were, didn't require it.

Then he knew. She'd never been through the priest-hole before. She'd commandeered his predicament to fulfil what was probably a childhood ambition. She'd actually read a book about it, for God's sake. He couldn't help a smile. Then it occurred to him it was probably unsafe.

Too late now. The way she was acting, she'd probably never come this close before. Worse, she'd reached the point where she didn't even need his company.

After climbing the staircase halfway, she lifted up four steps on hinges to reveal a dark cavity. A waft of icy, dank air greeted them. She flicked her torch on and off. "Ready?"

"Are you sure it's safe?"

"Perfectly. I'll go in front, since I know the way and there are quite a few false turns."

"Why would there be false turns?"

"To confuse the King's men. And because it was made from a pre-existing pothole. You don't think the family had enough money to build a tunnel a mile long, do you? The Anglicans kept them in penury."

"I know very little English history. When was the last time you went through here?"

"All the way to the end? About a week ago. I use it to sneak out. I just leave the Nintendo playing and Mummy and Daddy think I'm in my room. So long as things keep exploding, they're happy."

"What sort of condition's it in?"

"We had it renovated by Sarah Beeny last week," she replied tetchily. "Now are you coming or not?"

"Just one thing. When we get to the end, we say goodbye, agreed?"

She snorted. "You rejected my offer of marriage. What sort of a crazy desperado do you take me for?"

She switched on her torch and stepped inside the aperture. Orlov followed suit. Within a couple of seconds they alighted on a damp slate floor.

"Right," she said, "there's a hole in the ground in a second. We go down a ladder and then it's a fairly straight track. What are you thinking of doing, by the way, when I get you out of here? I mean, where will you go?"

"If you'd asked me that earlier today, I'd have said, to the airport. I need to get back inside Russia, but I've decided I don't need to be suicidal. No, I'm going to walk across Europe."

They were descending the ladder now.

"How long do you think that will take?" she asked.

"A couple of months. I can reach Vera Gruchov's people when I get there, I might be able to lie low for a while."

"Who's Vera Gruchov?"

"A liberal politician. One of the few powerful ones. She wrote to me in prison."

"Is she in love with you?"

He laughed. "She's your age."

They reached the bottom of the ladder and they shone their torches about. They were in a cave big enough to stand up in. Stalactites as long as a man's arm hung from the ceiling. Below them, Orlov could hear a stream rushing. In about five hundred yards, the path descended into muddy water.

"It's not very deep," she said. "Listen, what do you think of my brother?" she went on, in an obvious attempt to change the subject. "Do you like him?"

"We were only introduced yesterday. Since then, however, he's saved my life and resigned in defence of my honour. The more interesting question is probably, what does he think of me? I shouldn't imagine it's anything good."

"Yes, but he's not here to ask."

"I admire him."

"Even though he's a bit of a softie?"

"You mean, not macho? I'm afraid that particular characteristic plays no part whatsoever in my evaluation of men. I've seen how it can ruin things."

"What a pity you couldn't have worked with him a bit longer. He can really handle himself in a fight, you know. Even before he joined the police force. We were at school together. We had to go to a comprehensive because Mummy's a bit of a lush old communist, although I was two years below him. I mean, can you imagine being called Jonathan Hartley-Brown in a rough comp? But no one ever made fun of him. Or if they did, they'd stopped doing it by the time I arrived. Me, I became plain 'Marcie Brown' within a week of joining. I once saw him whip this kid in the year above him, a great big kid he was. I can't remember why. Squashing a bluebottle, probably."

They were up to their knees in water now. Orlov decided it was time to interrupt.

"I seem to remember you saying we'd barely get our feet wet."

"I meant it was nothing worth worrying about."

Suddenly, the ledge beneath their feet dropped six inches and they were up to their waists.

"And you do this journey often, do you? Take my hand. Can you swim?"

"Yes, thank you, I can. About … once a week. And it wasn't quite this deep last time."

There was a huge waterfall in front of them. They were going to have to pass through it to progress.

He laughed. "And when you get back, your parents never notice that you're a bit wet?"

"I don't necessarily report to them first thing," she replied.

They passed through the waterfall and found themselves confronted by a forty-five degree slope ascending ten or twelve feet to a narrow horizontal cleft in the rock. It looked slimy.

"How do you normally negotiate this?" Orlov asked.

"Fingernails. It's not as hard as it looks."

"And when you've squeezed through that cleft, what's on the other side?"

"Oh, just a straight track."

"Up or down?"

"A bit of both. *Okay, look, I admit it, I've never been in here before! Happy?* Look," she went on emotionally, "I'm always trying to get Jonathan to come in with me, but he won't, and Daddy says it's strictly out of bounds – he was going to have it closed up about a year ago. Satisfied? Shall we go back now?"

He sighed and shone his torch into the gap. "You go first so I can catch you if you slide back. Take your belt off and tie it round your torch and fix the other end back in your belt-buckle. I'll shine your way from here."

"You - you mean you're not going to make us turn round?"

"Tell me, is it really an old priest-hole?"

"That bit was true, promise. Like I said, we've got a copy of the last time a survey was done on it, in the library. In nineteen-seventy. It's a bit wet and treacherous in places, but it's still negotiable: that's what it says."

"In nineteen-seventy. Forty years ago."

She was already undoing her belt. "Yes ... Or I don't know, it may have been eighteen-seventy. I can't remember offhand."

He ground his teeth. "Don't go through that cleft until you're absolutely sure there's no danger. My guess is there's another cave with a gentle incline. No priest would ever come this way if it didn't start to get a little easier somewhere along the line."

She climbed up and slipped back four times. Orlov took her ankles and hoisted her up till she was able to clutch the lip of the cleft. She raised herself till her head was poking over and switched on the torch.

"*It is! It's a gentle incline!* Grab onto me and pull yourself up. We'll go in together."

There wasn't room, but he reached her level quickly and she pulled herself through. He followed.

The floor was sand, and there was no longer space to stand up. The tunnel disappeared into the darkness even with both torches full on it, and there was no indication that it narrowed.

"We'll have to crawl," she said. "Do you want to go in front or shall I?"

"Let me," he said. "We don't know what's up there."

"Well, you can't. I'm going in front."

Once she set off, it was impossible to change positions. The cave contracted to the point where overtaking or even turning round was impossible. It became increasingly hot.

"I hope you're not claustrophobic," she said.

"How's the air quality?"

"Good. I think we're about to descend."

"At what angle?"

"Down," she said. "Into water."

"We're going to have to go back then."

"Can't you swim underwater?"

"I don't want to."

"It's probably clear as crystal. You could open your eyes. And the torches are waterproof to a depth of ten metres. I bought them specially."

He was gasping. She was wrong about the air: it was getting thinner. "We've come probably half a mile," he said. "That means there's another half mile to go. Can you swim underwater for half a mile? Can anyone?"

"Someone must be able to."

"That doesn't necessarily follow."

"As for whether *I* can, I don't know. I won't know until I try. Neither of us will. You can swim, can't you?"

"I'm more than capable. That's not the issue. With the walls this tight, if you start drowning, you can't turn round. Have you any idea how painful it is to drown?"

She shook her head and laughed. "Have you?"

"I was interrogated for six weeks in a maximum security prison. I've an idea how painful most things are."

"As Elvis Presley once said: 'A little less conversation, a little more action'."

Before he knew what had happened, she slithered forward and disappeared underwater with barely a splash. He swore.

He inserted himself into the water. After the heat of the tunnel, the cold was like being electrocuted. He opened his eyes underwater and shone his torch in a circle. She was nowhere to be seen, but he'd soon catch her up.

He swam forward six or seven metres. But then just as his lungs were beginning to press, he reached a wall of solid rock, forcing him up. Two seconds later, he broke the surface again. This time, he was in a wide pool.

She sat on the edge, laughing. "You're supposed to say, 'You crazy fool, you could have got us both killed'. But think: how many priests do you know who can swim a full half mile with a monstrance full of communion wafers? It had to be only a short way."

He swam to the edge and hauled himself out. She was getting cocky, now. He wished he'd never indulged her. Not for the first time in his life, he'd allowed himself to be mesmerised by someone's yearning for something outlandish.

From what he could tell, they were in a cave as big as a warehouse. In places, the stalagmites met the stalactites, even though the ceiling lay in an obscurity beyond even torchlight. There were mounds of shale where the roof had collapsed and it echoed with a deafening dripping and sloshing and gurgling.

"It can't be far from here," she said.

"Next time you try something like that," he said angrily, "I'm going to grab you and punch you unconscious."

She laughed. "Don't be stupid. We're a team."

"We need to look for the exit."

"I know where the exit is. I've read the survey, remember."

"The eighteen-seventy survey? Have you seen how much of the ceiling's fallen in?"

"This cave's probably been here millions of years," she replied. "A hundred and forty years is hardly an eye-blink. Anyway, it could have been nineteen-seventy."

"Let's have a little less conversation, shall we?"

"It's over here. You have to go under water again."

"How far?"

She shrugged. "Ten yards. Cross my heart."

"And then?"

"And then that's it. We've done it. The exit's right above us."

"How far above?"

"I only looked at the survey, I didn't memorise it. Here it is."

He didn't wait for her. He jumped into the water and felt around himself for a tunnel. There was an opening in front of him. He waited till she appeared beside him and pointed. She nodded. He hoped there wasn't more than one.

Ten seconds later, they broke the surface again. They climbed out to find themselves in a muddy pit held intact with roots. She wrung her hair and re-tied it. A shaft of light shone from above. When they stood up, they were almost touching it.

"Lift me up," she whispered. "I'll go first, check the coast's clear."

He took a second to deliberate. If he did as she asked, he could follow her in no time, otherwise he'd have to hoist her up and that would take longer. He lifted her. She pushed on the area around the light source and it gave way. She poked her head through the hole she'd made.

"It's daytime!"

"Where are we?"

"In some undergrowth. I'm going to pull myself up. How long till you can follow me?"

"I'm coming now."

"There are two men. I'm going to create a diversion."

"No, stop!"

Again, he was too late. A moment later, he heard a male yelp. He jumped and caught the lip of the opening and fell back into the pool. He cursed and scrambled out and tried again. He caught the overhang and exerted all his strength to pull himself so he was half-clear. He grabbed a rhododendron stem and yanked himself the rest of the way and stood up.

Marcie was in the middle of a scrap. Two bearded men in suits towered over her without looking particularly threatening. One rubbed his head and looked at his fingertips. "She's drawn blood," he said plaintively.

She adopted a martial arts stance, right foot forward, hands at hip height like cleavers. "Come on, then."

"Just knock her out, John."

"She's the owner's daughter," John replied, talking about her as if she wasn't there. "Barry met her earlier. Do you know what she said? She said, 'Get out of my back garden'."

"You sit on her. Then I'll call Phillip."

She lunged forward with a kick. John grabbed her foot and raised it so she fell on her back. She rolled to the side with a grunt and freed herself. Then she threw a punch. But John was ready. He twisted her elbow and grabbed her under both arms. He lifted her without enthusiasm and threw her on her back again, winding her.

"Careful, John. You could break her spine."

She wheezed as if she was about to die. The two men looked down at her. Orlov approached them from behind, cleared his throat and they turned. He punched each in the chest simultaneously and cracked their heads together as they lost their balance. They fell in a heap.

The journey had been for nothing. The estate perimeter – a high brick wall fronted by hawthorns - was another two hundred yards west. He guessed the family must have increased its landholdings since the tunnel was built. He knelt down and took Marcie's hand as she fought for air.

"Give it time," he said. "It'll pass. You've just had the breath knocked out of you, that's all."

"You were - meant – meant – to run the other way."

He slid his arms under her and picked her up. "I think it's time we went back to the house, don't you?"

"Aren't you going to escape?"

"I don't think anyone here's going to harm me. Not any more."

"You haven't killed them, have you?"

"They'll be fine in about thirty minutes. Hardly even a headache."

Behind the house the sun rose, turning the sky purple and giving the clouds gilt fringes. A blackbird sang. After the tunnel, the air smelt of flowers.

"This has been the best night of my life," she said.

Chapter 6: How to Prove that $x^2(MI5 + MI6 - \sqrt{2y}) = MI7$

Marcie opened the back door than went to divert Jonathan. Orlov entered the house without incident and went straight to the bathroom for a shower. When he emerged onto the landing, Hartley-Brown was knocking on his door.

"Is everything okay?" Orlov asked.

"Everything's fine, sir. It's just ... Marcie's had an idea. It cost me a few moments off duty, but I think it's got mileage. There's an old tunnel under one of the carpets downstairs. If you like, I could accompany you through it and we could get you out of here."

"Have you - ever done it before?"

"No, but she swears there's a map in the library somewhere. I'm just saying it's a possibility."

He put his teeth together. "I think we'll take our chances."

Breakfast was a buffet of bacon, eggs, fried bread and kidneys. Joy and Sir Anthony were first downstairs and they waited for everyone to assemble before starting. The men wore suits. Joy was dressed exactly as she had been yesterday. Marcie wore a pinafore dress, heels, bronze lipstick and an air of self-consciousness, and Anya wore trousers. They helped themselves to food and sat down where they'd been last night. Geoffrey poured the tea.

"Bit overdressed for a fry-up," Marcie's father told her.

Her eyes flashed annoyance. She put a whole kidney on her fork and nibbled the edge of it.

"Only saying," he added. "You look marvellous, as usual."

"Please be quiet, Daddy."

"What are we going to do about the chaps outside?" Jonathan asked.

"Just bide our time," Sir Anthony said, in a tone of being pleased to change the subject. "They'll have to show their hand today, surely. And I don't suppose they can mean us any harm. No army in its right mind attacks in full daylight when it's had the place surrounded overnight."

"Eat your kidneys," Joy told Anya.

"They're all gristly," Anya said.

"They're good for you."

"I don't like them."

"Let her get the ketchup from the kitchen, Mummy," Marcie said.

Sir Anthony pointed at Orlov with a downturned fork. "I had an excellent idea last night. Believe it or not, there's supposed to be an old escape tunnel under the entrance hall. It's probably flooded now, but we could hide you there while they search the premises if it turns out they're hostile."

"You could even go along it," Marcie said. She winked at her brother. He winked back. "If it's really 'an escape tunnel'."

Sir Anthony scoffed. "You'd have to be mad. Slightest noise, the whole thing would probably come down on your head. Assuming there's even anything left of it."

The door opened and an elderly woman entered, wearing an apron and carrying an aerosol. She went straight to Geoffrey, addressed him in a whisper then left.

"What is it, Geoffrey?" Sir Anthony said with his mouth full.

"There are some gentlemen at the door to see you, sir."

"See me or Colonel Orlov?"

"See you in the first instance, sir, although going by what Geraldine's just told me, I believe that's a courtesy. They wish to request access to Colonel Orlov and Mr Bronstein and young Mr Hartley-Brown."

"They want to see us two as well?" Bronstein said. "Why?"

"I - I don't know, sir. I - "

"Ask Geraldine to put them in the lounge, Geoffrey, if you'd be so kind. Tell them we'll be about twenty minutes. More tea or coffee, anyone?"

Geoffrey opened the door and Sir Anthony entered the lounge – a hangar-sized room with a sofa and two armchairs huddled like orphans round a fireplace and an over-ambitious nineteenth century landscape - followed by Orlov, Bronstein and Hartley-Brown. Two men in their early forties with crew cuts and black brogues stood up. One had blond hair and wire-rimmed glasses. The other had brown hair and a Rolex. Otherwise, they were identical.

"Good morning and welcome to my house, gentlemen," Sir Anthony said. "I wonder if you'd mind telling me where my security team is and why you've cut the phones off?"

"It's quite simple, sir," said the blond haired man. "Yesterday there was an attempt made on Colonel Orlov's life. We've been assigned to protect him. Too many cooks spoil the broth, so to speak, so we took the liberty of sending your team home. They didn't argue. We cut the phones to stop you calling the police. We apologise for any inconvenience."

"Why have you been loitering in the grounds? Who are you?"

"We wanted to ensure Colonel Orlov got a good night's sleep," the blond man said. "We're MI5 operatives."

"The phones are back on now," the brown haired man said.

"What about my security men? Are they back?"

"They're ready to report for duty."

"Sit down, then," Sir Anthony said, "do sit down."

"We'd like to talk to the three gentlemen you've brought in, sir, if that's not too much of an imposition."

"Privately?"

"Please."

"Colonel Orlov?"

Orlov turned to Bronstein and Hartley-Brown and exchanged nods. Sir Anthony left with Geoffrey and closed the doors. The five men still in the room remained standing, facing each other as if they were about to draw Smith & Wessons.

"We've been instructed to request all three of you to accompany us to London," the blond-haired man said.

"Request or demand?" Orlov said.

"Request. The chief was quite specific about that. If you choose not to, we've money for your flight back to Moscow or wherever else in Russia you choose to go, by whatever means. We'll even arrange transit."

"What's the catch?" Orlov said.

"And what do you want from me and Jonathan?" Bronstein said.

"I'm not authorised to answer those questions. All I can say is that if we were considering forcing you to do anything, you wouldn't be in any doubt by now."

"I'm just thinking good cop, bad cop," Bronstein said.

"And you can choose never to find out," the brown-haired man said.

Orlov looked at his watch. "I'd like a few moments to thank Sir Anthony and his family for their hospitality, then we'll be with you. We'd like to travel together, if that's acceptable."

"We'll bring the car to the front."

Sir Anthony and his family stood on the steps to wave goodbye, exactly as they'd been assembled yesterday except this time Marcie was there. Hartley-Brown thought he'd never seen her looking so weary or miserable before. It was okay, though. Now he was unemployed he could take her to a flick or rent a caravan in Wales or whatever it took to put a smile back on her face. Time wasn't an issue. Maybe they could even get a flat together some place. House arrest was clearly sapping all the life out of her. Their parents obviously meant well, but they were suffocating her with their good intentions.

There was a lorry go-slow protest on the A1 so what should have taken fifty minutes took two and a half hours. The three men endured the crawl in silence until the London suburbs came into view. The tinted windows of the Land Rover didn't open or close, but the air conditioning worked well. The morning papers were all provided, so they read until the Post Office Tower came into view.

Bronstein leaned over to Hartley-Brown. "You've got a wonderful family."

Hartley-Brown folded *The Times* and looked out of the window. "We've got our problems."

"If there's such a thing as a family without, I'd like to see it. You must come and meet mine, now you've resigned."

"Certainly, if I'm ever in New York City."

"Purim's always a good time. We have lots of dressing up, so it's impossible to tell who's who, and you're commanded to get drunk."

Hartley-Brown smiled. "Commanded?"

"At least, that's how I interpret it. What about you, Colonel? Your parents got any quirks?"

"I can't remember. They died when I was young."

"Sheesh, sorry … Got a wife? Any kids?"

"A wife and one daughter. Both dead."

Bronstein furrowed his brow then said quietly, "How? … If you don't mind me asking?"

Orlov drew a breath. "I'm an ethnic Russian. I had the good or bad fortune - depending on how you look at it - to be born in the Chechen Republic. I married a Muslim woman and we had a daughter. Then in 2000, the Russians shelled Grozny. I was serving with the thirty-second tank regiment on the Polish border at the time. I thought – I was told - they'd long since been evacuated."

"Geez."

"Are you a Muslim, sir?" Hartley-Brown asked.

"No."

"Aren't you bitter?" Bronstein asked. "Why aren't you anti-Russian?"

"Because the men who killed my wife and daughter were conscripts. You have to understand what it is to be a conscript in Russia. I'm not anti-Chechen because of Beslan or Stavropol. There are evil people on all sides. When war happens, good people get trampled - on all sides. And we can get hoodwinked into a row about which side started it, but the answer's always in internal hierarchies rather than flags. The money, the preferments. It's why I went to prison."

They drove through the streets of the City without saying anything further. Twenty minutes later, they crossed Lambeth Bridge and turned into Thames House – a sombre grey cross between a Lancashire cotton mill and a Norman Keep - where they disembarked. Hartley-Brown realised that until now, there'd been nothing to prove beyond a doubt it really was MI5 that was transporting them. There were so many double-bluffs in this particular walk of life, anything was possible. Thames House confirmed it, though. He felt relieved before he even realised he'd been anxious.

The blond and the brown haired man accompanied them across a cobbled courtyard, through a set of double doors and into a carpeted foyer with a front desk stretching almost its width. Three receptionists sat with headsets, talking and writing and ignoring new arrivals. The blond haired man and the brown haired man signed a register and took them along a corridor to an open elevator. They stepped inside, the doors chimed shut and they seemed to descend for a long time.

When it opened, they found themselves looking along a long corridor with cream walls, closed entrances on each side, and a panelled door at the end. There were no windows. The complete silence augmented the air of something not quite right. Hartley-Brown felt the hairs on the back of his neck rising again.

"Walk straight ahead," the brown haired man said.

Orlov led the way to the end and stopped. The blond man knocked and someone inside the room – a woman – called Enter. He opened the door to admit Orlov and Bronstein and Hartley-Brown and closed it without following them.

By now, they were half-expecting a dungeon. Instead they were met by a late middle-aged black woman - grey skirt suit, court shoes and stiff hair – in a whitewashed room just large enough for a desk, a PC, In and Out trays, a large tropical fish tank and a variety of house plants on different levels. Three comfortable chairs had been set out. In the corner an old white woman with grey hair in a bun sat leaning on a walking stick looking oblivious. The aerator bubbled.

"Please sit down," the black woman said. "My name is Ruby Parker. You may have heard of me, Colonel, since you once worked in intelligence, although I think it's unlikely. I'm known in some quarters as the Red Maiden, although obviously I don't encourage people to call me that except in certain categories of official memoranda. You may call me Ruby."

Orlov looked to Bronstein and Hartley-Brown for any glimmer of recognition or sense that she was dissembling. None came. "I'm afraid you have me at an advantage," he said, at last.

"Maiden or not, there's something I need to get off my chest," Bronstein said. "According to Sir Colin Bowker, your people said I'm from the CIA, yes?"

She smiled. "We told him that because we were certain it would be the final straw. Which it was. Of course it was a lie."

"Why?"

"Because we want you to come and work here. The three of you. As a unit."

There was silence. The central heating awoke and hummed softly and the room filled with a renewed sense of unreality. Hartley-Brown felt it intensely. This was Thames House, he'd seen that. And yet – surely it wasn't.

"And what do you expect in return?" Orlov said, at last.

"Nothing."

He clicked his tongue. "No information about networks of dissidents, details of global intelligence strategies, names of agents, induction protocols, site locations – none of that?"

"As I said, no thank you."

Bronstein sat forward with a grin. "Let me get this straight. You're offering him – a Russian – a chance to come and work here, at MI5. That right?"

"Roughly, yes."

"Gee whiz, I thought I'd heard everything."

She smiled dryly. "You obviously don't know there are Russians working at the CIA Headquarters in Langley, Lieutenant Bronstein."

There was another protracted silence.

"I don't believe you," Bronstein said.

Hartley-Brown drew a deep breath. "With respect ... Ms Parker? ... I think I'm speaking for all of us when I – when I say it's difficult to understand what MI5 has to gain from what you seem to be proposing." It was more than that. He wondered if there could be two Thames Houses, and this was the dummy.

"I'm trying to take the whole thing in increments," she said. "I know from experience that someone sitting where you are now, with your background, offered this opportunity, is apt to experience a period of incredulity. I'm waiting until that's passed."

"May we assume it's passed now?" Hartley-Brown said uncertainly, scanning his colleagues' faces.

"The reason you're incredulous," she went on, "is because you haven't the faintest conception of how MI5, MI6 and the FBI and CIA now work. Which is very good news for us, very bad news for the Sluzhba Vneshney Razvedki, not to mention the Direction Générale de la Sécurité Extérieure and the Bundesnachrichtendienst. We've managed to keep our rivals in the dark for over a decade."

"Bravo," Bronstein said. "Now maybe you could fill us in on what the hell you're talking about." He folded his hands together. "No disrespect."

She sat down. "I won't bore you with the details. There is no MI5. Not any more. It merged with MI6 nearly a decade ago to create MI7, the result of an initiative to bring intelligence – in the cybernetic sense of the word – into Intelligence. We continue in public under the MI5, MI6 designation for obvious reasons. And because people seem to like it."

"Right," Bronstein said.

She chuckled. "We've had effective departments of spies in this country since Francis Walsingham in the sixteenth century, Lieutenant Bronstein. The author of *Robinson Crusoe* was a spy. There was nothing special about MI5 or MI6."

"So in what way is MI7 different?" Hartley-Brown said.

"Instead of a bipartite division we now have a number of 'levels', physical and conceptual, run by different colour 'Maidens'. Five of us. The White Maiden operates on the old MI5 and 6 remit, defending the realm, narrowly conceived. Beneath her, the Red, the Blue, the Grey, the Black. The latter works alone at a depth of two miles, one and three quarter miles beneath where you're sitting."

Bronstein blinked several times in quick succession, then drew back his head and grinned. "Five maidens, no misters. My kind of town."

"Maiden is a formal designation. It doesn't specify the gender of the role's occupant."

"And you all work together, yeah?"

"On the contrary."

Bronstein looked as if he was about to burst out laughing. "No?"

"The idea is that providing every individual does his or her job conscientiously, and every department sticks to its brief, the behaviour of the whole is more rapid and rational than anything the previous pyramidal model could hope to offer. 'Intelligence must be intelligent'."

"A bit like a beehive," Hartley-Brown said, diplomatically, though his head was spinning just as much as he knew Bronstein's was.

"Each of us knows the brief of those above her," Ruby Parker continued, tapping a small tub of flakes delicately over the fish tank and watching as a group of Gouramis came to feed, "although not what steps she's taking to fulfil it. More, she's authorised to facilitate or to sabotage her projects depending on whether she chances to discover them. But none knows the brief of those below. We make our guesses naturally – I happen to think the Blue Maiden has a more military remit than I do, for example - but precise knowledge isn't possible, even if it were desirable. MI7 today is a different animal to MI7 in say 2000 or 2005, and it'll be different again in 2020. And no one can predict how."

Bronstein was still grinning. "So you're actually authorised to sabotage operations carried out by your own organisation?"

"If we discover and disapprove of them, yes."

"It's original, I'll give you that."

"It's how intelligent systems sometimes work, Lieutenant Bronstein."

Orlov looked at her. "What's your brief?"

"I can't tell you everything. Very roughly, the Red Maiden exists to disrupt despotic and protect democratic regimes."

"And who defines democratic?"

"We all do. Everyone."

Hartley-Brown raised his eyebrows. "But what if we all decide that democracy involves getting the trains to run on time or killing all the Jews?"

"Then we define it as the separation of the powers, Mr Hartley-Brown, or as universal suffrage or Mill's Harm Principle. We may think we need a definition when we're having a discussion like this, but in practice it's nearly always unnecessary."

A silence fell. For the first time, Hartley-Brown had the sense that at least part of what he was hearing made some sort of sense. Maybe time and his subconscious were cooperating to weave a spell. It had happened before. Whether it was a good or a bad thing ...

Orlov stroked his chin. "Let's say, for the sake of argument, that I came to work for you. What would I be doing?"

"You'd be continuing the investigation with which Inspector Hartley-Brown and Lieutenant Bronstein have already made commendable progress. You recognised the gunman instantly, I imagine?"

"Dmitri Vassyli Kramski."

"Which was as much of a surprise to us as it probably was to you. Have you any idea what he's up to?"

"None at all."

"Then that's what you'd be trying to find out."

"Any news on the man who attacked me at the airport?"

"So far the police have drawn a complete blank. White, mid-thirties, six-two, almost certainly an illegal. You've got lots of enemies, so the rest is guesswork. They're still working on it, obviously."

Orlov lapsed back into thought.

"Lieutenant Bronstein," she said, "I've cleared it with the NYPD for you to work here, if you choose. They're anxious not to lose your services for good, so you may prefer to accept my offer as an extension to your secondment. You can confirm that in person. There's a CIA substation on Canary Wharf, I'll give you the address and a pass. Or you can contact One Police Plaza in Manhattan. Despite your surface antagonism, I very much hope you'll say yes."

Orlov shook his head as if he was still having difficulty. "And you're saying you don't want any information from me?"

"With respect, I doubt you could tell us anything we don't already know."

"And I wouldn't be ... betraying Russia?"

"We're not interested in that kind of war."

He let out a flute of air and nodded. "Provisionally then, I'm happy."

"And it just so happens," Bronstein said with a conciliatory shrug, "that I'm looking to escape from New York. It's why I came to London in the first place."

"Oh?" Ruby Parker said.

"My folks keep trying to marry me off to Sarah, Rebekah and Esther. I'll still have to check with HQ. But if they're up for it, I guess count me in."

She turned to Hartley-Brown. It was what the cliché called a 'no brainer'. If only she'd told them they'd be working on the Kramski case when they arrived, there would have been no need for her to explain the 'Maiden' business. Which frankly, still sounded bizarre.

He smiled. "If everyone else agrees, I see no reason to decline."

She handed each a large envelope. "This contains your new address, a month's pay, bank account details and identification documents to present at the desk each morning. This lady" – she indicated the woman with the bun, who had stood up without smiling – "is Celia Demure. She headhunts and trains new agents. If you know anyone you think might be suitable, tell me in the first instance. But I warn you, she's very discriminating. Settle in to your new addresses today. Report back here at eight am sharp and I'll show you your shared office. And Colonel Orlov, I was asked to give you this."

She reached into her drawer, took out a gun and placed it on the table. His Ots-33. He looked incredulously at it then slipped it into his pocket.

Chapter 7: Oh Jilly, My Jilly

They were given an office with three desks arranged in a triangle, each with a computer, a phone, a bookshelf, and a reading lamp. A filing cabinet, a trio of plastic chairs and a strip light completed the list of furniture and fittings. They spent ten minutes familiarising themselves with the IT network then went to see Ruby Parker. She was waiting for them. They all sat down and she passed Orlov an A4 folder full of photos of the same man. Swept back hair, wide grey eyes, a pencil moustache and a resolute jaw-line.

"This is Dmitri Vassyli Kramski," she said. "Born in Vologda, twelfth of September, 1970. Joined the Fortieth Red Army in 1988 and fought in Afghanistan before the withdrawal the following year. Following the dissolution of the Soviet Union, the Fortieth was reinvented as a Khazakhstani regiment and Kramski joined the GRU. His name doesn't recur until the Moscow Apartment Bombings of 1999. We have evidence, later corroborated by the dissident, Alexander Levinsky, that he was involved in the Buynaksk explosion in 1999 and the attempted bombing of Ryazan nineteen days later."

"What was he bombing apartments for?" Bronstein asked. "Sorry, I'm from the NYPD. I don't necessarily know much about Russian stuff."

"If you like conspiracy theories," she replied, "and in this instance I do, it was a false flag operation designed to bring Vladimir Putin to power and create the pretext for another Chechen war."

"A 'false flag operation'?" Hartley-Brown said.

"An outrage perpetrated secretly by one group of people for the purpose of indicting another," Bronstein said.

"He commanded a rapid deployment unit in the North Caucasus during the second Chechen war, and there's some evidence he may have been involved in atrocities, although nothing conclusive. Two years ago, he converted to Christianity and left the army. Since the death of Patriarch Alexy II in 2008, the Russian Orthodox Church has become much more nationalist and state-friendly, although it's very difficult to imagine it sanctioning or condoning murder.

"Six weeks ago Kramski entered Britain on a false passport, which strongly suggests he's collaborating with someone, although we don't know who or why. He's going by the name of Ivan Starkov. We don't know where he's living, but even if we did we'd probably hold fire for now. He's part of a bigger picture. Colonel Orlov, how do you like going to parties?"

"I don't."

"Unfortunate then, because you're going to one tonight. A fundraiser to help your friend, Vera Gruchov, run for Mayor in the forthcoming Moscow elections. Host, Valentin Tebloev. Ring any bells?"

"You'd have to have been asleep for the past twenty years not to have heard of Valentin Tebloev," Orlov said, "but I'd be very surprised if I can penetrate his wall of bodyguards. He's very sensitive to attempts on his life and if I was thinking of making one, it wouldn't be the first."

"I've never heard of Valentin Tebloev," Hartley-Brown said.

Bronstein sighed. "I haven't been asleep for twenty years but I haven't heard of Valentin Tebloev either. How can that be?"

"He's a Russian Oligarch," Orlov said. "He once owned just about every major business in the country. He fell foul of the authorities, alienated the public with showy behaviour and had his assets seized, or what could be traced of them."

"A Russian John D Rockefeller," Bronstein said.

Orlov nodded. "Maybe, although Rockefeller didn't have to go abroad. Four years ago, Tebloev was sentenced *in absentia* to ten years for extortion. The British government granted him political asylum in 2004."

Ruby folded her hands on the table. "He knows your background, Colonel. He knows there's no love lost between you and the authorities. I think he's looking forward to meeting you."

"What's his connection to Kramski?"

"They were converted by the same man, Bishop Hilarion Sikorski, so they have lots to talk about. And Kramski's recently become one of his bodyguards. When the evening's over, we've arranged for him to be tailed. You'll play no part in that. It's too risky for a single individual and he'll know you by then."

"So whose detail is it?"

"We use tag-teams. One of the men who escorted you here – Ronnie – will be first out of the stocks. You'll see him when you come out of Tebloev's if you look hard."

"Blond or brown?"

She smiled. "Blond."

"Anything else?"

"You'll be wearing a secret camera. We need to know who's at that party. You don't need to be aware of it. We'll provide you with a dinner jacket at Supplies on the fourth floor. Just make sure you keep it on."

"What do you want us to do?" Hartley-Brown said.

"Jonathan, I want you to interview the celebrities whose photographs they were chasing. It's just a hunch but I think they may be more involved than we've imagined, although I admit I don't presently see how. David, I'd like you to continue the interviews with photographers. See if you can access any more hard drives. And look at the post-mortems of those who died of alcohol poisoning. Question the morticians."

Bronstein grinned. "So Jonathan gets to hang out with Jilly Bestwick from Four Girls on Fire. I get to hang out with a bunch of winos."

"You can swap roles if you prefer," Ruby Parker said. "It's your investigation. After you've left my office, you'll run it yourselves. I expect to be kept informed, of course, and I'll offer advice on request, but I won't interfere."

"How soon can we be expected to know Kramski's address?" Orlov said.

"Ronnie has instructions to report to you as soon as he's got a result. It's for him to choose the precise time and manner. Any further questions?"

"I've got a gigantic one," Bronstein said. "Since we know who Kramski is, why don't we just tell everyone?"

"Why not get Crimewatch to do a feature about him?" Hartley-Brown said.

Ruby Parker shook her head and smiled. "We've got the full cooperation of the Russian embassy on this and they've specifically asked us not to go down that route."

"Their reason being?" Bronstein said.

"That the press would draw unwarranted conclusions about the Kremlin's involvement from Kramski's background. Thus providing the pretext for a wave of anti-Russian feeling. Bad for business."

Orlov nodded. "Perhaps that's even its purpose. We could be playing into their hands."

"We have retained the option to make Kramski's photo public if necessary, just not his name or *nom de guerre*. Any other questions, gentlemen?"

The three men looked at each other and said no. Ruby Parker stood up.

"I have a strong intuition about this case," she said. "Most countries are torn, when they're torn, by liberals and totalitarians. In Russia there's a third group. It comes and it goes. For want of a better phrase: militant mystics. At their worst they combine the most ruthless realpolitik with the highest idealism."

Bronstein smiled. "Sounds a bit Dan Brown."

"Or even al-Qaeda," Hartley-Brown added.

"I mention it because I don't want you to waste time looking for the crude hand of the GRU or the SVR in everything you discover. If the pieces don't fit, as you Americans say ..."

"Understood," Orlov replied.

"Now, if you need to do any interviews on the premises, we have rooms available at the police station on the embankment by Waterloo Bridge. Don't bring anyone here. Jonathan, you're officially Inspector Hartley-Brown again, although of course you're no longer answerable to your old employer. And if you've no further questions, it's time for you to get to work. Good day."

Bronstein tracked Garvey Simpson to the Shoulder of Mutton and Cucumbers on Beech Street. It was dark inside and the curtains were closed. The landlady shifted chairs and vacuumed around the scuffed brogues of pensioners with patterned cardigans and glasses of Olde English 800. Bronstein sat down on a stool and leaned on the sticky bar. Simpson pretended not to notice him. The landlord read the signals and went into the back.

"Hey, it's Garvey Simpson, isn't it? The photographer?"

Simpson curled his lip and went back to his drink. "What do you want? The police have already pumped me twice. I thought you'd been taken off the case."

"I have."

"What you doing here then?"

"I've given up police work, period. I'm going to be a manager at Sainsbury's."

Simpson smirked. "Yeah? So what are you after me for?"

"*Au contraire*, I'm here to celebrate. Bartender, could I have a Highball, please?"

The landlord came out from the back of the shop. "We don't do cocktails."

"Yeah, but you can mix some orange juice with some vodka, can't you?"

"No."

"Why not?"

"I don't want to."

Garvey Simpson started to laugh. "Give him a break, Samuel. He's celebrating."

"What are you having, Garv?" Bronstein asked, when the barman changed his mind and started cooperating.

"Triple vodka, since it's you."

"I'll do better than that. Barman, give him a Highball."

"I don't want a bloody Highball."

"With two triple vodkas in," Bronstein said.

"Okay, maybe yes."

Two hours later, Bronstein took Simpson home by taxi. He put him to bed in the recovery position and jammed a toaster behind him to stop him rolling onto his back and choking on his own vomit. Then he copied his hard drive.

The foyer of the Grand Hotel in Piccadilly was a self-consciously modern mixture of stainless steel, smoked glass and potted bay trees. Despite the profusion of polishable surfaces and a pot pourri on a coffee table, it smelt of nothing. Hartley-Brown walked up to the receptionist just in time to witness the summit of that day's activity: an elderly couple on chairs flicked through postcards with pictures of double-decker buses and beefeaters on.

The receptionist finished what she was doing and smiled. "How may I help you, sir?"

"I'm here to see Jilly Bestwick."

"Could I take your name?"

He showed his imitation police card. "I believe she's expecting me."

"I'll call up. One moment." She put the phone to one ear and her finger in the other to block out extraneous noise, although there wasn't any. "Hello? Could I speak to Miss Bestwick? Yes ... Oh. Thank you, that's fine, I'll let him know." She hung up. "I'm terribly sorry, sir. Apparently, she's at a rehearsal. She's appearing on the One Show tonight."

"Where's she rehearsing?"

"I'm not sure ... I guess wherever it's being recorded."

"If you don't mind my asking, who told you she'd been called out to the One Show?"

"I think that was Robert Vincent, sir."

"'Robert Vincent'?"

"From Simply Boyz?"

"Her boyfriend?"

She smiled. "I don't think I'm giving anything away if I say yes." She passed him a copy of *The Daily Mail*. To one side of the headline stood a photograph of a miserable-looking couple walking side by side in sunglasses. She was dressed in a grey T-shirt, grey leggings and pumps; he wore baggy trousers and a hoodie. The banner said, 'Oh, Jilly, my Jilly, can this really be the end?'

"Could you ask him if it's all right for me to speak to *him*?" Hartley-Brown asked.

"I'll call their room again. Just a second."

The elderly couple finished counting their postcards and left. A young woman in sunglasses came in and stood behind Hartley-Brown. The start of a queue: probably the second most exciting thing to have happen here today.

The receptionist put the phone down. "He says he's 'out of here'. Those were his exact words. You might meet him coming down on the lift."

The woman behind tapped Hartley-Brown on the shoulder. He turned round to find himself looking at the woman from the front of *The Daily Mail* in heels and a poncho and sunglasses perched on her hair. She was smiling.

"I'm Jilly Bestwick," she said, extending her fingertips for a handshake. "It's two o'clock so I suppose you must be the Inspector."

The lift doors pinged and a man of about twenty-five stormed out and ploughed to the exit, pointing and re-pointing his index finger in time with his words. *"You ain't gone dumped me, Honey! I dumped you! Y'understand what I'm sayin', bitch? I ain't been dumped on, you have!"*

The receptionist turned her head impassively, tracking his exit.

"I think you just missed Mr Vincent, sir," she said.

Jilly Bestwick had the tall healthy look of someone who had narrowly missed a career in pole-vaulting. She had long auburn hair held back from her forehead by a violet band, large eyes beneath neatly plucked brows, thick lips, and a 'Help For Heroes' bracelet. She couldn't face going back to the hotel room so she checked out permanently. She put her sunglasses back on because she'd just exfoliated and didn't want her public to see, and went for a walk with Hartley-Brown in Green Park.

"Haven't you any things you'd like to get from your room?" he asked her.

"Let the cleaners have them. I've nothing worth keeping."

"I'm sorry about you and Mr Vincent."

She laughed hollowly. "Don't be. It's not like breaking up with an adult."

They sat down on a bench. He opened a notebook. It was a sunny afternoon and the grass was strewn with lovers and drink cans and couples with children buzzing between them as if they needed pollinating. They had to speak up to make themselves heard over the traffic beyond the sward.

"Could I ask you about the shooting again?"

"I don't think there's anything more to say."

"I've been looking at your statement. And Mr Vincent's."

"I don't know what Rob said."

"According to him, just before the shooting, you said, 'I'm not bothered about us. I'm bothered about them.' Meaning the photographers. Do you remember that?"

"Not really."

"Has no one asked you about this before?"

"You're the first."

He wondered what on earth Sir Colin's men were doing. "I mean, *could* you have said it? Does it strike you as the sort of thing you might have said?"

"I sometimes do get 'feelings' about things. I can't explain it. My great grandma was psychic. She used to give readings. But you wouldn't need to be psychic to be scared. It's happened in other places. Like to Zane Cruse, for example."

"Have you ever been stalked?"

"Not that I know of."

He handed her a picture of Dmitri Kramski. "Have you ever seen this man before?"

"Never. Do you know who he is yet?"

"We're working on it. Can I ask you if you have any theories?"

"I think he's probably a stalker, like you say. But he's very shy, if that's the right word for a psychopath."

"Have you ever met any of the other celebrities present at the shootings? Bobby Keynes? Zane Cruse? Mikey Walker? Stallone Laine?"

"No."

"Sure?"

"I – I might have. I might have met Zane."

He smiled. "'Might have'?"

"Look, it's why Rob and I split up, okay? I get on with Zane, I'm not in love with him or anything. But Rob's too immature to get that. He thinks we've got to be having sex."

He closed his notebook and put it back in his inside pocket. "Thank you for being so cooperative. Are you going straight home? I'm only asking because if you have got a stalker, I wouldn't want to leave you alone."

"Would you like a cup of coffee?" she said. "I'll buy."

His mouth popped into a smile. "I - I'd love one. I wonder if you'd mind if I just step aside and call a colleague? Let him know where I'm going."

She knew more than she was letting on, he could see that. And whatever it was, she probably shared it with Zane Cruse. He'd go and interview Cruse next. But right now, it was Bronstein he needed.

Bronstein picked up on the third ring. "Hi, Jonathan. How's Jilly?"

"She's fine. Is there any possibility of you breaking into her house and bugging it?"

Bronstein laughed. "I've been drinking highballs since breakfast. I'm up for anything."

"It's just - "

"Tell me later."

Chapter 8: The Party Animal

Orlov climbed the steps from the street to the Port Royal Hotel and showed his invitation. The doorman took him inside and directed him to the right, where the lifts were cordoned off and three expensively dressed couples discussed flight-times to Saint Lucia. The hotel's regular guests came and went, regarding the newcomers with a mixture of contempt and envy, as if they weren't sure whether they or the guests were trespassers in the new order Tebloev's party had temporarily ushered in. Outside, long cars pulled up.

The lift took Orlov and three couples to the top floor and opened to reveal a group of professional greeters waiting to pounce on them with trays of drinks and offers of introductions to other guests. There was a jazz band in the left hand corner, a buffet to the right and a dance floor in the centre, on which no one was moving. The light was strong enough to disclose a face across a crowded room yet soft enough to conceal its defects. It was clearly a networking, rather than a real party.

Orlov's greeter – a tall, slim girl of university age: they had obviously been selected on the basis of looks - took his invitation and read it as if it was a wonderful surprise. "Colonel Orlov, I'm so pleased you could make it tonight. My name's Tanya. Mr Tebloev's circulating at the moment, but he's eager to make your acquaintance. Is there anything I can get you to eat or drink?"

He smiled. "I'd like an orange juice, please."

She summoned a waiter and passed the instruction along. "I'll be looking after you tonight," she told Orlov, "so if you need anything at all, at any time, just ask. Meanwhile, Mr Tebloev's left me a list of people he thinks you'll enjoy meeting. Just follow me."

She threaded her way through the crowds, smiling back every two seconds to check he was still there, and pulled up before a triumvirate of late middle-aged men, each attached at the elbow to a woman who looked like his daughter but probably wasn't. One of the men detached himself from his friends as if he'd been expecting this.

"Colonel Orlov," Tanya said, "may I present Lionel Edgeware, the Labour MP for Hayes and Harlington. Mr Edgeware, this is Colonel Sergei Orlov, the well-known Russian dissident. Colonel Orlov, Mr Edgeware has a particular interest in the case of the Khimki journalist, Mikhail Beketov. Could I get either of you anything?"

"I'll have another Scotch," Edgeware said. "Colonel Orlov, I'm very pleased to meet you," he said, shaking his hand. "This is my wife, Sylvia."

"I've heard of Mr Beketov," Orlov said, genuinely interested, as the greeter left them. "But I've been in prison for a year, so I have some catching up to do."

"Beaten up outside his own house and left bleeding in the snow. Brain damaged, his fingers had to be amputated, sodding police aren't bothered. All because he wrote about a few dodgy land deals. I've spoken to the ambassador in London three times now. Might as well have saved myself the bother, for all the good it did."

"We're fairly convinced Vera Gruchov will be vastly different," his wife said.

"She's certainly making the right noises," Edgeware said. "She won't get very far without a war-chest, though. Why we're all here, of course."

Sylvia interlaced her fingers. "Have you ever met her, Colonel?"

Orlov cupped his orange juice in both hands. "Not in the flesh. From what I do know, I can't help thinking tonight might be in vain. She's quite particular about accepting money from overseas organisations, especially regime-changing ones. And on his own admission, Valentin Tebloev's hardly a saint. If you were her, would you want him as a public benefactor?"

"We can but try," Edgeware said.

"Why are you here," Sylvia said touchily, "if you think it's a waste of time?"

"I didn't mean to sound negative. I'm simply advising caution."

"It's a bit late for that," Edgeware said. "We've paid now. Anyway, if she doesn't want it, I'm sure Mr Tebloev can be persuaded to find some other worthy cause."

A middle-aged woman with red hair who had been standing nearby, came over with her husband. "Excuse me. I'm Henrietta Clowes, and this is my husband, Tom. Did I just hear you criticise Mr Tebloev? Because we heard something to the effect that he wasn't quite the paragon he presents himself as, last week, but Tom said not to follow it up, didn't you, Tom?"

Sylvia raised her index finger. "Colonel Orlov says he's 'hardly a saint'."

"Can I take it you think the money we're raising might not be for Miss Gruchov's campaign?" Tom said. "Because that would be fraud."

"I wasn't suggesting anything of that sort," Orlov replied. Although now he thought about it he couldn't understand why it hadn't occurred to him before.

"The cat's out of the bag now," Henrietta said.

Edgeware accepted his Scotch from the greeter. "You must have known, Tom, that he's being investigated for extortion. Everyone knows that."

"I didn't," Tom said.

"Doesn't mean he's guilty."

Orlov saw Tebloev at a distance. Slightly smaller than average, bald and stout, with a trimmed black beard, velvet jacket and lots of rings. He was flanked by three minders with headphones – one Kramski; who were the others? - and introducing himself to a group of dowagers with ingratiating charm. They looked ecstatic. At this party, everyone seemed ecstatic to see everyone.

Except Tom and Edgeware, who were arguing. Orlov caught Tanya's eye as she passed by. She smiled. "How can I help you, Colonel?"

"I wonder if you could tell me who else is on Mr Tebloev's list of people for me to meet?" he said discreetly.

"Absolutely," she whispered. "Follow me."

He excused himself to Mr and Mrs Edgeware and Tanya took him on another winding journey through Chanel-smelling torsos. They came to a stop before an old woman with feather boa. She stood alone, clutching a glass of champagne and looking as if she was on the wrong side of her limit. She was thin and erect, with a black sequin dress that reached to her pointy shoes.

"Mrs Felicity Sykes," Tanya said. "Colonel Sergei Orlov, the well-known Russian dissident. Colonel, Mrs Sykes is the widow of Robert Sykes, the British ambassador in Moscow during the Gorbachev years."

"And for a few years afterwards," she said. "I come to these things because I'm always invited. But I hate them."

"Is there anything I can get you, Mrs Sykes?" Tanya said.

She drained her glass and handed it over. "Another glass of bubbly, please, sweetie. And a chair."

Tanya turned up thirty seconds later with the champagne and an armchair on casters.

"Mr Tebloev said to make you as comfortable as possible," Tanya said.

"Tell Mr Tebloev, *Ya tseloval nogi*," she replied, sitting down. "Is that right? I'm a little rusty. *I kiss his feet*. If I start snoring, Colonel Orlov, give me a good shake. What's your name, by the way?" she asked Tanya. "A commendation's coming your way."

Tanya flushed with pleasure. "Tanya, Mrs Sykes."

"Run along then. Keep an eye out for me, though. I might need a prod."

Tanya almost curtsied. "Yes, ma'am."

"I can get anyone in this entire hotel to do anything for me," Mrs Sykes said, when Tanya had left. "Because, of course, Mr Tebloev has to have me here. I'm the centrepiece in a sense. Old establishment. Added to which, I might have contacts in the right places. Is this your first time, Colonel? I don't recall seeing you at one of his fundraisers before."

"I've only recently arrived in the country."

"Are you enjoying yourself tonight?"

"I'm being well looked after."

"I was in Moscow for ten years when Robert was alive," she said. "Nicest people in the world, but they're their own worst enemies. The whole place is riddled with gangsters now, sad to say, right from the very top. You never get rid of that sort of thing except by amputation. Another 1917, that's what the country needs."

"Does our host know you think that?"

"Valentin? Oh, yes. He's all in favour providing he doesn't have to suffer in person."

"Maybe that's what this evening's really for."

She laughed. "To raise money for a revolution? I wouldn't put it past him, the rascal. I doubt whether Vera Gruchov's going to want it. With friends like Valentin Tebloev, she doesn't need enemies, that's for sure."

Orlov looked across the hall. Sylvia Edgeware was standing next to Tebloev, whispering something into his ear.

Tebloev frowned and looked directly at Orlov. Sylvia looked at him too, then apparently registered that he was looking back. She flushed and flapped away into the crowd. Tebloev began to make his way over, pointedly ignoring those guests who were trying to catch his eye.

"Take my word for it," Mrs Sykes said, "Vera Gruchov is another Benazir Bhutto, all glitter and no depth. You don't know what it is to deal with corruption until you're really and truly in office. Only when you have to physically confront the fact that everyone – I mean everyone, from the tea-boy upwards - "

Tebloev stopped before them. "Felicity, good evening. Excuse me, Colonel. I don't believe we've met."

Orlov felt the three minders' eyes digging into him. Tebloev wasn't offering a handshake.

"Sergei Orlov," Orlov said.

"You seem to have been upsetting my guests. Of course, any suggestion that their money isn't going to end up where they think it is is likely to cause them considerable anxiety, as it would me in similar circumstances. On what do you base such claims?"

"Does Vera Gruchov know about tonight?"

"I – I believe so, yes."

"Why isn't she here?"

"Why would she be? She doesn't like to leave the country, we both know that."

"Has she sent a representative?"

"No ..."

"Why not?"

"Look, Colonel - "

"I wasn't necessarily calling your intentions into question, simply stating a fact. You're wanted in Russia for extortion. It's not my business to prejudge your guilt or innocence, but is it credible she'll risk exposing herself to charges of receiving funding from a fugitive?"

"And you think I haven't thought of that?"

"What's your solution?"

Mrs Sykes leaned forward and cackled. "I was just saying, Valentin, 'With friends like Mr Tebloev, Vera Gruchov doesn't need enemies'. Wasn't I, Colonel?"

"I believe those were your words," Orlov replied tetchily.

"We channel the funds through a series of accounts," Tebloev said.

"I don't believe you."

Tebloev reared as if he'd been struck. He looked hard at his interlocutor. "I was actually looking forward to meeting you, Colonel. I thought I might supply you with a few contacts. You'll find London can be a very lonely place for an exile without connections. You'll have to excuse me now, however. You've done me an injustice and I have other guests to meet, men and women less cynical than yourself."

He withdrew without turning his back on Orlov then turned a sharp left. The bodyguards snarled as if covering his retreat.

"Well, there aren't many people talk to Valentin Tebloev like that," Mrs Sykes said. "I hope you've come armed."

Tebloev was clearly livid. He walked past his guests without acknowledging them again and left by the exit behind the band. A moment later, Tanya appeared, looking sheepish.

"I'm ever so sorry, sir. I – I've been asked to ask you to leave."

"That's okay," Orlov replied.

Two of the bodyguards, neither of them Kramski, were coming over to enforce the request. They took up position either side of Orlov and escorted him through the crowds. He knew what was coming.

They were both about ten years younger than him, and you probably didn't get to be Valentin Tebloev's bodyguard unless you knew how to comport yourself, but he wasn't worried. What worried him was that Kramski was probably already on his way home by another route.

The corridor was empty. He sensed the movement immediately and stepped to one side. A fist crashed into the wall, crunching plaster. He grabbed it and drew his knee up into the elbow, disengaging both forearm bones from their sockets. The other bodyguard was in the act of putting on a knuckle-duster when Orlov's heel whipped his jawbone and splattered blood and teeth on the walls and carpet. He collapsed like a tossed blanket. Meanwhile, his friend was screaming. Orlov kicked his feet from under him and put his foot on his neck, suffocating him just enough to render him senseless.

The lift arrived with no one in and he pressed Ground. Two seconds later, he was out on the street, blowing steam. He saw two things at once. Kramski departing on foot at speed, and Ronnie's presumably lifeless body, dressed as a jogger and propped up on a bench with its head at an odd angle.

Kramski rounded a corner three streets ahead, and Orlov broke into a sprint so he wouldn't lose him. It looked as if he was heading for the quieter part of town.

Tailing him was no longer an option. Sooner or later he'd reach a taxi, and no matter how films usually told it, nine times out of ten that meant he was away. He'd killed a man, so he had to be stopped and brought in. He probably didn't realise he was being followed.

Orlov rounded the corner and – nothing. Tenements with cast-iron balconies either side, cars parked both sides, a street light every fifty yards. It was too long for him to have cleared it already. He had to be hiding. Which meant he knew he was being followed. Orlov took out his mobile. If Kramski thought reinforcements were on the cards, he'd be forced to break cover.

Suddenly, Kramski lunged from behind a 4x4. Orlov barely had time to spring out of the way before he realised that was the idea. Kramski was double-backing, trying to get back to the hotel and Tebloev's protection. He watched him go then set off after him again.

But then Kramski turned and hurled something. Orlov was still regaining his balance from the last evasion and it came so fast he was unable to compensate. A wheel trim. It hit him square on the temple and he buckled. Kramski suddenly had him where he wanted. He strode over to him and kicked him in the stomach.

"You didn't really imagine I was running away, did you?" he said. He picked up Orlov's mobile. "I wonder what this will tell me about what the great Colonel Orlov's been up to since he arrived in England. But let's not waste time on pleasantries, eh?"

He raised his foot to stamp on Orlov again and a shot cracked out of the silence and Kramski yelped and collapsed.

Mrs Sykes stood behind them in a fur coat with a clutch bag, holding a silver pistol. "I'd back off if I was you, young man. I've never killed anyone before but I'm seventy-seven. A life sentence holds no fears for me."

The last thing Orlov was conscious of was Kramski dragging his leg as he fled into the darkness, and Mrs Sykes chortling before picking up his phone and calling an ambulance.

It suddenly occurred to him that he'd met her before tonight.

Chapter 9: More Ace Stuff About Jilly

As soon as she heard Ronnie was dead, Ruby Parker rushed to Thames House. She took some letter-paper from her desk and wrote: 'Information Request: were you in any way involved in the murder of Agent Ronald Giles outside the Port Royal Hotel this evening?'

She sealed it in an envelope and took it upstairs to the receptionist on duty, a sallow young woman with thin hair.

"I'd like you to see this reaches the Blue Maiden as a matter of priority, please," she told her.

Half an hour later she received a reply, bought to her in her office, as she expected, by a man she had never seen before. She tore open the envelope and read the single word, 'Negative'.

She expelled a sigh of relief.

"Celia Demure," Sir Anthony said. "And it's a great opportunity. Don't balk at it."

"I wasn't," Marcie replied.

The four Hartley-Browns were eating breakfast in the dining room. Anya and Marcie had Sugar Puffs, Joy and Sir Anthony cornflakes. Outside, spring was at its zenith. The leaves fluttered and sparrows chased each other in and out of the branches. In here, everything was exactly it had been for over four hundred years. Marcie could actually feel herself wasting away.

"Back to school tomorrow, Anya, eh?" Sir Anthony said.

"Don't remind her," Marcie said.

Anya put a spoonful of Sugar Puffs in her mouth. "I don't like school."

"You're not supposed to," Sir Anthony said. "You go there to learn useful information so you can qualify as an investment banker or an expert in corporate law."

"Who is this Celia Demure?" Joy said. "She's not one of your bits on the side is she?"

"She's seventy-something," Sir Anthony said. "And I'd hardly be introducing her to Marcie if I was knocking her off, would I?"

Marcie slammed her spoon down, making Anya jump.

The two parents sulked for a few moments then Joy reached for the toast and butter. "So what's going on?" she asked.

Sir Anthony smiled. "I've explained to Marcie, I'll explain to you. I bumped into Celia Demure the other day. She's not exactly a friend of mine, never has been, but she's a friend of friends and people speak very highly of her. She used to be a gymnast, Olympic standard. A few injuries combined to ruin her chances. As luck would have it, she's hoping to reopen the gym school she used to run in the eighties."

"Where does Marcie come in? Given that she's got all the athletic grace of an elephant?"

Marcie sighed. "Excuse me, Mummy, I am present in the room, you know."

"No offence intended," Joy said. "I'm just trying to work out where your father's going with this."

"Perhaps if you let me finish," he said, "you'll find out. You tell her, Marcie. She's obviously not prepared to listen to me."

Marcie swallowed what she was eating. "Pass me a piece of toast, please, Anya. The bottom line is, Mummy, Miss Demure can't do gymnastics herself any more and it's 'moved on' since her day. So she wants a guinea pig to order about, see if her methods still work."

"That's the beauty of it," Sir Anthony said. "She actually *needs* someone who's got all the athletic grace of an elephant, see if she can turn her into Olga Korbut."

"She'll have her work cut out with Marcie," Joy said. "Joke, dear. What's she paying?"

"Frankly, it wouldn't have to be much," Sir Anthony replied. "But as it happens, she's offering a very generous two hundred a week, plus accommodation in the heart of London, plus free evening meals."

Marcie put her toast down. "Wow. You never told me that."

"It'll be bloody hard work, though, don't get me wrong."

"I don't care. I can do hard work."

"And of course, you'd be able to go and see Jonathan," he said.

She'd just reached for the butter. She leant back again. "Is Jonathan in London? What's he doing? I thought he was unemployed?"

"He must have come to his senses and kissed an arse or two."

"Oh, how spineless," she said.

He scoffed. "You can't eat principles. They're only made of gas. He's finally growing up, if you ask me."

"Is he still working with Mr Bronstein?"

"I don't know. He hasn't mentioned him."

"What about Colonel Orlov? Have they sent him back to Russia?"

"I don't know."

"But Colonel Orlov could be in London, couldn't he? With Jonathan?"

Sir Anthony and Joy exchanged looks. He sat up. "Don't go falling for someone you know nothing about."

"I wasn't!"

"I've nothing against the Russians or anyone else, but you don't know a blind thing about him. And don't give me that wide-eyed innocent look, Marciella Hartley-Brown. You came down in a ne'er-seen-before dress and half a pound of greasepaint the day he was leaving."

"It's none of your business."

"Did he come on to you?"

"No, he didn't 'come on' to me! Look, Daddy, you're hardly in a position to lecture me on inappropriate liaisons. If you're up for a mud-slinging contest, though, fire away, because I warn you, I'll give as good as I get!"

He reddened and deflated. "I – I'm sorry. I just care about you, that's all. You're my daughter. And you're very attractive. And - and maybe you're even a bit lonely sometimes. I don't want men taking advantage of you."

"Apology accepted. Now I don't want to hear any more about it. Ever."

Anya climbed onto Joy's knee and put her arms round her neck. "I hate school, Mummy. Especially Janine."

Joy kissed her. "You don't have to become an investment banker or an expert in corporate law for me, beauty. I'll always love you whatever."

"So what do you say, Marcie?" Sir Anthony said. "Are you up for a spot of gymnastics?"

In a conference room on the fourth floor of Thames House, Orlov, Bronstein, Hartley-Brown and Ruby Parker sat watching a DVD of Tebloev's party. The tables were set out in three sides of a square, with a retractable screen making up the fourth. A junior intelligence officer called Gavin stood by the picture with a pointing stick and kept freeze-framing it to identify individuals. He was tall with a suit and had black hair and a white, pudgy face.

"Although you weren't at the party for very long, Colonel," he said, "you managed to get a good few three-sixties, so we've been able to identify a number of faces."

"Gavin's being polite," Ruby Parker said dryly. "The truth is, if it hadn't been for Miss Demure's involvement, we'd have very little footage."

"She gave me the impression she was a frequent guest of Mr Tebloev's," Orlov said.

"Of course, she would."

"Have you traced any of the money?"

Ruby Parker nodded. "Some of it. It's as he said. It passes through an intricate network of accounts, from direct debit to direct debit. Almost impossible for anyone outside to keep track of. I think you're right, though. It's unlikely any of it's going to Vera Gruchov."

He smiled. "I'd go further than that."

"Oh?"

"His sieving it through a matrix of micro-accounts indicates he wants to avoid embarrassing her. His throwing an ostentatious fundraiser in the middle of London indicates he doesn't care. It can't be both."

"Given that it's so conspicuous," Hartley-Brown said, "she must have heard of it. Why doesn't she say something?"

Bronstein rested his chin in his palm. "Perhaps she's hoping he'll go away."

"Maybe she's in a quandary," Orlov said. "Doesn't want to welcome Tebloev on board, doesn't want to set sail without him. Whatever else he may be, he's a talented businessman. One day soon, the wind in Russia will change – not necessarily for the good – and Tebloev will be pardoned. Then he's likely to become very powerful again, quickly. A kingmaker, like your Rupert Murdoch."

Bronstein laughed. "You mean, she's hardly the idealist she's cracked up to be? Golly gee."

"Sensible idealists in politics only expose themselves when all the cards are on the table," Orlov replied. "Those who show themselves too early aren't doing anyone any favours."

"I recognise those three men," Hartley-Brown said, pointing to the evening suits on the screen.

Gavin paused it. "The first, of course, introduces himself. Lionel Edgeware, the Labour MP for Hayes and Harlington. About a year ago he was deeply implicated in the expenses scandal. Bought a Queen Anne fireplace plus basket, a state of the art television, inter alia."

"'Inter alia'?" Bronstein said.

"It means, 'Among other things'," Ruby Parker explained wearily. "Gavin went to Balliol, didn't you, Gavin?"

"Sorry, ma'am, yes," he replied. "Unlike many other MPs in his position, Mr Edgeware decided not to resign or retire, but to show public contrition. He spends most of his free time nowadays doing good works in his constituency, and since it's a safe seat and he was always viewed as a bit of an eccentric anyway, he's expecting to retain it at the next election."

"Which is how far away?" Orlov said.

"Two months at the outside," Gavin said.

"Did he get a new wife on expenses?" Bronstein asked.

Gavin cleared his throat. "There's every reason to think Mr Edgeware's expressed concern for the case of the Khimki journalist, Mikhail Beketov, is genuine. We know he's raised the matter with the British embassy in Moscow, and that he's interested in several similar cases. Yuri Grachev, for instance, and Andrei Khmelevsky. It's likely, in other words, that he's at Mr Tebloev's party because he's a genuine idealist, not because he hopes to profit materially in some way."

"Despite the antique fireplace and the state of the art TV?" Bronstein said. "I think we should keep an open mind."

"Point taken," Ruby Parker said.

"The other two men are Herbert McLellan and Charles Inwood, the conservative MPs for Enfield Southgate and Gravesham respectively. Fared similarly in the expenses scandal, for similar reasons. Adopted similar means of coping. They're currently keeping a very low profile on the back benches, being nice to people, donating to charity, hoping to be forgiven."

"Anyone else we ought to know about?" Orlov said.

"We were hoping for a sighting of the mysterious Constantine Slope," Ruby Parker said. "He was supposed to be at the party somewhere. At least he was on the guest list. But we couldn't see him on any of the footage, yours or Celia's. Everyone who appears there is accounted for."

"Who's Constantine Slope?" Orlov asked.

"A businessman. Nothing intrinsically suspicious about him except that he's very rich and we've no record of a previous connection between him and Tebloev."

"Probably decided not to bother going," Hartley-Brown said. "My father's on the guest-list for a lot of parties. If he's busy or reluctant, he just sends his apologies and that's it."

"The question is, why he was invited," Ruby Parker said. "But it's a minor one for now. While we're all here, you might as well fill me in on how everything's proceeding elsewhere. What about you, David?"

"I've checked out the contents of eight separate hard drives, over six hundred photos. There was nothing on any of them that we didn't know already. Obviously, they were swapping significant JPGs hoping the potential for a scoop would grow to the point where it got lucrative. Now that we've put Kramski's picture out there, we've popped their bubble. I don't think they'll be withholding any more evidence."

"How close are we to finding Kramski?" Orlov said.

"No more than we were," Ruby Parker said. "We've renewed the All Ports Warning. The police got an address for him after they interviewed Tebloev about Ronnie's death. But he wasn't living there any more, if he ever was."

"And presumably Tebloev knew nothing about him."

"According to Tebloev, he was a compatriot with a talent for protection, that's all. He hardly knew him."

"Clean as a whistle," Bronstein said.

"What about the bugging device you installed in Jilly Bestwick's flat?" Ruby Parker said. "How's that coming along, information-wise?"

"Nothing yet," Bronstein replied. "Although I've a hunch it's going somewhere. I can't make out what she and Zane Cruse see in each other. He's got a girlfriend, so he's not interested in her. And she's not enticed by him. They don't even seem to get on very well. Very occasionally, they'll confide in each other. Something dumb, like he saw this hot girl in Tesco. Or what she read about Alesha Dixon in *Reveal*."

"Is it worth maintaining?" Ruby Parker said.

"Until I work out what they're doing together, yes. It was your idea to zero in on the celebs, after all. And I wouldn't remind you of that, incidentally, if I didn't think you were on to something."

"What about you, Jonathan?"

"I agree with David. I don't know quite what it is, but there's something not quite right about them. I've interviewed all the celebrities involved in the shootings now, and – I don't know, it's just a hunch – none of them have seemed fully candid."

"So what are we going to do to move the investigation forward?" Ruby Parker said.

"I'm going to attempt to draw Kramski," Orlov said. "I've contacted the editor of the *Russian London Courier* and I intend to denounce Tebloev's fundraiser a little more publicly. If Kramski's in league with him, as I think he is, he'll come after me."

She bristled. "That would be a mistake."

"Other than trying to follow the money and listening to the bug and hoping for another development, I'm not sure what options we've got."

"You saw what happened when you tried to leave Russia," she said. "As far as I know, the Kremlin now believes that if you *were* bent on divulging something it's too late to stop you. And since they don't know where you are, killing you for the sake of sending a message is likely to be too time consuming. If you go shouting from the rooftops, that may change. Leave it."

"I want to go and have a look at the house where Tebloev claimed Kramski lived," Hartley-Brown said. "There may be something the police have missed."

Ruby Parker shook her head despairingly and folded her hands on the table. "We're scraping the bottom of the barrel, gentlemen."

Orlov went to sit outside Tebloev's flat, and log arrivals and departures. Hartley-Brown and Bronstein went downstairs to their office in Basement One.

Bronstein donned a pair of headphones and listened to another tape of Jilly Bestwick in her flat. She had *Casualty* on and she was stirring something. Hartley-Brown took out a fountain pen, filled in a form then went out to the kitchen and made them both a coffee.

Bronstein removed his headphones. "Thanks, Buddy."

"Can I tell you something, David? I mean, in confidence?"

"Sure."

"I think I'm in love with Jilly Bestwick."

Bronstein whistled a long descending note and laughed. "Well, you did the right thing, informing a colleague. We wouldn't want you to be compromised. Are you going to ask to be taken off the case?"

"I think I probably should."

Bronstein seemed to consider something then make up his mind. "I was saving this for a rainy day."

"Saving what?"

"I thought it would crack you up. Sit down, sit down. Wait, I'll just rewind to … 4632, that's right, I made a note. Listen to this."

He pressed play. In the background, Rihanna sang *Umbrella*. There was a clunk, then Jilly said, "Can I tell you something, Zane?"

"Yeah, sure," Zane said.

"I think I've met someone I really fancy."

"Shouldn't be a problem, your bod."

More *Umbrella*.

"I don't mean I want to sleep with him," she said. "I mean, I do, but … "

"Who is he?"

"That's the problem. He's a policeman. Jonathan, he's called. You met him the other day."

"What? That fag?"

"He's not a 'fag'. Anyway, that's homophobic."

"All right, queer then."

"Bloody hell, Zane, you're a Nazi. I don't know what you're laughing for either. If your fans find out, you might as well kiss them goodbye. Serve you right too."

"Take it easy."

"No, I won't take it easy," she said. "That sort of thing gets right up my nose. I wish I'd never said anything now."

"Yeah that's right, you just keep your trap shut."

Bronstein pressed stop. "See what I mean about their relationship? Weird."

"I wonder if I should invite her home to meet my parents," Hartley-Brown said.

"She's one quarter of a girl band, so she's got three cute friends she could hang out with. There's no friction between them as far as I've been able to discover. And yet she chooses to chill with Hermann Goering."

"I agree, it doesn't make sense."

"How far has it gone already? You and her?"

"I've done nothing to reproach myself for."

Bronstein grinned. "Yeah, but seriously, what?"

"We went for a coffee and an ice-cream, then a day later I took her to dinner, then we went to the Tate Modern and yesterday to Hampton Court Maze."

"Sheesh. All in the line of duty?"

"I think so, yes, although obviously I enjoyed it. I filed a report."

"Paparazzi there?"

"She dresses down when she doesn't want to be recognised. But I suppose it's only a matter of time."

Bronstein hooted. "Don't you see?"

"What?"

"You heard what Ruby Tuesday just said. We're scraping the bottom of the barrel. This could be just what the investigation's looking for."

"I still don't follow."

"Whatever the connection between her and Kramski – whatever he was doing outside her guest house in the Lake District, if he's just some kind of twisted stalker – maybe the news that she's dating a cop will rile him. Especially if you're both seen in company with the Colonel."

"How could we do that?"

"You've got to persuade Jilly she could use a bodyguard. Then we get him to apply and you're there when she makes her choice."

Hartley-Brown thought for a moment. He sipped his coffee. "I think I love her. I don't want her to get hurt."

"And yet it's your job."

"Maybe I should resign then."

Bronstein clicked his tongue. "You've done that once already since I arrived in this country. You can't hand in your notice every time you hit choppy water. Anyway, she's a pop star, probably a millionaire. How many pop stars do you know who have boyfriends with no job and no prospects? Pop star plus cop has low enough odds already."

"Yes, yes, I take your point."

"Look, we'll look after her. We'll get the Maiden to put a few extra guys on. She'll be more than happy if she thinks we're up and running. And when it's all over, when Kramski's in the slammer and we've fed Tebloev to the lions, you can even tie the knot if you're still hot for each other. Meanwhile, here's a twenty. Go and buy Jilly a bunch of flowers. I mean it, boy. Drink up and scoot."

Chapter 10: The Disconcerting Photomatic

The door of 10 Downing Street opened. Theodore Ferguson – an old Gordonstounian with prematurely grey hair and a moustache - advanced to a podium followed at two paces by his spouse. Cameras clicked, whirred and flashed, otherwise there was an expectant silence. He rearranged a sheaf of papers and waited till his cabinet had assembled behind him with his wife to the fore, then smiled.

"This morning," he said, "I went to Buckingham Palace to ask the Queen to dissolve Parliament. She kindly agreed to my request, with the result that a general election will now take place on June the tenth." He paused to allow this information to sink in, although it had been universally anticipated, and continued, "I have always believed in the values of fairness, justice and equality. Over the last five years, my party has striven to weave these values more securely into the fabric of British life. Since the beginning of the global economic recession, our determination to live up to our ideals has not only remained intact, but has strengthened. We will say to the British people, we have your deepest concerns at heart. Let us continue to work together so we can all prosper on the most solid of foundations. Thank you."

He gathered his papers, smiled again and retired without taking any questions.

Jilly got up and switched the television off.

Hartley-Brown's flat had a bedroom, a bathroom and a living room. He'd painted the walls cream, hung Colourist prints of Iona and the Côte d'Azur and had a new carpet laid. The day he realised he was in love with Jilly he bought two new linen sofas and had the old ones put in storage in case they smelt of the previous owner in a way only a sensitive nose might discern. When she returned to sit down, he put his arm round her.

"Will you have to go electioneering now?" she said.

"I doubt it. My father's always told me to keep out of the way before. I mean, as in, pretend you don't exist."

"Yes, but you're older now than you were five years ago. And you're really good looking. I'd vote for whoever you told me to. I'd take one look at you - "

"I think he already has lots of helpers."

"I'm only asking because I thought we could do it together."

"What? Go canvassing?"

She shrugged. "Why not?"

"What about your fans? People don't like the Conservatives. Or they like to make out they don't."

"I've been talking to a lot of celebrities lately, friends of mine like Gary Boyler and Kim Flatt. Lots of us are going to get involved. Not like, 'I support this party', although we'll each have to choose one, but like, 'Don't give up on politics, it's important'. Young people have got to realise."

"I never knew you thought that."

She started to undo his shirt buttons. "There are lots of things you don't know about me, John."

He stood up. "Don't Jilly, please."

"What do you mean?"

"It's just I – I really like you," he said, putting his hands on his head and walking to the other end of the room. "Actually, that's wrong. I don't 'really like you'. I'm in love with you."

"What?"

"I didn't set out to be, honestly. I'm sorry. I know it's mixing the professional and the personal too fully. I mean, a day out at Hampton Court or walking round Hyde Park with a bag of doughnuts, that's mixing the personal and professional, but I was off duty, and it's not the same because - "

"Stop there, Jonathan. Just stop there."

"I'm sorry."

"Don't be, because the feeling's mutual."

"But you don't understand, Jilly. When I say I love you, I don't mean I want a string of dates and sex in a lift. I mean, I really love you. Like I want to be with you twenty-four seven."

"I can beat that. Three sixty-five."

"And a quarter. For ever."

She leapt on him and their mouths banged into each other, their eyes closed and they fell over on the coffee table.

"Stop," he said, gasping for breath. "Jilly, I've never asked you for anything like I'm asking this now. I love you. I love you. Put your coat on. We're going for a walk. Just trust me. I love you, just trust me."

He was already getting ready to leave. She got up, looking bemused, and put on her coat and shoes and linked arms with him. They went downstairs. It was dark and raining hard. They didn't have an umbrella. When they'd crossed six streets, he turned to her and kissed her passionately.

"I'm a secret agent," he said.

"But I thought you were a policeman."

"I was, once. I can't tell you much, Jilly, but I don't want to deceive you any more. I love you."

"I don't understand. What does a secret agent want with me?"

"We're looking for the man who shot the photographer, that's all. Someone thought it would be a good idea to interview the celebrities who were the reason why the photographers were there when each photographer was shot."

"So all this stuff about your father being a Tory MP - "

"That's all true. The only thing I lied to you about was being a police inspector. It's just, I don't want to sleep with you because I could be being filmed."

"What do you mean?"

"You've got to get used to the idea, when you're in my line of work, that people might be gathering information to blackmail you. By whatever means."

She laughed. "Jonathan, what century are you living in? Haven't you heard of *One Night in Paris*? Or Pamela Anderson and Tommy Lee? There are couples knocking all over the net. It's not as if they're hurting anyone. It's not like being cruel to children or animals, there's no shame. Well, yes there is, I suppose, I wouldn't want it, but no one could blackmail you."

"Apart from anything else, you'd look pretty stupid on film if you'd never had sex before."

"But I have," she said.

"I meant me."

She gasped then grinned. "Ah, I see."

"And my father would look ridiculous if they showed it in the multiplex in Hertford," he added by way of lightening the mood. "He'd probably lose his seat."

She started giggling and she couldn't stop. They had to find a bench so she could sit down.

"I love you," he said. "I may not be able to sleep with you yet, but I'm going to prove I'm serious. I'd like you to meet my parents."

"What? Really?"

"I've never introduced a young woman to them before, not on a 'this is my girlfriend' basis. They probably think I'm gay. Not that it matters what they think."

"Jonathan, how much money have you got? I mean, on you?"

"Not much. I've got a credit card. Why?"

"I've got about eighty pounds. We could find a random hotel. No one would have time to set up a camera and we could switch all the lights off."

His eyes lit up.

At midday Marcie got off the train at King's Cross and took the tube to Shoreditch. She had to cross the local park to get to the Leisure Centre where she was supposed to meet Miss Demure, and when she was halfway, she was attacked by a middle aged man in a donkey jacket and jeans wearing a wig as a disguise. She was on her back in front of him before she realised what was happening.

"Give me your bag," he said, wiping his mouth. She guessed he'd been drinking. Her heart raced.

She knew the sensible thing was to do as he said, but she didn't want to – her bag had her pocket money, iphone and credit card in. There were people around, so she knew she wouldn't have to run far to find safety. She bounced to her feet and was off across the grass.

But he seemed to have anticipated this. He gained on her and with her hair loose behind her, she was vulnerable. By the tennis courts, when he was almost on top of her, she threw herself on the ground and he caught his boot on her torso and flew headlong, landing on his neck.

She was in agony, but she put it out of her mind and bounced to her feet – this time into battle. She kicked him in the face as he was getting up. He flipped backwards like he was on a spring, his nose smashed. She kicked him again in the left temple when he began to raise himself. This time he didn't move.

She was gasping hard. All around her, she could see couples walking or lying on the grass, children running, dogs scampering. Why hadn't anyone helped her? She felt giddy and liberated and for a moment all she wanted to do was laugh.

Then she began to tremble and reached for her mobile and dialled 999. There was a CCTV camera nearby. Assuming it had film in, she wouldn't have to say or do much in court.

They were asking her for a description. She was light headed and short on focus. A description, a description …

But when she looked back to where her mugger lay, he'd gone.

On the other side of the park, Celia Demure sat in her flat and waited. A leather suite faced an unused coal fire, and a bookshelf stood beside the one window. Her only personal possession stood on a tea-table beneath a lamp: a framed photograph of herself – jet-black hair, heavy make-up and a cheongsam - with a rugged blond man, fifty years ago on a balcony overlooking the Larvotto in Monte Carlo. At its base, a strip of paper read: 'Like the hart desireth the water-brooks, so longeth my soul after thee. Psalm 42.1'.

It was about time now. She switched the television on and went to AV. The screen was hooked up to a closed circuit camera so she could watch her latest prospect fail to fend off Clive. Looking at the way she ambled across the park, she wouldn't put up much of a fight. Clive had instructions to challenge her and, if necessary, rough her up a little to test her reflexes. 'The police' would retrieve her bag for her later, minus Clive's fee.

When Marcie threw herself down and Clive had a crash Celia Demure realised she'd misjudged her and she thrilled. She inched involuntarily forward when Marcie went on the attack. Kicking Clive twice in the head – that was good thinking. Most people would have gone for his chest or stomach and left him relatively unscathed.

But what really struck her was what Marcie did when the battle was over and Clive had scrambled away.

She threw her head back and laughed.

She had a prodigy on her hands. Five minutes later there was a knock at the door. Miss Demure grabbed her walking stick and leant on it.

Marciella showed up even better than she had on camera. There was nothing of the ragbag about her, unlike of so many other girls her age. Smart grey mini-skirt, newly-ironed button up blouse and an Alice band.

"Come in, come in. You must be Sir Anthony Hartley-Brown's daughter, Marciella."

"Call me Marcie. Marcie Brown. I've never liked the 'Hartley-Brown' thing. It sounds like a bad kind of jam."

"Just 'Marcie Brown'."

"I hope this doesn't seem like too much of an imposition, but the police might be along shortly. I was almost mugged a moment ago."

"Oh, my. Are you all right? Sit down, please sit down. Let me get you something. A cup of tea with lots of sugar – or coffee?"

Marcie sat down on the armchair. She didn't appear unduly shaken. "I thought I'd better report it right away, otherwise he might pounce on some other poor woman. I'm not fazed."

"How did you manage to get away?"

"Oh, I – I kicked him in the head. Sorry if that sounds a bit unladylike." She laughed. "It was good gymnastics training, though."

For a moment, Miss Demure thought Marcie might know more than she was letting on. But then she saw her remark for what it was: an honest assessment of her own reaction. She had style, that was clear. She already liked her a lot.

"Do you want to interview me?" Marcie said.

"Not to decide whether to take you on. I've already told your father I'm happy about that. But I would like to find out a little bit about you and find out whether I'm suitable for you."

"You for me?"

"What I'm offering in the way of work is by no means permanent. When I terminate your contract, which eventually I'll have to, what will you do?"

"I'll find something."

"I don't want you to look back and feel that you've wasted a year of your youth humouring an old lady."

"Miss Demure - "

"Celia."

"Celia, my parents are very well connected. I know that sounds smarmy, but it isn't. It's just a fact. They'll find me something. Talking of that though, there's something I suppose I should tell you. It's ... I've a criminal record."

Miss Demure reared slightly. "Really?"

"That's why I'm here, I guess. If it wasn't for that, I don't know what I'd be doing."

"What sort of a criminal record?"

"Some boys were bothering a friend of mine outside this club in Hertford, about three in the morning. She was drunk. We both were, although I wasn't half as plastered as her. The rest of my so-called friends wanted to leave her, but I didn't – the guys were druggies, for God's sake, they'd probably have raped her - so they left both of us. Anyway, the boys started skateboarding at us so I picked up this guy's board and smashed his jaw then I threw it at the kid on the bike and he crumpled and the police happened to be driving by and it's all a bit hazy after that."

"I see."

"I always think that in most fights, if you haven't won in the first thirty seconds, you might as well throw in the towel. You don't save the big guns till last. I'm sorry if that's a bit off putting."

"On the contrary, it's nice to meet someone with a bit of pluck."

Marcie beamed. "Thank you."

"I don't exactly have an unblemished past myself. It may sound incredible – you'll probably think I'm making it up, but I'm not - I used to run a criminal gang when I was younger. You don't need to know the details. Suffice it to say, we're not as different as you might have imagined when you walked in here."

"I think I'm going to like this job."

"Don't get your hopes up. I'm not easy to work for. I demand one hundred per cent at all times. I don't necessarily hold the conventional working day sacrosanct, I may ring you up in the middle of the night and tell you to come over and start practising. I don't necessarily think eight hours a day is enough. There will be times when you hate me, whatever you might think now. The most important characteristic you can possess is a strong will. The will to see things through, whatever contrary emotions may grip you along the way. Do you think you're up for that?"

"Sure, but …"

"But what?"

"I thought you were starting a gymnastics school. You make it sound like a military training camp."

"Can you keep a secret?"

Marcie leaned forward as if there was a third person in the room, listening. "I've lots of secrets. Not mine, other people's. I've never let a single one go."

"Very well. It's going to have a self-defence slant. No one wants to do straight gymnastics any more. But martial arts, how to throw and fall and avoid - those sorts of things have street credibility. Of course, we're merely talking about City executives living out Ethan Hunt fantasies, but it's where the money is nowadays. And they're not going to part with their money for nothing. Most of them are intelligent enough to recognise an inferior product, and there's a lot of competition out there."

Marcie was nodding. "Cool."

"And so don't tell anyone. I mean anyone. Consider it an industrial secret."

Orlov and Bronstein sat in Orlov's flat, drinking bourbon and playing chess. The television was on in the background.

"Should we be worried about Jonathan?" Orlov said.

"He's utterly gone for this girl. I'm pretty sure he's going to tell her all about us. If he hasn't already."

"Do you think he'll tell her about the bug?"

"I've taken it out of her flat. I've told him that too, so he's nothing to tell her."

"Do you think it's worth my applying to be her bodyguard?"

"Nope."

"I'm reluctant to have him taken off the case, but if Ruby Parker finds out he's emotionally involved, she'll probably insist."

"We'd better make sure she doesn't then."

"Can we justify that?"

"Sure. If this had been old-style MI5, MI6, CIA, I might have been worried. But the way MI7's set up, no one's worth capturing or pumping for information. Imagine you're captured by some hostile foreign government and they start torturing you. What are you going to tell them when you finally crack? All you know is that you work underground with someone called the Red Maiden, whose agenda you barely know, and that there are other colour Maidens whose agendas you don't know at all. They'd probably think you were on LSD."

"Which may be precisely why she's got that designation."

"Besides, how many times is a guy like Jonathan going to fall in love? This is his big one, maybe his only one, him being a cop. And it's not like she's working for Dr Evil. She's just a kid and we're monitoring her because we're desperate."

"We're assuming she's not working alongside Kramski then."

"If she is, and she lets on, Jonathan's so honest he'll come running to us. Think about it. If you're in love, you tell each other things. If she's got anything worth telling, this is our best chance of finding out what."

"You don't think she could turn him, get him working as a double agent? Worst case scenario, but there's no point avoiding it."

"Some people will sell their souls for love. I'm not underestimating how badly Jonathan's been bitten, but I don't think he's one of them."

"He's an odd character."

"My grandmother survived the Holocaust. She lived with us when I was a kid, so I've spent a lot of my life listening to stories about genocide and survival and wondering why I'm so lucky to live in peacetime and how soon it'll be before it all comes crashing down again. She actually used to read me *Josephine the Singer or the Mouse Folk* at bedtime. You lost your wife and kids, I can't even begin to imagine what that must be like. Yeah, Jonathan looks odd to us, but it's only because he doesn't reek of the underworld."

"Do you think Jilly Bestwick has anything worth telling us?"

Bronstein moved his Bishop two spaces. "On balance," he said, "yes. For his sake, I hope it's not too much."

Orlov's landline rang. He stepped two places to the window sill, picked it up and nodded.

"Thank you," he said, after a moment. He hung up, resumed his seat and moved his rook five spaces to the left. "Check."

"Anyone I know?" Bronstein said.

"Julian, the doorman. Jonathan's on his way upstairs."

"You invite him?"

"No."

"Guess he must have had a eureka moment."

They stood up and went to the door. Hartley-Brown appeared, mounting the stairs in a jumper and jeans with a laptop under his arm. He looked sombre.

"What's up?" Bronstein said.

"I think I've found something," Hartley-Brown said.

Orlov laughed. "You don't look very happy about it."

"It's Jilly," he replied.

Hartley-Brown put the laptop on the table and switched it on. They all drew up chairs.

"I had an idea," Hartley-Brown said. "David, it was after you said you'd recovered six hundred photos from hard drives. It struck me we might be able to group them, put them into some sort of sequence, maybe even make a computer program to fill the missing links or reference different angles. To cut a long story short, I created the program and fed the images in as I thought they should go and pressed 'process'. What came out was a photomatic, not very good, but good enough to cast new light on what happened. "

Bronstein laughed. "Way to go, Jonathan, you're a dark horse."

"Ingenious," said Orlov.

"Firstly a control. This is Daniella Mordan coming out of the Dorchester last year, before the shootings began. The paparazzi are on the left. Notice how she eyeballs them in the early stages then focuses on her exit. Two modes of vision, one, hostile and two, reassured: two directions. Right from the start, her body's primed for a sprint. And ... there she goes. I've looked at five other instances of the same thing. The pattern hardly varies."

"Figures," Bronstein said.

"Now look at event code SL/Q01, Bobby Keynes, the first of our cases. I'll go four frames a second first so I can talk you through it. Keynes is here, on the left. Notice his eyes. He's clearly looking for something, eyes sweeping, expression, anxious. He's not even looking at the paparazzi. His body language is all wrong. I'm not just saying that. I ran the whole thing past the psychological profiler on floor two thirty minutes ago."

"Thorough," Bronstein said.

"I'm slowing it to two frames a second. Watch. Keynes reacts. He sees something right in front of him, rears slightly and then – that's when the bullet comes in. If we extrapolate from his gaze at that moment, it comes in from exactly the same place.

"Watch the same thing from a different angle. Watch his eyes. Now his reaction. No one else has reacted, just him. And remember his witness statement: 'The first I knew anything had happened, the man was dead. It took me a few seconds to realise what was going on.' Doubly significant because this was the first murder. How did he know?"

Orlov sat back. "Presumably, as regards the other cases, up to and including Jilly Bestwick, you could argue that similar behaviour simply indicates that they were reasonably nervous in the wake of the preceding murders."

"Except," Hartley-Brown said, "that I've checked these against other celebrity exits elsewhere at the same points in time, exits with no killings. There's nothing like the same degree of bodily anxiety. Now watch this."

He double clicked on SL/Q05. Jilly Bestwick appeared with Robert Vincent, coming out of a guesthouse.

"Notice the sunglasses. Her instinct is to frustrate the paparazzi, but she's obviously expecting something unpleasant. She removes them. Then – watch – she flinches. Before anything happens, she flinches at something in front of her.

She almost changes direction then – bang, another dead photographer. She's seen Kramski, she must have – the eye line's a perfect match, as you can see … from this frame here – and she knows what's coming."

Orlov sat back. "You've assembled a very persuasive argument."

"Don't forget," Bronstein said, "before she went downstairs that day she said she was worried for the photographers. And there are all those weird meetings with Zane Cruse, another of our cases. It all mounts up. I've no idea why any of them would be involved, but it does look as if they are."

"What do you want to do Jonathan?" Orlov said. "I think you deserve first say."

Hartley-Brown sat with his elbows on his knees and the flats of his hands together. He rested his nose on his fingertips. "Thank you. I'm going to ask her to tell me the truth. The funny thing is, I know she knows I know – at least she's aware I do on some level. I'm going to ask her to marry me. That's not part of the plan and she might well say no. If she says yes and it means I have to leave the service, so be it, but I can't see why it should, because I know she's not involved in anything really murky. Don't ask me how. I just do. If she really loves me, she'll tell me the truth, I won't even have to ask. And then I'll tell you."

"What's your timetable?" Orlov said. "Sorry to pressure."

"I'm taking her to meet my parents tomorrow morning," he said. "I'll confront her sometime during that, when we're alone."

"What if she is involved in something really murky?" Bronstein said.

"Then I'll help her get out of it. I love her."

Bronstein poured him a double bourbon and one for himself. He smiled wistfully. "I wish to God you were my boyfriend, Jonathan."

Chapter 11: Meetin' the Folks

Sir Anthony, Joy and Anya were waiting on the front steps of Mannersby when Jonathan's car pulled up. He sprang out in a camel suit, ran around the boot and opened the passenger door. Jilly wore a summer dress printed with blue flowers, and a mauve shrug. He accompanied her up the steps as his family came down, completed the introductions and went to park round the side while his father stood under the portico with his hands in his pockets to wait for him.

"We're very pleased to meet you," Joy told Jilly as she escorted her inside. "I won't pretend Jonathan's told us a lot about you, he's not one for confiding much, but I do know how much he likes you. I can read his tone of voice."

"We haven't known each other long," Jilly said. "But I don't think he can like me more than I like him. He's not like any other man I've met."

"Yes, I can believe that. I've spent many years wondering whether it's a good or a bad thing. I still can't quite make up my mind."

"Obviously, you know what I think."

"Although he hasn't told us much about you, we have looked you up on the Internet."

Jilly momentarily lost the rhythm of her stride. "Oh. Oh, I'm not sure what to think about that."

"I didn't discover anything you need be ashamed of, if that's what you're thinking. I simply meant I've listened to some of your LPs and seen some of the lovely awards you've won. You don't need me to tell you you're very talented."

"What's an LP, Mummy?" Anya asked.

"And of course, Anya's a huge fan of yours," Joy said. "I've just made a fresh pot of tea. Do come through."

"You're a little sweetie," Jilly told Anya. She turned to Joy, "Is she …?"

Joy sat down and removed the cosy from the teapot. "Anya's adopted. From the Sudan originally. Her entire village was wiped out by the Janjaweed, I don't know whether you've heard of them? They're a group of Arab militiamen who murder black African farmers for amusement. She was the only one left alive. Six months old and, as luck would have it, a very quiet baby. Do you take milk and sugar?"

"Milk, no sugar, please."

Joy poured the tea and they sipped in silence for a few moments.

"I wonder where Jonathan and his father have disappeared to?" Joy said. "I do know Anthony was thinking of asking Jonathan to help with the canvassing this time, but it's not very polite to buttonhole him when you've only just arrived."

"While we're on the subject, Jonathan and I were talking about helping Sir Anthony a while ago. I think we'd both like to get involved."

"You must be serious about him."

"I am."

Joy put her teacup and saucer down. "And he must reciprocate if he's thinking of working with his father. Who suggested it first?"

Jilly smiled. "I did."

"Yes, I thought so. Well, take it from me, if he agreed, it says more about his attitude to you than it does his attitude to the Conservatives."

"I don't understand. Aren't Jonathan and his father ..."

"Jonathan's father is what is euphemistically called a ladies' man. The only reason he's got so far is because he has a good brain and there are precious few of those in the Conservative party. School tie trumps brain, but brain plus school tie trumps school tie alone. He went to Eton then Cambridge and he's Mensa 153 so they're more than happy to forgive his indiscretions. I haven't voted for him for over twenty years."

Jilly shifted in her chair in response to the drop in temperature. "I – I see. Will you vote for him this time?"

"I doubt it. And there's a sea change in the country that means he may be unseated. Which is why he's grovelling to his son."

"You mean the Lib Dems?"

"The country's turning orange, so the papers say. I don't believe it myself, I've heard it too many times before, but it makes for good copy. And Anthony's petrified."

"I'm sure Jonathan will come to his rescue."

Joy picked up a finger biscuit. "You probably think it's rather odd, my being so frank. The fact is, I'd like Jonathan to marry well and I know he's not toying with you. He's incapable of that. I've done everything in my power to ensure he's as different to his father as any human being can possibly be. I stopped short of insisting he have a sex-change, but you can be sure I didn't stop that short."

Jilly waited for the jocose smile, but it never came. Her mouth popped open and she felt it only polite to use it to say something. "It's probably a little to early to start talking about marriage - "

"Unless you stop him," Joy said, "he will propose to you. Probably not today, probably not next week, but sooner rather than later. Believe me, there's not a frivolous bone in that boy's body. And the longer you let it go on, the more he'll be hurt. So you need to make up your mind what you want."

Jilly flushed and put her cup and saucer down. "I - "

"I'm not trying to frighten you, my dear. On the contrary, if he asks you to marry him, and you say yes, no one will be more pleased than me. I really mean that. But if you have no intention of taking things to that level you ought to tell him."

Jilly stood up. Her hands as well as her face were red now. "I probably need to find him," she said.

"Knock on the Study door. Turn right when you get out of here and it's the second door on your left. Please be gentle with him. And do stay to lunch and dinner, whatever transpires."

Ten minutes earlier, Jonathan mounted the front steps after parking his car, and laid his hand on his father's elbow. Joy, Anya and Jilly were just entering the Living Room.

"Could I have a word alone?" he whispered.

Sir Anthony looked at him as if he was mad. "I've actually taken precious time off to meet your ladyfriend. I should be out on the hustings."

"I know. I appreciate it. But this is important."

He sighed. "Come into the study then. Maybe we can scratch each other's backs."

The study held the books in the house that were actually used, as opposed to those in the Library, which were for decoration and never removed from their shelves except for dusting. It had a dark wood floor covered almost to the edges with a Persian green rug, a desk with a PC and three armchairs. A latticed window gave a view of the drive. Jonathan closed the door behind them. They sat down on the edge of their chairs.

"I'd like to give up work and give my time to managing the estate," Jonathan said. "I know that's what you and Mother want for me in the end, and I know I've always been pretty negative about it before. But I've changed my mind. I've some good ideas about how to raise revenue without compromising our privacy. If we can renovate the old priest hole, for example, and expand the stables and lease them to a commercial firm - "

"I take it you think you're in love with this woman, what's she called?"

"Jilly. Yes, I do. I am."

Sir Anthony sighed. "I'm going to pour you a drink, young man, and I expect you to listen to me while I give you the benefit of my experience." He opened a cabinet and took out a full decanter. "Scotch all right?"

Jonathan shrugged.

Sir Anthony poured him a triple. "I don't recall you ever saying you were in love before. In fact your mother and I had you down for a homosexual at one point. Then we discovered that little collection of page threes, torn out of the Sun, at the bottom of your wardrobe, all in plastic wallets in a ring binder. It was a very happy day for both of us. Not that we're against gay people, but we do want heirs, your mother particularly since she comes from an ancient family - all the way back to bloody Stonehenge if her brother's to be believed. How long have you known this girl?"

"She's not a girl, she's a woman. Not very long."

Sir Anthony leaned back. "I mean, exactly?"

"Six weeks."

"And all this talk of giving up work and managing the estate, it's all because of her, yes?"

"Everything's changed since I met her. I can't explain. It's - "

"You don't have to explain. That's how love works. You become completely irrational. And it's always worst first time. When I last talked to you about running the estate you described it as a living death, do you remember?"

Jonathan shook his head and drew a deep breath. "I wasn't thinking straight. Or rather I was. It's just, I don't like having my life all planned out for me like that. There's a world of difference between being plonked on the estate as a puppet and assuming the reins of my own free will."

"And that's what you thought I was about, did you?"

"Not consciously, no. I didn't mean to sound ungrateful, I know you've my best interests at heart."

"Damn right."

"Put it another way, if I was just to give up everything and look after the estate on the terms you suggested, I'd probably be quite lonely. It's a busy job, and my chances of meeting someone would be quite small. But with Jilly, there wouldn't be any of that."

"You've asked her to marry you, then?"

"Not yet, no."

Sir Anthony gave a laugh of relief. "Thank God for small mercies. Don't. First-time love is a beast. It's inevitably one third genuine affection, one third morbid infatuation and one third blind lust. Let it run its course and we'll have this talk later in the year, okay? Say round about Christmas."

"But that's - "

"Are you saying you can't hang on till then?"

Jonathan looked at the carpet. "I could, I suppose."

"I'm sorry to appear brutal, but when we get there I'd like you to look back and realise my analysis of some situations is often worth heeding. I'm willing to bet fifty pounds you won't be together then."

Jonathan looked at his father's outstretched hand without responding. "That's okay, I'd rather not."

"You see, you're already beginning to have doubts."

"I don't – I just don't want to – to make light of it like that."

Sir Anthony hooted. "Don't tell me, it's sacred. God, you have got it bad. Still, you are twenty-four, not sixteen like I was when I fell in love for the first time. And I suppose the higher they climb the harder they fall. Now I'm going to be frank with you again. This time, something a little cheerier. Depending on your point of view."

"Oh?"

"The truth is, I'd love to put you in charge of the estate. That would mean I could spend a lot more time in London, and if we're going to win the election, I'm probably going to be invited onto the cabinet, which means I won't have any choice. So it's either you or get some manager in."

"What about Marcie?"

"We both know Marcie won't touch it with a bargepole. She's made that abundantly clear on numerous occasions. Anyway, in default of her, it goes without saying I'd prefer you to some random chap – or chappess – no matter how skilled."

Jonathan wasn't sure how to take this. "Thank you."

"So, although in an ideal world we'd wait till Christmas to make a decision, in practice, circumstances might dictate otherwise. Now, before you start celebrating, there is flip side. I might lose my seat, and you might never get the estate. At least not until I die."

"But there's no chance of that, is there? You've one of the safest seats in the country."

"I did have. But then the Prime Minister, in his infinite wisdom, decided it would be sane to hold a televised debate between the party leaders, USA style. And thanks to all that twaddle about MPs' expenses, guess who came out smelling of roses? Mr bloody Tilden, that's who, the leader of the world's most boring party. And now everything's up in the air. I mean everything. You must have been listening to the news."

"Not much. I've been busy."

"Doing what?"

"Constructing a computer programme to make still pictures move."

"God help us. Let's cut to Hecuba, shall we? If you want the estate, you're going to have to help me slay the Lib Dems. That simple."

Jonathan nodded and finished his drink. "It's fine."

"What?"

"I said, it's okay. Jilly's happy to help too."

"She must be as besotted with you as you are with her then, which is a good start. Have you slept with her yet, by the way?"

"I don't - "

"Make sure you sleep with her at the earliest possible opportunity. On the whole, women tend to see intercourse as a contract. That can be a bad thing, of course, very bad, but if you're genuinely looking to hold on to her, it can only work in your favour. And start thinking about a pre-nup."

There was a knock at the door. Sir Anthony looked at his watch. "Bloody hell, I didn't realise the time. Your mother's going to be furious. Remember, ducking in here was your idea, Jonathan, not mine. *Enter!*"

Jilly put her head around the door. "Er, Jonathan, could I speak to you for a minute?"

"It's all right, my dear," Sir Anthony said, apparently changing his mind about whose fault it was, "I just needed to solicit his help. We hardly ever get to speak face to face. I do apologise."

"It's not that," she said as Jonathan met her at the door. "I – I'm very sorry, it shouldn't take too long."

Jilly led him out of the house and across the lawn. Her heels kept sinking into the soil but her pace didn't slow. The sky was clear with petite clouds plonked on the horizon as if they were snoozing. The grass had just been cut and little strips of mowings converged at the walls marking the estate boundary. She had obviously spotted the love-seat under the oak but when they reached it, she didn't sit down. She turned to face him, her eyes full of agitation.

"Jonathan, I've just been talking with your mother. She says you're going to ask me to marry you."

He'd already guessed she'd found out. What was his mother playing at? And how had *she* found out? She'd probably wrecked everything.

"I am," he said gloomily, determined only to salvage what little he could.

"When?" she said.

"Now."

She gave a laugh like a cough. "I can't believe it. How do you know you're sure?"

"Are you going to say no?"

"We've only known each other a short time. I don't want to make a big mistake."

"So you're not saying no?"

She sat down on the seat. "I don't know. Yes."

"What? You're saying no?"

"I … I have to," she said.

He took her hand. "You mean, you don't love me?"

"I do. I do love you. It's why I can't."

"I don't know what you mean."

Tears rose to her eyes and sat there for a second before jumping. Her voice rose a tone. "I know it sounds like a cliché, Jonathan. There are things you don't know about me. And if I was to tell you them, they'd put you off for good. I couldn't stand that. Either way, we're going to end up not getting married. At least if I say no, I can retain some sort of dignity."

They sat down together, still holding hands. "Nothing could put me off you."

"You say that. All men do."

"You mean, men have asked you before?"

"No one's ever asked me before."

"What, then?"

"I mean, men generally. They always make promises they can't keep."

"I don't."

She sighed. "It would be worse in some ways if you *didn't* give up on me. If I was to tell you the truth, and you kept insisting you wanted to marry me because you felt honour bound to keep what you thought was your word. That would be worse."

"Jilly, I already know."

She flinched. "Know - what?"

"The shootings. That you're involved. And that you're not the only celebrity. You're all involved."

She turned pale and snatched her hands away. "H – How did you find out?"

"I'm a policeman, or was. But that's not the point. The point is, it doesn't affect anything. I love you. I want to marry you. I don't care about anything else. Even if you have to go to prison, it doesn't matter. Sooner or later you'll come out and we'll look after the estate together."

She looked at him as if he'd sucked all the life out of her. Then she yowled, grabbed him and thrust her face into his chest as if this was her sole chance of survival and wept.

He tightened his arms round her. "Jilly, if I'm to protect you, I need to know everything. Then we're going back in to my parents and we're going to tell them we're getting married. If that's what you want."

She struggled to regain control, heaving and coughing and spluttering, then sat up. "I'm going to tell you very quickly, okay, and I'm not going to look at you, and I don't want you to ask any questions till I've finished."

He nodded.

She bit her lips, looked at the ground and took a deep breath. "When I was eighteen, I got a phone call from someone who wanted to sponsor me. A woman, an old woman she sounded like, and she said she'd seen me perform at the Lyceum in Cleethorpes, where I lived, and she wanted to covenant some money to help me. She said she thought I had talent.

Miss Burkinshaw, not her real name she said. She liked to do things anonymously, so she didn't want to meet. Anyway, I was a bit wary, so I talked to my dance teacher, and he said, yeah, go for it. He'd heard about Miss Burkinshaw. She'd sponsored other people, famous people, so I should jump at the chance.

"Anyway, Miss Burkinshaw didn't just send me money for courses, she gave me contacts, supplied breaks, put in a word for me every so often. Over the course of about a year, it stopped being Miss Burkinshaw on the phone. It became a man, middle-aged probably. But he obviously knew Miss Burkinshaw, and who was I to complain? They never asked anything of me, even to meet me.

"Gradually, I got to know the names of other people they were sponsoring: Mikey from Bad Lads Zero, Stallone Laine, Bobby Keynes, Julie Phelps, Connie Glaser, Soraya from Fully Magic Coal Tar Lounge. I don't know any others, but there must be more.

"Then one day, about a year ago, Julie Phelps came out of her house and the paparazzi were waiting in cars. You probably remember. It was after the England-Germany match, and she'd been in Robert Branden's hotel room the night before he missed that penalty and England got dumped. Everyone in the country hated her. She was a real mess, in her head. They chased her down the road in her Skoda and she crashed into a lamp post and split her head open. Fourteen stitches.

"The day afterwards, we all got phone calls. Miss Burkinshaw - whoever, whatever she was - was going to teach the paparazzi a lesson. And that's when the killing started. They trialled it in some other countries before they started over here, so as to create a false trail, but we didn't find that out till later. We couldn't say anything, because we were in too deep and there was the gratitude and the fact that they were obviously rich and powerful and violent. They obviously suspected we might crack, so they gave us 'buddies' to talk to about it, reassure each other. Zane Cruse was mine, another of their projects. He's a bit of a dork, but we share a terrible secret, so just being with him, you know ... We're not having sex, like Rob thought. We've never had sex, we wouldn't. I don't even like him much.

"You see what I mean, though, Jonathan? If I'd spoken out at the start, all those photographers would be alive now. I had a choice between fame and fortune and saving people's lives and I chose fame and fortune. And who knows who else these people have killed, whoever they are?"

"Is it okay for me to talk now?" he said, when she hadn't spoken for a few seconds.

She bobbed her chin.

"I still love you," he said. "As much as ever."

"I love you, Jonathan. Who do you think it is?"

"At a guess, the Mafia. The police think the assassin might be a Russian. That would fit. Russian Mafioso, Las Vegas by other means."

"Las Vegas?"

"They set up the first casinos there after gambling was legalised in the USA in the thirties. I'm guessing this is just another attempt to harness entertainments for profit."

She was shaking. "But I haven't given them a penny."

"They must be milking the subsidiaries. Whoever's giving you backing, whoever cashes in on you. I don't know - sponsorship deals, branding, that sort of thing."

"I haven't told you the most important thing. They told us to get involved with the political parties, this election. That's why I've been ... But I don't want to do anything to hurt you or your father, and that's one of the things that made me decide to tell you."

"Politics?"

"Any politics. Just get involved."

He got up. "We're wasting time. I've got to make a report on this now, then we've got to get you to London and transfer you to a safe house somewhere."

"But if it's Mafioso we're talking about, they never let you go. Once they've discovered it's me that told, I might as well be dead."

They were crossing the lawn now at speed. "It's not going to come to that. They're never going to find out it was you who told anyway."

"They'll know it was someone."

They cleared the grass, trotted across the driveway, entered the house, crossed the hallway into the study. It was empty. There was a thick silence, like death.

"Where the hell did I put my mobile?" he said. "Bloody hell. I need to write it down, write it all down, that's right, in case something happens."

"You can borrow mine."

"No, mine's got the numbers of my colleagues on. Where the hell did I put it? God, if I've left it in London ..."

"Can't you remember them?"

He switched the PC on. "E-mail, I'll have to e-mail them. I love you, Jilly. Let me just concentrate for a minute while I write all this down and send it, then we're on our way."

"I'm scared, Jonathan."

"I said I'll protect you and I will. All you've got to do is keep meeting Zane and acting like nothing's happened."

She closed her eyes and put her hands on her temples. "Zane already knows."

"Wh – what? How?"

"When you were in here talking to your dad, I didn't like to come in at first because you seemed to be so deep in some conversation. I listened at the door, then I couldn't stand it any longer, I had to talk to someone."

"What did he say?"

"He said he thought it was a good idea to tell you. He's on drugs, I don't even know if he knew what he was saying. But then I knocked."

"It's all right. We can still salvage things." His breath suddenly went the wrong way. "Unless – oh, my God. Jilly, give me your phone."

She handed it over. "What's the matter?"

He took out a miniature screwdriver from the inside pocket of his jacket, prised the back off, then the inside. There it was, welded to the circuitry. A nanowire, probably with a built-in location transmitter, since you could fit anything into anything using that technology. It meant they were already on their way.

Think, think. He couldn't just ditch the phone. That would mean they'd search the house and probably kill his parents. They had to take it with them, maybe drive randomly till they were far enough away to throw it out of the window.

"How long ago did you phone Zane?" he said.

"About twenty minutes."

He was typing furiously now, trying to get everything down, and yet he could see half of it didn't make any sense. London to Hertfordshire, but what if Kramski didn't live in London, what if he lived closer? Whoever the people Kramski worked for were, they probably had someone available who lived closer than London. His head throbbed like someone was blowing a million vevuzelas at him.

And then he realised he didn't have Orlov's or Bronstein's addresses in his contacts list. The depth of his ineptitude hit him in a wave of disgust that was almost physical. What he'd written had to go somewhere.

Marcie. It was the best of a botched job, but she was the only one who knew who Orlov and Bronstein were. He could retrieve it from her Inbox when he reached London, he knew her password. *If* he reached London, oh God. It had to go somewhere. Bloody, bloody hell. He was trembling now. He pressed send.

"We've got to get to my car," he said.

She took her shoes off. They ran out of the house onto the gravel and joined hands and kept running. They rounded the corner of the house to where his car was parked.

He had no chance to register what happened next. Kramski was waiting for them. He thrust a gloved fist deep into Jonathan's stomach and kneed him square in the face as he went down, almost snapping his neck. Jonathan fell unconscious.

Kramski grabbed Jilly's hair and kicked her in the solar plexus. He thrust a cloth into her mouth then taped over her lips and round the back of her head. He threw Jonathan over his shoulder and dragged Jilly to the car they'd been planning to make their exit in, flipping the boot and dumping them both inside. He hotwired the ignition and drove out of the grounds at speed.

In the Living Room, Sir Anthony sat at the coffee table counting election leaflets. There was a faint screech of tyres and he turned to Joy. "Did you hear that?"

"It sounded like Jonathan."

"It sounded like a car."

"He'll have gone after her. I was afraid it would end this way." She sighed. "It's a shame because I rather liked her."

"He cuts such a bloody earnest figure," Sir Anthony said irritably. Twenty minutes in the study getting Jonathan on board, probably wasted now. He licked his finger and carried on reckoning. "Ninety-eight, ninety-nine, a hundred. Someone needs to tell him the ladies don't necessarily find that appealing."

Joy sighed. "I hope he drives carefully, that's all."

Chapter 12: A Turn for the Worse

Orlov and Bronstein sat in their office, filing reports and waiting for the phone to ring. The BBC news website was loaded on Bronstein's computer and refreshed every two minutes. He accepted the *Guardian* Orlov passed him, folded over at page seven, *International News*. Under the banner, 'Gruchov Publicly Distances Herself From Disgraced Russian Exile' he read:

> A political storm was brewing in Moscow last night after Vera Gruchov, the *Vosstanovlenie* (Restoration) party candidate for mayoral office, denied that her campaign is being funded from London by the Russian exile, Valentin Tebloev. Speaking with rare emotion at a hastily-convened press conference, she insisted all such claims were fabricated by her political rival, the present mayoral incumbent, Boris Pyatin. Once a media magnate, Tebloev is wanted in Russia for extortion.
>
> "I have always kept my funding sources open for scrutiny," she said. "Anyone can examine them. I have received no monies whatsoever from Mr Tebloev and given the meticulous detail with which my campaign is planned within the existing budget, I do not expect to. It is a disgraceful slur."
>
> But in a twist to the tale, Mr Tebloev last night claimed he had raised money for *Vosstanovlenie*, only without seeking its approval first. He said he now plans to donate the funds to a Moscow children's charity. There was no hidden agenda behind his actions, he said. He apologised for causing Vera Gruchov any embarrassment.
>
> But Boris Pyatin remains deeply sceptical. Addressing his supporters at a rally in Promzona he said, "This

is a classic case of the right hand not knowing what the left is doing. Vera Gruchov put the fight against corruption in public life at the top of her political agenda and it goes without saying that a party funded by a known criminal cannot conceivably win such a fight." To loud cheers, he dismissed Vera Gruchov as "a Russian Eva Perón, all style and no substance".

The political editor of the Russian Courier in London, Mikhail Botov, says the affair is hugely embarrassing for Vera Gruchov. "Some commentators have accused *Vosstanovlenie* of being short on policies, saying its appeal rests largely on Vera Gruchov's youth, looks and perceived irreproachability. This could potentially be the moment she hits the rocks. The next week of the campaign should prove very interesting."

"What do you think?" Bronstein said, sitting down at his desk.

"I think we've been had. Obviously Tebloev was working for Pyatin all along. His 'fundraiser' was just a ruse to tar *Vosstanovlenie*."

Bronstein shook his head. "And yet it does kind of consolidate Tebloev's reputation as a two-bit criminal, it being the grounds on which both parties want to distance themselves from him. Why would he shoot himself in the foot like that?"

"A two-bit criminal who was only trying to help the anti-corruptionists and who's now patron saint of Moscow's orphans. I'm sure most Russians can find it in themselves to forgive that. As I'm sure Boris Pyatin can, once he's back in office."

"I see, yeah. When do you think Jonathan's going to call?"

"Sometime this afternoon. If he makes a breakthrough he'll take her to the police station by Waterloo Bridge. We'll meet him there."

"What if he doesn't? Make a breakthrough?"

Orlov smiled. "You're an American. What comes after good cop?"

"Maybe one of us should have gone with him. Keep an eye on him."

"You mean you don't trust him?"

"Sure I trust him. We've been through that. But if she knows the killer - "

"It's a risk he was prepared to take," Orlov said. "We're a team. We have to trust to each other's instincts."

"Guess so. Besides, his parents probably think we've left the country."

"They must do. He's still officially 'inspector'. It would only take a few phone calls for the Shadow Foreign Secretary to discover we're not working under Sir Colin Bowker any more."

"Presumably, that means we can never meet them again."

Orlov sat at his PC and began typing. "Not in this lifetime."

"That's a shame. I liked his mom. Strict but fair."

"They were a very agreeable family. I don't think Jonathan will be with us for long. I think he'll marry Miss Bestwick and leave to run his father's estate with her."

"You figure?"

"It's a foregone conclusion."

Bronstein sighed. "What are you typing?"

"Not typing. Something I've been meaning to do for some time. Googling Constantine Slope. You'll remember Ruby Parker said he was meant to be at Tebloev's party. 'A businessman. Not intrinsically suspicious but he's very rich and we've no record of a previous connection between him and Tebloev'."

"I can save you the effort. He's dead."

"When?"

"Week before last. It's probably why he didn't attend the party."

Orlov raised his eyebrows. "It's as good an excuse as any."

"Listen, boss, I don't want to sound critical, but the Internet's for mail, porn and talking dogs on YouTube. There's a perfectly good library on the third floor and we share a bunch of researchers with the House of Commons. Write your question on a yellow form and they'll provide you with a brief. Sorry if that sounds a bit preachy."

"On the other hand, if someone's taken the trouble to put a lot of disinformation on the web, surely that has to be significant?"

"Yeah, all right. Just checking."

"So what does your brief on Slope say?"

Bronstein grinned. "It's less than a side of A4. He's a businessman. Originally from Albania. Not intrinsically suspicious but very rich. And he's kaput."

"There can't be many businessmen whose biographies fit on a single sheet of paper."

"He's religious."

"Even so."

The smile fell off Bronstein's face. "My God."

"What?"

"Jilly Bestwick. She … She's dead. Come round here. Come and look on my monitor, quick. Shit, this can't be happening."

Orlov arrived just as Bronstein was unticking 'mute' and going to the video channel. A woman reporter in her late twenties stood outside a suburban house that was surrounded by police vehicles and cordoned off with yellow tape. She held on to her hair as the wind teased it out of place.

"The police are still refusing to comment," she said, "but I can definitely tell you, Jane, that the bodies are those of the Four Girls on Fire singer, Jilly Bestwick, and her boyfriend, the

Li'l Baby Boy frontman, Zane Cruse. It is understood they died from gunshot wounds to the head and body. It's not yet clear whether this is a murder inquiry."

"Is there any reason to think it might not be?" Jane said from the studio.

"Some witnesses I've spoken to say they heard voices raised between Miss Bestwick and Mr Cruse in the moments leading up to the shooting. It is known that they were very close, but that Miss Bestwick seems to have begun seeing someone else very recently. I understand the police are desperate to contact that person and are prepared to offer a reward for information identifying him. They're expected to make an appeal for him to come forward within the next twenty minutes, when of course, they will give us more details."

Orlov was already on the phone. "Get me Ruby Parker."

Jonathan didn't come back to explain to his parents what had happened, but since it was obvious, they didn't feel it worth discussing. Sir Anthony ate his lunch and returned to Campaign Headquarters. Joy took Anya to her piano lesson, went shopping in Hertford and picked her up again an hour later. She didn't expect to see Anthony again till after nine pm, and she assumed Jonathan was either pleading with his now ex-girlfriend or on his way back to London and work.

She was therefore surprised when, arriving home at four, with Anya, she found her husband striding to meet her as she got out of the car. She wondered what it could possibly be, then her heart crumpled. "He's had a crash, hasn't he?"

"I take it you haven't been listening to the news. Because it could be worse than that."

"Anya, go inside."

Anya ran off at speed.

"His girlfriend," Sir Anthony said breathlessly, "Jilly Bestwick. She's been murdered."

"What?"

He swallowed. "Apparently she was seeing someone else. Some rock band chap by the name of Zane Cruse. Someone shot both of them dead."

Joy's fingertips tried to find her face. "Oh, oh, oh my God."

"Take a few deep breaths," he said, putting a hand on each of her shoulders. "Just breathe deeply."

"It isn't Jonathan that did it. It isn't Jonathan! *Tell them, Anthony -* "

"Get a grip on yourself, Joy. No one's accusing Jonathan – yet. Although they probably would be if they knew of his involvement with her. I know I would be."

"But – but - I don't understand how ..."

"It's like this. She was seeing someone else, he brought her here, she probably thought they were just friends - you know how girls are with Jonathan - they had an almighty row, she cleared off back to her boyfriend, he followed her. And now she's dead, and so is her boyfriend. What is anyone supposed to think?"

She started crying. "It isn't Jonathan, Anthony, *I know it isn't!*"

"You heard them shouting at each other in the study, Joy. Look, no one knows she was even seeing Jonathan yet. But her murder's all over the news, so wherever he is, he must know about it. The obvious question is, why hasn't he come forward? If he's innocent?"

She looked round herself like she was floating in white. "What are we going to do?"

"He's got to ring us sooner or later. You're just going to sit at home and wait. I'm going back to base to get on with some canvassing. It's horrid, I know, utterly ghastly, but I haven't the least choice. We've got to make things look normal or someone will suspect. We've got to think about Jonathan."

She seemed to have regained a measure of control. She was still deep breathing. "Have you tried ringing him?"

"Of course I've tried ringing him. It just keeps ringing. It's not switched off or anything. I've been ringing him since I found out. He's not answering."

"Why doesn't he switch it off if he doesn't want to talk to us? He must know it's us."

He ran his hand back and forth through his hair. "I don't know, Joy. I don't bloody know."

"Try again, now."

"I'm not sure - "

"*Please*, Anthony."

He shrugged and took out his mobile. He scrolled through the names and pressed call. "It's ringing."

"I – I can hear something," she said. "It's coming from the house."

They ran inside and into the study. Jonathan's phone was on the floor next to where he'd been sitting earlier. Sir Anthony picked it up, ashen-faced. He switched it off. Joy cast her arms round him and thrust her cheek against his tie and wept.

Within an hour of Orlov's call, Thames House obtained the Home Secretary's permission to clear the crime scene of policemen. MI7 agents swarmed into the building and began scrutinising every detail, bagging, dusting, swabbing, taking photographs, measuring distances, calculating angles. It was a large two bedroom flat with new furniture and a water bed on which the murdered couple lay with their arms round each other. Within thirty minutes, the investigative team established that Jilly Bestwick had died of suffocation long before the bullet entered her temple and that Zane Cruse could not have shot himself. These were therefore murders, not, as elements of the press were already beginning to speculate, suicides. They were premeditated – which strongly ruled out Jonathan Hartley-Brown. And the murderer was still at large.

At two-fifteen, Ruby Parker sat down at a table in the crime-scene Living Room with Orlov and Bronstein to write the statement the police were due to read to the press. The families of the murder victims arrived and were received in a tent set up outside. At half past two, Agent Forsby came in.

"Bingo," he said.

"Kramski?" Ruby Parker said.

"Same description."

"From how many people?"

"Two."

"Thank God. Thank God." She blinked slowly. "Did you contact Jonathan's parents?"

"I pretended to be an old school friend in Hertford for the day," Forsby replied. "He's not with them. They say they haven't seen him all day. They sounded cagey but composed."

"He must have told them he was bringing her to see them," Bronstein said.

"Not necessarily," Orlov said. "He might have told them he was bringing his girlfriend, but not named her. The English usually do names face to face."

"Guess so," Bronstein said. "Maybe that was why they sounded cagey. Maybe they were expecting a girl and got nothing. Maybe they think there's been a tiff."

"I contacted his sister too," Forsby said. "She hasn't seen him for weeks."

"Give the police Kramski's description," Ruby Parker said. "Tell them he's their man. They can take it from here. Our number one priority now is to find Jonathan."

"I'm going back to see Tebloev," Orlov said.

"I don't think that's a good idea," she said.

"What choice have we got? It's a race against time, you know that."

"I'll have Tebloev brought in for questioning," she said. "It's cleaner and the fewer forms we have to fill in afterwards, the better."

"You need to put more pressure on the Russian embassy," Bronstein said. "I can't believe they don't know someone who knows someone who knows Kramski. It's horseshit."

"If Jonathan turns up dead, they'd *better* get more proactive," she said irascibly. "We'll give them a timetable and a rocket."

"I'm trying to think where the hell I'd go if I had a man to get rid of," Bronstein said, running his fingers through his hair.

"We've got the Thames River Police on full alert," she said. "I've contacted the Road Policing Unit and told them to disseminate a nationwide ANPR. Other than that, I'm not sure we can do any more than wait."

At one thirty the next morning, Bronstein sat in the office with a cup of coffee, grinding his teeth and clenching and unclenching his fists. He was thinking about what he'd do to whoever had done whatever to Jonathan, when Orlov walked in and sat down.

"Tebloev still missing?" Bronstein said.

"Apparently. I want to be here when they find him."

Ruby Parker came in with a folder under her arm. "They've found Jonathan. Brace yourselves, it's bad. Beachy Head, 162 metres. They've taken him to an intensive care unit in Eastbourne but he's not expected to last the night."

Neither Orlov nor Bronstein spoke for a moment, then Bronstein shook his head bitterly. "I guess he had the murder weapon planted on him?"

"Yes."

"Car?"

"Parked on the clifftop. If it hadn't been for the local Chaplaincy Team – they actually keep watch up there, hoping to dissuade suicides - he'd have washed out to sea."

"Fingerprints?"

"No."

Orlov pinched his forehead. "I have to ask. Is there any possibility …?"

"His car had been hotwired," Ruby Parker said. "And there's blood on the inside of the boot, not just his: Jilly Bestwick's. Kramski tried to burn it out, but he was out of petrol and it was raining hard. It's obvious what he wanted us to think. If we hadn't taken over from the police when we did this afternoon and slapped a DA Notice on the press, the whole country would have been taken in."

"I take it we can't go to the hospital and see him," Bronstein said.

"Out of the question. I've arranged for the police to inform his parents. They're going to tell them he crashed his police car in the line of duty. I don't want them to think anything other than that he was an exceptionally fine officer."

At two o'clock the next morning, Joy and Sir Anthony sat in the morning room listening to the clock tick and waiting for the phone. Every hour, Sir Anthony poured himself a brandy. Joy fell into a snooze and awoke with a start and a groan. Mostly, they sat holding their heads in their hands.

"I don't know whether we've got a duty to tell the police," Joy said.

"Don't be an idiot, Joy."

"You heard the news. They've started looking for a man who looks nothing like Jonathan. What if they find him?"

"What if they do?"

"What reason have they got to assume that that man killed them?"

"We don't *know* what reason. They may have a very good reason."

"Oh, come on, Anthony. Think of the Birmingham Six and the Guildford Four. Once the police get an idea fixed in their brains? They don't know what we know. All they're aware of is that some poor fellow who looks nothing like Jonathan was seen nearby, round about the time of the murder, acting suspiciously."

"I repeat: we don't know what they know."

She scoffed. "They certainly don't know what *we* know."

"As I recall, it was you who said it couldn't be Jonathan."

"But if it is - "

"Just let's wait till we've talked to him, shall we?"

"Have you rung Sir Colin Bowker?"

"How do you think that would look?"

"You could find some excuse," she said frailly.

"You're not thinking, Joy. Circumstantially, everything's against him, *everything*. Any false move on our part, no matter how superficially innocuous, might tip the scale later. I've never rung Colin Bowker before and I'm not the kind of man who rings the Metropolitan Police Commissioner about his son unless something's very wrong. Added to which, I'm the Shadow bloody Foreign Secretary. Could you tell my son he forgot to pick up his packed lunch just won't cut it."

She cried again. "There's no need to be sarcastic."

"I - I'm sorry. I'm as much of a wreck as you are. I'm just trying to keep a grip on reality."

"I know."

She put her arms round him, something she hadn't done in a long time. He kissed her hair. There was a knock at the door.

"Oh, God," she said.

"You stay there."

But she followed him into the hallway. He opened the door to find himself looking at a policeman and a policewoman.

The policeman removed his hat. "Sir Anthony Hartley-Brown? Sir, we've come about your son, Jonathan. There's been an accident, I'm afraid. We've been instructed to offer you a lift to the hospital."

Joy fainted.

Marcie finished dodging tennis balls and doing backward flips at midnight. She went home, showered and fell fast asleep in bed. It took her a few moments to realise that that sound was her mobile. She crawled out of bed and looked at the screen. *Daddy*. Something must be very wrong for him to be calling at this time. She picked up.

"Hi, has something happened?"

"There's been an accident," her father said. "It's Jonathan. He crashed into a lamp post chasing some slimy little bastard in a modified car."

"Shit, oh shit."

"You need to get over - "

"How bad is it?"

"About as bad as it gets, I believe. Your mother and I are on our way. Eastbourne District General Hospital. Get a taxi, I'll give you the money when you arrive."

"*Eastbourne?*"

"Look, I haven't time for an interrogation. You can imagine the state your mother's in. I need both arms. Just get there."

They got out of the car and gave their names at the front desk. A middle-aged consultant with a moustache and half-rim glasses took them to Intensive Care. Jonathan was bruised and swollen to the point of being unrecognisable and punctured with wires and tubes connected to monitors and drips. A nurse stood watch. There were three chairs and a smell of disinfectant.

"Is he …?" Sir Anthony said, not knowing how to complete the sentence.

"He could go at any minute," the doctor said. "We've done everything we can. I'm very sorry, but there's just too much internal damage."

"Tell him … tell the doctor we're with BUPA," Joy instructed her husband through her gasping.

"Sorry, doctor … my wife … I'm … I'm the Shadow Foreign Secretary …"

The consultant shook his head. "Again, I'm very, very sorry."

Marcie arrived at 4.30 and, after hearing the bare details, sat down to join the vigil. The darkness seemed to breed in the corners of the room and ooze down the walls. Somewhere in the far distance, a dog barked patiently. They all heard it, though none of them tried to account for it. Marcie held hands with her mother and looked at the floor. Occasionally, her father stroked her back.

A nurse sat by the life support on the edge of her seat, her eyes glued to the ECG screen, her hands folded on her lap. At 4.50, the signal jumped high then levelled to a line and a monotone. The family all whimpered. Four staff came in and surged to the patient. Someone said 'Stand back' and there was a bang and Jonathan's body bounced. The pulse resumed and the screen showed troughs and peaks and everyone sighed.

But then the signal flattened again. There was another 'Stand back' and Jonathan bounced, but this time nothing happened. A squealing noise filled the room. The doctors and nurses looked at each other and seemed to deflate. Their hands fell to their sides and they separated as if they'd been disgraced.

When they re-converged on Jonathan, it was without the slightest urgency.

Chapter 13: Nichole Moore, Superstar

After Jonathan died, Sir Anthony went outside to the car park and wept. By this time, the press had learned what had happened, so he was flash photographed and persistently asked how he was feeling. When he gathered his senses and stumbled back inside, Joy was missing. She had told Marcie she was going to the toilet and she didn't return. According to the woman at the front desk, she'd asked for a taxi and left in it ten minutes ago. Her mobile was switched off.

The police picked her up two hours later on one of the roads along the cliff tops. Dawn broke. She was wet and bedraggled and her expensive shoes were caked in mud. She said nothing to anyone. When they all got home at nine, she went straight to her room and locked the door without saying hello to Anya.

For the first three days leading up to the funeral, she ate nothing and spoke to no one. Meanwhile, Buckingham Palace and the Prime Minister sent condolences and bouquets of flowers and cards arrived hourly. Sir Anthony resigned from the Shadow Cabinet. Marcie rang Miss Demure and told her she might not be coming back. Miss Demure said she'd seen the news and she would keep her post open indefinitely.

On the fourth day, Joy came down to dinner for the first time. She ate without acknowledging her husband or her two daughters. Then Sir Anthony put his knife and fork together.

"Joy, we all understand what you're feeling. We're all going through exactly the same thing. I know we're never going to get over it, but it might help if we could at least talk to each other. Just a bit. One step at a time, that's all we're asking."

She narrowed her eyes. "Oh, and you'd know all about 'getting over it', wouldn't you?"

"I'm not obliged to wear my heart on my sleeve, Joy. You've no conception of how devastated I am. I haven't even known where to walk these last few days. How dare you say that?"

"I know the truth, Anthony."

He put his wine glass down. "What do you mean?"

She turned to Marcie. "Would you like to know the truth, Marciella? Would you?"

Marcie swore under her breath. "Mummy, what the *hell* are you talking about?"

"I'm going to tell you then. Not because I think it'll do you any good, but because I think you deserve to know why I've given up. I'll go to the funeral tomorrow, but I won't stay to the reception and if any of his friends turn up, they can go to perdition for all I care."

Marcie and Sir Anthony sat immobile, waiting for whatever nuclear bomb Joy thought it was in her power to detonate. Anya began to cry. She got off her chair and climbed onto Marcie's knee.

Joy stood up. "It's like this, you see. It seemed odd from the start, very odd. Jonathan's with the Met, why was he in Eastbourne? And who was in the car with him? Policemen usually patrol in pairs, not alone. But there was no one at the hospital, not a soul. So after he died, I did a little digging. I went to find the Beachy Head Chaplaincy Team, you know, who look out for suicides and try either to dissuade them or pick up the pieces if it's too late? And would you believe it, they knew all about Jonathan. Because – as of course, you already know, Anthony - there *was* no police chase, no car crash. No, Jonathan was in the state he was because he jumped off a cliff. And guess what else they told me? He had a gun on him when they found him. And then I got to thinking: wait a minute, who could conceivably have covered all this up? It's not like my husband has friends in high places, oh no."

"A *gun*?" Marcie said.

"You see, Marcie," Joy said, laughing, "your brother was here that morning with his new girlfriend. I bet your father didn't tell you about that, did he?"

Sir Anthony stood up. "Joy!"

"Jilly Bestwick, she of girl-band-shot-in-the-head-with-her-lover fame. And our Jonathan was the murderer. That's right, your older brother was a filthy, rotten murderer, and he couldn't even face up to it, which makes him a coward to boot. And your father thinks that's worth keeping a lid on."

"Joy, that's not true!"

She was addressing herself solely to Marcie now. She stopped laughing and her voice cracked. "I loved that boy more than any mother ever loved any son. Because I knew right from the outset the moral danger he was in. I did everything, *everything* to turn him to the good, to nullify the effects of his father's sordid, philandering genes. But of course, I was wasting my time. I was always wasting my time. My whole life's been one stupid, miserable joke. And now it's over."

She threw down her napkin, put her chair in and left the room.

Bronstein flicked though the phone bill noting the handwritten names next to each number. Nichole Moore, Nichole Moore, Nichole Moore, John Dobson, Directory Enquiries, Conway's Wine Bar, Nichole Moore … And yet Nichole Moore had a boyfriend and Stallone Laine wasn't even into girls. He put the bill back in the file, picked up the laptop and went to the first of two interview rooms.

Nichole Moore was twenty-two with platinum blonde hair and blue eyes. She wore a 'Little Miss Happy' T-shirt and a mini skirt. When Bronstein came in, she was looking in a compact and refreshing her lipstick. She looked frightened.

He sat down. "My name's Detective Bronstein," he said. "There's no need to be anxious. You're only here to answer a few questions for your own safety."

She cleared her throat. "Are you … are you a Jew?"

"A Jew?"

"That's right. Because I'd rather not talk to a Jew."

"Yeah, I am a Jew."

"I'd rather not talk to a Jew, if that's okay."

He shrugged and stood up. "Any particular reason?"

She sighed and rolled her eyes. "I'm trying to get into Wicca. It's, like, difficult, learning all those spells. And when I started I said to myself, 'Nicky, if you want to do this properly, you mustn't have anything to do with the Jews'. Like, ever again. Comprendez? It's nothing personal. You don't smell or anything."

He ground his teeth and went to find Edward, the duty sergeant. He wasn't in the mood for an argument, not after Jonathan. It was an evil day, but the only way to get at the throat of the bastard that did it was to soldier on and not get riled. Edward was in Evidence Storage with a cup of tea. He was thirty-one and stubbly in a creased suit.

"Could you go and talk to Nichole Moore?" Bronstein said. "She doesn't want to speak to me."

Edward's eyebrows shot up. "You serious?"

"I'm not having the kind of day where I do practical jokes."

He grinned and drained his cup. "My friend," he said, "I have lurid fantasies about that girl and they always begin like this."

In the second room, Stallone Laine was a twenty-four year old goatee in a baseball cap and a white nylon tracksuit with black stripes on the forearms. He sat alone with his sunglasses upside-down on the table. The room was tiled and strip-lit with a soundproofed window looking onto a busy corridor. This was to be a more a serious encounter.

Bronstein sat down. He switched the laptop on without speaking and showed Laine the photomatic of himself leaving the Odeon that Jonathan had put together.

"Not sure what I'm supposed to be looking at," Laine said when it finished.

"We've had a psychological profiler look at it. We know you know how it ends right from the start."

"Er ... what?"

Bronstein put Kramski's photo on the table again. "Take another look at him."

"Ain't never seen him."

"You know why Jilly Bestwick's dead, don't you?" Bronstein said.

"It's nothing to do with me."

"Sure."

Laine laughed. "You think I murdered her?"

"She's dead because she wouldn't cooperate with us. But we put it out there that she had, just to see what would happen. And we'll do the same for you."

Laine shrugged. But Bronstein noticed him bristle.

"Of course, given what a calamity that was, we'll keep a closer eye on you than we did on her. Nothing's guaranteed though."

"You're bluffing. The police wouldn't do that."

"Go figure. We've got to draw the murderer somehow."

"I need to see my lawyer. I'm not speaking until I see my lawyer."

Bronstein looked into the corridor and saw Katie nod to him. He winked at her. "I'm not a policeman, buddy. What are you going to call your lawyer for?"

"I'm supposed to be allowed a phone call."

"You're free to go."

"How do you mean, 'go'?"

"Whenever, wherever you want."

Laine scraped his chair back as if he suspected a trick and picked up his sunglasses.

"Just one thing," Bronstein said.

"Talk to the freakin' hand, man."

Bronstein talked to the hand. "What's Nichole Moore to you?"

"What?"

"Nichole Moore. You know, the singer."

"Yeah, yeah, I know who she is. What do you mean?"

"Just asking. Because she told us a lot about you."

Laine turned pale. "What did she say?"

"Sorry, I thought you were leaving. I've got work to be getting on with."

"No, no, what did she say?" He tried to sit down again. Bronstein took the chair away and replaced it at the side of the room. They stood looking at each other for a moment.

"I get the impression there's something you're not telling me," Bronstein said.

"I've got to get out of here."

He charged into the corridor. Katie bumped into him and they both fell backwards, sending the papers she was carrying all over the floor.

"Oh, my God," she said, getting onto all fours and putting her glasses right, "I'm *so* sorry. I'm so, *so* sorry."

He gave a scowl of recognition. "You're the same muppet that bumped into me on the way in, yeah? Why can't you people watch where you're going?"

"I'm ever so sorry, I'm so clumsy, people are always saying … Since we're here, Mr Laine, I'm a really big fan of yours, could I have your - "

"Get *off* me, bitch!"

She burst into tears. Laine got to his feet and charged down the corridor and left the building.

Katie stopped crying and turned to Bronstein. "There's already something in there."

"What do you mean?"

"A listening device stroke transmitter. Someone's already hanging on every word he says."

"But you put ours in, right?"

"As instructed. He's probably ringing her now."

It was bright sunshine as always and a light wind swept across the grass, combing upwards in waves to where it met the forest. In the distance, the mountaintops looked like a row of children's desserts. Orlov's wife and daughter were on their hands and knees further towards the village, gathering pyrethrums. It was always like this, so he always knew he was dreaming, but for some reason his participation was never optional. They were going to die and he had to warn them.

He was trapped behind a window pane. Zainab and Fatima ran through the streets of Grozny in the pitch black, dodging explosions. He knocked frantically on the glass but they couldn't hear him. And then they died and it was time to wake up.

He'd had this dream a lot when it first happened. Recently, it had become less frequent. Since Jonathan's death it was nightly. He awoke in the room he was sharing with four other illegals and stepped over their sleeping bodies – they all worked night-shifts - and out into the afternoon. It was time to tie together the loose ends he'd been picking up the last few days.

Half an hour later he took out his gun and stepped off a ladder into a dripping corridor beneath a basement in Soho. The lights shone twenty watts every two hundred yards and rats strolled around as if they owned the deeds. The doors alternated with a big one straight ahead in the gloom. Tebloev was somewhere down here. Plus minders.

There was a small chance none of them knew he was coming, but since he'd spent the last four days making enquiries amongst Russian expats probably someone would have told. He listened at each door as he progressed. And pushed.

The third door gave way, opening into a darkness that was almost complete. And the fourth. There could be anything in there. It might open onto a bottomless pit for all he could tell from looking. But at least no one was shooting.

Suddenly, he saw it. A light coming from beneath the door at the end. He pushed as many doors open as he could, and stepped into the one just before it. His eyes were adjusting now. He could see barrels, piles of scrap. God knows what it had ever been used for.

"*Tebloev!*" he shouted.

He heard them panicking. The end door burst open and two men appeared at right angles to him, holding pistols in outstretched arms. He trod on the ankle of the first and clawed his gun off him as he staggered. Once he had it, he put it to the second's head.

"Put your weapon down and no one will get killed," he said. Out of the corner of his eye, he saw Tebloev sitting at a desk inside the room.

Suddenly, from every doorway along the corridor a man stepped out with a pistol aimed at Orlov's head.

Tebloev smiled. "You're pointing at the wrong man, Colonel. I don't care what happens to him and you'll be dead before you can switch. Game, set and match. Now put the gun down."

Orlov put his revolver on the floor. The man whose head he had aimed at hit him in the face and stepped on his chest.

"That's enough," Tebloev said. "Bring him in here and shut the door."

The man sighed as if he was expecting this. He put his gun in his inside pocket, dragged Orlov into the room, and shut the door on him and Tebloev and two minders. Tebloev put a chair out and gestured for Orlov to sit down. Then he went behind the desk, folded his hands, and leaned forward and smiled.

"Now how may I help you, Colonel?" he said.

"What do you intend to do with me?"

"This room is directly below the Thames. We're going to chain you to the wall and detonate a bomb by means of a timer switch. After that, it will flood inch by inch and we'll watch you die on closed circuit television while we eat truffles and drink fine wine with our business associates and a select bunch of Eastern European ladies."

There was a prolonged, sombre silence. Then Tebloev and his men began to laugh.

"I'm *joking*, Colonel! The truth is, I'm not going to do anything with you, and I probably wouldn't recognise a truffle if you stuck one up my nose. Wait outside, boys."

"I don't understand," Orlov said as the minders left.

"I'm appealing to your better nature because I know you have one. I haven't got a weapon. You could easily overpower me and threaten to break my neck unless everyone disarms and lets you through. But I don't think you will."

Orlov paused. "Okay, I'm listening."

"I've known you were coming after me for a few days now. I knew if you held all the cards, you'd never believe anything I said."

"I'm not obliged to believe you because you've turned the tables."

"If I needed to lie, I'd probably also benefit from killing you."

"Presumably, you're going to pitch me your version of the truth. And whether I get to leave here alive depends on how convincing a job I can do of pretending to believe you."

"It sounds like you're already jumping to conclusions."

"Am I right?"

"Just because a person has the power to murder, it doesn't mean they'll use it. And I won't. You have my word on that, for what it's worth. I don't kill people."

"Why don't you come with me then, and we'll finish talking somewhere else?"

Tebloev sighed. He put his wrists together and held them out. "If it really makes you happy, Colonel. I'm sure you carry a pair of handcuffs nowadays. But it's completely unnecessary."

Orlov grunted and backed down. "Very well."

Tebloev took out a 75cl bottle of Gordon's and two mugs from the desk. He poured himself a generous measure. "It frees my mind to speak. Want one?"

Orlov waved his hand.

"Last time we met," Tebloev said, "you accused me of embezzlement. I'm very sensitive to that sort of thing."

"It turns out I was right, though. We both read the papers."

"That's precisely the thing. It did turn out you were right. But you weren't right at the time. Those guys asked me to raise money for them."

"What guys?"

"Vera Gruchov has 'representatives' in this country. At the embassy. It's not in their interests, or yours, for me to divulge their identities."

"And they asked you to raise money for her?"

"I did think about naming names, since right now I'm the one taking all the flak, but I decided not to. I have seen them since. They know how I feel."

"I'd give them up if I was you. They're almost certainly working for Boris Pyatin."

"Once bitten, twice shy. I won't be falling in with them again. On the other hand, I can't afford to make enemies at the embassy."

"I'm not interested in this. I'm interested in Kramski."

"I've told the police all I know. We were converted to the faith by the same man, so I thought we had a connection. I do a lot for Russian émigrés in this city. I know everyone, high and low, and most of them owe me. The point is, a new face in town, down and out of work? I like to do what I can. It's good PR. And Kramski knew how to handle himself."

"You really believe you're influential in this city?"

"Do you honestly think I could have lured you here if I hadn't told nearly all the people you've questioned what to say about me and what not? I'm loved, Colonel, and I didn't get to be loved by kow-towing to the likes of Dmitri Vassyli Kramski. If I say I don't know him, I don't."

"If you've got that much influence, you should be able to find out where he is. Someone must know."

"I've got exceptional leave to remain in this country so I've got to be seen to be behaving myself impeccably. I'm not prepared to let Kramski put a spanner in that, and just by being in my pay that time, he nearly did. So I've tried to find him. And if I'd succeeded, you'd have been the first person to know."

"Despite what happened at your party?"

"You humiliated me in front of my guests. What did you expect?"

"I didn't go there intending to show you up. I was thinking out loud. I wasn't the only one. Although I was the sole individual scrupulous enough to admit it."

"Is that supposed to be an apology?"

"I'm prepared to put my suspicions to one side for the moment and declare that, for the sake of argument, yes, I apologise."

Tebloev laughed. "Congratulations, Colonel. That has to be the most grudging apology in the history of the entire world. So, friends now, eh?"

"I don't have any friends in my profession. And even if I did, I only make friends with people I know are on the same side as me."

"*Vosstanovlenie* again, eh? What can I say to convince you?"

"I don't know."

"Okay, have you ever met Boris Pyatin?"

"No, thank God."

"He's forty-five and he wants to be mayor for ever. Imagine – as I suppose you must have done – that he came to me and said, 'Valentin, I'll make you a deal. You're seen in Russia as a filthy criminal, so I'd like you to cosy up to Vera Gruchov. And if she's besmirched by the association and I win the election, I'll arrange for you to be pardoned in five or six years'. Do you really think I'd be stupid enough to fall for that? Its premise is that I'm a crook and that anyone who associates with me is unlikely to win a mayoral election. I don't like being taken for a ride, Colonel, and this one's an articulated lorry with a ten thousand megawatt 'I'm stupid' sign on top."

"I admit, you argue your case well."

"I've had a long time to think about it. All the time you've been looking for me. Incidentally, some people say you're working for the Brits now, that you're a traitor."

"I've been granted asylum. Like you, I want to earn my passage. Information's not hard to come by in Russia these days. If the British want it, they don't need me to provide it."

"What about this 'list' you're supposed to have of potential dissidents?"

"A myth. Anyway, what would the British want with it? It's not like the Cold War. Any dissidents nowadays are anti-Putin, not pro-Western."

"You're not working for anyone?"

"I do odd jobs. I've got to make a living."

Tebloev leaned forward and lowered his voice. "Is it true you knew Anna Politkovskaya?"

"We corresponded briefly, yes."

"I worship the ground that woman's feet trod on."

"I doubt that was her aim."

"How about if you were to come and work for me?"

Orlov laughed. "Thank you, no."

"I'll pay you double whatever the British are and it'd be permanent. I'd provide accommodation too."

"I wonder what Vera Gruchov would make of that."

"Ah, the lovely Vera Guchov again. Are you really so beholden to her?"

"She stands for what I believe in. I don't want to do anything *Vosstanovlenie* might … misinterpret."

Tebloev scowled and poured himself another gin. "Very tactful, I don't think." He tipped the contents into his throat. "I'm not guilty of extortion, you know. I'm the kindest man in the world, I really am. But that's the way of the world. Mud sticks."

"You need to clear your name properly. Less PR, more of the sort of rigid argumentation you displayed earlier."

"I love Russia, I love it with a passion. But after Gorbachev, it needed *The Wealth of Nations*. It got *Il Principe*."

"Am I free to go?"

"You've been free to go since the beginning. But I didn't lure you here just to convince you of my innocence. I thought I'd give you a little help, so to speak."

"How can you give me 'a little help' if you're innocent? It implies you're withholding something. Are you?"

"I know lots of people, I hear lots of stories. When I hear something that particularly interests me, I try and put it together with other stories. I speculate. But my speculations are better informed than most people's."

"Go on."

"Constantine Slope."

Orlov raised his eyebrows. "What about him?"

"That's what I think you need to find out."

"He's dead."

Tebloev put his mug down and sat up straight. "I'm sorry, that can't be true."

"What makes you say that?"

"You can't believe everything you read on Wikipedia."

"What was he doing on your guest-list?"

"When? The night you were there? He wasn't – I don't think … Who told you he was?"

Orlov realised he'd blundered. "Felicity Sykes. The late ambassador's wife."

Tebloev considered this. "Yes, Mrs Sykes would probably know him if anyone does - did. If he mentioned it to her, I suppose that must mean he considered coming at some point."

"Maybe the reason he didn't turn up was because he was dead."

"What else did Mrs Sykes say about him?"

"Not much. That he was a businessman, extremely diverse, extremely reclusive. Eighty-eight, not in the best of health lately. Why would Mrs Sykes think he'd been invited?"

"He may have been. It was a fundraiser. People buy tickets in blocks and give them out to their clients or friends. My secretary vets the names and compiles the list. I don't necessarily approve of, or even see, everyone on there in advance. Put it like this: I'm not complaining, but I've no idea how you got on the guest-list."

"What's so odd about Slope being dead?"

"You'd have to have met him to know that. There's something about him. Colonel, are you a superstitious man?"

"No. Are you?"

Tebloev looked into his mug. "I – I might be. Have you ever heard of the Upir? It's a corpse possessed by the devil. It lives during daylight hours."

"And you believe in such creatures, do you? I'm surprised."

"Don't believe Constantine Slope is dead, that's all. Trust me."

"You seem anxious that I should investigate him."

"It's up to you what you do. I'm only trying to help you."

Orlov stood up. "Time for me to leave."

Tebloev put the mug and the bottle back in the drawer. He escorted Orlov back along the corridor and up the metal ladder and opened the door to let him out of the building.

"Wait, there's something I forgot to give you," he said, and rushed back inside. He came back with a small box tied with a pink ribbon. "Take it. A token of friendship."

"What is it?"

"Biscuits. The best. You have to taste them to believe them. Listen, I'm sorry Karl hit you earlier, but you pointed a gun at his head. Please take them."

Orlov hesitated, then accepted the box and the handshake Tebloev was offering.

"Thank you," he said.

As soon as he finished talking to Katie, Bronstein went to his car where the receiver was and put the headphones on and pressed play and record. It was ringing already.

"What's up Stall?" Nichole Moore said.

"Nicky, what have you been saying about me?" Stallone Laine replied.

"Huh?"

"I've just been talking to the pigs. They said you dumped some bad shit on me, girl. Is that right?"

Her voice sped up. "No, no, it isn't. Absolutely not."

"How do they know about us?"

"God, I don't know. I didn't even know they did. Listen, I swear – Look, we shouldn't even be talking like this any more.

You heard what the man said. He was like, no more phone conversations."

"I just want to know - "

"I'm going to hang up, baby. I don't want to get in trouble, and nor do you. Kiss, kiss."

"Meet me in the park in ten."

"But I - "

Bronstein unplugged the wire from the recorder and plugged it into the Location Finder. They were currently in Drury Lane. So what 'park'? Then suddenly, the dot that was their phone sped up. Obviously, they'd taken a taxi. He watched until they stopped at Green Park.

He shook his head. *No more phone conversations.* Obviously, they were going to have to start working on the assumption that Kramski knew a hell of a lot more about them than they did about him.

Chapter 14: The Return of Nicholas Fleming

It rained the day of the funeral. The Church was packed with Jonathan's school and university friends and Facebook associates, all in black. The family sat on the front pew, Sir Anthony with Marcie, Joy with Anya. The vicar – an elderly man with long white hair - spoke of Jonathan's devotion to duty, his love of animals and his kindness to strangers. Joy sat dry-eyed and winced. They sang, 'O Lord, to whom the spirits live' and 'Now the labourer's task is o'er', then went to stand under umbrellas as the coffin was lowered into the grave.

"Man that is born of a woman hath but a short time to live," the vicar said, "and is full of misery. He cometh up and is cut down, like a flower. He fleeth as it were a shadow, and never continueth in one stay. In the midst of life we are in death. Of whom may we seek for succour, but of thee, O Lord?"

The rain increased as if the sky was angry and people huddled closer. Joy broke down and hugged Anya and heaved gently. Marcie squeezed her father's arm and felt his emotion like electricity chaining them to the spot in anticipation of their own deaths. The sky was grey, the earth was grey.

The family shuffled to the graveside. They sprinkled soil on the box. The vicar said the Collect and everyone either sidled away or moved in to offer support. A group of Townswomen's Guild ladies took Joy over and ushered her to the car. The Leader of the Opposition and six of Sir Anthony's parliamentary colleagues came to confirm their condolences in person.

Suddenly, Marcie found herself alone in her complete immobility. Someone was coming towards her, though. She could see him out of the corner of her eye. She didn't want to be consoled. Perhaps if she pretended not to see him he'd go away.

"Marcie, I ..."

She turned to face him. Good God. "Nicholas Fleming."

He looked as emotional as she was. "I was in America when I heard. I chucked everything to get back. I've never been so gut-wrenched. As for you, Marcie, I can't begin to imagine what you must be feeling."

She looked at him for a moment as if he'd said something exceptional then she clutched him and burst into tears.

Apart from the moment the life support machine failed she hadn't allowed herself to cry yet, not properly. It was a full time job just keeping Mummy and Daddy apart. It shouldn't, but it felt good. She saw her hat fall into the mud.

Fleming kissed her hair and picked up her hat for her. "If there's anything I can do, please tell me."

"I'm – I'm so glad you came," she said, regaining some of her former self-control. "You're right, it's been utterly, utterly horrible."

"Bloody kids in cars. No conception of the consequences."

She drew a sharp breath. "Are you coming to the reception? I'm sure Daddy would love to see you again."

"It's not really my thing. I know that sounds selfish."

"What were you doing in America?"

"It was a secondment. Strictly temporary."

"Anything new going on in your life?"

"Yes, I, er, I might be getting married in a few months time."

She swallowed. "Anyone I know?"

"A woman I met in New York. Margarita ... Martinez. Damn and blast it, Marcie, no there isn't anyone in my life. I was just trying to put you at ease."

She gave a weak smile. "How would that put me at ease?"

"We both know I'm no good at small talk, so I might as well just come out and say it. I don't think Jonathan died chasing a boy racer."

Her heart plopped into a lake. "What?"

"There's no smashed car, no official police report, no hunt for the suspect, nothing. I don't know how he did die, but I bloody well intend to find out."

"My God, Nick, this isn't the time or place."

He laughed bitterly. "I'm not very good on times and places. You know that better than anyone. What do you know about a Mr David Bronstein?"

But she was already walking away, pulling her hat onto her head

He drew parallel with her. "Look, I really cared about Jonathan - "

She tried to change direction to shake him off, but there was nowhere to turn. The lych-gate was blocked by a couple sheltering from the rain, and it was the sole exit. "Get away from me, Nick, just - get away. I don't want to talk to you any more. You just can't stop being a policeman, that's your trouble. Everything's got to boil down to some stupid mystery or other. I think if what's left of his family – Mummy and Daddy and I – can live with the fact that he died in a car chase, you should be able to. Or is that too much to ask?"

"I know it isn't what you expected me to say."

"Just go back to America, okay? I don't want to hear your silly little theories, nor does anyone. I've just lost my big brother."

She increased her pace, barged past the couple, passed through the gate and opened the rear door of the car into which her father had just climbed. Before she sat down, she looked back at Nicholas and shook her head. She made herself as comfortable as she could, considering, and the car pulled out. She watched him from the window, standing motionless in the rain like a crow in a field.

"Is that Nicholas Fleming?" he father said. "Bloody odd chap. Don't know what you ever saw in him, but I suppose you were a lot younger."

"It was only a year ago, Daddy."

"Is he coming to the reception?"

"I've told him he's not welcome."

Sir Anthony shifted in his seat and stroked his chin. "Maybe ..."

"Maybe what?"

"It's just that ... well, whatever your shared history, we both know Jonathan thought the world of him."

She scoffed. "Jonathan's not here."

All the rest of that day she couldn't shake the idea that Nicholas Fleming was here to destroy them. He wasn't the kind of person who took no for an answer, not when he thought the truth was at stake. So he'd dig and dig until he found out what really happened.

Then what? He'd be horrified. But it would be a spreading horror. It would spread to her – she'd become the unspeakable monster for him - just as it had spread to her for Mummy. And it might even go further. It might end suffusing him with the sense that no matter how nice people seemed on the surface, underneath they were all woodlice and dry rot. A kind of reasonable misanthropy next door to nihilism.

At the reception, she drank two large glasses of wine and tried to shield her mother from the sentimentality of the crowd. But Joy left after half an hour, taking Anya with her, and didn't say goodbye. Marcie wandered out of the hall into the housing estate and got a bus into Hertford. The rain stopped and the sun came out. She went to the park and sat down and cried again, and again she felt better.

Half an hour later, she bought a bottle of gin in Waitrose and went back to the park. She realised she was making matters worse after drinking about a third. She was spoiling for a fight now, but at least she knew she was spoiling for a fight, which meant she'd be able to forestall it. And that was a big improvement on last time. She was growing up.

Bloody Nicholas bloody *bloody* Fleming, she wanted to punch him.

Maybe she could phone him, try to distract him somehow. Tell him she loved him, that would work, the sap. Maybe tell him everything, trust to his better nature. Ask him, beg him to keep it a secret.

No, why should she? And she didn't love him.

Everything was ruined now. Like a Greek tragedy, it would run its course, disaster following disaster until the epic catastrophe and the curtain. The Fall of the House of Hartley-Brown. She had to get away. There was nothing else for it. Go back to London.

Her head swam. She was still dressed in her funeral gear. Big black hat with a veil, skirt-suit, nylon tights, heels, clutch bag, half a bottle of gin. She poured the rest on the grass. No wonder she was attracting odd looks.

Her phone was ringing. *Nick.*

Bloody hell, you'd think 'get away from me' would be pretty clear, but no. Her stomach rolled onto its back and groaned. She switched it off on the fourth ring.

Then she switched it on again. She scrolled down the names until she came to Miss Demure and pressed call.

"Marcie Brown?" an elderly voice said.

"Hi, Miss Demure."

"How can I help?"

"You - you said you'd keep my job open for me. I quite understand if that's not been possible, but - "

"You poor dear. Come back whenever you like. Really."

"How about tomorrow?"

"I understand it was the funeral today. There's no hurry. I told you I'd keep your job open. I'm not the sort of employer who has second thoughts."

"I know, and thank you. But I don't think there's anything more I can do here. I'm getting under my parents' feet. And I want to come back."

"I've retained your flat for you just as you left it. Pick up the keys tomorrow morning and be at the gym at midday. Of course, you must understand that there can be no easing you in gently. I only know full ahead."

"I look forward to seeing you."

She wondered how long she had before the time-bomb that was Nicholas Fleming detonated. It inevitably would. Once Hercule Poirot arrived in town you might as well put your own handcuffs on. Daddy would be disgraced, he'd probably die of shame. Mummy would stay alive for Anya, a corpse in all but name. And she'd be the spoilt little ASBO whose parents used to pull strings for her. Miss Demure wouldn't want to know her, no one would. Nick included.

She suddenly had a plan. It wasn't a happy one, but it avoided the worst of what was coming.

She'd train as intensively as she could. Whatever Miss Demure asked of her, she'd do double, triple. And when the truth about Jonathan looked like it was about to emerge, she'd join the army and go to Iraq or Afghanistan.

End of her.

She sat in the central library until four o'clock, researching army careers and waiting to sober up. She went outside and bought a litre bottle of water, twenty paracetamol and a Mars and flagged down a minicab. Twenty minutes later she was home. She felt terrible.

She went straight to her room and lay down. Two hours later, Geoffrey came to tell her it was dinnertime. She showered, changed into a long blouson dress and a pair of pumps, tied her hair in a bun, and went downstairs. Joy, Sir Anthony and Anya were waiting. Marcie sat down and attacked the soup. As usual, Joy wasn't speaking.

"Your friend rang this afternoon, Marcie," Sir Anthony said.

"Who?" she said, although she already knew.

"Nicholas Fleming. He said it was very important. He said if you don't want to speak to him, please read his e-mail."

"I definitely don't want to speak to him."

"We spoke for quite some time. I've never had a prolonged conversation with him before. Turns out he's a very decent chap. I've misjudged him."

"What did you talk about?"

"Mainly Jonathan, I'm afraid. Shared memories. He really rated him, you know. From what I can make out, he saw Jonathan as a role model."

Joy scowled. "If he only knew."

"Which is exactly how Jonathan saw him, of course. Joy, we all know what you *think* you know, but you weren't in your right mind that night. I've told you, I've actually been back to Beachy Head and I couldn't find anyone who remembered Jonathan or a gun or anything. And I spoke to the chaplaincy team."

"Liar," she said.

He sighed. "You carry on thinking what you want to think. It's up to you."

"I'm going back to London tomorrow," Marcie said.

"Probably best," Sir Anthony said. "To Celia Demure?"

She nodded. They finished their soup and ate a curry and Marcie went upstairs to switch on her computer. She might be able to judge how close he was to a breakthrough and whether it was even worth the effort of packing for London.

She went straight to her e-mail. There it was, right at the top. 'Nick – Re: This Afternoon II'. Right above another from him, sent one minute earlier, 'Nick – Re: This Afternoon'. How very methodical, how exactly like a filing clerk, how typical. She clicked on the earlier one first.

> *Dear Marcie,*
> *I'm going back to the USA tomorrow, but I couldn't leave without letting you know how sorry I am about my behaviour at the funeral. You were right about everything: it wasn't the time or the place and if you're happy with the coroner's verdict, what the hell right have I to come sticking my idiotic nose in? Sometimes, you can't see the wood for the trees and I haven't been myself lately. I haven't just been grieving for Jonathan, I've been angry. I don't really know what with. Probably with the way the world unfailingly seems out to hunt down and kill its very best specimens and leave all the villains intact. Anyway, I've got a grip on myself now and I really hope you'll forgive and forget. No more conspiracy theories. Let sleeping dogs lie, etc. In any case, tomorrow I return to the fictional arms of Margarita Martinez, so you never have to see me again if you don't want to.*
> *Nick.*

She closed it with grateful relief and opened 'Nick – Re: This Afternoon II'.

> *But that would be a shame because I don't love Margarita Martinez.*

She smiled and wiped her eyes, then went back to her Inbox. Message after message of sympathy, scores of them, just as she'd expected. She'd been putting off facing them until after the funeral. She couldn't possibly reply to all of them before tomorrow morning, could she? Tammy, Edie, PhilippaG, Greg, Josh345, HotJake, Stinkadore, Hannah ... She'd have to try. She scrolled to the bottom. Nick, there he was again – oh, but that was another Nick. Darren56, Gill, Priscilla, JonathanHB, Carlos ...

Er ... *JonathanHB?* She looked at the date. My God.

> *Orlov, Bronstein.*
> *Told Jilly about we know. She contacted by group, starting with a woman years ago, Miss Burkinshaw not her real name, then man afterwards. Put her where she is. Others too, all sponsored same, buddies. Russian mafia, poss, but told J to involve in politics, so doesn't fit. Nanowire and location transmitter IN HER PHONE, so coming. She phoned Zane!!! Coming back by B roads with J. Will ditch her phone at safe distance. Call me asap. JHB.*

She read it twice but her mind was blank. She read it a third time and it was blank. She was trying to do two different things and they cancelled each other. She was trying to work out what it meant in itself and what it meant for the idea that Jonathan was a murderer.

He wasn't a murderer. He'd been frightened when he wrote this. It sounded like he thought someone was coming after him. Not him, though: *them*. 'With J'. He'd been with Jilly Bestwick when he wrote it.

She felt like she was reading the Rosetta Stone, as if her head might float away. For a moment she considered running downstairs and telling her parents, but she thought better of it. There was only one person she could trust to deal sensibly with this and get to the bottom of it. She lurched for her phone. She could tell him everything now. Her hands shook.

"Nick, hi, yes, this is Marcie. I need to see you right away … Immediately, that's right … Yes, I got your e-mail, it made me cry … Both of them, yes … No, I'm not angry, far from it … Come to the house, I'll meet you in the grounds. And, er, shit, there's no easy way to say this … Is it possible for you to put off going to the USA for a while?"

Chapter 15: Reading *The Stage*

A box of biscuits stood on Orlov's desk, next to the PC. He reached in, ate one and passed it to Bronstein. By coincidence, the two men had arrived at work in roughly the same clothes: polo-necked jumpers and dark trousers. Bronstein thought they looked like a couple of U-boat commanders. He resolved to stick with turtle or V-necks from now on.

He took a biscuit and tut-tutted. "What's espionage coming to when the main villain gets you a present?"

"I don't think he's the 'main villain'. I'm not sure he's a villain at all."

"Aren't you worried they might be poisoned?"

"If he'd wanted to kill me he had the opportunity."

"They're in the shape of hearts, for God's sake."

Orlov shrugged. Bronstein took another and turned to the notice board behind him, where paired portrait photos of celebrities with their names beneath were pinned. Stallone Laine and Nichole Moore, Connie Glaser and Rick Teal, Beth Corea and David Pike. If he looked often enough, something would come to him, it had happened before.

Orlov pushed his chair back and pulled his coat on.

"Off to meet Tebloev's secretary?" Bronstein said.

"I need to know who invited Slope to that party."

"Slope's a red herring. Unless he's not really dead after all. But you've seen his grave. You've spoken to people who knew him, who were there at his funeral. It wouldn't be so bad if he had some kind of successor."

"We don't know he hasn't yet."

"If he has, we don't really know what he or she's successor to. Not in terms of the investigation."

Orlov went to the door. "Feel free to have another biscuit."

Bronstein's phone rang. Gavin. He put on his sports jacket and took the lift to the conference room on the fourth floor. Gavin stood adjusting the audio visual equipment. He switched out the lights, pulled the blinds down and turned the projector on. Bronstein sat down.

"It's quite rare for us to be asked to do lip-reading, Mr Bronstein - "

"Call me David."

"David. But it's an excellent idea. You must have been very patient."

"I'm a man of many virtues, Gavin. And I used to work for the NYPD so I've done my fair share of stake outs. I know how to cope with boredom."

"What sort of camera did you use, if you don't mind my asking?"

"You'd have to ask the technical department. All I know is that it's a video camera with a telescopic lens. Nothing fancy. They told me just to point and press the red button."

"If you want me to pause it, please say. I've added subtitles so you can watch each film again later. Of course, the subjects are facing away from us a fair bit of the time, so we've only snippets of what they say. It's interesting that they all choose the same park to come to."

"Probably implies that I'm not the only one watching them."

"I hadn't thought of it like that."

"Well, that's NYU one, Oxford nil. It's partly what I'm looking out for. Press play."

Gavin obliged. The screen showed Stallone Laine towering over Nichole Moore, jabbing his finger at her. The subtitle said, "LAINE: I don't believe any of that astrology shit. What do mean, 'What star sign?'"

Bronstein waved his hands. "Stop, stop. Press pause."

"Is there a problem?" Gavin asked.

"I didn't mean to diss your university back then. I was only teasing. Obviously Oxford's very good, otherwise I wouldn't have heard of it."

"Thank you, sir."

"Press play again."

"Is it okay for me to do a little paperwork in the background while you watch? You probably won't have many questions. I don't think there's very much that's suspicious in there, although I'm not an expert. But I'll still be here."

"Sit next to the window. Pull the blind up a touch so you don't ruin your eyes." Bronstein realised he'd become his mother.

Gavin pressed play again. The subtitle said, "MOORE: 'There's no need to be so prissy. I heard you were a Pisces and if you are, that explains a lot'."

LAINE: Yeah, like what?
MOORE: Because of your tattoos.
LAINE: What do you know about my tattoos?
MOORE: Like you've got one of a man carrying water.
LAINE: That's not a man carrying water. Anyway, Pisces is a fish.
MOORE: No, way. You're thinking of Aquarium.

An hour later, Bronstein was still watching, taking the occasional note on a pad. Gavin had pulled the blind up a little more and put reading glasses on.

GLASER: You don't like it when it's happening, no one does, but I wouldn't change it. I had rows with my parents. I wouldn't change it now for anything.
TEAL: It may be too late for me, though.
GLASER: It's never too late for orthodontic treatment.

TEAL: Do they do, like, part-time braces? Like only put them on at night?
GLASER: Yeah, they do that.

The film came to an end.

"That was the last of them I'm afraid," Gavin said.

"Right, okay. I need you to go back to Laine-Moore episode one. Four minutes thirty-three seconds."

Gavin double-clicked on the film. He dragged the button along the play bar and hit pause. Stallone Laine's hands were spread. Nichole Moore was reaching in her bag. The caption: "LAINE: 'I don't like chocolate but I once dreamed I was working in a Twix factory'."

"See that guy in the background?" Bronstein said. "Twenty paces behind Moore?"

"Do you recognise him?"

"Never seen him before. But, to begin with, he's in all the films. And in every one, he's doing what he's doing here. Looking straight at me."

"Shit."

"Steady, Gavin."

"Sorry, sir. I meant, what's it mean?"

"It means they're playing with me."

"What for? Do you think they're going to try and kill you?"

"They could have done that already. This is still quite a small investigation, despite Jonathan. But you kill two agents, suddenly you've got a war on your hands. No, I think they're just trying to waste my time, giving me lots of lovely lips to film. But they're also curious about me. Hence, the mystery man."

"Presumably, you'd like me to print off the stills and distribute them."

"We might salvage something yet. Get to it, boy."

Orlov came back later that day to find Bronstein at his desk eating an apple and drawing a flow chart. He took the personnel file from the cabinet and sat down.

"How did you get on with Tebloev's secretary?" Bronstein said.

"It's Edgeware. Edgeware's the one who invited Slope."

"Not Tebloev, then. You sure Tebloev didn't tell her to say that?"

"The secretary? What makes you think it's a 'her'?"

"Is it?"

Orlov smiled. "No."

"Could I have another biscuit?"

"The problem is, now I have to interview Edgeware. Or someone does."

"I see what you're thinking. You're a Russian. He's never going to swallow the idea that you're from the English police."

Orlov glowered. "I met him at Tebloev's party. That's why he won't 'swallow' the idea."

"And not that you've got a Russian accent."

"I spent three years perfecting my English accent at the Russian Ministry of Defence. You hardly notice it unless you're looking for it. Do you?"

Bronstein laughed. "The Brits are experts at spotting accents. They've built an entire social system on it."

"Maybe we should send you."

"No, thank you. I know my limitations."

"This is where Jonathan would have come in very useful."

"What about Gavin?" Bronstein said.

"Projector Gavin?"

"The only Gavin we know."

"You can't just pick a name out of a hat. MI7 probably has protocols. I'm guessing you look in a file, select x, then submit a written request."

"Then you wait till x becomes available. How long do you think that's going to take? Time is of the essence."

"I can't believe it would drag out."

Bronstein stood up. "Don't bet on it. Wait there."

"Where are you going?"

"I'm going to ask Ruby Parker. Relax. I'll just say, 'What form do we fill in to get someone to interview someone like Edgeware?'"

"Don't mention Gavin. I don't want her to think we're dilettantes."

Bronstein walked the ten paces along the corridor that separated Ruby Parker's office from theirs. He knocked and heard 'come in'.

"Close the door behind you," she said, looking hard at him. "We need to talk."

"We'd like to borrow Gavin. Orlov and I. To interview Edgeware."

"Sit down."

He sat down with his legs apart and leaned forward. He adjusted his glasses. "Is something the matter?"

"Presumably, you've heard of Kyrgyzstan."

"Central Asia, right?"

"There's a potential genocide out there. Kyrgyzs are killing Uzbeks – only a hundred and thirty eight so far, but rising, and it's got the potential to become a new Rwanda or a Goražde. Moscow hasn't ruled out sending in peacekeeping troops, but it's reluctant to act unilaterally. The Kremlin's asked for our help and the US is keen to get involved because it has military bases there acting as stopover points to Afghanistan. Can you see where this is going?"

"You're folding us."

"Absolutely not, no. But we're going to have to reassess our budgetary priorities. No more lip reading technology, for example."

Bronstein shrugged. "Seems more than fair. Certainly if we're talking about genocide."

"There's also the possibility that Colonel Orlov might get to go home."

"What?"

"If we cooperate with the Russians, they're willing to consider pardoning him."

"And you believe that?"

"There would be very serious consequences for them if they gave us their word at the highest diplomatic levels – which is what this is – and then they were to renege. They wouldn't risk that, believe me."

"If that's what he wants."

"It's important you realise, Lieutenant Bronstein, that I've been very impressed with you since you started here. You've hardly made a wrong move, and you've made lots of right ones. Orlov too. I'll be very sorry to lose him, but you're right: it's what he desires. First and foremost, he sees himself as a Russian."

"I guess you're going to tell me I mustn't let on to him."

"If that's okay."

"Mum's the word."

And David?"

"Yeah?"

She held out a wadge of photos. "Firstly, yes to Gavin. It'll be good experience for him and he needs an airing. And this man you identified in the stills this morning. Well done. We didn't recognise him, so we got through to the Russian embassy. Valdim Yakinterev, an ex-field officer from Irkutsk. They sent us fingerprints, DNA profile, mug shots, the works."

"Connection to Kramski?"

"Same line of work."

"Any notion how he entered the country?"

She smiled. "We're working on it."

"The Russians must have a view on this. What do they think's going on?"

"They think it's Russian mafia."

"And what do you think?"

"They're a long way from home if it is. And they haven't announced themselves in any previous enterprises. At the same time, I've dealt with the Russian embassy on several other occasions and my feeling is that they're not up to anything. I think they're as baffled and perturbed by this as we are."

Bronstein returned to find Orlov reading *The Stage*.

"Any jobs?" he said facetiously.

Orlov turned it round and put it on Bronstein's desk. "Essential reading for anyone involved with celebrities."

Bronstein picked it up. Under the banner, 'Celebrities in "Unprecedented" Rush to Political Parties', it ran:

> In what one media commentator last night dubbed a "cultural sea-change of major significance", this general election sees an unprecedented number of A-list celebrities signing up to campaign for the main political parties.
>
> Among the raft of names, the Conservatives boast Rick Teal, 2009 BAFTA award winner for best actor, the Bling Bling Bubbly Gum singer, Connie Glaser, and Christopher Temple-Main, last month's winner of the X Factor. Leading the charge for Labour are, among others, Ted Vallania (Super Coolkidz in Dumpsters), Soraya Snow (Fully Magic Coal Tar Lounge) and Ronald Wakehurst (*Death on the Golden Fireplace, Ten Inches of my Girlfriend*). The Liberal Democrats are also significant beneficiaries.

Celebrities have always been involved in general elections in all countries. In the UK, Joan Collins, Antony Worrall Thompson and Delia Smith declared allegiances in 2005, while Geri Halliwell famously served tea to pensioners in a party political broadcast in 2001.

But according to Tim Cloipes, lecturer in Modern British Politics at the London School of Economics, the current phenomenon is unparalleled. "The difference is not just of scale, it's that many of the celebrities are seen as role models by the young - of the sort 'your parents would tend to disapprove of'. And of course party politics in this country has traditionally been something with which young people fail to engage."

Asked what he thought had brought about the change, he declared himself at a loss, adding, "The evidence is that celebrity involvement does little or nothing to change people's voting habits, but it definitely makes for a more colourful spectacle."

Underneath there were portrait photos of over a hundred celebrities, arranged into groups with blue, orange and red frames.

Bronstein hm-hmmed. "The whole gang. Why isn't it in any of the other papers?"

"You would expect *The Stage* to join the dots first. It's in their job description. The others will carry it tomorrow."

"What do you think's going on?"

"At a guess? Assuming they're all being remote-controlled by whoever Kramski works for, it's obvious."

Bronstein spread his hands. "I don't do obvious. What's your theory?"

"One or more of them is primed to assassinate one or more politician. The more senior, the better."

"To what end, pray tell?"

"Do we need to know that now? We know Kramski's collaborating with them. Have you a better theory?"

Bronstein clicked his tongue three times like a kangaroo. "Not yet, I admit. But I'm going to work on the assumption your theory's wrong if that's okay."

"It's more than that. It's what I expect. There's no point in putting all our eggs in one basket."

"I've got Gavin, by the way."

"You didn't ask for him by name, though, did you?"

"No, it was her idea."

"You're not making eye contact with me."

"She said he needed 'an airing'. Her exact words."

"We might as well start now then. Let's go and get him."

The lifts were out of order but they intercepted Gavin in the stairwell on the third floor on his way to meet them, carrying a briefcase with a dossier under his arm. He smiled and nodded a greeting.

"I've got an updated report on Constantine Slope for you, sir," he told Bronstein. "Courtesy of Gabriella in Research and Reports. She says she's dug a little deeper, but she doesn't think there's anything obviously suspicious there."

"How come the elevators aren't working?" Bronstein said.

"Oh, that happens every afternoon – and morning - at about four. The lifts and shuttles close down for ten minutes while the Black Maiden leaves the building. I believe it can be overridden in an emergency."

"How does he or she get out of the building if all the elevators are shut down?" Bronstein said.

"No one knows. At least not on our floor."

"Could I have a word with you?" Orlov asked Gavin.

"I was just on my way home, sir, but I'm happy to stay behind for a while if it's what I think it is. My train doesn't leave for an hour. It's about Edgeware, isn't it?"

"I promise it won't take any more than thirty minutes," Orlov said.

"And I'll meet you on the way to work tomorrow morning, Gavin," Bronstein said. "You've just set me thinking. There are a few things I'd like to ask."

Chapter 16: Sacred Texts

Joy stood in her bedroom holding Anya's hand and looking out of the window. Rain dribbled down the casement and jiggled the ivy on either side. It was warm in here, but outside the gale drove the clouds as if they were sheep, and the downpour lashed the lawn. It was evening. A sheet of lightning seared the sky followed by a bang like a cannon. The storm was overhead now.

Joy was interested to see what would happen if the lightning destroyed the oak where Marcie and Nicholas Fleming were sheltering. They would probably be killed. Why didn't they come in? They must know the risk they were taking. Ah, but they were in love, the fools, their selfish genes kicking in.

It was academic, but all things considered, it would probably be best for everyone concerned if they *were* killed.

"I can see why your mother would think that," Fleming said.

"Let's walk," Marcie said, linking arms with him. "It's not any drier under here. And it's probably not safe in this weather."

"It's obvious what the truth is."

"The secret service, yes, I know. I wonder how long he'd been doing that."

"Quite some time, I think. Before I went on secondment."

"Presumably, he and Mr Bronstein were looking after Colonel Orlov. That would explain the men outside the house just before they all had to leave."

"It must be bigger than that. What does 'contacted by group, starting with a woman years ago' mean? And 'all sponsored same, buddies'? And where does Jilly Bestwick come into it?"

"If we can find Mr Bronstein - "

"And if, as we both suspect, he's a member of the CIA …?"

"Then what?" she said.

"He won't say a word. I'm not sure what you want from this, Marcie. There's enough information in this e-mail to prove that Jonathan didn't kill Jilly Bestwick and Zane Cruse then commit suicide. He was murdered and MI5 tried to suppress the facts by re-invoking his Metropolitan police cover."

"I know, but that's not enough."

"You wouldn't be thinking about revenge, would you?"

"Of course not."

"Because that would be very, very silly. I mean it."

She frowned. "On the contrary, I think it would be only natural. Speaking theoretically."

"Whoever killed him probably didn't do it for any personal reason. That's how the secret service works. And if you go around looking for revenge because your knight's just been taken you're likely to be checkmated very quickly."

"If I wanted revenge, I'd throw the board away."

"That's an over-extension of the metaphor. Anyway, if you don't want vengeance, what do you want?"

"I want to persuade Mummy. She thinks she's been lied to once about Jonathan – by Daddy and whatever chinless string-pullers she thinks he has behind him - and that she had to find the truth by dint of her own resourcefulness. She thinks more or less everyone was in on the conspiracy, probably even me. If I go to her now and say, 'Look, Mummy, I've found this e-mail. It proves Jonathan didn't commit suicide after all', do you think she'd give it or me a second glance? She hates Daddy and she hates Jonathan's memory, and I've got to prove to her she's got it all – wrong."

He nodded. "I see."

"My mother's never been very forthcoming. But she's always been there for me. Which is more than can be said for Daddy. Jonathan really loved her. And I really love her …"

"Are you okay?"

"Not really."

He put his arms round her and turned her to face him. "You know I'll help you, whatever."

"Listen, I'm going to tell you something I've never told anyone."

"Go on then."

"Seven years ago, when I was fifteen, Mummy had a miscarriage. It was just after one of Daddy's 'dalliances'. I would have had a baby sister ... And then, quite by chance, she heard about Anya. She literally came across her. And ... I know this sounds weird but ... I've always thought that's because God wanted me to have a baby sister."

He smiled. "You believe in God?"

"I'm a confirmed member of the Church of England, Nicholas. What about you?"

"I, er - "

"The point is, if I lose Mummy, I lose Anya too. I imagine you can appreciate why that would destroy me."

"Yes, I can."

"So that's why I don't want you to go back to America. You've got to help me amass so much evidence to show Jonathan died honourably that it becomes undeniable, even if you're in the grip of the world's strongest delusion."

"Maybe you're being too pessimistic. It's a Hotmail address. It contains the date and time of sending. You can't forge that. Your mother would have to believe you."

"I'm going to ignore your naïve belief that you can't whip up a counterfeit Hotmail document. Consider this: if I show it to Mummy and she doesn't believe it, it'll reinforce her defences. Because that's how conspiracy theorists are. They surround themselves with a protective shell of dogma and every new attack that fails to break through actually fortifies it. Like a science-fiction film. Your second attempt has to be doubly good, your third quadruply and so on."

"I understand, yes."

"You run out of options sooner than you can possibly imagine. I've seen it happen."

"So we've got possession of the trigger, now we've got to build the gun."

"I don't want to ruin your career, Nick. If you can't get out of going back to the US, I'll understand, really."

"And what will you do?"

"I don't know yet. But I'll think of something."

"Marcie, I've already got out of going to the US. My mother 'suddenly fell ill' when you told me you wanted me to stay. They quite understand. After all, no one in their right mind would chuck up that sort of an opportunity unless there was a bloody good reason. And I've got one. Just not the one they think."

She kissed his cheek. "You're a wonderful friend."

"Are you still going to London tomorrow?"

"Of course. But that's where you'll be, won't you?"

"How about dinner?" he said. "And I'll tell you what I've found."

"Really? You'll start tomorrow?"

"No time like the present."

Ten minutes later, she was back in her room, folding cardigans and bunching socks into pairs to go in her suitcase. She wanted a photograph of Jonathan, maybe one of him and her together, although she wasn't sure she could go through the process of choosing one without breaking down again.

Joy stored all the keepsakes in the sideboard drawer in the parlour. Hardly anyone ever went in there nowadays, so she'd probably be able to sort through whatever was inside at her convenience. She crept downstairs. Mummy had almost certainly gone to bed now. Daddy was most likely staring into the empty grate in the living room again. She went into the parlour and closed the door and switched the light on.

There were two boxes of photos in the drawer, side by side. She opened the first.

Jonathan's mobile. What was that doing in there? She remembered Daddy telling her how he'd rung and rung it that day, then discovered he'd left it at home by mistake. Mummy must have put it away.

She had an idea that hit her like a punch in the heart. What if …? She switched it on. Low battery, but not flat. Names. Sally, Gordon, Daddy, Will, Charles, Spike, Mummy, Marcie, O – yes! – James, Matthew, B – yes!

For a moment, she thought of calling 'B', but then she remembered Nicholas - *And if, as we both suspect, he's a member of the CIA, he won't say a word.* It didn't matter, she held a trump card. It was a question of knowing when to play it. Not now, no. But the time would come.

Just out of interest, she went to his Inbox and pressed 'messages'. It took her a second to realise what she was looking at, then she had to put her free hand against her face to stop it trembling.

> *I lov u, Jonathan. ILU W evry atom of my hart.*
> *Jonathan, I've nvr met NE1 lk u, you're ll I wnt n lyf.*
> *I can't liv w/o u Ny mor Jonathan, I don't care w@ hpns 2 me now, I lov u.*
> *I cnt stop thnkn bout u. I want u so mch it's painful.*
> *I didn't knw twas posbL 2 lov NE1 dis mch. It's scary.*

There were more, many more. She swallowed hard and went to his Outbox.

I can't believe I've been lucky enough to meet you. I just can't believe it.
You're the most beautiful, most elegant woman in the world, Jilly. I'd follow you anywhere.
Jilly, you're sacred to me, I'd die without you.

She was dripping onto the floor now. She put the phone into her pocket and ran back upstairs.

It was early morning. Bronstein and Gavin walked through Green Park together eating cereal bars. Bronstein wore a V-necked jumper and chinos and had his left hand in his pocket. Gavin wore a pinstriped suit and carried an umbrella and a briefcase. Everyone around them was fixed on their destinations, all places with polished floors and strict dress codes involving jackets, haircuts and a recent dry clean. Only the pigeons looked relaxed.

Bronstein threw his wrapper in the bin and took out another bar. "You know yesterday, when you were talking about the Black Maiden?"

"About the lift being temporarily out of order?"

"I'm only asking because, when Orlov and I arrived here, Ruby Parker told us her department was authorised to sabotage operations carried out by the others if she disapproved of them."

"I didn't know that, but go on."

"So what if this whole Kramski thing is an operation by one of those others? It's not like we know what their agendas are."

"It's likely Miss Parker has explored that already. I'd imagine it would be the first thing on her list."

"But it's possible she hasn't closed the book on it."

"With respect, sir, you're asking about things I'm too junior to comment on. I can speculate, but that probably isn't going to be of much use to you."

"What do you know about the Black Maiden?"

"Nothing at all. Except that she – or he – comes in at four in the morning and leaves at four in the afternoon."

"Someone must have seen her. Or him."

"We've probably all seen her - or him - "

"Let's stop saying 'or him', shall we?"

"But seen her without knowing it. I know stories. I don't know any facts."

"What stories?"

"Stupid things, like she's incredibly aged. Or she's not entirely human. Or again, that she doesn't really exist, she's just an empty room. All hooey, as you Americans say."

Bronstein knitted his brows. "Sounds suspiciously like Tebloev's version of Constantine Slope."

"I've also heard it's someone's job in MI7 to keep such stories going."

"And you believe that?"

"No."

"Cushy number if it is. Are you ready for Edgeware?"

Gavin rubbed his hands together. "As I'll ever be. I'm to catch the train in an hour and a half."

"Nervous?"

He smiled weakly. "I guess everyone is on their first outing, aren't they, sir?"

"Don't take any risks."

Chapter 17: No Blancmange in Lebanon

Between two platforms dangling ladders, seven ropes hung from the ceiling. Each ended thirty feet above floor-level. Beneath them stretched a safety net.

The gym smelt of Marcie's sweat. She wore a black leotard and plimsolls. Miss Demure's long dress and lace blouse were perfectly suited to her detachment from today's lesson. She obviously had no intention of teaching by example. The two women faced each other. When they spoke their voices echoed slightly.

"To begin with," Miss Demure said, "I simply want to see how long it takes you to get from the floor at this end to the floor at the other. Once you've succeeded, we'll repeat the exercise, but with one of the ropes – you won't be able to predict which, of course - detaching on contact. Then two. You may start whenever you're ready."

Marcie ascended the ladder as she'd been taught, right foot and left hand, left foot and right hand, ignoring the rungs and using her arms to pull her up. She scrambled onto the platform, paused to size up what remained and launched herself at the first rope. Her momentum carried her to the second without difficulty but she'd lost ten inches of height. She tried to regain it on the third but overstretched herself and dropped on to the safety net. She crawled to the edge and let herself down to the floor.

Miss Demure smiled. "What do you think you did wrong?"

"Too fast. More haste, less speed."

"How long do you think it ought to take?"

Marcie shrugged. "Four minutes?"

"The world record is one thirty-six. Four would be acceptable for now."

"I lost height on the second rope and I guess I panicked."

"As soon as you came in here, you should have been thinking about what I was going to ask you to do and how you'd achieve it. Think now. Assume you've got longer this time. How do you think you're going to address the loss of height?"

"Transfer the oscillations from one rope to another before I switch?"

"Very good."

"And use one arm at a time."

"Try it."

"Do you think my biceps are big enough?"

Miss Demure laughed. "Your muscles are more than adequate for your weight. Don't go bodybuilding or taking steroids."

"I wasn't going to."

"Are you sure you want another attempt so quickly?"

"Try and stop me."

Nine minutes later – after two more falls - she succeeded in completing all seven ropes. Miss Demure laughed.

Marcie grinned and wiped her forehead with a towel. "What's so funny?"

"It normally takes people two or three days."

"You think it was a fluke, eh? Maybe it was. I'd better try again, just to be sure."

"Aren't you tired?"

"I can't let that hold me back."

Miss Demure sat down on a bench. "Take five. I hope this doesn't sound as if I'm prying, but you seem to be possessed of a new resolve since your brother died. I sense you've discovered some sort of vocation."

"I'm going to join the army."

"The *army*?"

"At first I thought it was just a negative reaction, like an escape from certain things. My mother's taken Jonathan's death badly and I'm not sure she'll ever relate to me in the same way again. And there's my criminal record. It's difficult to get a normal job with one of those."

"Have you been to the army careers office?"

"I've looked at their website. They say they won't necessarily turn you down. They believe in giving young offenders a second chance."

"And that's why you've been working so hard for me?"

"I thought you might give me a reference. Plus the self-defence skills."

"But what if they send you to Afghanistan or Iraq?"

"I'm hoping they will."

"What if you're killed or badly wounded?"

Marcie sighed. "Someone's got to do it."

"You must realise not everyone would agree with that sentiment."

"I don't know whether we should ever have gone to war or not. I'm not talking about that. But I do know that now we have, we can't just walk away."

Miss Demure paused and looked at the ground. "I think we should call it a day for today. Start again tomorrow."

"You're – you're not angry with me, are you?"

Miss Demure turned to her with an expression that was impossible to read. "On the contrary," she said. "I'm very, very pleased with you."

Marcie showered and went home to change. She put on a red dress, a string of pearls and her court shoes and tied her hair in a bun. Fleming arrived at eight in a brown suit, and she made him sit in the lounge while she finished her make up. Half an hour later, they set off on foot for the restaurant.

"I've never eaten Lebanese before," she said.

"Neither have I. Not knowingly. I suppose I might accidentally have consumed some Lebanese food at some time in my life."

"What on earth do you mean?"

"I may have eaten something Lebanese without knowing its country of origin."

She hooted. "Vintage Fleming."

They went into the restaurant and stood behind a sign that said, 'Please wait for an attendant to guide you to a table'. Four chandeliers with dark red shades – the same colour as the carpet -hung low enough to peer down on. The wallpaper was blue arabesque on a cream background. In the background Nawal al Zoghbi sang Ma Loom.

The attendant – a bald, middle aged man in a white evening jacket – came over and bowed from the neck slightly.

"We have a reservation," Fleming said. "Table for two, name of Nicholas Fleming."

"Yessss," the waiter said, as if their arrival was a great relief but also the cause of considerable resentment.

They sat down. Fleming ordered a bottle of wine. They pored over the menu, ordered Saiyadit al-Samak and Hareeseh and crossed their fingers.

"I like the fact that you've brought me here," she said.

"It's supposed to be a very nice place."

"You've never been here before? I like that doubly."

"I'm not sure what you're getting at."

"Nicholas Fleming will always be Nicholas Fleming, he'll always try to reduce the element of uncertainty to nil, but at least he's trying."

He smiled. She reached her hands across the table to him and he took them.

"I think you'll find I've grown up a bit since we last met," she said.

"In what way? You were fine as you were."

"I don't see spontaneity as so much of a virtue now. I mean, I still value it. But next to reliability and loyalty, I can see it's rather a paltry thing."

He sighed. "I still care for you, Marcie. I don't want to scare you off, but when I form an affection for someone, I tend to stick with it, even when that someone throws a blancmange at me."

"Yes, I'm really sorry about that."

"I deserved it. You're right, I was Hamlet."

"Neither of us has anything to be proud of. I was the proverbial bull in a china shop that day. Yet they say opposites attract."

"Do you think there's any possibility of us ever getting back together again?"

"I'm going to join the army."

"Pardon me?"

"If you can put up with that and wait for me, then I'm not ruling anything out."

"I don't believe it. The *army*? But you might get killed."

"Back up, Nick. You're going to have to accept me on my terms or not at all."

He withdrew his hands and used them to hold his head up. He looked at the candle in the middle of the table as if it was something he'd just lit for a memorial service. "And there's absolutely nothing I can do to dissuade you?"

"I'm not sure you'd have a leg to stand on, having been in the army yourself."

"But that was different."

"Oh, really."

"Yes, because the Coldstream's a family tradition."

"I'm not getting into your bloody snobby family again, Nick. We're in Lebanon now. There isn't a blancmange to hand."

"Sorry."

"Anyway, my mind's made up."

He pursed his lips then offered her a handshake. "Okay, yes, I accept."

She grinned and shook his hand. "I'm only saying I'm not ruling anything out, mind. I'm not saying yes. You might turn out to be just too much of a fastidious, nitpicking fusspot for comfort. And it's not as if I'm not a complete screwball."

"I'll start seeing a psychotherapist right away."

"You'd better not."

"For your part, you need to promise me you won't run off with some barrel-chested sergeant major."

"It's you or no one, I've known that for a long time. But I'm not frightened of spinsterhood, so be warned."

He kissed her hand. The waiter brought them their food and a loaf of sliced bread and Marcie unfolded her napkin and laid it on her lap. Suddenly it was time for the main business of the evening.

"Did you find anything out about Jonathan?" she said.

"I ransacked all the filing cabinets and searched all the hard drives but there wasn't much to discover. I do now know for a fact that he was in the secret service. He resigned from the Met just after I left for New York."

"I knew that too. Daddy gave me the impression he'd begged for his job back. I'm glad he didn't."

"Do you think your father knew Jonathan was working for the secret service?"

"If Daddy ever knew the truth, he'd have told Mummy. Right now, he thinks Jonathan committed a *crime passionnel* and topped himself."

"Damn shame."

"What else have you found?"

"I've 'found' nothing," he said, "as you might expect. But I have been doing a little thinking. I may have come up with a plan."

She beamed. "I knew you would."

"I happen to know that before Jonathan resigned he was particularly interested in the paparazzi who were being gunned down by that unknown marksman, you remember?"

"Vaguely."

"Jonathan contacted Interpol. Sir Colin went ballistic, but it turned out Jonathan was right. There had been similar murders elsewhere. Four in the USA, five in Russia. So Sir Colin put Jonathan in charge of the operation."

"I suppose he can't have been all bad then, although Daddy did call him a farty-arsed squirt."

"Think about it. England, the USA, Russia. Jonathan, Bronstein, Orlov."

"You think they were part of a special unit?"

"It would make sense. Created by the Met for MI5. Orlov was an intelligence officer, not a policeman."

"No, sorry, Nicholas, that doesn't work. Orlov was an *ex*-intelligence officer. He was expecting to be shipped back to Russia and executed when I met him. And Jonathan wouldn't have had to resign if his unit had been custom-built for MI5."

"Okay, so what must have happened was the Met created the unit then disbanded it, and MI5 snapped it up in the fire sale."

"That would explain all the men outside our house that day. But it still doesn't work. Why would the Met create a unit like that only to disband it?"

"Maybe they were ordered to."

"But why didn't MI5 just say, 'Thanks, guys, you've done a great job, we'll take charge now'? Why all the unpleasantness? Because I know for a fact Jonathan *thought* he'd resigned. He was almost crying at one point. Anya told me."

Fleming finished his Saiyadit al-Samak and put his knife and fork together. "So we've established there's something we still don't know. And it's pointless speculating, because we don't need to know for what I've got in mind. Would you like a dessert?"

"Only if you can afford it."

The waiter arrived to take their plates. "Enjoy your meal, sir, madam?"

"Very nice indeed," Marcie and Fleming said together.

"Could we have the desserts menu?" Fleming asked.

"So what's your plan?" Marcie said, when they were alone again.

"I know Jonathan was in the secret service because I saw the DA Notice covering his death and Jilly Bestwick and Zane Cruse's. It's likely they were all killed by the same person."

"What's a DA Notice?"

"A government request to news editors asking them not to publish details of something for reasons of national security. It's not binding but it's usually respected. Remember, the press went with the notion that Jilly Bestwick and Zane Cruse were the victims of some sort of suicide pact, probably because MI5 thought anything else might create a trail that led to Jonathan."

"Maybe."

"But what they failed to notice – or maybe they did, but they were asked to steer clear of it – was that Jilly Bestwick and Zane Cruse were both celebrities who had paparazzi shot before their eyes."

"And Jonathan thought Jilly was being manipulated by the Russian mafia."

"And of course, where did he meet Jilly Bestwick in the first place? You don't just bump into a global superstar. He must have still been investigating the paparazzi shootings. And that's why he was killed."

"Of course … That makes perfect sense … It's the only thing so far that does."

"And it's also why she was killed."

Marcie bowed her head slightly and ran her thumbnail along the underside of her lower eyelid. "I – I'm sorry … I'll be okay in a minute."

"We don't have to have a dessert. We can talk about this at my place. Or yours. I promise not to make a move on you."

"I'm not a child, Nick. If I don't want you to make a move on me, I'll tell you."

The waiter arrived with the dessert menu. They ordered peremptorily as if they'd been eating Lebanese all their life.

"What's your plan?" she said afterwards.

"There are other celebrities who had paparazzi shot in front of them, and it's likely they're working for these Russian Mafioso too. What we've got to do is contact one of them and pretend to be from the organisation. Ask for a meeting."

"Any name in particular?"

"Have you ever heard of Nichole Moore?" he asked.

"The? We'd need her address and phone number."

"I'm a policeman, I can get all that. First of all, I need to perfect my Russian accent."

"Wait a minute. You? What about me?"

He drummed his fingers on the tablecloth. "I expected you'd say that."

"She'll open up to a woman. She won't open up to a man, especially not one in a brown suit."

He smiled thinly. "Us, then. But we need to be very careful. We've no idea what we're dealing with yet."

Chapter 18: How Do You Solve a Problem Like Marciella Hartley-Brown, ASBO?

Orlov sat opposite Gavin in the staff canteen on floor two. They wore open-necked dress shirts and sipped bottles of J2O. The kitchens hissed and clattered. Office workers sat before triangles of quiche with friends and sheaves of paper. In the corner, a woman lay asleep on a paisley cushion. The rain pattered on the windows.

"So Edgeware effectively blew up," Orlov said.

"I'm very sorry, sir. I'm not sure what else I could have done. Maybe I should have gone in as a journalist."

"We discussed that. There was no way he'd have been prepared to speak to a reporter about anything as tangential as Constantine Slope when he's supposed to be fronting a local election campaign. It had to be police."

"It was quite difficult."

Orlov folded his arms. "Explain how."

"Treading a fine line between asking him for information and avoiding giving him the impression that he's in trouble. Because he isn't, is he? And if he gets on to the local police station to clarify matters, he's going to realise he's been duped."

"By which time, we'll be far away."

"But it might set alarm bells ringing. I mean, if he talks to – if he knows anyone who ..."

"Who's in league with Kramski? You're allowing your presuppositions to mould your behaviour. Don't."

"Yes, I see that was a mistake."

"Once you make the decision to go in as something, you have to be that thing. No halfway houses. And if you hadn't noticed, alarm bells are already ringing. They killed Jonathan and they've been watching David. They know we're after them."

"Maybe I should take you through what happened. With Edgeware. I made some additional notes on the train back so I wouldn't forget."

Orlov nodded. "Go on."

"Well, I introduced myself. I said I thought someone might have been impersonating Slope, that there are no pictures of him out there on the Internet. I asked him if he had any pictures. He didn't. He'd never been photographed in public with him."

"I expect he used the magic word 'reclusive'?"

"Yes, he did."

"Odd how that word's supposed to explain everything. You asked for a description, yes?"

"He said Slope was about five-seven, lean, usually wore a suit and tie, a big coat and a trilby. Face: longish Roman nose, thin lips, pale blue eyes, clean-shaven, hollow cheeks, a lot of the sorts of features old men have everywhere. He was in his eighties, after all."

"The important thing is, Edgeware knew him. He physically met him. I was beginning to think we were dealing with a phantom."

"He went to his funeral as well."

"Who else was at that?"

"I didn't ask that. Sorry."

"It's a roundabout way of asking who else might have had face-to-face contact with Slope. You asked that, didn't you?"

"Herbert McLellan and Charles Inwood, the conservative MPs for Enfield Southgate and Gravesham. They were with Edgeware at Tebloev's party."

Orlov stroked his jawbone. "Confirming that they were there on a group ticket, and they invited Slope on the same basis."

"It would seem so."

"Did Edgeware ever meet Slope in company with either of the two?"

"I don't know. It was at that point that he became angry. It seemed to sink in that I was a policeman and I was investigating Slope. He told me Constantius Slope was the noblest of men, had never aroused suspicion in any quarter before, was universally - "

"'Constantius'? Not Constantine?"

"That was how he referred to him throughout. Is it significant?"

"I don't know yet. Listen, this is very important. When Edgeware became angry, did he seem to you in any way ... scared?"

Gavin sighed. "To be honest, sir, I don't really have enough experience of this sort of thing to be able to judge. Just off the top of my head, I'd say probably not."

"Okay, here's what we're going to do. Your cover expires in just under eighteen hours. I'm authorising you to go and speak to McLellan and get a photo or a description of Slope from him, then Inwood. It's only four o'clock - "

"It's okay, sir, I don't mind getting home late. I told my wife - "

"Good."

Bronstein came over and sat down next to Gavin, eating a cheese sandwich and dropping gratings. "Guess what?"

"Is it about Slope?" Orlov said. "Because it may save Gavin a journey."

"The mystery deepens. I'm not even sure there was a Slope."

"Edgeware met him," Orlov said. "Or thinks he did."

"'Thinks', yeah. Gabriella's just been on the phone. She found a 'Konstandin Sopa' who arrived in this country from Albania in 1946. Aged twenty-four, that's how he told it back then, and they had to believe him since he didn't bring a birth certificate. No relatives, no connections. Settled down and lived quietly in Hampstead until 2004, when he shimmers into invisibility. Then, in 2008, he suddenly reappears with a fortune. Or his successor does. My guess is that the real Slope – Sopa - ran out of luck and money and died in a Salvation Army hostel somewhere. Identity theft, pure and simple."

"What makes you think so?" Orlov said.

"Because nothing I was given in the Slope dossier matches what we know about Sopa. Slope's supposed to have had long-standing connections with wealthy American socialites, until recently when he became a – ho, ho – 'recluse'. He's supposed to have founded several of his industries in the '70s and '80s at a time when Sopa was so hard up he was fed by Meals on Wheels. Slope's supposed to have had the ear of Reagan and Thatcher, for God's sake."

"Maybe he's a little ashamed of his past," Gavin said. "People sometimes are in this country. The class thing. They make things up."

Bronstein finished his sandwich and clapped his hands together. "Nope, he's an impostor. Money you inherit. A clutch of industries?"

"It's probably pointless going to interview McLellan and Inwood," Orlov told Gavin. "We need to go straight to source now. Exhume the body."

"Don't waste your time going to see Ruby Parker," Bronstein said. "She's already said no. Too sensitive for a start – he had a lot of friends in the Edgeware category who'll kick up blue murder at the merest sign of a trowel, and too costly."

"Too costly?"

"We're diverting spare monies to Kyrgyzstan at the moment. Her mind's made up."

Orlov leaned forward and rested his chin on the back of his hands. "Well, luckily I wasn't the one who asked her."

Ruby Parker stood at one side of her office while Celia Demure sat on a chair and faced her down. Relations between them had always been like this. Celia Demure inspired awe, even on a first meeting. Seniority of rank counted for nothing. At best it levelled the playing field.

Ruby Parker nodded. "It could have been foreseen. Criminal record, spirit of adventure, deep in mourning."

"Of course, we've got to stop her."

"Have we? Why?"

"I have the highest respect for the services, but the army will be disastrous for Marcie Brown. Utterly ruinous."

"I'm not sure why you would think that. It could be the making of her. It is of many others."

"She's in mourning. Do you really think a stint in Iraq is going to help?"

"I can only think - "

"She's likely to come back even more traumatised. And the Ministry of Defence will do nothing to help her, it never does. Given that about eight per cent of the current prison and probation population have seen military service in the last ten years, what do you think her chances of reoffending are? Not to mention mental illness."

"MI7 isn't a holiday camp. If she can't cope with the army, what's our interest in her?"

"We both know we're the opposite of the army. We train individuals to accentuate their individuality. The army's about corporateness."

"So what are you suggesting?"

"I think the time's come to be frank with her and tell her what we're about. At least offer her the choice – us or the forces. I think she'll leap at it. If she joins the army we've lost her, but at least we tried."

"How good is she?"

"I've told you already, she's outstanding. As good as anyone I've trained."

"As good as you were?"

Miss Demure smiled. "That's hardly for me to judge. I honestly don't know."

Ruby Parker sat down. "I'm highly reluctant to bring her inside right now. The first thing she's going to want to know is who recommended her."

"We could make something up, couldn't we?"

"We're secretive enough with the outside world. I like to think that once we're within these walls, there are no lies, no double deals, no half truths, we are who we say we are and we do what we say we do. Of course, I know it can't be like that, but that's the ideal."

Miss Demure sighed. "I see your problem, then."

"Once she knows it was Jonathan who recommended her and Sergei who confirmed, she's going to want in on the Kramski case."

"'The Kramski case'? Is that what you're calling it?"

"What do you suggest?"

"I thought Kramski was a mere foot soldier."

"That's the supposition. But in the absence - "

"You mean you're making no progress?" Miss Demure said.

"On the contrary, but in one direction only. We're finding everything out about the mechanism, to the point where we might even be able to shut it down."

"But?"

"But we know nothing whatsoever about who's turning the handle, or what whoever's turning it wants."

"That will come, surely?"

Ruby Parker paused. "To get back to Marcie Brown. I take it you can appreciate the danger of her wanting to get involved."

"I won't pretend she isn't emotional from time to time, but I was impressed by how quickly she was back at work after her brother's death."

"That may not necessarily be a good sign. She's hurled herself back, and I would guess she's doing twice as much as you require because she's desperate to get into a war zone. That sounds suspiciously like a death-wish to me."

"Yes, perhaps."

"I haven't met her, but she sounds pig headed."

Miss Demure seemed on the point of saying something, but changed her mind. She sat up. "Maybe we can reach a compromise. It's a question of keeping her away from the Queen's shilling until after we've closed the Kramski investigation. If she's as good as I think, she's an asset we can't afford to lose."

"Very well, here's what we'll do then. Lieutenant Bronstein was in my office earlier, asking permission to exhume the corpse of Constantine Slope. I said no, but if he asks again, I'll reconsider. Henceforth, any opportunity for a resolution, however small, however expensive, I'll take it. Although obviously, in this case, I don't personally think it'll come to anything."

"And at my end?"

"She could be quite useful to MI7 in Afghanistan. In any case, you're going to have to maintain the pretence that you think that's where she's going. Have you given her to understand you're supportive?"

"Very much so."

"Tell her you've had a word with an army contact. Tell her you might be able to get her in at officer level but she's got to learn Pashto. And a few trips to the solarium wouldn't go amiss."

"Pashto? Do we have an instructor locally?"

"Several. Have a word with Gabriella on the way out. She'll never pass as a native of course, but given the population drift out there and sufficient ingenuity, she could make a convincing refugee."

"It should kill a bit more time. What if she turns out to be as good at languages as she is at everything else?"

"We'll show our hand and ship her off to Kandahar before she can ask too many questions. There are plenty of things a bright girl can be doing over there, trust me."

The terraced houses along here were among the most sought-after in London, although in most other cities they'd have been ordinary. Big windows with heavy ledges, all the stone work re-pointed and the timber freshly painted. The door was three steps above street level and behind a set of iron railings. Orlov knocked and looked up to watch the cumulus clouds drifting across the pink evening sky while he waited.

A bald man of about fifty in a suit opened the door. "Colonel Orlov, I presume? You're expected. Please follow me."

Orlov followed him through a dark hallway into the living room. Tebloev sat on an armchair surrounded by the sort of furnishings that might have looked at home in a Chekhov play. A sofa, a sideboard and a medicine cupboard. A table in the middle of the room. Tebloev sat in a wingback chair opposite the window, smoking a cigar. He got up and gestured for Orlov to sit on the sofa.

"Do you mind if I carry on with this? I thought I'd have it finished long before you arrived. Bit of a slow burner unfortunately."

"I'd like you to feel comfortable while we talk."

Tebloev sat down again. "Thank you. If I stub it out now I'll only throw it away and it's a Havana. What can I do for you?"

"I'm here to ask a favour."

"'Shoot away', as the English say."

"I want to exhume the body of Constantine Slope."

Tebloev guffawed. "Well, I certainly didn't see that coming."

"I need your help. You're the only person I know who could conceivably muster the manpower."

"You mean besides the legal authorities?"

"They're not interested."

"I have my position here to consider. If I was caught, I'd be deported. No."

"I wasn't asking you to do it in person. I just need contacts."

"No, Colonel, absolutely not. Apart from anything else, I'd rather not be hunted down by the Upir."

"The *Upir*? You mean, as in the mythological vampire-creature?"

Tebloev ignored him. "Because I can tell you for a fact, there's no corpse in that coffin."

"How can you be so certain?"

"A man like yourself could hardly be expected to understand. No, I'd love you to 'exhume the body', or rather dig up the coffin, because that's all it'll amount to. But I'm not prepared to drag the curse down on me."

"Did you ever meet Constantine Slope?"

"In person? Who knows?"

"But you never knowingly met him."

"No."

Orlov laughed. "And yet you're sure he's some kind of supernatural being. I'd like to think you'd at least do me the courtesy of seeing my face before you reached such a conclusion about me."

"You're not the Upir, Colonel."

"What I'm asking is, what sort of second-hand impressions have you received to make you form such a low opinion of him?"

"You know of course he's supposed to have fled the genocide in Albania?"

"What genocide?"

"In 1917."

"Don't be absurd," Orlov said. "You know that's well-nigh impossible. Unless he was a new born baby."

"But new born babies don't flee. And I think you'll find he arrived in Albania from somewhere else in around … the eighteen-fifties?"

"And you've got hard evidence for all this, have you?"

"Colonel, I'm of peasant stock. I didn't get my first taste of the big city until I was twenty-five and I liked it so much I thought I'd buy one or two of my own. Unfortunately, it didn't turn out that way - as we both know. But I've never lost the conviction that there are things we in the countryside know that you city dwellers only ever scoff at."

"Have you ever talked to Lionel Edgeware about Slope?"

"The MP? No."

"Who then? You've never met him in person and yet you've formed the most singular opinion of him anyone's ever formed of anyone. Something must have prompted you."

"Last time we met I told you that I know most Russian émigrés in this town. Rich and poor, high and low. And many of the low ones have crossed paths with Constantine Slope. He's a businessman and we can all do with the odd bit of cheap labour from time to time."

"Why didn't you tell me this earlier?"

"I didn't want to get him into trouble. Or those who inherit his interests. My default position is not to talk of tax avoidance where I know there's an investigation going on. Honour among thieves, I suppose. Even now, I'm talking off the record."

"Go on."

"It's these people – Russian and Ukrainian lumpenproletarians, if you like, and a few others – who say he's the Upir. They're the ones who say he arrived in 1917. When you hear that sort of tale from one mouth, you might discount it. When it comes from two or ten or thirty, you start to have second thoughts."

"Names?"

"I tend not to ask for them unless I'm employing people. And even then, I tend to forget them. If you go back and see my secretary again, he'll give you a rough list. If you run it past me, one or two might stand out, but I would imagine they'll have left the country and even if they haven't you'll struggle to find them. I'm sorry I can't be of more help."

"Did Kramski ever mention Slope?"

"Not that I remember. We weren't that intimate."

Orlov stood up. "Thank you for your help."

Outside, Orlov turned the collar of his jacket up and took out his mobile. It was dark now and a jet roared across the quarter moon. He went straight to his contacts.

"Hi, buddy," Bronstein said.

"I need Slope's address."

"Any luck with Tebloev?"

"He's not interested. He's getting his secretary to draw up a list of people who might have run into Slope."

"And you're on your way to Slope's, yes?"

"Only if you can find me that address," Orlov said.

"Little village just outside Oxford, name of Borlforth. Nice property, I looked it up on Rightmove. One and a half million list price. Why not just go to the estate agent?"

"Who is the estate agent?"

"Royal and Finch. Shall I meet you there?"
"I'll ring if I need you."

Chapter 19: Inside a Big Old House

Orlov got off the train at quarter past midnight and took a taxi straight to Borlforth. The street lamps were all off, so there was little to see. A stream ran by the road, and a dormant pub and the village green ascended gently from its far side. To the north, a church spire scratched the clouds. Orlov switched his phone on, opened a satellite map and began to walk across country. Five minutes later, he stood outside the grounds.

'The Manor House' lay in an acre of garden fenced off with wire netting - which probably meant it was guarded by dogs. It had two floors, two wings and a mansard roof and looked searchable in about ten minutes. There were lights on inside, presumably activated by a timer.

He couldn't see the dogs, then he realised there weren't any. Someone would have to feed them, and in this country, if that didn't happen it would probably catch the attention of the animal charities. He switched his mobile off, checked his gun, fitted the silencer and scaled the fence.

It was a short journey to the front of the house. He registered the security lights and gauged the strip between the sensors. Just wide enough for him to get through … maybe. Where was the burglar alarm? Two wires, one for the alarm, one for the outside lights. If he could hit both – which he could - he'd be through. Assuming anyone was inside they might hear the ricochet, but so be it. Drawing them out might solve half his problems.

He took the two shots and a moment later, he was at the window. The room was lit by a central pendant light and he couldn't see anyone in there, so he moved to the next, lit in the same way. Three minutes later, he'd done a circuit of the building. Time to try the back door, enter through the kitchens so as to retain the element of surprise, should he need it. In the distance, an owl screeched.

The back door was secured with a simple cylinder lock. He inserted a screwdriver into the keyhole then thrust a pick to the end of the plug. He pulled it out quickly and felt the pins fall on the ledge. He turned the screwdriver and was inside. After closing the door gently behind him, he secured it.

He already had a strong sense he wasn't alone. He crept into what looked like the living room. Suddenly the lights went off and the door slammed hard into his side. His attacker grabbed him by the neck and pitched him to the ground. He rolled forward to avoid the bullets that were churning the floorboards. Suddenly, clicks replaced shots and the attacker was on his way to compensate. Orlov kicked upwards and lifted him off the ground by his groin. He landed on the far side of the room, rolled and grabbed a sword from an ornamental suit of armour. Orlov sprang to his feet. An assessment of his assailant flashed from his brain to his body. Thirty-ish, lean, as tall as he was, shabby.

He grabbed the man's arm as he swung the blade, and kicked his feet away. They went to ground with Orlov on top. Orlov put all his weight into turning the man's hand and smashing it into the floorboards. The man relinquished his weapon only to swivel behind Orlov and put him into a head lock. Orlov threw himself upwards, nearly snapping his own neck, and slammed his heels into his attacker's knees. Their bodies scattered and they lay apart. He heard the man groan.

Orlov was the first up and he made to stamp on the man's spine – he knew now this was to the death – but he rolled and grabbed his foot. Orlov twisted and lurched backwards and freed it. They were both upright now. For a few moments they parried each other's attempts to find a hold, then the man stepped back three paces, drew a knife from his jacket and advanced at a swift walk. He lunged, but Orlov caught his hand

and rotated and kicked him in the armpit. His shoulder momentarily dislocated, but he wrenched it back into its socket with a gasp and came forward again, retrieving the knife on the way. His face was bloodied and he looked like he knew he was losing. He thrust at Orlov's heart, but Orlov evaded, grabbed his arm and twisted, dislocating it a second time, more drastically now. He kicked him in the stomach and took the knife.

The man repaired his arm at nearly the same speed as before, but he was clearly flagging. He picked up the sword and hurled himself at Orlov. Suddenly, Orlov caught sight of the man's phone flashing on the table. He meant to stab him, but his instincts saw another opening and he twisted his neck. He clapped his hand over his mouth to ensure he lost consciousness quickly.

The man's associates were about to arrive, the pulsing phone left no other possibility. They wouldn't come in through the front door either. They'd do a circuit of the house, just as he had, then they'd –

The far window exploded and there was another man in the room. Orlov grabbed the wrong end of the sword but the man ducked and reached for a gun. Orlov bounced back to his feet and kicked it. He reached for his own – he had no idea why he hadn't thought of it before – and shot his assailant point blank.

Someone else was already coming through the window. He ran to the kitchen, but two men were on their way in, struggling with the bolt. He dashed upstairs, locked himself in one of the bedrooms and threw the window open. The guttering was low enough for him to pull himself up where things would be more evenly matched. Down in the garden, he could see eight or ten of them, pouring inside in response to the all clear.

He pulled himself onto the roof and the open air and felt a bullet pass through his calf. The tiles in front of him were ploughed from the inside by machine gun fire. He waited for the hiatus then jumped across the rift and fired downwards and saw the gunner lurch.

Suddenly he was inside. He killed the two men on his flanks and picked up the machine gun and went out onto the landing.

He was back in charge again now, but he could hear gunfire outside. He switched his phone back on and it immediately began ringing. He picked up without a second thought.

"Orlov?" Bronstein's voice said.

"Speaking."

"Thank God, I thought you'd be dead."

"Right, thank you."

"You sound out of breath, though. Take it easy. We're mopping up outside. I'll join you in a minute. Where are you?"

"Upstairs."

Orlov looked out of the window. Army trucks, scores of men, mostly soldiers. He gave a sigh of relief. They might be able to catch one of them alive.

There was a knock.

Bronstein emerged through the door, frowning. "Ruby P nearly had heart failure when she heard what you were up to, before you ask. On the phone to the Ministry of Defence like Thor on a bad day. But it looks like it's been worth it. She'll probably kiss you on the lips now ... I don't think."

"Have we got anyone alive?"

"One. Ten dead."

"Any escapees?"

"Four we counted."

They began to move downstairs, Orlov limping. "What about Kramski?"

"Not that we've identified but the evening's just beginning. You should really get that leg seen to before it ruins the carpets."

Ruby Parker stood at the bottom of the stairs glaring ominously at Orlov, hands on hips and feet apart.

"Uh-oh," Bronsten said, moving to one side slightly so he wouldn't be caught in the blast.

She narrowed her eyes. "This had better not be down to some misguided enchantment with machismo, Sergei Orlov. Because macho men tend not to last very long in my organisation, if, thanks to some clumsy oversight, they ever get in it to begin with. I may be a woman, *but don't think I won't crush your cojones and smear what's left of them in your face if I take exception to your way of working!*"

"It's nothing to do with cojones," he said quietly.

She took a deep breath, ground her teeth for a second and smiled sardonically. "Let me put it in plain English then, so you'll understand. It's normal in this sort of case to fill in a risk assessment form. If you'd marked it 'priority', I'd probably have rubber stamped it within the hour and given you some sort of back up. Instead of which we've ten people dead, nearly including yet another of our agents. If you'd taken just *two seconds*, you'd have realised it's *bloody pointless* even having an MI7 if we're all just switch to gung ho mode when the whim takes us! It's not as if you're in some far-flung part of the globe where you can't even get radio contact and you have to act recklessly or not at all. This is Britain, *we've got bloody tanks and bombers if we need them!*"

"David told me you were reluctant to exhume Slope. I assumed you'd be equally reluctant to break into his house. But I didn't keep it secret. I told David. I expected he would pass that information on sooner or later."

"It's a damn good job for you he did."

"I had the situation under control when you arrived."

"You were extremely lucky, that's all, as I expect your exhaustive written report will show. In anything like this, no one survives through skill alone. Believe me, I know. And don't be so bloody self-justificatory. You were wrong, pure and simple. Unless you can appreciate that, there's no place for you with us. We're a team. We do teamwork. We don't do mavericks."

Orlov took a breath and nodded. "I take your point."

"What partly annoys me about this is that you assumed I wouldn't be cooperative. I bend over backwards to help my agents, and when I say no, as sometimes I have to, it's because there's a very good reason."

"Would you have said no to this?"

"As a matter of fact, I wouldn't. Not only that, I'd actually changed my mind about exhuming Slope this afternoon. I want this investigation to move forward as much as you do. But it's no use trying to put me on the defensive, Colonel. I have nothing to answer for."

"If you'd sent, say, ten men with me, the way events unfolded at least two of them would now be dead. As understand it, the casualties were all on their side."

"Don't bloody argue with me. You just said you took my point."

"I promise not to undertake anything like this, ever again, without informing you first."

She looked hard at him as if she thought he might be being sarcastic. Her glower dissipated. "Go out to the ambulance and get them to take a look at you. Then go home. And that's an order."

Marcie sat alone on the back seat of a London taxi outside Nichole Moore's house. She wore a black suit, a clutch of fake diamonds and high heels for intimidation. This was a quiet Golders Green terrace with flowerpots on the front patios and lines of maple trees verging the pavements. The sun shone hard on the stucco and made the water in the bird baths glisten.

She slid the window shut between herself and the driver and took out her mobile. She texted *I'm ReD* to Mr Brown. The message came back, *I'm outside Keynes's house now. On count of 3.* She trawled the names till she reached 'NM' and pressed call.

"Yeah?"

"Miss Moore," Marcie said, in the Russian accent she'd practised, "I must speak with you this minute on a matter of grave urgency. You shall say nothing to anyone, but come downstairs. I await you in taxi."

She heard Nichole's heart drop and lodge in between her stomach, kidneys and other impediments. "I – I'll be right down. I won't be a minute. I've just got to put some clothes on. I'll be there in a few seconds, that's all."

Bingo. She pressed end call. A few seconds later, she held the car door open as Nichole came out of her house and double locked it with her key. She wore a T-shirt and leggings and trainers. Her hair was held up with a comb and she carried a black bag.

"I'm sorry I took such a long time," she said breathlessly.

"You bring mobile?"

"Yeah."

"Go back to house. Drop through letterbox, quick. We go."

"But wh – why?"

Marcie immediately saw that she was one of those people who see their phone as a kind of portable oxygen tent. She had to be firm. "No ask questions! Do as told!"

Nichole jogged back up the drive, wrapped her mobile in a wad of tissues to break its fall and popped it through her letterbox. She already looked traumatised.

"Now," Marcie said, as the taxi pulled out, "we go to Starbucks, yes? Nice treat. We eat cake, drink coffee, have friendly little chat. You are involved in politics now, yes? As instructed?"

"I joined the Tories. My grandma says she's never going to speak to me again."

"You prefer the Labour?"

"We've always voted Labour in my family."

"Time for a change then, da?"

She folded her hands and put them in front of her mouth. "Please can I change to Labour?"

"No."

"Pleeeeease?"

"No."

"*Pleeeeease?*"

"*No!*"

She slumped. "Okay."

"I am here to tell you that you should no longer meet at the usual meeting place."

"What meeting place?"

Marcie glared at her, trying to force the answer to the surface.

"You mean … Green Park?" Nichole said eventually.

"Da."

"Da? That's Russian for yes, right?"

Marcie nodded.

"What's Russian for, 'I'd like to come round and check out your flat sometime, dude, I think you've done some awesome stuff for Chelsea'?"

"Who you meet in Green Park?"

"Stallone, usually."

"Anyone else?"

Nichole paused. "Can I ask who you are? I mean, what organisation? I mean, if it's not too rude?"

"Russian mafia."

She blood visibly drained from her face. Her mouth popped open and her eyes bulged. She swallowed.

"Who you think we were?" Marcie said.

"Oh, my God, no."

"What is the - "

"You're going to kill me, aren't you? You're going to kill me! That's why you made me leave my mobile at home! *Oh my God!*"

"Stop making - "

"You're going to kill me! I'm going to die! Just like you killed Jilly and Zane! It all makes sense now!"

She started to scream. The taxi driver hit the brakes, and suddenly Nichole had the back door open. She threw herself into the road and a car swerved to avoid her. She leapt to her feet, and although her legs and arms were badly grazed she broke into a run.

Marcie went to follow her, but her heels buckled and the taxi driver got out and grabbed her arm. "Are you going to pay up, or do I have to call the police?"

"I've got to - "

"To *what?* Get away without paying?"

"Bloody hell! Get off me. How the hell can I pay you when you've got hold of my arm?"

"Get back in the car. I'm calling the police."

Marcie got onto the back seat and took out five ten pound notes. "*Here.* Keep the bloody change!"

"But it was only fifteen pounds. Hey, did you steal this?"

"What? I'm supposed to get a Criminal Records Bureau check to give you a tip now?"

"No, of course not. Sorry, no, I'm not thinking. Looks like your friend's done a runner. Sorry about that."

Marcie looked in all directions. She was nowhere to be seen. "Shit, shit, shit, shit, shit, *shee-it!*"

"Would you like a lift home? On the house."

She was so furious she couldn't bring herself to answer. She began to walk towards a bus stop, but the adrenalin took over and she passed it and sped up. After five minutes, she took out her mobile and went through the names till she got to Mr Brown and texted *UR gunA B furious. Iv 404 her.*

She waited a full five minutes. Presumably he was still busy with Keynes. Then a loud beep.

Don't worry. I know how we can retrieve this.

A large tent had been erected over the grave. Orlov, Gavin and Ruby Parker waited inside it with an elderly funeral director in a suit, a young man in jeans representing the department of environmental health, and the vicar. Two men with spades worked inside the hole, which was far wider than the original so as to give Slope's coffin berth as it ascended. The soil was still loose from the interment.

The area outside the dig had been cordoned off to a radius of two hundred yards, causing traffic diversions in the village. Twelve policemen with walkie-talkies stood at intervals round the ticker tape, fending off enquiries and giving directions. A clutch of journalists with cameras and notepads drank and ate at the Coach and Horses or loitered in front of Costcutter. Outside the tent, a refrigerated van stood ready for the corpse. The sky threatened rain and a strong easterly wind shook the canvas.

At last the men inside the hole began fixing the ropes. They called done and threw up the ends. Gavin, Orlov and the funeral director took an end each, and the men climbed out. Together with the environmental health rep, they took the ends on the other side.

"Whenever you're ready," Ruby Parker told the funeral director.

"Hand over hand and I'll tell you if I need you to stop," he said. "Everyone set? On my command: one – two – three - "

The coffin rose to the surface as slowly as if the hole beneath it was being gradually flooded. It seemed an age before it stood apart on the surface. The funeral director took a small crowbar and went round the lid, tactfully prising it open. He nodded to Orlov to assist, and they lifted it off.

It took them a moment to realise what they were looking at. A pile of soil.

Chapter 20: Serve the Lord With Gladness

Ruby Parker took the lift to the twentieth floor and stepped into the corridor. Just as she remembered it. The walls needed a new coat of paint, but there was no graffiti and the floor tiles looked clean. She knew how many steps to the flat by heart, because she'd lived here herself, an age ago. She knocked and took a carton of grapes from her bag. It was one in the afternoon, he'd have to be up by now, however 'unwell'.

The door opened. Bronstein stood holding the latch fully dressed plus a yarmulke and a pair of phylacteries. "Look," he said, "I don't want – oh, it's you. Sorry, boss. Okay, enter. I don't normally answer the door looking like this."

She followed him inside. He'd kept the place looking nice: no clutter, just his suitcase and a few old newspapers. The sofa, the armchair and carpet still looked as they might in an estate agent's catalogue. She gave him the grapes. "Gavin tells me you reported in sick. I brought you these."

"Thank you. The vine shall give her fruit and the ground shall give her increase, and the heavens shall give their dew and I will cause the remnant of this people to possess all these things. Zechariah eight-twelve."

"That's okay. The branch cannot bear fruit of itself, except it abide in the vine. John fifteen-four."

He showed her the grapes label. "See this? 'Product of Israel'. Some of this stuff comes from Gaza, but the Israelis won't even let them sell it under their own name."

"I thought that was tomatoes."

Bronstein sat down. He unwound the straps on his arm. "I don't know. All I know is this. In all vineyards shall be wailing, for I will pass through thee, saith the Lord. Amos five-seventeen."

"You're not actually unwell, are you?"

He looked at the floor. "Not really."

"It's about last night, isn't it?"

He clicked his tongue and turned himself into a sigh. "I didn't realise it had affected me at first. Joking around as usual. Then it sank in."

"What? Anything I should know about?"

"I killed a man."

"Go on."

"Not just anyone. I went and turned him over, see if it might not be fatal. No such luck. Valdim Yakinterev."

She nodded, inhaling. "Yes. I saw him on the list of casualties this morning, your bullet."

"All that time he was watching me in Green Park, just looking. He could have put a slug through me any time he felt like it, but he didn't."

"Did you shoot him in self-defence?"

"He was aiming for one of the soldiers. I got him first. I was aiming for his shoulder, but, well, there you go."

"And when you turned him over he was covered with blood, yes?"

"Look, I don't want to make too much of this, okay? I realise it's an occupational hazard. It just – shook me a bit, that's all. I joined the NYPD because I like puzzles. That, and I wanted to shave my beard off. I'm not really the OK Corral type. But I knew the day would come, had to."

"So you thought you'd stay at home today and pray, yes?"

"Pretty much sums it up, yeah."

She smiled. "I find it quite touching that there are still people left who believe in a god."

"Hey, until I was twenty-five, I thought everyone did."

She crossed her legs and leaned back. "Lieutenant Bronstein, I didn't come here to bring you grapes or check you were really ill. I came here because I put two and two together and I want to put your mind at rest."

"Tall order, but go ahead."

"Valdim Yakinterev didn't die from a gunshot wound. He died from ingesting a capsule, probably when he saw he was going to be captured. Your bullet entered his shoulder. In other words, you saved a man's life – Lance-Corporal Geoffrey Smith's of the 23rd Pioneer Regiment, to be precise. And Smith has two devoted parents, a wife and a baby daughter."

Bronstein said nothing for a moment. His mouth wobbled. Then he went to the window and threw it open and leaned out over London. *"Make a joyful noise unto the Lord, all ye lands!"* he yelled. *"Serve the Lord with gladness! Come before his presence with singing!"*

Ruby Parker got up. "So, er … can I take it you'll be back at work tomorrow?"

He looked at her as if she was mad and picked up his jacket. "What do you mean? Let's go."

The report lay on the desk between them. Orlov sat as if there were such things as sit to attention, sit at ease, sit easy and he'd been ordered to do the first. Ruby Parker sat at ease. Bronstein sat easy. They were in her office being fragranced by a plug-in.

"Your written style is very elegant," she told Orlov.

"I spent a lot of time at the Russian Ministry of Defence perfecting it. My accent also."

"Although you'd save yourself a bit of time if you cut down on the adjectives. Well done for finishing it so quickly. And … for taking on board what I said last night."

"I would be failing in my duty if I was to backtrack from my view that had you sent men with me, some would be dead."

"They'd have been under your command, Colonel. If you wanted to keep them in the background while you took the lead that would be up to you. But at least they'd have been there."

"Yes, I see."

"Now let's go through what we've got. We took four bin bags from that house, most of it very interesting, some of it - though it pains me to have to admit it - pure gold. They seem to have been using it as an *ad hoc* operational command centre, although – fortunately for you, Colonel - not a barracks. We'll begin with the letters to and from Ross Henshall. Bronstein, you're going to see him this afternoon. You've an appointment at four outside the National Theatre. You'll approach as a journalist from *The New York Times* who's received a copy of the letters from an anonymous source. Buy him a coffee and a flapjack and see what you can get him to divulge."

"Will do."

"The mere fact that he agreed to meet you at such short notice speaks volumes. Unite is Britain's biggest union. As its leader, I would imagine his diary's fairly full."

"Even more so on the eve of a general election," Bronstein said.

"And don't forget: this is of marginal interest in the US. You can offer to sit on his story for a while in return for a little more openness."

"I don't know why we don't just go in as MI5," Orlov said. "Offer to keep his name clean in return for all the information he can offer."

"That's Plan B. Since he's obviously compromised on some level, I'd rather not commit us to protecting him in the first instance. He knows the game's up anyway. Bronstein could be wearing a hidden microphone for all he knows, or he could have a colleague snapping away with a telephoto. We're probably turning up to hear his swansong."

"Understood."

"The real question is, what are we going to do with the man we captured, Ivan Ryazantsev? Because so far, he's not talking."

"Maybe he just needs more time."

"Whatever this is, gentlemen, it's big. We've got the police working on it full time now as well. As you rightly say, Lieutenant Bronstein, there's a general election just around the corner and your theory, if I understand it correctly, Colonel Orlov, is that there may be assassinations in the offing. 'More time' is the one thing we don't have."

"Your tone of voice suggests a decision has already been made," Orlov said.

"The Russian embassy's been very cooperative since day one, and for our part we've kept a lid on those aspects of the case that might result in a kind of Russophobia. They're very alarmed by what we found at the Manor House. They think – and I believe they're right – it may have implications for their own national security."

"But not everyone we killed was Russian," Bronstein said. "There were two Georgians, two Ukrainians - "

"What does that remind you of?"

"You mean … the Soviet Union?"

"Perhaps better described nowadays as 'Greater Russia'. I said at the beginning of this case that we might be dealing with some sort of mystical Slavophilism. I'm more convinced of that now than ever."

Orlov raised his eyebrows. "Don't you think it's coincidental that it's precisely the building of 'Greater Russia' that Chairman Putin's often accused of? Economic dependence for the CIS countries, the Orange revolution, the invasion of Georgia, etcetera? It must have occurred to you that maybe we're being taken for a ride?"

"And yet I don't think we are," she said. "The Russians' cooperation is too complete. And one could argue that Vladimir

Putin is hardly more than a monkey on a red carpet, that virtually anyone's better qualified to carry through the Greater Russia programme than he is. Don't you think that's likely to make him feel a little scared?"

Orlov shrugged.

She smiled. "Of course, I'm not ruling anything out." She pushed a small black and white photo across the desk towards him. "What do you make of this? We found it in Ryazantsev's pocket."

Orlov looked at it. It showed Vera Gruchov in a long coat and a smile shaking hands with Ryazantsev. He sucked air. "I honestly don't know. It seems incredible the leader of *Vosstanovlenie* could be knowingly connected to a den of killers."

"And yet, first Tebloev, now this."

"Tebloev's no killer."

"All I'm saying is, that young lady keeps turning up."

"'Keeps' is an overstatement. Tebloev genuinely supports her. As regards that fundraiser, he didn't foresee the opprobrium his name would inspire. This is … well, I don't know what it is."

She took the photo back. "Let's put it to one side for now then."

"Interlude," Bronstein said. "A question I keep meaning to ask. This 'Anna Politkovskaya'. Is she worth reading? Ruby."

Ruby Parker smiled. "Her, 'How to misappropriate property with the connivance of the government' is probably the most significant piece of journalism since Voltaire took a liking to Jean Calas. You ought to read it. In fact, I require it."

"How do the Russians propose to deal with Ryazantsev?" Orlov asked.

"How do you think? They propose to do the one thing we're not permitted to do under human rights legislation."

Orlov scowled. "Presumably the idea is that standing by while someone else commits an atrocity is morally better than committing that atrocity yourself."

"We're probably talking about lives here, Colonel, maybe hundreds, maybe thousands. Ryazantsev's free to talk whenever he wants. The longer he holds out, the more serious things probably are. It's no time for squeamishness."

"Orlov shook his head. How do you know that once the Russians have Ryazantsev they won't just 'lose' him?"

"There will be hell to pay if they do."

"Maybe they don't believe in hell," Bronstein said.

"Apart from anything else, it would be incredible if we hadn't considered the possibility of their spiriting him away, and if they hadn't considered we would. No, they've offered to take four of our personnel as observers of everything that happens to him."

"On strict condition they don't intervene," Orlov said.

"On strict condition they don't intervene."

"I'm as uneasy about this as the Colonel is," Bronstein said. "And I accept your point that if we say no, and six weeks down the line we're looking at a pile of corpses, we'll wish we'd waterboarded him ourselves."

"But?"

"There may be a third way."

"I'm willing to listen to any suggestion within the limits of reason," she said.

Bronstein folded his hands. "It's a shame we didn't think of this earlier – while he still had an open wound somewhere - but what say we bury a location transmitter under his skin somewhere, then he 'escapes' on the way to being tortured, and we watch and see where he ends up. I've got a map with every Slope business address on. We simply look for a match."

Ruby Parker put her thumb on the corner of her mouth and stroked her cheek.

"If we don't get one," Bronstein added, "we might even be able to pick him up again."

"What if he jumps straight off a cliff?" she said.

"Psychologically unlikely that he'd run that program when there's still a possibility he could be useful to the organisation – whatever it is."

Orlov nodded. "If we hand him to the Russians, they could easily end up torturing him to death or disability."

"Because he's obviously trained to keep schtum," Bronstein said.

"If he ends up unable to walk and he hasn't talked," Orlov said, "and six weeks down the line we're looking at a pile of corpses, we're going to wish we'd followed Lieutenant Bronstein's plan."

Ruby Parker let out a long breath. "Very well … very well, let's give it a try. Bronstein, put a copy of that map on my desk before you set off to interview Henshall, understood?"

Her phone began to ring. She picked it up. "Gavin, I thought I gave instructions we weren't to be disturbed." She paused and her expression changed. "Ah … Yes, that's different … Yes, put them on then, please."

Orlov and Bronstein looked at each other.

"Thank you," she said into the receiver. "Yes, that's very interesting. Yes, you were right to. If you leave an address at reception, I'll send a member of staff round right away. Of course, of course."

"The Russians?" Bronstein said when she put the phone down.

"Scotland Yard."

"You're looking … pleased?" Bronstein said.

"Nichole Moore's disappeared. She was due to meet her friends last night but no one's seen her. Her boyfriend says she left in a taxi with a Russian woman yesterday afternoon. We've located the taxi driver and he's confirmed that story.

Here's the crux, gentlemen. Nichole Moore jettisoned herself from his car just after our mysterious woman revealed exactly who she was. Russian mafia."

Bronstein and Orlov toasted each other with raised eyebrows and smiled.

"Finally progress," Orlov said. "I suggest that's Vera Gruchov absolved too."

"And I guess it puts your Slavophile theory to rest," Bronstein said.

She smiled. "To be honest, that's one I won't be sorry to see the back of. Profit and loss we can deal with. Ideas and ideologues – no thank you. Especially when we don't even know what their ideas are. Bronstein, I want you go and see Henshall right away. Ring his office and ask for an earlier time, he won't say no. Orlov, you go and see this taxi driver. Get a full description and get someone to produce an E-FIT then wire it to the Russian embassy priority. I'll launch a full-scale search. If we can find Nichole Moore before the mafia do, we might be able to close this case fast."

Chapter 21: Securitavan Shenanigans

The afternoon crowds outside the National Theatre wore loafers and had cotton jumpers tied round their necks and drank lattes. Waiters came out, scribbled numbers in notepads and went back inside without ever making eye-contact. By the embankment wall an ice-cream van sold cornets. Schoolchildren on trips hugged haversacks and clipboards and looked moody. There was a blue sky.

In the midst of all this, Bronstein lounged at an aluminium table with a milk shake, a wad of papers and *Putin's Russia* in a Waterstone's bag. He knew his man by sight, but he was nowhere in view. He wished he was back at Thames House. Things were picking up now, and although what he was doing here ranked high on the list of priorities, he still couldn't help feeling he was temporarily on the fringe.

What he and Orlov needed was a Brit of some description. Someone who could blend in better. Like Jonathan. Gavin wasn't ready yet, despite his good intentions, and no one else looked likely to step up. Hell, they didn't even know anyone else. Which probably meant they'd be dismantled when the Kramski case was over, then teamed with others alongside whom they could provide more net balance. A shame, because he liked Orlov, although he couldn't quite figure him out most of the day.

Suddenly, Henshall came into view. Just like his photo he was stocky, tanned with narrow eyes, faded sports jacket, matching trousers and slip-ons. He had his hands in his pockets and he walked with a shuffle as if he was on his way to his own execution. He was in his early fifties, but he looked ninety.

Bronstein stood up. "Ross Henshall?"

Henshall shook his hand limply and sat down.

"What are you having?" Bronstein said.

"Whatever you are."

"Waiter, another banana milk shake, please."

"No, sorry. Scratch that. I'll have a latte. No, I'll have a cup of tea. Thank you."

The waiter wrote and crossed out, wrote and nodded, then left them.

"How bad is it?" Henshall said in a low voice. "I don't need to see what you've got. Just tell me."

"I know you've been blackmailed and I know they've got some extremely compromising pictures of you and several ladies at the Blackpool conference last year. I can sit on all that in exchange for a fuller story."

"Fuller in what sense?"

"Ideally, I need to know who was blackmailing you and why."

"You don't know?"

"Obviously if I just go to press with what I've got, people will assume the worst. It's just human nature."

Henshall almost burst into tears. "You bloody journalists!"

Bronstein had come prepared for this. "Now that Rupert Murdoch owns *The Wall Street Journal*, Mr Henshall, *The New York Times* is the world's greatest newspaper. We don't do tacky. We do news, the real deal. You're not some B-list celebrity found *in flagrante* with a fan. This is blackmail and you're the leader of the UK's biggest union."

Henshall stepped down a rung. "Of course, yes, yes, you're right ... You said you might sit on the story for a while?"

"For a week or two, in exchange for a better one. Call it deferred gratification, if you like."

"And you'll sign something to that effect, will you?"

"I need the information today. For all I know you could be planning an exclusive with one of the weekend dailies."

"I wouldn't trust those sharks as far as I could throw them. Promise you a mint, take the story and leave you high and dry. I've seen it happen loads of times."

"So where does that leave us?"

"I – I've brought a document, drawn up by my solicitor. The deal is, I tell you all I know if you put off going to press for a minimum of two weeks from today. I don't want it witnessed by a person, obviously, so I'm going to photograph us together and you signing with my phone. If you agree, that is."

"Show me the dotted line."

Henshall removed two sheets of A4 paper from his jacket pocket. He put them on the table, ran his hand over them to gets the folds out and passed them to Bronstein. Bronstein read them for a few moments then signed while Henshall snapped him. Then Henshall signed and put them back in his pocket.

Bronstein took out a Dictaphone, placed it on the table between them, and pressed record. "Who's blackmailing you?"

"I don't know them personally. They work for a van firm. Trucks, vans, lorries. Securitavan, they're called."

"That's - a Constantine Slope company, isn't it?"

"Yeah. I've never done any direct dealing with the old crook. He tends to rely on his managers and supervisors. Or did. I believe he's dead now."

"And it was Slope that was blackmailing you?"

"Maybe not him personally, I don't know. Like I say, I never got close enough to find out."

"Despite the fact that you're a pretty powerful guy in your own right. Didn't that strike you as odd, him holding you at arm's length like that?"

"Not really. He held all the cards."

"The photos."

"Yeah."

Bronstein sipped his milk shake. "You've seen a copy of them."

"Yeah."

"Why didn't you go to the police?"

"Isn't it obvious? That's how blackmail works. I'm supposed to be happily married. I've got two grown up kids. Emma's doing politics and history at Sussex. She's got severe asthma. God knows how this is going to affect her."

"The blackmailers must have testimonies, yes? I mean, these women, what's to stop you claiming it's a Photoshop mock-up? They must have affidavits."

"They say they can get them."

"Thought so. Anyway, you never dealt directly with Slope."

"I didn't expect to. He's a good tactician. He's not going to expose himself in something like this."

"Who *did* you deal with?"

"No one, face to face. Voices on phones."

"But none of those voices was Slope's."

"That's right."

Bronstein scratched his head. "How do you know?"

"Age of the voice, and deduction. Why would he deal with me personally, when he could get underlings to do it? Anyway, what's it matter? He's dead, isn't he?"

"Let's move on. What did Securitavan want?"

"Unite to back off. Look, you may have heard of the miners' strike in the 1980s, Mr …"

"Bronstein, David Bronstein."

"The government didn't approve of the miners' politics so it took away their livelihoods. Well the same thing's happening now, except this time it's lorry drivers in the firing line. And it's a Labour government, not a Tory."

"I don't get it. How are they trying to crush you?"

"Come to think of it, you could do an article on that for *The New York Times*, couldn't you? How they're determined to undercut us at every turn, how hundreds of drivers are looking at the dole simply because Slope's running Securitavan as a loss-leader, how none of his drivers are in our union and ours can't get jobs with him. I'd love to talk about that."

"I thought that's what we *were* talking about."

"Yeah, but you could do an article on it."

"Let's concentrate on one thing at a time, shall we? You tell me what's going on and I'll be the judge how newsworthy it is. Or not."

Henshall nodded. "Okay, okay. It's what I just said. Every contract that comes out – especially the public service contracts, the biggies – has to be put out to tender. Like anything, there's only so low you can bid before you start losing money. Slope wins every time. Putting hundreds of drivers elsewhere out of work. God knows why he was doing it. We did the sums a while back. He was losing millions."

"He was running the business at a considerable loss."

"And of course, he had the Three Stooges on his payroll. Herbert McLellan, Charles Inwood and Lionel bloody Edgeware. Obviously if you've got friends in the government, the usual rules needn't apply."

"They were working for him?"

"They're 'consultant directors', whatever that means. A big, fat salary and the odd backhander for services rendered probably. We all know what those three are like. You've heard of the expenses scandal in the US, have you?"

"Just about. It wasn't big news. Mind you, forty-five per cent of Americans have never even heard of England."

"Lucky them."

"Things might change now Slope's dead, right?"

"You know what I think?" Henshall said. "I think he became senile. You know how it is sometimes with old people when they start losing it. Like Howard Hughes. Suddenly, they get obsessive about something."

"And you think Slope became obsessive about Securitavan?"

"That would explain it, wouldn't it? How he couldn't deal with me personally? How he threw millions down the drain for no tangible reward?"

"It's not implausible, I grant you. But you still haven't explained how you came to be blackmailed."

Henshall flinched. "Unite decided to make things difficult for them. Protests outside their branches, go-slows down the M1 or roads we knew they'd be using on particular days. You see, it wasn't just that they were undercutting our members, they also had this unassailable reputation for reliability. Check out their website. Customer satisfaction one hundred per cent. We decided we'd have to hit that, if we hit anything."

"And that's when it got nasty."

Henshall wiped his head in two different directions. "I swear to God, I don't even remember going to the bloody hotel room, except in snatches. They must have spiked my drink. But it's too late for that any more. Who's going to believe me? It's like something from Monty bloody Python. A honey-trap to secure van contracts."

"Their idea was that when the union considered any plan to put a spoke in Securitavan's wheels, Ross Henshall would vote against it, yes?"

"That's what it amounted to, yes."

"Did they suggest they'd let you off the hook if you played along for long enough?"

"I believe that's standard in blackmail."

"Any indication when that might be?"

He smiled bitterly. "They said 'soon'. But obviously, not soon enough."

Bronstein finished his milk shake. "That's probably all I need to know for now. I'll be back in touch if I need to ask anything else."

Henshall shrugged the shrug of the dead. "Sure."

"So what are you planning to do now?"

"Speak to my wife, obviously. Then to the press. I may need to spoil it for *The New York Times*, but we do still have a deal, yes?"

"Hey, I signed your contract. And even if I hadn't, *The New York Times* always keeps its word."

"Yeah, okay, sorry about that. I mean, for doubting *The New York Times*."

Bronstein folded his arms. "Listen, Ross. I've got a journalist's hunch about this one. Why not wait a while to tell your wife? Like, say, twelve days? I've a feeling things may not be as bleak as they look."

"What do you mean?"

"There may be more to this than meets the eye. Keep it to yourself, but I've been speaking to one or two high-level off-the-records in the British security services. The question is, would you be prepared to take radical action at short notice? If it gets Securitavan off your back permanently?"

"If – if MI5's on board, yes." He laughed. "Even if it isn't. Of course."

"I can't promise anything, but at the very least I might be able to discover something that will put a different spin on matters. Make them look not so Monty Python."

Henshall was trembling. "Twelve days?"

"I'll be back in touch then if I can't."

"So you believe me?"

"I'm a roving reporter. I don't go in for beliefs. It's a story I'm prepared to investigate, that's all. Having said that, Ross, I'm good. Very good."

On the opposite side of the road from Nichole Moore's house, Marcie Brown looked out of the bedroom window of a detached house with a 'For Sale' sign in the garden. Next to her, a video camera on a tripod pointed at the road through a gap in the net curtain, its red light flashing. She pressed 'eject', inserted another disk and pressed 'record'. She took out a pen and wrote '1.10-2.10' on the disk she'd just taken out and returned it to its case. A car drove by. She picked up her laptop and typed 'LA51UJR Ford Focus Hatchback blue, 2.11' and saved.

She yawned. If this was the sort of thing Nick did all day, he could keep it. She wondered how he was getting along outside 45 Scarborough Avenue. They'd discovered a vacant property opposite there yesterday and rung the police anonymously to report a sighting of Nichole Moore. They would report fresh sightings of her tonight, at properties yet to be identified, and keep watches on the roads fronting them tomorrow.

She reached into her bag and took out a Marmite sandwich and a litre bottle of lemonade. Another car went by in the opposite direction. She typed, 'LY52VCG Volvo XC90 silver 2.11' and saved. Another Orthodox Jew in the driving seat. She wondered why Nichole Moore chose to live among so many Jewish people. Maybe she was Jewish.

Shit, LA02CCF Fiat Punto red was on its way, Joyce the estate agent.

Marcie knew it was pointless panicking. She dismantled the camera, put it in the bag with the laptop and switched off her mobile. She climbed into the airing cupboard and crouched down behind the wooden panel that had once screened an old-fashioned immersion heater. A few minutes later, the bedroom door opened and she heard Joyce's voice.

"It's very sizeable, and of course the window's north-facing so it stays cool in the summer."

They clopped backwards and forwards on the bare floorboards for a few moments and a woman's voice said:

"I like the amount of space but there's a real smell of Marmite."

"I like Marmite," a man said jocosely.

"Nice to eat maybe, but not an attractive smell for houses. Do you think we could we have another look at the address in Lambeth, please, Joyce?"

The taxi driver wasn't happy that he was losing money talking to the police. He and Orlov stood by the car in a bus stop on Ridgeway Road breathing the passing fumes. The driver had his hands in his pockets. Orlov pretended to be taking notes.

"She closed the window between me and the back seats," the driver said, "but it's a very loose fit. Crap. I probably need to get it seen to."

"But you heard practically every word they said."

"Practically. She was definitely a Russian. I heard her say 'da', apart from anything else. 'Da'. It means yes."

Orlov nodded. "But you say she sounded English when she got out of the car."

"I think that was put on. She was very annoyed about losing Nichole. She said 'shit' a few times, but the last 'shit' was what I'd call really Russian."

"I'm not sure what you mean."

"Like, 'shee-it'. As if she couldn't help breaking into her own language because she was so furious. 'Sheeeeee-it!'"

"Yes, I see."

"Of course, I don't speak Russian."

"You've given the police a description of her?"

"Sure. She was a pretty girl, although if you ask me, her head was a little too big for her body. She made Nichole look a right minger. Mind you, Nichole didn't have any make-up on. She was in such a rush to get out of the house."

"You must pick up lots of celebrities in your taxi. In your experience, is it rare for someone like Nichole Moore to leave her house without make-up?"

"Listen, I've got a theory. I don't think this is an actual gangster we're dealing with. I think it's a gangster's moll."

"Thank you."

"Celebs never leave their houses without their make-up, no. Or at least, looking good."

Orlov's mobile pinged. He took it out and read the text. *Picture coming through.*

The next moment, a composite appeared. A young woman with big eyes, big lips, a small nose and dark hair brushed away from her face. Pretty, but also formidable-looking. And very Russian.

Orlov showed her to the taxi driver. "Is this her?"

"Bloody hell, you've found her? That was quick."

"It's a software realisation of your description."

"It's a beauty."

"Is it accurate?"

The driver grinned. "Totally. Bloody hell, we've moved on since the days of Identikit, haven't we?"

Orlov looked at the picture again. Something rang a bell. He tried to think back. It had to be someone he'd known before he went to prison. Judges, lawyers, court officials? ... No. Journalists? ... No. A woman soldier, perhaps? ... No. Whoever she was, his efforts weren't bring her closer. He'd been in situations like this before. He needed to switch off and let his subconscious do the work. It would come to him when he least expected.

And yet he couldn't switch off.

"I'm telling you," the driver said, "that's a gangster's moll. Not a gangster. A moll."

After an hour in bed, Marcie went to the fish and chip shop while Fleming switched on his computer and loaded the data they'd collected that day onto his hard drive. She returned twenty minutes later with two pieces of Pollock, a jumbo bag of chips and some mushy peas in a pot, and they got back in bed to eat and express affection. Afterwards, she washed the plates, he dried them, they returned to work on the investigation.

"What are we looking for?" she said.

"Matches, to begin with. I've combined the car data we collected under two headings. We're looking for the same vehicle appearing more than once."

"But that might just mean we're looking at next door neighbours, mightn't it?"

"I've downloaded all the relevant data from the DVLA mainframe onto here. Quite illegally I should add, but love is blind. We can call up names and addresses of registration numbers at the press of a button and so eliminate the neighbours fairly quickly."

"I don't want you to get into trouble. You'll delete it afterwards, obviously."

"Then I'll dump the hard drive and get a new one."

"What else are we looking for?"

"If we find the same registration at the two different addresses we were at, that's good. Then out of town numbers. Every licence plate begins with a letter showing where the car was registered. We can eliminate L for London, and also the surrounding counties at a stretch, G for Kent and Sussex, and so on."

"Then what?"

"We search for suffix matches. Look, I'm saying 'we'. I mean the computer. If it finds anything, I load the videos, look for drivers' faces. I'd like you to get some sleep while I sit here and click on stuff. I'll wake you up at eleven when it's time for you to go back to the gym. Are you sure you're up for that today? You're burning the candle at both ends."

She kissed him. "Good night."

She went into the bedroom, got into bed and turned off the light.

Three hours later her alarm rang. She wondered where she was at first and why she hadn't dreamed. The she went for a shower. She'd brought a change of clothing, so she put it on and thrust her old clothes into a bag. When she went into the living room, Fleming turned to her and stood up. He smiled.

"I take it you've found something," she said.

"Someone's been driving up and down in front of us all day in unmarked vehicles, seven in all, both locations. All the way from Bedford. I wonder if you've ever heard of Securitavan?"

"What? A van company?"

"Sounds odd, I know. But that's not all. When you play back the videos, the drivers – and I emphasise the plural – are always looking for someone. And there's been an unusually high proportion of cars from that part of the country passing by too. All of them looking, looking, looking."

"Sounds like we've hit the jackpot."

"I'm going to pay them a visit tomorrow in Bedford. See what I can dig up. It'll mean throwing another sickie, but it's a price worth paying."

"What are we going to do ultimately? Shouldn't we hand everything over to the police?"

"Not yet."

She smiled. "I hoped you were going to say that."

"It's going to be pretty difficult explaining how we came by all this information without ending up in serious trouble. No, we need to catch them red-handed."

"I'm not sure you should go alone. These are the people that killed Jonathan. They're not going to think twice about killing you."

He grinned. "You think I should take you, presumably?"

"Obviously."

"Out of the question. While you were asleep I watched the news. The police have put out an Identikit picture of 'a woman they'd like to interview in connection with the disappearance of Nichole Moore'. If it is Securitavan that's behind all this and they see you within a hundred miles of their depot, they'll twig. No, I know how to handle myself, and I'll take a gun just in case."

She beamed. "Gosh, this is getting really exciting."

He shook his head with a sigh. "If only we knew how to contact David bloody Bronstein we might be able to hand everything over. This is probably more his sort of line. As far as I can make out, he's disappeared off the face of the planet. Listen, I've written down everything we've done in a notebook. I'm going to tape it to the underside top panel of the wardrobe, just in case anyone comes looking for it. If anything happens to me, I want you to take it straight to the police, understand?"

She swallowed and hugged him. "Be very careful. And ring me as soon as you get out."

Chapter 22: Rumble at GCHQ

Ivan Ryazantsev sat on his bed staring at his feet. His blond hair and filo-pastry face contrasted oddly with the grey walls and floor tiles, which looked as if they had been gnawed by rats, especially in the corners. The cell had a toilet and a barred window above head height. The halogen lamp was out of reach and protected by six centimetres of Perspex. Orlov and Gavin and a guard stepped inside and closed the door behind them.

"Time for a trip to the Russian embassy, my friend," Gavin said. "Are you absolutely sure you don't want to reconsider? We can set you up with a new identity anywhere else in the world. The mafia need never know."

Orlov translated all this into Russian. For all the prisoner's expression changed, they might as well not have been there.

Orlov snapped the cuffs on him and on his own wrist. He stood up and the three men went out to the waiting van, unmarked, with blackened windows. Three 'observers' were waiting to meet them: Shaun, Katie and Paula, all in office wear. Gavin made up the fourth. Orlov and the prisoner got into the van and sat down. The observers followed suit in various states of uneasiness. There was a little jerk and they pulled out onto the road.

Ten minutes later, they pulled to a sharp stop. They heard shouting. Shaun went for his gun, but suddenly the back door to the van was rived open.

They found themselves face to face with an armed teenage gang. The leader – a muscular-looking boy in a hoodie with a chain – had his arm in a lock round their driver's neck and a gun to his head. Four other boys pointed guns at them.

"Jus' bring out the money, right, and no one gone get hurt, yeah?"

"Jus' do as he says," the boy behind him said. "And get out and get down on the ground."

"Jus' bring out the money, right, and no one gets hurt!" the first screamed a second time. "Now!"

"Now!"

Orlov and the observers got out.

"We – we haven't got any money," Paula said.

The second in command punched her in the chest and she fell back against the open door. "*Get down on the ground now, bitch!*"

"Jus' bring out the money!"

Orlov held his wrist up attached to Ryazantsev's, demonstrating the gang's mistake.

The leader's face fell. "Bloody shit, it's a bloody police carrier." He turned incredulously to the second in command. "*We're robbing a bloody pissing police carrier, you dipshit! What the hell we doing robbing a bloody pissing police carrier?*"

"Shit, how the hell was I supposed to know?"

"There's probably a bloody *fleet* on its way!"

The second turned his gun on Orlov. "Let him go. Unlock him."

"*What the bloody hell you talking about?*" the leader yelled at him. "*We've got to get out of here!*"

"Fighting for justice, man." He turned back to Orlov. "Undo the lock! *Now, or I'll blow your ugly head off!*"

They could hear the approaching sirens now. Orlov went in his pocket and returned with the key. He released Ryazantsev and held up the key and tossed it. Then he pulled a gun from his side and discharged it.

The leader loosed his hostage as he slumped and Ryazantsev began to run. The second shot Orlov in the heart as his gang dispersed in all directions. Six panda cars screeched round the corner followed by an ambulance. Gavin and Shaun pulled out guns and went after Ryazantsev.

Once the three runners had rounded the corner, everyone heaved a sigh of relief. The gang leader got to his feet and brushed himself down. Orlov stood up with a disgruntled look at the fake blood on his chest.

"Let's hope this works," Paula said. "Well done, everyone."

Bronstein met Ruby Parker outside Government Communication Headquarters in Cheltenham. He'd only ever seen it in aerial images before – as far as he could tell, no one thought it worth photographing from ground level – so he knew it looked like a particle accelerator. But he wasn't surprised to discover that particle accelerators look like supermarkets when you can't even see the roof.

She'd told him this was going to be her 'party'. She had to hold one each year to keep members of the Joint Intelligence Committee and the Defence Intelligence Staff happy. She liked to hold it as far away from Thames House as possible, preferably here, where the gadgetry and pyrotechnics could be relied on to mollify them for another twelve months. When she'd begun in the post, they'd been quite fractious. Nowadays, she had them in the palm of her hand. A security officer clicked his heels and saluted as she got out of the car.

Bronstein followed her inside. He held a wad of papers marked urgent, but he'd already decided to wait till the shindig was over before breaking its contents to her. He hadn't even told Orlov yet. When he let this one out of the bag her jaw was set to hit the ground so hard it'd smash like a windshield in a write-off. Orlov even more.

They went through three sets of double doors and up a flight of stairs into a room with two projector screens, both turned on. The lights were low, and a committee of men and women, some in uniform, others in three-piece suits, stood up with an appreciative sigh as she entered.

"Ladies and Gentlemen, please sit down," she said, smiling and making eye-contact with all of them as she made her way to the front. "You'll have received my report into the Kramski case. It is a good example of what my department is working on at present. Like most of what we focus on, we began with only a vague inkling of the threat it posed to national security, but we've come a long way. I've invited you here to observe a crucial juncture in the investigation.

"You'll be aware that two days ago we captured a potential terrorist, Ivan Ryazantsev, and that – since he steadfastly declines to speak - the Russians expressed an interest in eliciting information from him by use of force. Of course, no one here needs reminding that since our recent discomfiture in Guantanamo Bay, we prefer not to sanction such recourses, but we're in a dilemma. Because there is no denying that failure to tap him may have serious consequences. We've planted a location transmitter inside a wound he picked up the other day and we're releasing him into the wild to see where he ends up. If all goes well, we will re-arrest him later. I'll hand you over to Michael for the technical details."

A stout man of about thirty in a black suit stood up. "First of all, on the left hand screen, you're going to see CCTV footage of the simulated robbery of the van carrying Ryazantsev. That's coming up ... now."

The screen showed a blurry gang in hoods at the back of a van holding its driver hostage, and Orlov and the Ryazantsev getting out, followed by four intelligence officers. Punches were thrown, shots were fired, bodies crumpled and the prisoner made a run for it, followed by Gavin and Shaun. The screen switched off and the next screen showed a computer-generated facsimile of the map Bronstein had drawn up, with Ryazantsev represented by a barely moving flashing dot.

Michael picked up a pointer. "The pulsating dot is Ryazantsev, of course. The illuminated yellow lights are businesses owned by Constantine Slope. We have reasons to believe he'll make for one of them, as outlined on page thirty-seven. It may be some time before we can ascertain which."

One of the men in suits raised his hand. "Have you any reason to think it'll be one location rather than another?"

Ruby Parker folded her hands. "Most of Slope's companies are shell corporations. They've nearly all come under the scrutiny of the Serious Organised Crime Agency at one time or another, usually in response to suspicious activity reports from various sources, but they've always come out clean. However, his biggest company is real. Securitavan."

A woman in a khaki tunic raised her hand. "I would imagine you think SOCA hasn't delved deeply enough into these shells? That one or more of them really is more than it looks?"

"That's one avenue we're exploring. Obviously, no one sets up that many shells without a good reason. If Ryazantsev makes for one of them, we may be on to something."

"What if he makes for a branch of the one 'real' company, Securitavan?" the man in the suit said.

"That's progress too."

He smiled. "But less of it, I would imagine."

"I'm sure you'll understand, Tim, that I prefer not to make such assumptions so far in advance of any subsequent investigation."

"No, no, of course not. I was just asking."

Michael switched another screen on. A satellite photograph. "This shows Ryazantsev's progress as seen by Planetsat 6," he said. "Ground sample distance 0.35 metres, updated once every ten seconds. That's him making his way across a field."

"Is he a danger to the public?" someone asked.

"Now we know where he is," Ruby Parker said, "we're never likely to be more than twenty metres away from him. If he was to try and hitch a lift, it would be one of our operatives that stopped to pick him up. But we're doing more than that." She took out her mobile phone and pressed call. "Charles? Yes, thank you, I wonder if you'd mind updating me on Mr Ryazantsev's travel arrangements ... Excellent, that's very good news. Well done." She put her phone down and turned to the men and women in front of her. "In approximately two minutes' time, Mr Ryazantsev will emerge onto a motorway. There he'll find a car with its engine idling and a lone driver relieving himself behind a tree some distance away. If he's got two brain cells to rub together - and he has - he'll do the sensible thing and no one will get hurt."

Two minutes later, the flashing dot sped up and the satellite picture showed a Ford Fiesta pulling out of a lay-by, chased by a man in his late thirties holding his trousers. The room purred and settled into silence as the spectacle of the minutely monitored fugitive fixed it with a grim fascination. A few people wrote in notepads. One by one, large numbers of Slope's shell corporations were eliminated as the flashing dot passed them by. An hour later, it stopped at the Securitavan headquarters in Bedford.

"Now what?" someone said.

Ruby Parker stood up. "Now, assuming he stays put and doesn't look likely to move on to another Slope enterprise, we discreetly retrieve him. Then we'll send in a reconnaissance team, probably tomorrow under the guise of a Ministry of Transport inspection. Then ... we'll see."

The flashing light suddenly started to move. "He's leaving," Michael said.

Everyone felt simultaneously that something wasn't right. Ryazantsev was on his way back to London.

Ruby Parker picked up her phone. "Charles, does anyone know what's happening? Why's he on his way back here? ... No, okay. Get back to me in five minutes." She put it down with a glower.

Suddenly everyone in the room was talking. Then Ryazantsev's flashing stopped and they lost satellite contact.

"I think he must have discovered the transmitter," Michael said.

Ruby Parker sighed. "Since we know his destination, this changes nothing. Although since they're now aware we're tracking them, we'll have to proceed more quickly. I'm sure you'll understand therefore, ladies and gentlemen, when I say I'm now obliged to return to my desk. My apologies, I do hope you'll excuse me."

Bronstein sat next to her on the back seat of the Daimler back to London. He clutched his bundle of papers and stretched his legs.

"What do you think happened?" he said.

"I know what happened. Charles told me. Ryazantsev's dead. Given the amount of time that elapsed before that light started moving again, I guess they killed him as soon as he showed his face. I half suspected they would. In that eventuality, I gave strict instructions that the location transmitter was to be switched off. Kramski's men are probably dumping the corpse as we speak."

"On the plus side, they don't know we're onto them."

"Not that we know of. It sounds callous - I regret Ryazantsev's death of course - but it got us out of that meeting a little more quickly than I'd hoped."

"I take it you're not keen on meetings."

"Not those. One or two of them always get slightly drunk before it starts. They're in their posts because the job-title feels important and they think you won't notice a little slurring. One or two of them like the sounds of their own voices, so they make miniature speeches and then they look cross when you ask which of the thousand points they only raised implicitly they'd like you to tackle first. Then there are the trip-wires, or that's how they see themselves. And none of them know anything, not really. They might as well all get drunk."

"Brace yourself, I've got some bad news. I mean apart from Ryazantsev."

They were entering London now. Flocks of sheep and clumps of Meadow Barley were giving way to industrial estates and corner shops. She turned to him.

"I've discovered the identity of our Russian lady."

Her eyes widened. "Really?"

"It's Jonathan Hartley-Brown's sister, Marciella."

"You're - joking."

"First of all, the Identikit's a dead ringer. But secondly, as you know, I've been keeping tabs on the phones of the celebrities meeting in Green Park. Nichole Moore's Nokia bill shows she was called just before she disappeared. When we traced the caller, guess who."

Ruby Parker took a sharp breath. "You may or may not know we're considering recruiting her. Jonathan recommended her. Orlov seconded. She's in training."

"Shit no, I didn't know."

"There's no reason you should have. Nor does she … yet."

"But you can get hold of her at short notice, right?"

"In theory. My guess is that she's trying to get even with Kramski's men and she's blundered."

"So how do you think she got hold of Nichole Moore's phone number?"

"I've heard she's very resourceful. At least Celia speaks very highly of her. That sort of thing would present no trouble to an intelligent girl, sufficiently determined."

"Does the name 'Nicholas Fleming' ring a bell?"

"Not at all. Should it?"

"We were exchange students. When I came to Scotland Yard, he went to New York. He's a police inspector, a friend of

Jonathan's from university, and Marciella Hartley-Brown's former lover."

"And he fits into this how?"

"First of all, he's not in New York. He's back in England."

She shrugged. "Colin Bowker probably recalled him when he gave you your cards. He wouldn't want to be left short staffed."

"He's been taking a lot of time off work lately. And he's in constant contact with Marciella. And that's not all."

"Please get to the point, Lieutenant Bronstein. I have a lot of time for you, but we're going to arrive back at Thames House in a minute and I need to have some idea of the magnitude of what we're dealing with if I'm to respond effectively."

He passed her an A4 colour photograph. "This is a print-off of one of the satellite pictures Michael just showed us at GCHQ. That's the car Ryazantsev arrived in. See that fellow on the edge of the picture, there? That's Nicholas Fleming."

"Good God. You're – you're sure?"

"Here's another one. Slightly clearer because I asked Michael to put some software to work on it. And yup, that's him all right."

"You think he was involved in Ryazantsev's murder?"

"What do you think?"

The car pulled into the forecourt of Thames House and they walked inside and took the lift down in silence. They went straight into her office where Ruby picked up the phone. "Gabriella, could you ask Terence and Mahtab to come down to my office immediately? Tell them it's urgent. And could you get Celia on the phone and ask her to do the same? Ask her to drop whatever she's doing, she may be in danger. And recall Colonel Orlov."

As she was speaking, Terence and Mahtab arrived. Mahtab wore a hijab, otherwise they were both in their twenties in casual wear with notepads and pens at the ready.

"Thank you for coming so promptly," Ruby Parker said. "I need a deep-level search on one Marciella Hartley-Brown, daughter of the former Shadow Foreign Secretary, Sir Anthony Hartley-Brown. I want you to run a full check on her phone bill and ideally I'd like to listen to her conversations. I want access to all her Internet profiles - Facebook, MSN, Twitter, etc, etc, as applicable, all her e-mail accounts. I want you to get into her flat and the house she used to live in, in Hertfordshire, and check for documents, real and virtual, indicating communications with foreign nationals. Go through her waste disposal. I want her watched twenty-four seven, and I need details of all her trips abroad in the last three years. And I'd like the same for one Nicholas Fleming, an inspector with the Metropolitan police. Deploy as many personnel as you need. Effective immediately, please. And I'd like a preliminary report on my desk in an hour. Mahtab, take this note to reception and ask them to deliver it to the Blue Maiden. That will be all."

Chapter 23: The Other Side of Nichole Moore

Fleming left his Vauxhall Insignia on the street alongside the Securitavan headquarters, and walked through the open gates into a large compound with low level warehouses enclosed on all sides by aluminium shutters. He estimated the forecourt where the vehicles turned to be about thirty-five by fifty metres. A few vans - Ford Transit Mk 3s, grey, with the company logo - stood parked in the centre next to a black Range Rover. The perimeter was fenced off by green PVC Hexagonal wire netting to a height of approximately seven metres. A two storey office-block faced the gates from the other side of the compound, twelve by ten. Two burglar alarms - Elmdene make - and a CCTV camera.

He couldn't see any personnel. Overhead, the clouds were grey and high and uniform. A small pile of litter and dead leaves had been shaped by the wind.

Suddenly, a man in green overalls with blond hair emerged from the office block and slammed the door behind him. "Excuse me!"

"*My name's Roger Lazenby!*" Fleming called over, showing his card. "From the Department of Transport! I'm here to do a spot check on some of your vehicles, if you'd wouldn't mind?"

The man came over, gave the card a cursory glance and handed it back. "You are expected?"

"We tend not to announce these things."

"We very busy. You might come back?"

"I'm afraid it doesn't quite work like that, Mr ...?"

"Ostrowski. From Poland."

"Are many of your workers from Poland? Just out of interest?"

"You want look at safety, no?"

"Er, yes, please."

"How long you need?"

"Between ten and twenty minutes, depending on how well it goes."

"Wait minute, please. I must confirm."

He walked away. Fleming already knew he wasn't from Poland. He wasn't accenting the middle of his sentences nor the wrong syllables the way a Polish speaker with his grammatical command would. Fleming didn't know what inflection he did have.

He waited a long time. Doors on the warehouses opened and closed, and he caught glimpses of what was going on inside. Men working on the vans somehow, he couldn't tell how. It didn't look like engine maintenance.

Suddenly, he heard shouted commands and after another interval the workers filed out of the warehouses and lined up sullenly against the perimeter fence. The man with the blond hair returned.

"Please to accompany me."

"There was no need to make everyone down tools," Fleming said, trying to sound chastened. "I usually work round people."

"Is done now."

Fleming followed him at a brisk walk into one of the warehouses. He felt the workers' pupils sticking antagonistically to the back of his neck.

"I don't necessarily need you to be present, Mr Ostrowski," he said, when they were inside. "I'm sure you've got other things to be getting on with. You could just leave me a set of ignition keys - "

"Please to hurry up."

They stood between two rows of twenty vans with brake lights facing each other. Ten double strip lights overhead provided the illumination once Ostrowski closed the door. He had his hand in his right pocket and he was holding something. Fleming suddenly had the strong conviction it was a gun. If it came to a draw, Fleming's still had its catch on. He wouldn't stand a chance.

With an effort, he managed to stop his voice shaking. "Could you step into the cabin, please, and turn the engine on?"

Ostrowski ground his teeth and did as instructed.

"Now check it's in neutral and press your foot on the accelerator!" Fleming shouted.

While the engine screamed, he opened the rear doors and looked inside. Two bundles of newspapers tightly wrapped in polythene. Some panels had come away from the ceiling. The loading dimensions looked smaller than they should. There were scraps of paper lying on the floor. He snatched a wadge and thrust them into his briefcase. He quietly re-closed the doors, located his pistol, released the catch and put it ready to hand. He pretended to examine the tyres.

"You can stop now!" he shouted.

He suddenly wondered whether there was a CCTV camera in here. He looked up. Shit yes, and it was pointed at him.

"I think I've got the data I need," he said, as Ostrowski stepped out. "I can be moving along now. Thank you for your cooperation."

Ostrowski looked nonplussed. "That is *it*?"

"We can tell an awful lot from the way an engine turns over nowadays. And of course, your treads are beautiful."

Suddenly, there was a loud screech of tyres. He heard a man shout, then an argument, all in another language, then a gunshot. Ostrowski blanched and apparently forgot all about Fleming in his haste to get outside.

Fleming followed him. He was just in time to see one of the workers get into a blue Ford Fiesta and put his foot so hard on the accelerator the tyres burned. And then the car was out of the compound and roaring into the distance. Fleming walked and kept walking, although he guessed no one's eyes were fixed on him for the time being. Once outside, he broke into a run and didn't stop until he reached his car. Marcie sat waiting for him in the driving seat wearing a leather jacket and an Alice band.

"What are you doing here?" he demanded. "You're supposed to be in London."

"Don't be angry. I came up to meet you on the train. I was worried."

"You're in the driver's seat. Swap over, quick."

"It took me ages to find you."

He looked back along the street. Ostrowski was walking towards him and, when he saw he'd been spotted, he broke into a run.

Fleming got into the passenger seat and tossed his briefcase in the back. "You need to pull out now, Marcie, and put your foot down. We haven't time to argue. Drive anywhere."

She started the car and pulled out at speed. Ostrowski stopped running and watched them until they turned the corner.

They'd escaped by the skin of their teeth. And he had no idea what he and she were going to do next. At least not in the long term.

"Pull over and give me the wheel," he said.

"Don't be silly, Nick. How am I ever going to pass my test if I don't get any practice?"

They drove for about ten minutes till they reached the suburbs. He looked in the wing mirror. Behind them, a black Range Rover was recklessly overtaking in an effort to pull closer.

"Don't fret," she said. "I've seen it."

Ruby Parker waited in her office with Orlov and Bronstein. She looked at her computer screen. The fish tank hummed. Bronstein read a comic. Orlov sat with his hands in his pockets. There was a knock and Gavin opened the door to admit Miss Demure. She looked about the room with a glower.

"Please sit down, Celia," Ruby Parker said. "It's about Marciella Hartley-Brown. We've a suspicion - though as yet it's no more - that she may be working for Kramski's men. Have you seen the Identikit?"

"Of the Russian lady who put the fear of God in poor Nichole Moore?"

"The same."

"Now you come to mention it, the resemblance is striking. And yet I'd be surprised if it was what it seems. She wants to go to Afghanistan, which would be unusual for that sort of a criminal."

"The other thing," Bronstein said, "is that the taxi driver was adamant she spoke with a Russian accent."

"She said 'da'," Orlov said. "Apparently, it means yes in Russian."

"Just thinking about it," Bronstein said, "she didn't have to do that. Surely she wouldn't imitate them if she had their backing?"

"Young people tend to imitate the accents of people they admire," Ruby Parker said. "Think of all the white middle-class Londoners who go round speaking Jafaican."

"Simply because they've heard a few Dizzee Rascal songs," Miss Demure added.

Ruby Parker sat forward. "Her father's the Shadow Foreign Secretary – or was. She'd be an excellent feather in the cap of any recruiting officer. Celia, do you think she knows who you are?"

"I don't think she suspects a thing."

"We chose her," Orlov said. "Not the other way round. At no stage did she hint that a life in the secret service was something she'd find attractive. To the extent that we've guided her in that direction, we may bear at least some of the responsibility for her behaviour, whatever she does or doesn't consciously know."

"What are we here to discuss?" Miss Demure said tetchily. "An *a priori* analysis in an underground office isn't going to determine her guilt or innocence. The evidence alone will do that. If you've asked for a comprehensive search, we'll probably know the answer in thirty minutes."

Ruby Parker smiled. "We're here because I need to know how to react to the worst-case scenario. As you rightly say, Celia, there may be very little time before we know whether that's what we're up against. If so, it probably won't be much use confronting her directly. We saw how Ryazantsev clammed up. No, we're probably going to have to tap her by stealth. I need ideas, suggestions."

There was a knock on the door. She got up. Gavin. He handed her a note and she closed the door and unfolded it.

"The White Maiden," she said. "She wants to know whether we're investigating Nicholas Fleming. It turns out he's been illegally downloading information from the DVLA. Names, addresses, registration numbers." She picked up her phone and keyed in a number. "Gavin, send a message to Vauxhall Cross. Tell her affirmative and that she's to pass any information she's gathered my way asap, please."

"Do we know where Marcie is?" Miss Demure said.

"She's not at home or in Hertfordshire," Ruby Parker replied. "And her phone's switched off."

"Which means she's probably in Bedford with Fleming," Bronstein said and grinned.

"This isn't a laughing matter," Ruby Parker said.

Miss Demure sighed. "I hope she's not in any danger."

"Is it possible Fleming's working for anyone on any of the floors beneath us?" Orlov said. "I remember you saying that you don't necessarily know what the Blue Maiden is up to. Could they both be working for her?"

"Good thinking, but I've already asked. The answer's no."

"What we need is a pliable celebrity for her to talk to," Bronstein said. "Someone we already know is involved on some level, like Stallone Laine or Connie Glaser or Rick Teal. Then we just wire them up and arrange an introduction and see what emerges."

"It's a very good plan," Ruby Parker said, "but horribly long-term. And if they're suspects, they're too tightly - "

Another knock at the door.

"I'm afraid I was banking on this meeting being disrupted on a frequent basis," she said, getting up. "Yes, Gavin, what is it?"

"I thought you'd like to know we've got Nichole Moore. She's been sleeping rough for a few days on Hampstead Heath but she spent last night with her grandmother in Stamford Hill, and she persuaded her to turn herself in. They're on their way to Waterloo Bridge. She's expressed a strong desire to speak to Lieutenant Bronstein regarding a change of identity."

Ruby Parker hooted. "A change of identity? That's a bit melodramatic, isn't it? Who does she think she is?"

"You sure she wants to talk to me?" Bronstein said. "Because it's a bit of an about-turn if she does."

"She was quite adamant," Gavin said.

Bronstein shrugged and grabbed his coat.

He crossed the river by motor-launch and reached his destination in just under ten minutes. He showed his pass at the desk and a WPC escorted him to a first floor interview room outside which a middle-aged woman in a calico blouse and mules was waiting, one hand on the doorknob as if to stall his entry.

"Janine Thompson," she said, shaking his hand. "I'm a counsellor. I just thought I'd better warn you, before you go in, that Nichole's not likely to be very forthcoming. At least not today. She's still deep in shock."

"I thought she'd asked to see me?"

"I doubt it. That was probably her grandmother. I'm not saying don't interview her. You're a policeman and it's in everyone's interests to find out what happened. Just don't expect too much, that's all. Or anything."

Bronstein looked through the small window in the door. Nichole sat next to her grandmother on a plastic chair. She wore her 'Little Miss Happy' T-shirt, jeans and ballet pumps and her roots were coming through black. She stared at the ground as if she was about to retch. Her grandmother was hard-faced and miserable-looking, and probably in her mid-sixties. She wore a lime shell suit and crocs over bare feet. Bronstein knocked and opened the door.

"All right to come in?" he said as cheerily as he could. He let the counsellor in first and closed the door behind them. They sat down.

"Bronstein's a *Jewish* name, yeah?" the grandmother said. "You're a *Jew*, yeah?"

"Is that a problem?"

"Nichole told me about you. She said she'd spoken to you, and she thought you were a Jew. You are a Jew, right?"

"I am a Jew."

"Good, because it'll be a breath of fresh air for her to speak to a proper man, instead of that *fershtinkiner* she usually hangs out with. Wicca my backside, pardon the expression."

"Nichole's Jewish?"

"We need to talk about her changing her identity," her grandmother said. "If there are gangsters after her and - and she talks to you people, she'll probably need plastic surgery."

"It's a -"

"And I thought maybe you could get her into one of these tight-knit communities in Brooklyn or Miami. No one would find her there. Or Israel. She's even willing to go there, but not the West Bank. She doesn't like the ultras. She needs to be amongst people with a sense of humour, not some *schmucks* who're going to smack her head for wearing heels on Shabbat."

Bronstein trembled. "Let's take one thing at a time, shall we?"

"She needs to know if it's possible first," her grandmother said. "I don't want her *fercockt* like my daughter, God rest her soul in heaven. I want to know she's going to be taken care of."

"I give you my word," he said. He picked up one of the Tzitzyot protruding from under his shirt and made a show of clutching it. "As a Jew."

The grandmother nodded solemnly. "Good enough."

"Nichole, can I ask you about the Russian lady - "

"Are you married?" the grandmother said.

"I think we should concentrate on – no, no I'm not married."

"Do you live in a tight-knit community?"

"I live a quarter of a mile underground with a black woman."

"Well, each to his own, I suppose. So long as you're not married. It's not as if Nichole hasn't been round the block a few times. No one's perfect."

The counsellor leaned over. "I think perhaps we should leave Mr Bronstein alone with Nichole for a while."

"I always say, it's not what a couple's done that's important, it's what they're going to do. *Afh yenems tukhes is gut sepatchen*. Look to the future, don't brood on the past."

"Yes, I - "

The WPC who had accompanied Bronstein in knocked and put her head round the door. "There are some paparazzi gathering outside. I thought I'd better let you know. And the Conservatives have just been on the phone. They want to know if Nichole's okay to attend the party at 30 Millbank after the polls close tonight. I told them no. I hope that's okay."

"Sure as hell it is," Bronstein said.

"I think we'd better leave Mr Bronstein alone with Nichole, just for a few minutes," the counsellor told the grandmother again.

"That's fine by me," she said, standing up. "I'm gasping for a cigarette, anyway. Nichole doesn't smoke, though," she told Bronstein. "And she's a very good cook, and she knows how to clean - a real *Berryer* - and she loves children, and her great great grandfather – that's my grandfather – was a rabbi in Bucharest. She's going to be on *Who Do You Think You Are?* on BBC One next year. Oh, and she's had her Bat Mitzvah, she knows the names of all the Jewish festivals by heart. Tell him the names of the Jewish festivals, love, go on. Just for - "

The door closed. Nichole's grandmother obviously had more to say, but the counsellor put a friendly yet firm arm round her and guided her away.

Nichole was still looking at the ground but she was speaking now, although in a whisper. He got off his chair and crouched down next to her, so he could look into her eyes. She was crying and he could just make out her words.

"Rosh Hashanah … Aseret Yemei Teshuva … "

"Nichole?"

She looked as if she'd been switched off for a moment. Then she turned to face him, her eyes swishing as if she was trying to make him out. She put her arms round his neck and whimpered.

"Okay, okay, that's enough. Sit up. I only want you to do one thing for me - "

"Will you – will you help me?"

"I promised your grandmother. So yes."

"What about the gangsters?"

He smiled. "I'm going to get the gangsters. This Russian lady you spoke to. I'd like you to ring her back – I've got her number here – and arrange to meet. You won't have to be there, in fact I forbid it. But when she turns up we'll capture her and put her in prison."

"What if she gives me a knowing look when I take the witness stand, and I look up and there's my grandma sitting alongside that lady's cousin in the gallery with a knife to her throat?"

"We'll put your grandma in the witness protection program. You too."

His phone started ringing.

"Give me your hand," he said.

She passed her fingers. He held on to them and answered. Ruby Parker.

"Excellent news," she said. "They're both on our side, after all."

"Have you spoken to them?"

"Not yet. We got into her e-mail and we discovered a notebook in Fleming's flat detailing what they were up to, in case of an emergency. It turns out he's an inspired sleuth, a real brain. With all due respect, he'll be an excellent replacement for Jonathan assuming he agrees to join us."

"If he's been stealing files from the DVLA I shouldn't think the Met will want him any more."

"That's what I'm hoping. I've sent personnel to both their flats. We'll be dealing with them face to face before long. Incidentally, Marcie Brown's Inbox. It contained an e-mail from Jonathan to you and Orlov. It doesn't supply us with any new information, but you might like to look over it when you get back."

"To *us*? So how did it end up with her?"

"We don't know. It reads as if he was anxious when he wrote it. Speculation is he simply clicked the wrong name in his address book. Alphabetically, 'Brown, Marcie' would be just below 'Bronstein, David'."

"I guess."

"You can leave Nichole Moore now. Report back here."

He felt Nichole squeeze his hand. "Er, it may not be quite that simple."

"Lieutenant Bronstein," Ruby Parker said, "I … I …"

"Are you okay? What's the matter?"

There was silence.

"Hello?" he said, getting suddenly panicky. "Is everything all right?"

He heard her swallow. "Fine. Marcie Brown. And Nicholas Fleming. They're on the news. Sorry, I have to go."

He put his phone is his pocket, rubbed his forehead and took Nichole's other hand. "I have to leave now but I'm going to get a car to take you and your grandma to my house. It's a police-owned building, so it's guarded, and I'll be home later tonight. But don't wait up because that's how this job works. I tend to come in late. There's a double bed straight ahead as you go in. You and *Bubbe* can have that. My bedroom's on the left. There's some kosher beef and some latkes in the fridge and a whole heap of stuff in the cupboards. Help yourselves, what's mine is yours. But you don't have to. You can go home if you want, it's up to you. The Russian lady left the country. That phone call was to tell me she's been arrested in Calais. She won't be back for a long time."

She shook. "I'd – I'd like to go to your place, please."

"I'll call a car."

"Do you - think it'll be okay for me to vote Labour now?"

He laughed. "Honey, you can vote for anything. The way it works, no one can check."

She turned her eyes to full. "God can."

Chapter 24: The Obligatory Car Chase & Sundry Other Business

Marcie geared down into third and pulled out fast into the opposite lane, overtaking a Ford Ka and plonking her bumper on its headlights. An oncoming Mercedes flashed and sounded its horn.

"I always think if they've got time to do that, they've got time to slow down," she said. She put her foot down and left the Ka behind. "The trouble is, there are far too many drama queens on the road."

"I think we should - should drive to a police station," Fleming said, clutching the armrest.

"Hang on, I'm going to pull out again."

"You haven't – *room!*"

The car on the other side veered onto the pavement. But there was clear space in front of them now. She went into fourth and crushed the pedal underfoot.

"How the hell are we going to find a police station?" she said. "Do you know where there are any in Bedford?"

"I've got SatNav."

"Yes, I thought you might have." She screeched round a corner onto the wrong side of the road then accelerated. "Look, Nick. We both know those people in the Range Rover are coming after us, right? And we both know what they did to Jonathan. We'll be dead before we've opened the car doors. Besides, what's the point in going to the police station if you can get the police station to come to you?"

"*Watch out!*"

She veered to avoid a bike. "Where are they?"

"Look, this isn't a film. It may be all right for Jason Bourne to have a car chase in a built-up area, because there are never any children around when he's in town. But this is real life. How are you going to feel if you mow down a school trip?"

"I won't."

"Don't go up on the pavement again. I mean it."

"We're going to head for the motorway. Where are they?"

"They're right behind us," he said.

She looked in the mirror. "They won't take no for an answer. What the hell did you do to them, Nick? You must have really pissed them off. What the bloody hell did you do?"

"I haven't had time to find out yet. Took something. Papers."

"Whoa, hold tight!"

They mounted a roundabout and became airborne, then crash-landed with a bang on the other side. She slalomed to avoid a traffic island then sped up.

"Look out for motorway signs," she said.

"I can hear a siren."

"Good."

"M1, four miles. Pull down here."

She braked, rived the steering wheel back into line and sped up again. A stench of burning rubber puffed from the air conditioning. A bullet smashed the rear windscreen and went through the roof just in front of them.

"Get your gun out," she said. "Climb into the back. Two can play at that game."

There were more sirens now. They were on a straight road and she was doing eighty and climbing. But the Range Rover was gaining. Fleming thrust back hard against his seat and snapped it from its fixings. He climbed into the back and fired. The Range Rover's windscreen shattered.

"Hopefully the wind in their faces will be enough to stop them!" he shouted.

The Range Rover slowed for a few seconds. The passenger reached into the back and took out a pair of motorcycle helmets. They were still decelerating. He could see a pair of police cars, gaining on them. If they slowed any more, they'd be out.

But they'd seen the police too. They began to accelerate again.

"*We're coming onto the motorway!*" Marcie yelled.

She swerved into a gap in the traffic, then built the engine to a roar. In less than a minute they were doing a hundred and fifty, zig-zagging between cars and lorries on both sides. Still the Range Rover was closing fast. She looked in the mirror. The passenger was aiming a rifle. But suddenly there was a pop from the back seat and she saw him fall back with a deep split in his helmet.

"*It's kill or be killed now!*" Fleming shouted.

"*They're down to one! I bet he can't drive and shoot at the same time!*"

She was wrong. He undid his seat-belt, kept one hand on the steering wheel and reached across for the gun and fired. Their windscreen punctured with a clean hole but didn't smash. She could hear a helicopter now.

"*How about a burger?*" she yelled.

She pulled onto a slip road and went through the red light at the top without stopping. Two cars coming from opposite directions braked hard, but neither Fleming nor Marcie saw whether they hit each other. The Range Rover followed as if they weren't there. Suddenly, they were in a service station. They slowed a notch for the one way system and skidded onto the exit lane, past the petrol station and back onto the M1.

"*Sorry!*" she shouted. "*I didn't know it was a KFC!*"

"Bloody hell, I told you not to go anywhere there might be children!"

"Oh, but when I was a girl I was expected to climb the old oak and these bloody kids can't dodge a car?"

"What?"

"Nothing."

"*Keep it steady, I need to get another shot.*"

Above them, an electronic variable sign read, 'Urgent Police Warning: All Vehicles Leave Motorway at Next Available Exit.' Then the next: 'All Vehicles Follow Diversions to A1'.

"*We might have a clear road ahead!*" she shouted.

"*They'll be getting ready to throw a spike chain. Puncture our tyres!*"

"*It can't come soon enough for me! When's the next exit?*"

"*About two miles!*"

She overtook a lorry and hung there next to it till she saw the Range Rover behind her. Then she sped forward and skidded two lanes to the left and braked, allowing the lorry to overtake. Then she overtook it again. Suddenly, they were behind the Range Rover.

She tried to imagine what would happen if she rammed it. Then she had a better idea. She decelerated and overtook the lorry on the inside again. She couldn't see the Range Rover, so she guessed it must be where she'd left it, wondering what she was doing.

"*Get back in the front seat!*" she shouted to Fleming. "*Quick!*"

She pulled sharp to the right, crossing two lanes in front of the lorry and missing its bonnet by a hair's breadth. Then she slammed her brakes on. The Range Rover smashed into the back of them. The driver left his seat and flew through his empty windscreen and over their roof. They bounced as they ran over his body. Behind them, the Range Rover ploughed the crash barrier, throwing up sparks, and then tumbled over and over.

"*Good news!*" she shouted. "*There's a Burger King coming up!*"

"We've just bloody killed two men!"

She was braking now. "Don't expect me to feel any remorse, Nick. These are the people that killed my brother and they'd have killed us too if I hadn't had my wits about me." She pulled to a halt in the hard shoulder. "Sorry about your car, by the way. I hope it's insured."

He laughed. "I'll send off for a claim form when we get out of prison."

Ruby Parker was on her way to the surface of Thames House by lift. On either side of her, Terence and Mahtab hugged clipboards.

"When did it happen?" Ruby Parker said.

"About an hour ago, ma'am," Mahtab said. "Probably while you were on your way back from Cheltenham."

"We've only just found out about it," Terence said. "Apparently they tend not to broadcast these things live because they're over so quickly and there's a feeling they might inspire - "

"Where are they being held?"

"Luton, at the moment."

"Casualties?"

"Only two, from what I understand. Both drivers of the vehicle pursuing them. Both armed. So far the police are treating it as a gangland feud."

"Have the police released their names to the media?"

"So far it's just 'a man and a woman in their twenties'."

"Tell them not to. Get the Chief Constable of Bedfordshire on the line and the head of Counter Terrorism Command. Bloody hell, just as everything was starting to go right for a change. Are either of them hurt?"

"Not a scratch from what I've been told."

"There's no justice then. We're going into that van compound tonight. I want to know what's in there. Where's Colonel Orlov?"

"He's driving up there, ma'am. As ordered."

"Ordered? By whom?"

"Er, we thought you."

Fleming sat in a room with a rickety table and two plain clothes detectives, a Chief Inspector in uniform and a WPC taking notes. He had no anticipation of anything other than the hard slap of the book as they threw it at him, so he felt calmer than he had for a long time. His posture made no secret of this, and it was with difficulty that he restrained himself from drumming his fingers.

Clive and Ian didn't like him – as a matter of policy, they despised coppers gone wrong - but they admired him, he could see that. Any law-abiding citizen who shot a gang member in the head with a short-range pistol couldn't be all bad. The Chief Inspector was dying of asphyxiation caused by ever-increasing doses of incredulity.

"Even if we put aside the murder you just committed," he said, "and chalk it up as manslaughter – say, that's how the courts can finally be persuaded to see it – we've still got the fact that you hacked into the DVLA database and took information away for your own personal use, and impersonated an officer from the Department of Transport. I can't believe you just did that on a whim. It's all connected, isn't it? Now obviously you've been a bloody fool. It goes without saying you've got no future in the force, but if you at least tell us what it is you were doing, we might be able to get you *something* in the way of mitigation."

"The courts tend to be very unsympathetic towards bent coppers," Clive said.

"Thank you, Clive," Fleming replied. "I too have a rudimentary acquaintance with the *de facto* workings of the criminal justice system."

"And of course when you get inside and they find you're an ex-copper, they won't show you any mercy."

"They'll bum you to bits," Ian said. "So why not just co-operate?"

"Simply tell us what it was you were trying to do."

The Chief Inspector put his knuckles on the desk. "Look, Fleming, as far as I can tell there are only two alternatives here. One: your recent activity's in some way connected to your job, which is to bring criminals to book. We might call that the hyper-optimistic alternative, although in fairness, it may not be too generous because I've been looking at your record and everyone speaks very, very highly of you. But ... according to the second alternative, you've been led drastically astray by your girlfriend, a convicted criminal with violent tendencies, and you've ended up wallowing in sewage. Either way, the question is, what were you up to? Because the best you're looking at here is a reduction in sentence and, without your full cooperation, even that small mercy's going to elude you."

Fleming leaned forward. "I'm absolutely prepared to tell you what I was doing, but first of all I'd like you to read it for yourself. I imagine you've probably got men inside my flat now, going through my things. I'd like you to contact whoever's in charge and tell them there's a notepad sticky-taped to the underside of the shelf in my wardrobe. Ask them to remove it and fax its contents over here, then I'd like to call my lawyer."

"Wait here," the Chief Inspector said.

He left. Fleming gave in to temptation and drummed his fingers. Ian and Clive eyeballed him but didn't speak.

The Chief Inspector came back with a sigh. "There's nothing there."

"*What?* There must be! Whoever it is can't have looked hard enough. Tell him to go back and try again."

"They've had a very good look. And they've found nothing."

Fleming scowled and put his fingers to his forehead.

"Things not looking so bright now, eh, son?" Ian said.

The Chief Inspector frowned. "On the plus side, I have been ordered to stop questioning you. You're to go up to the canteen for a cup of tea and a Digestive and await further instructions. Clive and Ian will accompany you."

"What?" Fleming said. "What do you mean, 'further instructions'?"

"MI5. They'd completed a thorough search of your flat before we even knew you existed. Maybe they've got your precious notepad."

"Not that it's going to mean a damn thing," Ian said.

"You're still going down for a long, long time," Clive said.

"Actually, I wouldn't mind a nice cup of tea," Fleming said. "Not too strong, Clive, that's a good fellow. And Ian: two sugars, please."

Four doors further along the corridor, Marcie was in an identical room with two WPCs. She had a cup of orange in front of her and she felt calmer than she knew she was entitled to. The policewomen both looked as if their uniforms were designed to pad them out. There was a tape recorder on the table.

"We know all about your criminal record," the first said.

"We need you to make a statement now we've brought you a glass of orange," the second said. "Where did these two men come from? Were they friends of yours?"

"You might as well tell us everything. We've got lots of witnesses. We've got it all on camera too."

"I'd like my phone call, please," Marcie said.

The first WPC sighed. "We don't do that. You have the right to have someone notified of your arrest, but not to make a call."

"Listen, if you let me use my mobile, I'll talk. We'll all get out of here much quicker. Just one little phone call, one minute. You don't even have to leave the room."

They looked at each other.

"I'll have to ask," the first said. She got up and left the room. Two minutes later she returned with a mobile phone in each hand. "These both yours?"

"I'll take the one on the left," Marcie said. "And thank you for being so understanding."

Her heart went into her throat. She hoped he didn't have it turned off. She scrolled down the names until she came to 'B', then pressed call.

It began to ring.

"Hello?" said a voice she recognised.

"Hello, Mr Bronstein. This is Marcie Brown, you may remember me. The fact is, I've just been arrested and I'm in Bedford police station. I happen to know that you're in the CIA and you know a lot more about my brother's death than anyone's letting on, and if you don't come down here and help me out – and my boyfriend – or at least arrange for that to be done, I'm going to tell everyone here the truth about who you are and what we both know happened that night. Is that understood?"

Twenty minutes earlier, Bronstein bought an *Independent* and took the motor launch back to Thames House. He arrived to find Ruby Parker on the fourth floor, looking out of the window and wringing her hands. This was one of the conference rooms overlooking the river. It doubled as her office when she felt claustrophobic.

"We're going to raid Securitavan headquarters in Bedford," she said. "Three o'clock tomorrow afternoon. Bedfordshire Special Branch and Metropolitan Counter Terrorism Command are backing us. You're directing."

"Wouldn't it be better to strike while the iron's hot? Like ... now?"

"I've done my level best. Unfortunately, it's election day and there's a nasty little rumour going around - started by us - that there may be assassinations in the offing. All police leave has been cancelled everywhere. The security forces are literally at full stretch."

"What about the army?"

"I called the Home Office who called the Ministry of Defence. The Director of Special Forces doesn't think it's urgent enough, apparently."

"Sheesh."

"Major General Tim Reynolds. You met him at GCHQ. He's never liked me, but I made the request through the proper channels and stamped it 'urgent' so if anything goes up there tonight, he'll be the one picking shrapnel out of his face. I almost hope it does."

"Maybe that'll give us time to find out roughly what to expect, then. Have you spoken to Fleming?"

"We're about to. I've sent a helicopter."

"And Marcie?"

"I've sent Celia to get her. She has instructions to stall her, so they're coming back separately. I don't want Marcie anywhere near this, she's too involved. She's going to Afghanistan."

"That's a bit drastic, isn't it? Does she know?"

"It was her idea."

"Why do you want me to lead the operation?" Bronstein said. "Orlov's in charge."

"Not any more."

"Excuse me? What's happened to him?"

"You saw how I reacted when he broke into Slope's property in Oxfordshire, so you know how I feel about mavericks.

I specifically warned him never to try anything similar again. He said he took my point."

"I take it he's changed his mind, then."

"He's on his way to Bedford. Without any authorisation whatsoever, without filling in any of the requisite forms, without consultation, or even the pretence of seeking permission."

"Which of course means he could be about to get killed."

"You just heard me, Lieutenant Bronstein. There's no help to be had today or tonight. Besides, I've no mandate to risk the lives of my more conscientious operatives bailing out swashbucklers. Where would it stop?"

"Has it occurred to you that he might want out of MI7 even more than you presently want to see the back of him?"

"What do you mean?"

"Take a look at this." He passed her his copy of *The Independent*. "Vera Gruchov's thrown in the towel. She can't take the jibes about Tebloev any more. She wants to be above reproach."

Ruby Parker scoffed. "She's hardly cut out for politics then, poor petal. What's this to do with Orlov?"

"Permission to speak frankly."

She narrowed her eyes. "Granted …"

"I recall you saying that Orlov shouldn't act recklessly. I also remember what you said when you welcomed us to MI7. I quote: 'It's your investigation. After you've left my office, you'll run it yourselves. I expect to be kept informed, of course, and I'll offer advice on request, but I won't interfere'."

She blinked slowly. "I did say that, yes."

"On the other hand, you know how Britain works, you know how MI7 works, you know the acronyms and initialisms – GCHQ, SO15, SO13, JIC, DIS - you know who works here by name and rank and all the codes and protocols, White Maiden, Blue Maiden, Grey Maiden. You know the job intimately enough to inhabit it. There's no way we can compete with that, and for the record, we wouldn't have made a third the progress we have if you'd kept your word. But ... the last thing you had him do was interview a goddamn taxi driver."

She sat down and looked at the table.

Bronstein sat next to her. "You saw how quiet he was in our last meeting. He hardly spoke two words. He wants to go home. On any terms."

"You're ... sure?"

"He hasn't told me straight, but he's no fool. Like you say, you made it clear to him what would happen if he took matters into his own hands again. He won't be expecting you to overlook it if it all ends happily. You didn't last time."

She sighed. "I wanted so much to keep him here."

"He won't stay. He's not a team player in the sense that you understand it."

"What other sense is there?"

"Someone who forges ahead without waiting for the green light then wins a medal. They do it because they see things the team can't. And thanks to what they achieve, there's still something left to call a team."

"I still don't understand what this story about Vera Gruchov has to do with anything."

"He's the kind of guy who likes to support his friends. And when your friends are retreating, the best thing you can do is get back and man the barricades. I bet he worked out we wouldn't be able to get any manpower tonight."

"I've never been in this position before. It's utterly unprecedented. I hope to God there isn't a national emergency."

"Can't you call on one of the other Maidens? The Blue, say, or the Grey?"

"It doesn't work like that. Even if it were permissible - which it isn't – they only have their own remits, they don't have their own private armies."

"Pity."

She ran her hands through her hair. "Should we go and help him, do you think?"

"You and me?"

She shrugged. "Everyone else is on duty."

"I'll tell you what. I want you to get on to the Russian embassy and negotiate concessions for Orlov's return. Strictly hypothetical. Don't concede an inch. I'll wait for Fleming and we'll put our heads together over what we've got. We'll keep the helicopter here and our phones on, and if we so much as hear a squeak from Bedford, we'll pounce."

"It's a long time since I was in the field."

"Don't build your hopes up. Orlov's a Russian, he'll blend in. Me? I don't speak the language, yet I might just pass if I keep schtum. But a middle-aged black woman with a penchant for skirt-suits? That may be stretching things a bit."

"We'll see. When Fleming arrives, he'll come straight to me. He'll need briefing and inducting. If he agrees to join us, which he will, his working day starts now and for as long as you need him. Where will you be?"

His phone started to ring. He looked at it. "That's odd ... it's from – Jonathan?"

Ruby Parker smiled. "So she found his phone, eh? I was half expecting this. Put it on speakerphone, let's see how she plays it."

"Hello?" he said.

"Hello, Mr Bronstein. This is Marcie Brown, you may remember me. The fact is, I've just been arrested and I'm in Bedford police station. I happen to know that you're in the CIA and you know a lot more about my brother's death than anyone's letting on, and if you don't come down here and help me out – and my boyfriend – or at least arrange for that to be done, I'm going to tell everyone here the truth about who you are and what we both know happened that night. Is that understood?"

Bronstein grinned. "We're on our way, baby." He pressed 'end call' and turned to Ruby Parker. "You've got to admit, she's got balls."

"Well, well, well, the little minx. I'd better let Celia know."

"I'm not in the CIA, though. Where the hell did she get that idea?"

Marcie put the phone down on the table. That was it, then. A cute little quip from Mr Bronstein and the ropes were cut. What the hell had she been expecting? Yes, she could tell everyone all about him and what really happened to Jonathan, but no one would even care. She was a criminal, for God's sake. She was in here because she'd broken the law. All anyone here was interested in was where did these two men come from and were they friends of yours. She might as well get the statement over and done with. God, she hoped they hadn't told her parents yet.

The door opened and a uniformed policeman put his head in and swept his eyes from one WPC to the other. "Could I have a word, please? Outside?"

The first WPC swept up the mobile phones.

The man grinned. "It's okay, neither of you is in trouble."

They went outside and Marcie heard them walk away. She wondered how long it would be till she could slit her wrists, have done with it. Her whole life had been one long failure and she'd sown disaster wherever she went. She'd always hoped that as she got older, things would get better. They hadn't. They'd got worse. Wherever Nick was now, he was almost certainly wishing he'd never met her.

Maybe if she killed herself, she could be with Jonathan again. She was crying uncontrollably now, leaning forward in her chair as the tears splashed everywhere like some kind of Chinese water torture.

"Please don't be upset, my dear," someone said.

She looked up.

Miss Demure?

It was. In a cream blouse and a beige skirt and new shoes. What the hell - ?

She wiped her eyes. Bloody hell. "Did – did Daddy send you?"

Miss Demure smiled. "Sir Anthony has us to thank for the death of his only son. We'd rather not add the incarceration of his daughter and the probable loss of his parliamentary seat to our list of credits. He knows nothing about this, nor is he ever likely to."

"What? What do you mean? I don't understand."

"The truth is, Marcie, I haven't been entirely above board with you. Ever. I'm not a gymnastics teacher, I'm a senior training officer for MI6. Your brother recommended you to us and we've been very impressed with you. We persuaded the police to desist from their enquiries on the grounds that when we get you into a mess, we get you out. Usually. Anyway, we got you into this one, make no mistake. Shall we go?"

Marcie stood up. She felt light headed. "What - what about Nick?"

"I understand you've been on the phone to Lieutenant Bronstein. He says he admires your chutzpah, although we all know no one would believe you or care if you were to carry out your threat. Your boyfriend's on the way to London. We're very interested in both of you. Now come along, I'm sure you've got lots of questions."

Chapter 25: Fleming at Thames House

Bronstein waited in his office for thirty minutes looking at Orlov's empty seat and scrutinising Securitavan headquarters on Google Maps, when there was a knock at the door. Fleming came in, followed by Ruby Parker.

"I believe you've already met," she said. "David, I'm delighted to say Nicholas will be joining us. You'll be working together for the foreseeable future. You're in charge, David, and I've briefed Nicholas on the details of the case."

The two men shook hands. "Welcome to the revolution," Bronstein said.

"I'm heading off to vote," Ruby Parker said, pulling on a pair of gloves. "Then I'm going home. Nicholas, have you voted yet?"

"This morning before I set off for Bedford."

"You're in no rush to get away, then. If you need to contact me, you know where I am."

She closed the door as she left. Bronstein indicated Orlov's chair and the two men sat facing each other across the joined desks.

"You've been inside the compound," Bronstein said. "What did you find out?"

"Very little. I only looked in one warehouse, but I chose it at random. No guns, no sign of anything suspicious, except they seemed pretty cheesed off to see me."

"What do you think annoyed them?"

"I don't know why they seemed so riled to begin with, except that they were busy. Then I got the crazy feeling the fellow showing me around was pointing a gun from inside his pocket. I realised mine had the safety catch on, so I took it out and undid it. They'd been watching me by CCTV – I didn't realise till afterwards."

"So you had a weapon. That's no reason to chase you along a freeway with a bolt-action rifle. There must be more. You must have stumbled on something important."

"I was a witness – or as near as wasn't worth taking a chance over – to the killing of Ivan Ryazantsev. They must have deduced from my gun that I didn't belong to the Department of Transport, which meant I must be working undercover. The fact that I'd witnessed a murder meant I was probably in a position to bring the roof down on their heads. What do we know about Securitavan? I mean, have we got a list of its recent and pending contracts?"

"If only. We only really latched on to them this morning. Since then, we've been trying to hack into their computer."

"And?"

"And we don't think they've even got one. If they have, it's not networked. We're guessing they do things the old-fashioned way, pen and paper."

"There's one other thing. While I was in there, I managed to get a look inside the back of one of the vans. It had a false ceiling. Some of the panels had come away, and there was a big gap between that and the actual ceiling."

"Which probably indicates smuggling. So we need to watch for them going abroad. Anything else?"

"There were some scraps of paper on the floor. I didn't get a proper look but looked like leaflets. Roughly identical, about A5 size, crumpled. Something left over from a previous job maybe. I scooped up a few and put them in my briefcase."

"Where are they now?"

"Still in the back of the car my girlfriend wrote off, hopefully. Ruby Parker's been on to Bedford constabulary, but they shipped it to the scrap depot when we told them to stop the investigation. They're going to fax us the contents as soon as they've retrieved them."

"A bunch of Pizzaland flyers, maybe?"

Fleming looked at the table and folded his arms. "That's a very good point, actually. No, no, they weren't."

Bronstein grinned. "Hey, I was joking."

"Sorry, yes, I realise that. I meant your standard commercial flyer would be three hundred grams per square metre silk art board, or similar. One hundred and thirty grams minimum. But these can't have been any more than seventy."

"So ... just normal paper, yes?"

"But if you can't afford better than normal paper, you probably wouldn't hire a company like Securitavan to do your deliveries."

"Assuming they *were* deliveries. Let's not get carried away."

There was a knock at the door. Gavin entered with a sheaf of papers. "These have just arrived for Inspector Fleming, sir. Courtesy of Bedford police."

"Talk about expert timing," Bronstein said. "Spread them on the floor, Gavin. And make mine a twelve-inch Margherita, please."

Gavin fanned them out and they gathered round to see. It took them a few moments to recognise what they were looking at, then they stood stupefied.

Ballot papers with the names of parliamentary candidates down the left hand side and a cross next to a different name on each.

"You don't think someone could be trying to rig the General Election, do you?" Bronstein said eventually.

Ruby Parker went back to her office and put her coat on. She thought she'd give the potted plants some water before she went home – the Peace Lily was looking a little thirsty – so she took out the plastic bottle she kept in her drawer. Mahtab knocked on the door.

"Message for you, ma'am. There are some solicitors waiting to see you at Waterloo Bridge."

"Solicitors? In connection with what?"

"Representing Slope Enterprises. They're alleging police harassment."

She chuckled. "They must have a pretty slim case then. Who sent them?"

"Lionel Edgeware, I believe."

"Ah." She screwed the top back on the bottle. "Mahtab, if you're going past the kitchen, would you mind running a drop of fresh water in here and putting it in my pigeonhole for tomorrow morning? This, I've got to hear."

She considered driving herself, but a chauffeur would make it look as if she was someone to be reckoned with, so she asked Terence. She arrived at the police station five minutes later. Terence accompanied her upstairs, carrying her briefcase.

They were waiting for her in the foyer: two men in charcoal suits like advertising executives, both in their early fifties, one thin, the other thinner.

"Ruby Parker?" the thin one said.

"I am Ruby Parker. What do you want?"

He took a sealed envelope from his inside jacket pocket. "We represent Steven and Goldsmith, corporate lawyers. We've been instructed by our client to issue you with this."

She took it without looking at it. "I'm a busy woman, gentlemen. I hope you're prepared to summarise its contents."

"To begin with, it alleges institutional harassment of individuals under contract to Sockpuppets, a theatrical agency owned, until recently, by Constantine Slope and now under the temporary direction of Mr Lionel Edgeware, MP. It contains an itemised list of dates on which you pulled clients of the firm in for questioning, including principally, Nichole Moore, who we've been given to understand has now been with you for five hours without charges being pressed. We need to know where she is and how to contact her."

Ruby Parker laughed. "She's not with me."

"You're sure about that? Because you should really file another missing persons report if you think she's genuinely gone astray again."

"Just because I personally don't know where she is, that doesn't make her a missing person. Someone has to report her missing."

"In that case, I hereby report Nichole Moore as missing."

Ruby Parker held his eyes. "You'd better go downstairs and file a missing persons report, then."

"Except that we all know where she is, don't we? You're holding her."

"Why don't you phone her?"

"Because we both know she's not in possession of her mobile. The taxi driver's witness statement makes that abundantly clear. What's going on, Ms Parker?"

"You think I'm interrogating her? What do you think I imagine she's able to tell me?"

"She was due to attend a victory party at Conservative Campaign Headquarters after the close of polls tonight. When a party representative rang this address to confirm, earlier today, he was told in no uncertain terms she would not be available. We have a recording of that conversation. We allege that the police officer who gave the assurance – and we would like to know her name – had no time to consult with Miss Moore with a view to obtaining her consent or refusal."

She took a breath. "I didn't know that."

"She's not at home and neither is her grandmother. Her boyfriend doesn't know where she is and neither do any of her friends or relatives. If this sort of thing was to happen in a developing country, Ms Parker, one would probably describe it as scandalous."

"Is that all?"

"By no means. Mr Edgeware has also been given to understand that an official claiming to be from the Department of Transport paid a visit to the Bedford Headquarters of Securitavan this morning, another Slope company. He wishes it to be known that he is in possession of CCTV footage of the gentleman in question, and if it subsequently turns out that he is a member of the police force or the security services, he will make life very awkward for you."

"As far as I'm aware, most of Slope's companies were shell corporations. They're hardly worth making anyone's life 'very awkward' for."

"You're prevaricating, Ms Parker. If you suspect any wrongdoing on our client's part, you should have taken it up with the Director of Public Prosecutions long ago."

She smiled. "I'm sure 'very awkward' isn't a legal term either. What exactly does Mr Edgeware want from me?"

The two men looked at each other. "I believe Mr Edgeware is particularly concerned that Securitavan should be allowed to fulfil its contractual obligations tonight unhindered by interference from the law enforcement authorities. He's been given to understand - by a source whose identity we're not at liberty to disclose - that you were planning a raid on the company's central office in Bedford tonight."

She flashed with rage. "Major General Tim Reynolds, well I never."

"You may or may not be aware that Mr Edgeware has devoted a considerable amount of time and energy to persuading the Chair of the Electoral Commission that Securitavan's irreproachability more than qualifies it for the minor task of transporting ballot boxes from polling stations, under the auspices of the various Presiding Officers, to Returning Officers at the Count Centres. He's staked what remains of his... slightly tarnished reputation - after the expenses scandal - on the notion that here is a company that can deliver significant goods in the public interest. The service is free, but its advertisement value is worth millions, and of course, if you sabotage it, you could find yourself footing a very large bill."

Ruby Parker handed the envelope they'd given her back to them. "I hope you didn't spend too much of your valuable time and money making that document up, gentlemen, because tomorrow morning, the boot's likely to be on the other foot. Incidentally, don't forget to fill in that missing persons form before you leave. You might as well waste a little more of your day."

When Marcie and Miss Demure went outside, there was a black Jaguar waiting. The chauffeur got out and opened the rear doors for them. They left Bedford by the same route Marcie had driven with Fleming earlier, and she saw her tyre tracks on the roundabout where they'd momentarily become airborne.

When they got onto the motorway it was relatively traffic-free, and the driver accelerated to a hundred and twenty in virtual silence. At one point, they passed a police car in the slow lane. It looked for a moment as if it was about to give chase, but then thought better of it and slipped off sheepishly at a junction.

"Where are we going?" Marcie asked.

"London. I told you. Slow down, Tomlinson, please. You'll cause an accident."

"Whereabouts in London?"

"To meet your new employer, hopefully."

"Who were those men that were chasing Nick and I?"

"We don't know yet. Have you voted?"

"No."

"We'll stop off in Hertfordshire then. I don't want your parents to think we don't care. Tomlinson, did you hear that? We're taking a diversion to Hertford."

"Very good, Madam," he said.

"Do you know Daddy well?" Marcie asked.

"I met him for the first time in connection with you. We haven't met since."

"Is Celia Demure your real name?"

"I never disclose my real name. I've too many enemies, and if I don't tell you it, you can never give it away."

"Did you ever meet Jonathan?"

"Yes, and I liked him very much."

"Do you think he died ... heroically?"

"He died trying to save an innocent woman, after attempting to get vital information to his fellow operatives. In the armed services, he'd probably have been awarded a medal. So yes, indubitably."

"Would you mind telling my parents that?"

Miss Demure put her head on one side and smiled. "They know he died in the course of duty, don't they? Surely, that's the important thing."

"Actually, they think he murdered Jilly Bestwick then threw himself off a cliff."

She sat up. "I - I beg your pardon?"

"After he died, Mummy went to see the Beachy Head Chaplaincy. They told her he'd been found broken to bits on the coastline with a gun on him."

Miss Demure closed her eyes and put her hand to her mouth. "Oh, good God, your poor parents. I'm so, so sorry." She leaned forward. "Tomlinson, speed up, please. Forget about Hertford. Make straight for Thames House."

Chapter 26: Bedford then Kafka

Bedford. The train smoothed to a halt and the doors swished open. Orlov stepped out at the back of a crowd which immediately dispersed to the station exit. Ideally, he knew he should wait for dark, but lighting-up time was still some four or five hours away, and once Ruby Parker worked out what he was up to, she'd undoubtedly try to pre-empt him. The longer he waited, the longer it gave her. And that would mean endangering more lives. No, it had to be now.

It was a quiet afternoon. Commuters returned home and all the platforms were busy. Next to where Orlov stood, a man with a golf umbrella sat on his suitcase and ate a toasted sandwich. The smell of fried bread drifted. The metal benches were all occupied with people reading tabloids or scrolling menus on phones. In the eaves, sparrows chattered and bobbed.

He switched on his mobile just long enough to locate the Securitavan headquarters. Four miles as the crow flies. He had a plan now. Not a very novel one, but originality wasn't the greatest virtue in a situation like this. Sometimes you had to play it by the manual. He bought a packet of cigarettes and a lighter in the newsagent's and slipped them into his pocket for later.

It took him forty-five minutes to reach the company's perimeter fence. It stood in the heart of a housing estate through which one main road ran in an arc. He didn't intend to circumnavigate the compound in one movement, that would be too conspicuous. There were six side roads leading up to it. He'd do a bit of walking, he'd do part of it by taxi, watch out for a bus that ran by, borrow a bike if possible. He looked at the satellite picture on his phone. About an hour probably, all told, then he'd act. He checked his pockets: wire-clippers, binoculars and gun still intact.

Ninety minutes later, he had a more detailed plan. He'd seen the workers up close. They wore overalls, but there was apparently no uniform version. He took a taxi to a builders' merchant in Bedford and brought some for himself, half a litre of engine oil to sully them with and a cap to conceal his face from above where the cameras probably were. He changed, and fastened his coat over the top and returned by bus.

There were six numbered warehouses backing onto a wire netting fence. A footpath ran alongside it with windowless house-ends on the far side. A witch hazel grew on the grass between the path and the fence. He waited till the coast was clear, slipped into the foliage and cut a hole in the wire behind it.

No doubt they'd heard what had happened to their friends in the Range Rover by now, and were anticipating a visit from the police. The gates were open to make it look like nothing was amiss. If there was anything illegal in here, it would be well hidden by this time. He crept along the space between warehouses five and six.

He could hear voices. He was expecting Russian but it wasn't a language he recognised. Something Slavic. Not Polish. He knew a bit of Polish from his stint on the border, an age ago. More South Slavic – Bulgarian, maybe, or Serbo-Coatian? He hoped they weren't all from the same area. He'd banked on Russian. Without it he might as well go back to Thames House.

Then suddenly he heard his own language.

"What are you two men doing? Get back to work, we've no time to hang around. You! You should be packing! Get on with it!"

He heard them shuffle off. Whoever they were, at least they understood the language. Perhaps the Russians were in charge.

He took out his cigarettes and lit one and stepped out of the gap.

"You!" the foreman yelled. "What are you doing?"

"Sorry, boss, cigarette break," Orlov replied. He held out the packet. "Want one?"

"Just get back to work. What are you supposed to be doing?"

"Packing. But we just finished."

"Follow those two then. And give me those cigarettes, the packet."

Orlov handed the cigarettes over with a shrug. He stamped out the one he was smoking and jogged slightly to catch up with the two packers.

"He's a miserable bloody sod, isn't he?" he said.

They sighed and turned right into warehouse three. Two rows of twenty vans stood with their open rear doors facing each other. Inside each vehicle, ceiling panels had been removed, and men were stuffing crumpled wads of paper into the cavities by the fistful. Orlov looked up. CCTV, pointing right at him.

He pulled down his cap and climbed into the van his companions had just entered. He grabbed some wads of paper – men were handing them inside now – and began to thrust them into the cavities.

One of the papers floated to the floor. He picked it up.

A ballot paper with the names of parliamentary candidates down the left hand side and a cross next to Charles Landon, Liberal Democrat.

He heard a gun cock and looked up.

Valentin Tebloev in a blue business suit, pointing a revolver at him and glowering. Behind him, yet others were aiming rifles.

"We've been watching out for you all day," Tebloev said. "It's a good thing you arrived when you did, you almost missed the whole thing."

Fleming sat next to Bronstein, reading a PDF file called 'Handbook For Polling Station Staff: Supporting a UK Parliamentary Election'. The phone on Bronstein's desk rang.

"Hi."

"Ruby Parker here."

"You don't sound very happy. What's up?"

"I'll ask you this once. Where's Nichole Moore?"

"At my place. I hope."

"Well now, that's what I call a fast mover," she said superciliously. "And completely unethical. From what I understand, David, she's deep in shock - "

"Hold your horses, you've got the wrong end of the reins. She's scared to go home because she's petrified, period. I told her she could crash at my place, and for your information, her grandma's there too. They're Jewish and they appealed to me as a son of Abraham. The way things are panning out, I'm not likely to get home tonight anyway."

He heard her sigh. "I - apologise. I've just had Vholes and bloody Tulkinghorn in my face, wanting to know where the hell she is."

"Who are Vholes and Tulkinghorn?"

"*Bleak House*. Except in this case, they've joined forces to represent Slope's interests."

"So they're looking for Nichole, eh? What do you think they want to find her for? Find out whether she's sung is my guess. Same reason they'd have wanted to find Jilly Bestwick under similar circumstances."

"You think she's in danger?"

"I'll give my flat a ring, check she made it over there. I'd be surprised if she didn't. I sent her by police car."

"*What?* Why didn't you tell me any of this?"

"You were a bit put out by Orlov, last I saw of you. And relatively speaking, it didn't seem to count for much. She was scared, I took care of her. She's okay. Let's prioritise."

"Have you heard from him?"

"Not a squeak. Listen, Fleming and I think they may be about to rig the General Election."

"Nice idea but it's impossible."

"Famous last words?"

"I had the same thought myself ... for about ten seconds. Apparently, Securitavan is contracted to transport ballot boxes from polling stations to count centres tonight. Probably not all of them – there are in excess of two and a half thousand – but a fair number."

"And that doesn't set alarm bells ringing with you?"

"The polling officer has to close the ballot box at the end of the poll with a certified seal in the presence of officials. He or she is then obliged to deliver it - usually no more than four or five miles down the road - to the Returning Officer in person. At no point between A and B is he allowed to leave the box unattended, otherwise it becomes void. You'd have to bribe an awful lot of very respectable people to interfere with that."

"You remember those pieces of paper Fleming gathered up in Bedford? They were crossed parliamentary ballot slips. Stamped with an official perforation in the top left-hand corner."

He heard her gasp and step up her pace. "I'm on my way back."

Celia Demure ordered the car to stop on the threshold of Thames House. She turned to Marcie. "We call this 'The Castle'. Have you ever read any Franz Kafka, my dear? The fact is no one knows quite what goes on here and once you're truly inside, you can never, ever leave."

Marcie shrugged. "Suits me."

"Drive in, Tomlinson."

They drove in at walking pace. They were just in time to see Ruby Parker entering in a hurry through the main doorway.

"Speak of the devil," Miss Demure said. "Stop the car, Tomlinson, there's a good man. Take Miss Brown through to reception and wait for me. This shouldn't take long."

She saw Ruby Parker take the stairs. She guessed she was heading for the third floor, so she walked into the open lift and pressed 3. The doors opened just as Ruby Parker was passing.

"Marcie Brown's here to see you," Miss Demure said.

Ruby Parker stopped and looked around, then saw the speaker. "Celia? What are you doing back so early? I thought we agreed you were going to Hertford to see - "

"I was, yes. But then Marcie told me something that persuaded me taking the long way round wasn't the kindest option."

"What do you mean?"

"Her mother thinks Jonathan killed Jilly Bestwick then committed suicide."

"I beg your pardon? But he didn't."

"But that's what Kramski wanted us to think, and it turns out he's succeeded with the very person that information is likely to hurt most. Can you imagine what it must be like, thinking your son's a murderer and that he committed suicide rather than face the consequences?"

"I don't understand how - "

"She spoke to the Beachy Head Chaplaincy the night of his death."

Ruby Parker closed her eyes and massaged her forehead. "I'm really – I'm in the middle of what could be a national catastrophe here, Celia. I admit I've botched this badly. I'll go and see her parents first thing tomorrow. But right now - "

"I'm afraid that's not good enough, Ruby."

Ruby Parker frowned and threw up her hands. "It'll have to be. What more can I do?"

"I don't want to hear, 'she's too involved' any more. I want her in on this case as of this minute. From what I understand, you need all the help you can get. And if she's going to Afghanistan, she needs you as much as you need her. In any case, you owe her hugely, and this is where you start making reparations."

"She's still determined to go to Afghanistan, I take it."

"She's still perfectly willing."

"Willing, Celia, or eager? Have you ever stopped to wonder why – despite everything in the news about car bombs and soldiers coming home in coffins – she's so desperate to get into the combat zone?"

"You have me at a disadvantage, as you English say."

"I've done a thorough background check on that girl. It's not the slightest wonder she's gone off the rails. What's amazing is that she's still sane."

"She is what she is. If you persist in saying no, you can expect my written notice on your desk by eight am tomorrow. Not only that. I'll sit up all night composing the letter. It'll be the most detailed letter of resignation anyone's ever written or read."

"You really feel that strongly about it?"

"I don't like it when we make mistakes. And this is a big one."

Ruby Parker sighed. "Send her upstairs then. We'll be in Room N11. And bring yourself."

Bronstein and Fleming appeared from the conference room, just as Miss Demure pressed a button and disappeared behind the lift doors.

"We think we've discovered what they're up to," Bronstein said.

"Go back to N11. We've a new recruit. Is it serious?"
"More than you can possibly imagine," Fleming said.

Chapter 27: Kramski Opens Up

They tied Orlov's hands and three men in their early thirties, plus Tebloev, took him to the first floor of the office compound. He was thrust into a room with a filing cabinet, a fax machine and a computer on which a screensaver was playing the Windows logo back and forth. Box files stood haphazardly on shelves and a desk backed onto a large single-paned window.

Tebloev waved his pistol. "Sit down, Colonel."

Orlov did as he was told. The three men went into the filing cabinet and took out several coils of rope. They spent the next few minutes tying Orlov to the chair. They were in no hurry. They left when they'd done an expert job, and closed the door behind them.

"Comfortable?" Tebloev said.

"I've felt worse," Orlov replied. "So what now?"

"Relax, no one's going to hurt you. We're your friends in here, all of us."

Orlov looked down at his ropes. "Odd way to treat me, then."

"Just because we like you, it doesn't mean you reciprocate. We're well enough acquainted with you to recognise that."

"So what's going on here?"

"We're going to fix the British election."

"A tall order. Why?"

Tebloev stood up and went to the window. "It's quite complicated. I've never really been one for long explanations. We'd like you to join us, by the way."

"I don't even know who you are."

"I'll take that to imply you're keeping an open mind."

"I know enough about you to say no."

Tebloev chuckled. "That, I doubt."

"I know you killed Jonathan Hartley-Brown, Jilly Bestwick, Zane Cruse and a whole raft of press photographers. Innocent people."

The door opened and a tall man with a cuboid jaw and hard eyes entered. Kramski himself, dressed in overalls, like Orlov. He rubbed oil off his hands with a cloth. He looked vacantly at the prisoner then turned to Tebloev. "Let me talk to the Colonel, Valentin. He's not likely to get much sense out of you."

"I've already told him I'm not one for long explanations," Tebloev said.

"You may as well go back to London now. There's only the driving left for us to do. We should be all finished up here by eleven."

Tebloev got up with a sigh. "I suppose to divert suspicion from myself ... "

Kramski shook his hand. "You've been very helpful throughout this whole thing. I'm not sure we could have done it without you. In fact, we couldn't. Thank you again."

Tebloev closed the door behind him. Orlov heard him descending the stairs.

Kramski sat down. "I don't know whether Valentin told you we'd like you to join us? I don't suppose that means much at present, of course. I'm sure you have very little idea who we are."

"One can tell a tree by its fruits."

"And every tree that bringeth not forth good fruit is hewn down and cast into the fire, eh? Are you a Christian, Colonel?"

"No."

"A shame. It might have made my task easier. You're a Muslim, I take it?"

"I'm an atheist."

"That must have been a source of unease for your wife. She was a practising Sunni, wasn't she?"

"Let's cut the chit-chat."

"I'm not one of those who hates Chechens, incidentally. Quite the contrary. The war's over now, but it was a stupid waste of life provoked by the Kremlin."

Orlov had no reply to this. He wasn't even sure one was required.

"What do you think of Russia, Colonel?" Kramski asked.

Orlov paused. "I - "

"You see, it's quite difficult, isn't it? Whenever I ask any decent Russian that question, the reaction's always the same. There are lots of reasons to love it. Our history, our geography, our religions, our architecture, our traditions, our culture. But then there's the Mafia and the Kremlin and the racism and the fact that it's as good a place as any to fleece honest, decent people and set yourself up as a tin pot dictator."

"And you propose to get rid of the bad and keep the good, do you?"

"There would nothing interesting or original about that. It's the world's oldest, most widespread ambition."

"It's the way you propose to do it then."

"If you'd looked into the family trees of the men you killed in Constantine Slope's house in Oxfordshire, you'd have emerged with a clue."

"There never was a Constantine Slope, was there?"

"Oh, there was. Only he's not called Constantine Slope. Someone had to coordinate all this and he's about the right age. He's left the country now, I believe."

"What 'clue'?"

"We're all descended from the nobles of old Russia. Pre-1917 Russia."

Orlov laughed. "I don't believe it. You're going to tell me you've found Anastasia, last of the Romanovs, aren't you?"

Kramski grinned. "Pretty much, yes. Although it's not quite that simple. You see, it doesn't matter whether we have or not. What's important is that we can get people to believe we have."

"Why would you want to?"

"We'll come to that later."

"Presumably, to pull it off, you'll have to control the state media."

"On the contrary. We simply have to control the evidence."

"Fabricate it, you mean."

"There's an old philosophical thought experiment, Colonel. I'm sure you've heard of it. It says, Imagine the world came into existence ten seconds ago, complete with everything you see around you, including you and what you now think are your memories. How would you ever know?"

"I'm not sure what you're trying to say."

"The world could be full of manufactured facts, for all we know. A fabrication that no one knows is such and which no one can discover is such – for all practical purposes that's the same thing as a hard fact, isn't it?"

"It's a pretty difficult stunt to pull off, though."

"But of course you *would* think that, because you only ever heard of the failures. If you only ever hear of X in association with Y, after a while you come to think all X's must be Y. But don't you see? Where Y equals 'unveiling', the situation's completely different."

"I'm missing something here. History lessons when I was at school weren't exactly impartial, but I've never yet found reason to revise the view that the Romanovs were a gang of dim-witted anti-semites."

Kramski beamed. "I entirely agree."

"So why would anyone want to resurrect them?"

"Not to give them any real power, that's for sure."

"Which is no answer."

"It's where the Church comes in."

Orlov smiled. "So you want a theocracy now, as well."

"We want a liberal democracy. But there has to be an absolute standard for public life. People may not adhere to it – that's in the nature of democracy: people are people. But unless they know what that standard is, your democracy lacks justice. Which is precisely the problem with the present setup."

"And the Church is going to provide that standard, is it?"

"'The Lord said, "Look, I am setting a plumb line among my people Israel".' The Orthodox Church has always required a monarch at its apex. It was designed that way from the days of the Romans. Ours would merely be constitutional."

"I've still no idea why you want to rig the British general election."

"You must have. The British have what we want, but they're losing it. This is designed to restore it and spread a fashion for it across Europe. Prepare the ground."

"I'm still in the dark, I'm afraid."

"The British, Colonel Orlov, have lost their plumb line. Their politicians have their snouts in troughs of swindled expenses, their senior executives are given huge bonuses for failing, their journalists are either stymied by defamation laws to the point where Britain's actually become a global centre for libel tourism or they're hacking into people's phones, they've flushed their manufacturing base down the toilet and what's taken its place is a nothing run by armies of nobodies. Shall I go on?"

"And yet they've got a national church headed by a constitutional monarch."

"Our purpose is simply to complete the process of disillusionment by ordinary people with their putative rulers. Once they discover the election's been manipulated, their faith in parliament will finally crash. It will throw them back onto the one person in this country who's widely considered beyond reproach."

"Only a foreigner could think the British see the Queen as irreproachable."

"Even only relatively speaking, she is."

"There are lots of Republicans out there."

"We're not talking about what *is*, Colonel. We're talking of what's to come. Republicans come and go. By and large, they lack a plumb line."

"Well, assuming you get your way, we'll see, I suppose. Who's going to be the monarch in your new Russia, by the way? Difficult post to fill, I'd imagine."

"Haven't you guessed? It's why we thought you'd join us."

"Surprise me."

"Why, Vera Gruchov, of course."

"Vera Gruchov?"

"We'll be 'going public', as the phrase has it, in 2017, for obvious reasons. So there's lots of time. Of course, she doesn't know it yet. We've been grooming her for years."

"I … I see."

"Think about it for a moment. It's inconceivable that someone like her could have come this far under her own steam. All those complaints she's made about what happened to poor Mikhail Beketov, all that railing against corruption in the Mossovet, all that standing up for Chechens and Nenets and Gypsies and speaking out against skinheads? No, without us to protect her, the FSB would have had her hide for new boots years ago. She's entirely our creation."

"And – that's why she withdrew from the Mayoral election?"

"Simply a piece of theatre designed to fix her moral irreproachability in the minds of ordinary people. Yes, Tebloev had to take a bit of a fall, but he's an idealist so he didn't object. Of course, if we'd let her run, she'd have won by a landslide. That would have been bad news for us. The last thing we want is her getting her hands dirty with the day-to-day business of real politics."

"The last thing, yes."

"I can't help feeling you're disappointed with her."

Orlov looked at the floor.

"I take it you're not prepared to join us, even after all I've told you."

Orlov shook his head. "No."

Kramski shrugged. "I may have murdered a lot of people to get here, Colonel, but I'm not a natural killer. I'm a soldier just like you and I fight to defend the cause I serve. Whether you join us or not, I'm not going to kill you. None of us is. Do you know why? Because even if you were to tell Vera Gruchov all about us, she wouldn't believe you. Secondly, I know that you will join us. Maybe not today, maybe not even next year. But there's a long time to go till 2017. You will relent."

He left the room and went downstairs. Outside, Orlov could hear the vans starting up. They started to peep their horns all together.

He assumed they were celebrating.

Chapter 28: Call for the Cavalry

Ruby Parker followed Bronstein and Fleming into the conference room and they sat down. Gavin took a chair at one of the tables with the pile of faxes he had just gathered. It was seven o'clock. Outside, the rush-hour traffic on the embankment was starting to thin. In bars, restaurants and takeaways, men and women in company uniforms exchanged shifts. Random street lights came on early.

The door opened and Miss Demure entered, followed by Marcie. The two women drew level and Miss Demure put her hand lightly on the younger's back. The men stood up.

"Marcie," Miss Demure said, "you already know Mr Bronstein and Mr Fleming. This is Gavin Potter, and this is Ruby Parker, your new employer. For reasons she'll explain later, we sometimes refer to her as the Red Maiden. Ruby, gentlemen: Marciella Hartley-Brown, or as she prefers, Marcie Brown."

They exchanged handshakes.

"Nice tan," Bronstein said. "Been away?"

"I've been going to the solarium," Marcie replied.

Everyone sat down again.

"I believe Mr Bronstein and Mr Fleming are just about to tell us what those men in the Range Rover wanted," Miss Demure said.

The two men looked at each other to decide precedence.

"Some of this is speculative," Bronstein said. "But not much. Would you like to kick off, Nicky?"

Fleming folded his hands. "Securitavan declared itself *Bona Vacantia* last year. Its assets then passed to the Crown under section 1012 of the Companies Act 2006. No debts, no liabilities, no one sought redress. It's fully functioning – just ownerless. Investigations are ongoing. Word is that the workers want to buy it out – that's probably just a smokescreen - but it's presently owned by the Crown."

Bronstein picked up a sheet of paper. "Parts of the company were secured by loans from the Royal Bank of Edinburgh, But in 2009, RBE was bailed out by the government. Thus Securitavan is, by extension, a nationalised concern, owned by the state.

"The three MPs we saw at Tebloev's party - Lionel Edgeware, Herbert McLellan and Charles Inwood - are directors of and lobbyists for Securitavan. We've just spoken to the Chair of the Electoral Commission and it turns out that the company's going to be bringing Presiding Officers and their ballot boxes to the count centres in three hundred and forty-five constituencies tonight, with Presiding Officers from single wards sharing a ride. There's no cost to the taxpayer – it's supposedly for the publicity."

"Their plan tonight is simply to provide the transport," Fleming said. "They have thirty-five branches spread out around the country from which vans are set to leave in just under forty minutes, so you can appreciate the near impossibility of stopping them now. Tomorrow they'll anonymously tip off the police and the press that the ballot boxes have been compromised and counterfeit votes swapped for real ones. Raids on Securitavan compounds will reveal hundreds of thousands of marked, crossed ballot papers, concealed behind ceiling panels. Some ballot papers will probably turn up in rubbish tips, rivers, and so on.

"The obvious question will then be, who's rigged the ballot? Well, Securitavan is run by the state and it's fronted by three long-standing MPs. So the state itself is your answer. The 'why' doesn't matter. The important thing is that the British public come to despair of democracy as it's hitherto been understood. I don't know whether anyone's ever read Ben Goldacre's, 'The Power of Election Smears'? All the evidence suggests that smears work and corrections only reinforce them. Given that people in this country are already very disillusioned with politics and politicians generally, what do you think they're likely to conclude?"

"The beauty of it is that they're not going to rig the General Election at all," Bronstein said, "because doing so's not within the realms of practicality. But the truth is irrelevant. What matters is what people can be brought to believe."

"They've chosen a very good time to pull something like this off," Gavin said. "After all those leaders' debates on television, lots of people are expecting an unprecedented swing to the Liberal Democrats. But of course we all know the British people aren't like that. The strong likelihood is that the current government and the opposition will come first and second, in whatever order, with Mr Tilden trailing a weak third. Which could set alarm bells ringing in some minds from the outset."

"And the celebrities are merely there to tie up the police force while this is going on?" Ruby Parker said.

"And the media," Fleming said. "But it's longer-term than that. Tomorrow, we're likely to end up with a hung parliament. The next government will probably be a coalition, with an inherently weakened authority. Add to that the notion that this government – however it pans out – will be thought to have triumphed by subterfuge and you'll imagine it may be disposed to curry popular approval in any way it can. Of course it'll be the kind of government that listens carefully to celebrities. And if the celebrities are merely the puppets of - "

"But it won't get that far, surely?" Marcie said. "The Prime Minister will simply call another election, won't he?"

"Not necessarily," said Miss Demure. "The difficulty of forming a workable coalition at all may persuade him he's unlikely to get a second bite of the cherry."

"But surely the Queen will tell him he has to?"

"The damage will have been done," Fleming said. "Firstly, no one will know quite how the election was rigged. A proportion of the energies of the police will be devoted to solving the riddle for years to come. Secondly, however, if you can do it once, you can probably do it again, this time covering your mistakes. It's all about undermining faith in an institution."

"And of course, the longer it all goes on, the more juddery the City's likely to get," Bronstein said. "The pound could crash within a fortnight if all the signals are bad. We all know what wusses stockbrokers are."

"Any idea yet who it is we're dealing with?" Miss Demure said.

"We hope to discover that very soon," Bronstein replied.

"What about Edgeware? Will he know?"

"We doubt he and his parliamentary colleagues have the faintest conception of what they're involved in," Fleming said. "Edgeware's a decent enough fellow, though he can be a bit bullish. In any case, everything's set down ship-shape in the Register of Members' Interests."

Ruby Parker cupped her face in both hands and squeezed. "I hope to God you have a plan. Because I haven't."

"Surely, it's obvious," Miss Demure said. "We need the help of the army."

"Except that the DSF isn't interested."

"Go over his head, then."

"Oh, would that it were that simple!"

"Ladies, please," Bronstein said.

They looked at him.

"You asked if I had a plan," he said. "I've already put it into operation. It's been unfolding since the moment you walked in here."

"It had better be good, then," Ruby Parker said.

"When I first joined this outfit, you told me there was a CIA substation on Canary Wharf. So I gave them a buzz.

Turns out that under the 1951 NATO Status of Forces Agreement there are nearly fifteen thousand US troops at RAF bases round the country. They can be deployed to stop vans leaving compounds at the drop of a hat."

"What's the catch?"

"What do you mean, 'catch'? What happened to the Special Relationship?"

"'The reason for having diplomatic relations is not to confer a compliment, but to secure a convenience'. Winston Churchill."

"Yeah, well Winston Churchill's not here. All you've got to do is go to Canary Wharf and authorise it in person. Gavin's agreed to drive you – and you too, Miss Demure – and once they've confirmed that you are who you say you are and you want what I've told them you do, they'll move heaven and earth to make tonight's election as dull and uneventful as any other. Here." He held out an envelope.

Ruby Parker took it. "What is it?"

"It's a sealed set of authorisation codes. Only to be opened by the Section CIA Chief in your presence. It proves I sent you."

"And what about you?" Miss Demure said. "What are you going to be doing while we're on our way over there?"

"We're going up to Bedford by helicopter. It's a long time since we heard from Orlov and I'm getting jumpy. I'm assuming it's okay for us to take Marcie? We'll look after her."

Miss Demure smiled. "I think you'll find she's perfectly capable of looking after herself nowadays. Shall we go, Ruby?"

Gavin went to the yard to pick up one of the fleet cars and drove round to the front of the building, where the women waited for him under two black umbrellas. The sun was setting now and more street lights were coming on. It rained a thin drizzle carried by wafts of cold air from the river.

The women got onto the back seat.

"This is probably the most humiliating thing I've ever had to do," Ruby Parker said. "I'm not even sure how it's going to look in the morning."

"I expect the PM will be very grateful," Miss Demure replied. "You'll have saved the country."

"Correction, the Americans will have saved the country. And don't think Mr President won't milk it for all it's worth. It's not just third world democracies he's propping up now, it's us. We'll be an international laughing stock."

"Tush, we don't call it 'the third world' any more."

"He'll simply ooze schadenfreude."

"Why not just let events take their course if you feel so strongly?"

"Because whatever else the Americans may be, they're still our friends. Nobody likes it when their friends laugh at them, but sometimes it's a price worth paying. We don't know what these Russians are like."

Miss Demure smiled. "And yet there's that remark of Bismarck's: 'The secret of politics? Make a good treaty with Russia'."

"Times have moved on. Neither of us is that old."

"I still don't understand why you can't go over the DSF's head."

"Because if I ring a bloody Field Marshal, the first thing he'll want to know is why I haven't rung the Home Office, then when I explain that the DSF isn't interested, he'll put the phone down. It's not about the country's interests, it never is. It's about the chain of responsibility. So long as everyone knows the buck stops with the DSF, they'll cry off. It might be different if he was popular, but he isn't."

"Ruby, if the buck stops with the DSF, I honestly think you should just file your report and go to bed."

"Don't think I haven't considered it."

"And?"

"Both my parents came to this country from Montserrat in 1956. I've never felt the slightest affection for Montserrat or the slightest inclination to visit it, although of course I've nothing against the place. All my affection is invested in this country. Every last bit. Don't you see? I can't bear to see it sink."

"Even at the expense of the profession whose exercise is your sole means of expressing that sentiment? That's absurd, Ruby. This is absurd." She took her mobile out. "I'm going to ring Field Marshal Willoughby."

"You've got Field Marshal Willoughby in your address book?"

"It was after tea at the Dorchester. He insisted. I'd rather not talk about it right now but he owes me a favour."

She pressed 'call' and waited and frowned.

She pressed 'end'. "Damn and blast it, what's the point of giving a girl your number if you're going to turn the thing off just when she needs you most? Don't despair, all is not lost yet. Here … yes, General Sir Steven Polkinghorne. Before you ask, I met him at Farnborough air show."

"He's retired, isn't he?"

"He still wields considerable influence. And beggars can't be choosers."

"We're clutching at straws."

Miss Demure listened, then removed the phone from her ear and glared at it as if it had spat at her. "Hell's teeth, no such number." She put it back in her bag. "To be fair, he did strike me as rather a technophobe. 'May I have your cellular mobile telephone number, my dear' probably speaks for itself."

"It looks like we're still going cap in hand to the CIA then. Thank you for trying, though."

"I don't know Lieutenant Bronstein very well. Is it possible he manipulated this case to put us in the power of the United States?"

"I'm a pretty good judge of character, Celia. I'm sure he wouldn't do anything like that."

"Er, have you noticed anything unusual?"

"We're certainly taking the long way round. Gavin, what's going on?"

"Diversion, ma'am," Gavin said. "Don't worry, we're there now."

"'There'? Where?"

But they knew where they were, and it wasn't where they were supposed to be. This was a side road near Covent Garden. Gavin got out and opened the door for Ruby Parker then Miss Demure.

"I hope you're not thinking of killing us, Gavin," Miss Demure said, "because this is a public place and I have a very loud scream."

"Don't be silly, Celia," Ruby Parker said. "If Gavin was going to kill us he wouldn't have brought us to Covent Garden. I'll only ask you one more time, Gavin: what is going on?"

Gavin walked up some steps and opened a glass door. A stocky, tanned man in a sports jacket skipped down into the street and walked uncertainly up to the two women. "I, er ..."

"Mr Henshall," Gavin said, "may I present Jill Abramson and Susan Edgerley, the Managing News Editor and the Assistant Managing Editor, respectively, of *The New York Times*. Jill, Susan: this is Ross Henshall, General Secretary of Britain's largest union, Unite."

Henshall broke into a smile. "Welcome to our headquarters. We've got another property in Holborn, but I understand this one's more convenient. I got Mr Bronstein's fax showing the location of Securitavan's depots. We've parked an articulated lorry across the entrance of every one, as per your request. Or a container where we feel they might be awkward. No one'll be leaving or entering any of them any time soon, believe me."

It took Ruby Parker an entire breath and an inhalation to digest this. She beamed. "Mr Henshall, I really don't know how to … "

Henshall lowered his voice. "I don't know why you want this, but as Mr Bronstein said, mine not to reason why. And it certainly suits our purposes. It's just ... about those photos …"

Ruby Parker nodded. "Rest assured, that is one story we will never run. And nor will anyone else, you have my word."

"Come this way," Mr Henshall said. "I'll show you our command centre. We can follow the chaos we're causing on Twitter. Do either of you drink beer, by the way?"

"We both love beer," Miss Demure said.

Gavin was holding out an envelope to Ruby Parker. "You forgot Lieutenant Bronstein's letter, ma'am."

She tore it open and smiled.

"What does it say?" Miss Demure asked.

"It says, 'I don't know anything about the CIA'."

Chapter 29: Burning Rubber

"Burn the vans," Kramski said bitterly. "It's over."

Twenty Ford Transits stood wedged in the compound forecourt unable to exit. Incoming call after call said the same was happening at Securitavan branches across the UK. As far as he knew, not one had embarked. All that was left now was to get the men away and destroy as much evidence as possible. A helicopter roared overhead and hovered. It looked to be landing somewhere nearby.

"There's a crowd on its way," Rogozin said, wiping his hands.

"Close the gates and lock them with the chain," Kramski said. "Get the men through the fire exit and tell them to make for the ports. I'll contact Tebloev. Keep your phone about you."

"What about the account books?"

"I'll make sure they're destroyed."

"What about Orlov? You still going to spare him?"

"That was before."

A stench of petrol hit them thick as a rug. A whoosh accompanied a billow of flame from warehouse six.

"Make sure it spreads," Kramski said. "Wait till the men are all out then torch the fuel supplies."

"You're leaving?"

"Not until after you, old friend. A captain doesn't leave a sinking ship till all his men are accounted for. Now let's get busy."

The helicopter touched down in a cul de sac two streets away from its objective. Bronstein was first out, followed by Fleming and Marcie, then it roared away as children waved. It was dark now, but they could see the blaze where they were headed.

They ran as fast as they could to the compound. An orange shipping container was parked across the entrance, but there was no sign of the lorry that must have brought it. The gates were chained and topped with razor spikes and behind them, twenty white vans stood abandoned, as if a Vesuvius had petrified them going about their daily business. Six warehouses flared like furnaces. A crowd was gathering and sirens blared in the distance.

"Is there any other way in?" Bronstein said.

"Not that I remember seeing," Fleming said. "But there must be. At the very least, a fire exit."

"They'll all be abandoning ship then. Not that there's much we can do. In any case, we're here to rescue Orlov, not make arrests."

"I don't think we're authorised to make arrests, anyway."

A panda car pulled up and two policemen jogged over, jabbing torches. "Move away, please. *Right now, move away.*"

"We're with MI6," Bronstein said, showing his card. "Radio my security number over to base and they'll confirm. Do you know where there's another exit to the compound?"

Fleming scrutinised his mobile. "From the satellite, it looks like there's one on the opposite side."

"I - I think that's right," the policeman said.

"We need an armed response unit as soon as you can. Then get as many men over there as you can and arrest anything that comes out. It's urgent, code one."

"What's code one?" Marcie whispered, when the policeman was on his radio.

"No idea."

"I've a plan for how we can get in," she said.

Bronstein nodded. "Have you got your gun, by the way?"

"In my pocket."

"You know how to use it? We should have gone through this in the helicopter, but - "

"I've seen how it works in films, Lieutenant Bronstein. You point the barrelly thing and pull the triggery thing."

He smiled. "So what's your big plan, wise guy?"

"There's a gap in the gates. In the middle."

"And you think you're going to squeeze through, yeah? It's too narrow."

Fleming nodded. "Actually, I can see what she means. If we both push, we might be able to increase the width, and she might just be able to make it."

Bronstein laughed. "Then what? We'll have locked her in the den with the lions."

"I'll hotwire the van at the front and drive it against the gate until the chain snaps," she said.

"You know how to hotwire a van?"

"I've got a criminal record," she replied. "I know how to do anything evil."

Bronstein thought for a minute against the sound of muffled explosions only yards away. "The fire's spreading fast. It'll eat that front van up in a flash and you might burn to death inside the cabin. I don't want that on my conscience."

"Then what's *your* proposal?" she said.

He sighed. He hadn't one. "You'd better be quick. If one of us two slips when you're halfway through you'll be snapped in two from crotch to forehead. And that's before you burn to death in the cabin. You up for this, Fleming? She's your girlfriend."

"She doesn't belong to me," Fleming said.

Marcie stamped her foot. "We're wasting time! Colonel Orlov's going to fry if we don't hurry up! Assuming he's even alive!"

The two men went to the gates. They were wide enough from latch to pivot to make Marcie's plan credible, but they were already hot to the touch. "On count of three," Fleming said. "One, two, three."

At first it looked like they were making no headway at all. Then a gang of teenage boys in hoodies came over and started laughing.

"What are you waiting for, you dorks!" Marcie screamed. *"Come over here and get pushing!"*

The boys shuffled forward looking cowed and started to push. She inserted herself into the slot.

"Harder!" she shouted, then she fell through with a laugh. "I'm inside! I'm inside! Thanks, boys!"

"Get away from the van!" Bronstein yelled as she went to yank the door open. "Shit, it's on fire! Now what?"

The seats were burning. Bronstein realised that of course they were going to go up even faster than he'd thought with all that crumpled paper inside. They were no more than tinderboxes on wheels. He'd been an idiot.

"I tried my best!" Marcie shouted. She blew them a kiss and ran into the compound.

"Where's she gone?" Fleming said.

"Does she even know how to hotwire a van?"

Fleming held his head in his hands. "She'd have tried. We could have told her what to do."

"What's her criminal record in?"

"Fighting, I believe. I don't even think she's much good."

"We'd better find another entrance before they jump her."

A fire engine screeched to a stop. Four men leapt out and started ordering people to stand back.

"Talk about the cavalry!" Bronstein said. He ran over. "Guys, *guys!* I'm with MI6. How long will it take you to cut a hole in that fence?"

The Station Officer climbed back into his cabin and flicked some switches. "About ten seconds, mate. First thing we're going to do. Now stand right back if you wouldn't mind, please."

As far as Marcie could tell, there was no one left in the compound, which was a good job because a girl would probably stand out a mile. She guessed they didn't have an equal opportunities policy.

A narrow gate right on the other side of the forecourt swung on its hinges. That was probably where they'd all gone. The warehouses growled like open kilns and blasts inside shook the metal walls on their rivets. If Orlov was in one of those, she was wasting her time.

She checked her gun and took it out and tried to fire it. Nothing. That must mean she hadn't released the safety catch, the oldest cliché in the world.

She looked for it. Then realised she wouldn't know it if it sprang back and snapped her fingers off. Some sort of hook?

She didn't have time now. Anyway, if she needed a gun, Miss Demure would have told her how to use one. She put it in her pocket just in case she had to bluff or throw it at someone.

Assuming he wasn't dead, where would they have put him?

There was an office-block, behind some of the vans. But no lights on and no signs of life.

And yet it was as good a place to start looking as any. She had no idea where else they could have taken him.

Kramski hurled six sealed bottles of petrol at the entrance to buy a few extra minutes. He went behind the office block and slit a gap in the fence wide enough to fit through, then pulled it together and smoothed it so it wasn't visible unless you came looking for it. He went to the gate he'd just ordered Rogozin out of, locked it and set a fire going outside with another bottle of fuel and a match.

He looked about himself. It had been a bold idea and it had almost worked. But it was merely one battle and every campaign had its Sevastopols. It was time to burn the account books and kill Orlov. Not something he was looking forward to.

He swung open the door to the office block and mounted the stairs at a walk. He knew from experience not to call on his reserves of adrenalin by over-exerting himself prematurely. It had been a long day and, in a few moments, once he prised that gap in the fence apart, he was going to need every ounce of energy his body could muster.

He threw the door open. Orlov sat in the darkness with one side of his face bathed in the ghastly light of the burning vans outside. He turned to face Kramski and smiled.

"You said you were descended from a Russian nobleman. That wouldn't be Count Rostopchin, by any chance?"

"Very funny, Colonel. You probably know why I'm here."

"And yet I thought you weren't a natural killer."

"I don't want you to burn to death, which is what will happen if I abandon you. If I untie you, you'll try to overpower me. I killed your colleague and his girlfriend because they presented an obstacle. I'm going to kill you out of kindness. It's far more of a reparation than a continuation. Have you any preference as to the manner?"

He was suddenly aware of a movement in the room – not just a stirring but a looming up of a substantial shape. From behind the desk. A young woman stood up with hatred in her eyes. Who - ?

He went for his gun, but she leapt over the desk and kicked his hand, then his thigh, then his shoulder. He fell backwards against the door and recovered and lunged at her with a chop. She evaded it as he expected, but she also evaded the stab from his right with which he'd hoped to gain the advantage. He rolled over and emerged by the desk and swept her feet from under her with a scything kick.

She fell expertly and kicked Orlov's chair so it tumbled on top of him. As he cast it aside, her boot smashed into his jaw and he felt his teeth dislodge.

He spluttered blood. His energy was ebbing fast. There was only one way he was going to win. It had to be one apocalyptic burst, like he'd been shown in training. He sprang to his feet and aimed his best kicks and punches at her as fast and obliquely as he could, but he still couldn't get through.

Change tactics again. His fist. Concentrate all his weight into one blow – shatter her defences by sheer brute power.

But in the small time he took to load the bolt, she kicked his solar plexus so hard he felt the skin tear and his soles leave the floor. The desk behind him half-broke his fall, but she came at him with the chair again, and almost before he had time to register the fact, she thrust him back-first through the window. He tried to grab the frame but realised with horror that it was too late. His fingers clutched empty space and, accompanied by a million shards of glass, he descended into the cold black.

It was no longer about waiting till the fire crew cut a hole through the fence. Not when someone was hurling Molotov cocktails from inside the compound. News crews arrived and unloaded cameras and presenters from vans.

"Come on," Bronstein said. "There must be another way in."

Fleming nodded. "Let's go round to the rear exit. The police must have got there now."

They followed the fence round its course, cutting through back gardens and a corner shop car park until they came to the back gate. The patch of ground around it was burning, but a crowd of police officers - some armed - looked as if they had it under control.

"*Sir!*" Fleming called.

Bronstein turned. Fleming was holding open a six foot slit in the wire.

"How the hell did you do that?" he said.

"I found it like this."

Bronstein squeezed through and Fleming motioned for the police officers to follow. They took out their guns. They heard two shots in rapid succession from somewhere.

"Did you hear that?" Fleming said.

"There's someone still in here."

"Unless it's Marcie?"

"Even then, she must be shooting at someone."

Fleming indicated the office block. "I think that's the nerve centre. If either of them is still in here anywhere, that'll be where."

"It's where those shots came from, I think."

They advanced crouching and paused to converge on the crumpled body before the front door. Kramski. Bronstein peremptorily felt his pulse. "Dead."

They heard an ear-splitting scream from upstairs.

"*Marcie!*" Fleming yelled.

They charged upstairs and threw the door open and swept the room with their guns. Orlov sat on the ground next to Marcie. To one side of him stood an upturned chair swathed in ropes.

"It's okay, it's okay!" Marcie yelled. "I kicked a guy through the window and dislocated my hip, that's all. We've just put it back in." She rubbed her side and grimaced. "Whoo, man. Never again."

"We thought we heard shooting," Bronstein said.

"I shot through the Colonel's ropes," she said. "Lovely to see you fellows."

Orlov turned to her. "I don't think I've ever seen anyone fight like that. Man or woman."

She beamed. "I ... I ..."

They waited to hear her speech. But it never came. She stood there with her mouth open looking dazed and disorientated.

Bronstein put his gun away. "Yeah, well, can't stand here gossiping all day."

"Are you okay to walk?" Orlov asked her.

She nodded. Fleming gave her his arm for support. They descended the stairs in silence.

The fire brigade looked as if they were starting to get the blaze under control. The night sky was a shimmering mixture of reds and blacks. Marcie's phone beeped a text. She took it out.

22.52 BST. Houghton and Sunderland South. Labour hold.

Chapter 30: Hung Parliament

In an upstairs office hastily tidied to accommodate two transatlantic VIPs, Ross Henshall and five of his staff sat with Miss Demure, Ruby Parker and Gavin watching the election results come in. The chaos of the Unite blockade had occupied newsreaders for an hour, then it became clear the election was going to proceed as it always did, with Presiding Officers making their way to the count centres by their own means. Then the fire in Bedford. At ten-fifty, the first results began to arrive and the celebrities were wheeled out in their best clothes to town halls, campaign headquarters and TV studios.

At two in the morning, all channels switched to Hertfordshire South West. The Returning Officer, a woman in her late fifties in a trouser suit, stood on a town hall stage before a microphone, with the candidates lined up behind her looking impassive. She read out the results in alphabetical order. There were jeers for the BNP candidate then mounting cheers and applause and she ended by saying:

"And I hereby declare that the said Anthony Hartley-Brown is elected to serve as Member of Parliament for this constituency."

The cheers reached a crescendo. The other candidates looked glum. Sir Anthony came forward and thanked the Returning Officer and her team then the police, and the screen cut back to the studio where David Dimbleby sat looking impassive.

"Not unexpected there for Hertfordshire South West. A safe Conservative seat since it was created in 1950. We'll do a little more analysis in a moment, see again how the country's shaping up, but, er, right now I believe we're about to get the result for Bolton North East. Adam."

"I guess we're looking at a hung parliament," Henshall said.

"It's what most of the newspapers have been predicting," Miss Demure remarked, to break the silence.

More silence. Ruby Parker stood up. "I think we'd better be leaving now, Mr Henshall. Thank you again for such an enjoyable evening."

"You sure you won't have some more Earl Grey? Or another shandy?"

"We've a plane to catch," Gavin said. "And a meeting with Anna Wintour to discuss how we Brits are going to conquer New York."

"It's amazing how they seem to like the English accent over there," Henshall said. "I've never understood that. But I suppose the grass is always greener."

When Ruby Parker left 35 King Street, she got Gavin to drop Miss Demure off at home then went straight back to Thames House. Mahtab met her in reception. Ten of Kramski's men, she reported, had been captured en route to the coast.

"Where are they?"

"They're bringing them to Waterloo Bridge," Mahtab said.

"Assemble an interrogation team. I shouldn't think we'll get anything out of them, but we have to try. Keep me informed."

She collected a folder of documents, photocopied them and put them in a briefcase. She dismissed Gavin and called Reception to provide a driver to take her to Hertford. She gambled that neither Joy nor Sir Anthony would be sleeping until all the results were declared – probably not till well after the working day began.

She arrived outside Mannersby at 5am. It was well lit and crowded with cars of all makes and conditions. Inside a party was obviously in progress, but there was very little noise, just gentle strings, and heads and shoulders with glasses of champagne, framed in illuminated casements. She rang the doorbell and waited.

A middle-aged balding man in a plum waistcoat and smart black trousers answered. "Good morning, madam. How can I help?"

She showed her card. "I'm here to see Sir Anthony and Joy Hartley-Brown about a personal matter. I'd like speak to them in private, please, at their discretion. I'm happy to wait if they're busy, but I need to be back in London by eight."

He took her to the study and asked her to sit down, closing the doors on her as he left. A moment later, Sir Anthony entered, his expression a blend of anxiety and indignation.

"My name's Ruby Parker," she said. "I'm - "

"Yes, yes, I know who you are. I used to be Shadow Foreign Secretary. What's the matter? Has there been some sort of irregularity? Because I'm guessing if there has it must be pretty serious - "

The door opened again and a small woman in a dressing gown and a hairnet entered with bare feet and sleepy eyes. She looked indignantly from Sir Anthony to Ruby Parker and back again. "Are you going to introduce us then, Anthony, or not?" she said, at last.

"Very well, this is my wife, Joy. Joy this is Ruby Parker, head of MI5, or one of them. Now look here, Ms Parker, we're in the middle of a quiet celebration here and I can assure that if there have been cock-ups of any kind - "

"It's about your son, Jonathan."

Sir Anthony took a step back as if he'd been burned. Joy let out a whimper and seemed to shrink in the act of sitting down.

"Wh – what about him?" Joy croaked. Sir Anthony put his arm around her.

"I'm here to talk to you about the manner of his death. I need you to listen very carefully, and I won't beat about the bush. I happen to know you're labouring under a serious misapprehension."

Sir Anthony looked at the carpet. "Go ahead, then."

Ruby Parker drew herself up. "I might as well tell you everything. Jonathan wasn't working for the Met when he died, he was working for MI5, spearheading an investigation into an attempt by foreign nationals to rig tonight's election. For the usual reasons we had to conduct that investigation in secret. He was murdered in an attempt to save the life of Jilly Bestwick and to pass critical information about the criminals' agenda to the proper authorities.

"The killer worked hard to create the false impression that Jonathan killed Miss Bestwick and Mr Cruse, then committed suicide, but every scrap of forensic evidence – described in detail in the documents in that briefcase, should you have difficulty believing me – shows that none of that is possible. In short, he was framed by the perpetrator to stall the enquiry.

"Because publication of the bare facts of his death would have led the media to the conclusion the murderer wished it to reach, MI5 chose to suppress them with a fabricated report that he died in a car chase. We didn't have much time to consider the details, but we wanted to convey the notion that he died obeying the call of duty - although in fact his actions went far beyond that. Whatever you may think you know to the contrary, he behaved with exemplary courage.

"In a recent conversation I had with your daughter, Marciella - whom Jonathan recommended to us as a recruit - it came to my attention that you'd succumbed to the murderer's deception after a visit to Beachy Head Chaplaincy. I can only say that I am very, very sorry for the distress this must have caused. I came here almost as soon as I found out."

Joy stood up and looked for a moment as if she was going to have a seizure. Then she went to the mantelpiece where five portrait photographs of the family stood in a row. Jonathan's had been turned to the wall slightly. She picked it up, trembling, and looked at it. She hugged it. Then she looked at it again, as if she were seeing it anew, and left the room.

Sir Anthony looked thunderstruck. His expression hadn't changed since Ruby Parker began speaking. "I would – I'd - "

Joy screamed.

"Could – could you come back tomorrow?" Sir Anthony said. "We – I'm sure my wife – and I – we'd like to ask …"

"I'm at your disposal."

"I'd better go and see Joy."

Ruby Parker left the briefcase on the table and went to her car. As she was driven away, she saw the couple on the grass. Joy knelt in the mud with her head on the soil, clutching the photograph and rocking. Sir Anthony was trying to comfort her. The guests emerged onto the front steps with expressions of consternation.

The man in the plum waistcoat ran out at speed.

Marcie took a taxi to Hertford to be with her father, then on to London as soon as she heard the result. Bronstein and Fleming went straight back to London and got off the train at King's Cross.

"Fancy a drink before we turn in?" Fleming said. "There won't be any pubs open now, but there should be a few clubs."

Bronstein remembered Nichole. "It's a great thought, Nick, but I think I'd better be getting home. I'm beat."

"Sure?"

He remembered Nichole's grandma. "On the other hand, why not?"

They drank two pints of Theakston at *Madrigals*, while people hoorayed the election results on large screen TVs, booing the BNP and anyone well-known. This was the most glamorous election anyone had ever seen, with celebrities popping out all over the country and rumours of assassinations abounding. At ten past one, Soraya from Fully Magic Coal Tar Lounge fired a cork from a pop-gun at the Independent candidate for Hastings and Rye and was wrestled to the ground by policemen with Tasers. Ten minutes later there was another deafening cheer.

"What's happened now?" Bronstein said.

"The Greens have just won a seat. Somewhere in Brighton."

"When will Marcie's old man be on?"

"Could be any time. Depending on how long it takes to count."

"Will they put it on YouTube afterwards?"

Fleming laughed. "I think YouTube has to draw the line somewhere."

They drank for a few moments.

Fleming sighed. "She's going to leave me, you know."

"I hear her heart's set on Afghanistan. What's she want to go there for?"

"I don't know. I wish she loved me a bit more. But she doesn't."

"It's probably more complex than that."

"Maybe."

"In my experience, some people feel they've got to prove themselves. You never know why. It's no use persuading them they don't have to either. You've just got to let them get it out of their system and ... and wait."

"Have you got a wife or girlfriend?"

"My mum keeps pestering me to get hitched, but luckily me and Kurt Russell escaped from New York. It's easier to keep a low profile here. I've only got to speak to her twice a day."

"So it's only a matter of time, eh?"

"She's a very determined lady."

They parted just after the appearance of Hertforshire South West, and Bronstein walked home. Nichole and her grandma were probably in bed by now, but they might just be the kind who liked to watch the results district by district. He hoped not. He was tired.

The sky was cloudless but there was no moon he could see. Fireworks went off in the distance. He climbed the stairs to his flat and couldn't help noticing that the closer he came, the stronger the smell of cooking and perfume. He hoped to God they hadn't found out, but he had a feeling Nichole's grandma was the sort of woman from whom nothing was secret. She'd probably been through his mail.

He opened the door to find the flat full of candles. Nichole and her grandma were dressed in expensive skirts and full make-up. Nichole's hair was black. They stood up when he came in and looked at him with an admiration bordering on awe. It was the same look he'd seen a thousand times before. It was one reason he'd crossed the Atlantic.

"I'd have brought some flowers if I'd known you'd be up," he said.

"Nichole cooked you a meal," the grandma said. "This is her natural hair colour, what do you think? We've tidied your flat a bit, not that that's a criticism, it isn't. Nichole, *ainikle*, go and get the casserole out of the oven. I spoke to your mother on the phone, David, I hope you don't mind. It rang, I was going to ignore it, but she left a message on the answer phone. She sounded so worried, poor thing. I told her about you and Nichole, I hope you don't mind. Not that you're getting married or anything, I didn't tell her that. Obviously."

Bronstein took his coat off and sat down. "I don't suppose she told you anything about my father?"

"Now why would that make any difference if she had?"

"So she did?"

"Look, Nichole's last boyfriend, he was a *nebbish*. All the time she was missing, he was round at mine asking, have you seen her, have you seen her. In the end I said, Why don't you cast one of your spells and find her yourself, you *shmuck*? She's much better off with you. And now we know your father's a rabbi, my mind's at rest. And not just any rabbi."

"No."

"There can't be many rabbis who make two hundred men burst into songs of praise when they enter the synagogue. And they say that when Rev Jacob Bronstein goes back to Israel, that will be the beginning of the Messianic age. Of course, I'm only an old woman - "

"Grandma, leave it," Nichole said. "Please, just shut up."

There was a long silence.

"Can't you see you're embarrassing him? This is exactly why I left home in the first place. You don't know when to stop."

"I'll just go to bed, shall I?" her grandma said.

"That might be a good idea," Nichole said. "Yes."

"Without any supper?"

"You could have had the bloody casserole at ten o'clock. That's when it was ready."

The grandma retracted into her shell then peeped out as if she might still get her feelers bitten off. They expected her to mutter something about wanting to watch the election.

"I just wanted to stay up and see David," she said.

Nichole melted and hugged her. "I'm sorry, I'm sorry. You're just so ... I don't know what the bloody Yiddish is. *Full on*. I don't need a matchmaker. I need a walk. The casserole's in the oven. Eat it up and get some sleep."

"Where are you going?" her grandma said.

"Just - out. To get some air."

Bronstein met her as she opened the door. "Mind if I tag along?"

She looked at him, her eyes searching.

"I've run three and a half thousand miles to get air," he said. "I know how it feels, believe me."

"What about the casserole?"

"Have you eaten yet?"

"No."

"I've got some Tupperware," he said. "We could go on the roof for a picnic and watch the fireworks. And you could point out the sights. And I could show you the constellations and if it doesn't get too cold we could watch the sun come up – it won't be long now - and listen to the birds and we can guess their names … I mean, if you like that sort of thing."

She swallowed, smiled and nodded. "That sounds really nice, yes."

Chapter 31: One Out, One In

A black Kaliningrad BMW pulled up in the forecourt of Thames House. Four SVR agents in suits stepped out and stood to attention in the early morning sunshine, waiting. Orlov shook hands with Fleming, hugged Marcie and shook hands with Bronstein.

"We *will* meet again," he said.

He lowered himself onto the back seat. The secret servicemen got in around him and they drove off. Marcie cried.

Ruby Parker had already said farewell. She was in Hertfordshire for her second meeting with Joy and Sir Anthony when he left. She arrived back at her desk two hours later, receiving two unconnected pieces of news - that his departure had gone as planned and that the DSF had resigned - without emotion. She sent for Bronstein and Fleming.

"Close the door behind you," she told Fleming. "And sit down, both of you. We'll regard this conversation as your debrief then I'm going to set you to work on something else. Feel free to ask any questions."

"What's wrong?" Bronstein said.

"Nothing. Don't be impertinent."

"We're not off to a very good start. You just said feel free to ask any questions."

She sighed. "Oh well, use your imagination. I've just lost one of my best men. And it's not as if I've wrung any significant concessions. He's going back to prison with two years remission for what the Kremlin's calling 'good behaviour'. The Russians promised not to torture him to get at what we all agree he knows but isn't telling us. And we've been given an assurance that we'll be able to call on him again if we're ever in desperate need. And that's it. I feel a wretched failure."

Fleming put his hands together. "Once the Russians realised he was determined to come home, they knew they didn't have to negotiate. And it wasn't you that gave that away."

"It always amazes me," she said bitterly, "that people never feel so attached to their own patch of earth as they do when they're lying face down in the mud."

"Hang on," Bronstein said. "'What we all agree he knows but isn't telling us'? Who 'agrees'?"

"We do with the Russians."

"Oh, come on, it's only in movies that the baddie ties up the good guy and makes a speech about what he's up to and what his motives are. Why should Orlov know anything?"

She smiled. "Why didn't they just kill him immediately? It's only in films that the 'baddie' ties the 'goodie' up first."

"There would have been no reason to kill him," Fleming said. "So long as the vans did their job and the press found the fake ballot papers afterwards."

"Plus he's a Ruski," Bronstein said. "It probably struck them as unpatriotic."

"Look at the facts," Ruby Parker said. "In Marcie's presence, Orlov reminds Kramski he's 'not a natural killer', then quips that he might be descended from Rostopchin, the man who ordered Moscow razed when Napoleon was set to take it. He's undeniably referencing a prior conversation, prompted by immediate stimuli. Now which of these alternatives seems more plausible? One, that he revisited the whole of that conversation in Marcie's presence? Or two, that he revisited two points out of a possible n? Because if it's alternative one, given that she only overheard two seconds' worth of conversation, that makes Marcie ridiculously lucky."

"So what do you think?"

"I think he's told us only what he knows Marcie knows because he realised she'd tell us anyway. Everything else he's concealing. Except one thing, maybe. He's convinced there really is a Constantine Slope. He said it was just a hunch, but I wouldn't be surprised if he got it from Kramski."

"Do you think he's right?"

"I wonder who sent those lawyers to see me on election night. It can't have been Kramski. It wasn't Edgeware, although Edgeware knew they were coming. Looking back, they were more concerned to find Nichole Moore than anything else, and it's difficult to see why that would have exercised Edgeware at that point."

"If Orlov's hiding anything," Bronstein said, "I don't think it can be very important. I remember just before Jonathan made those photomatics. Orlov and I were sitting round talking about whether Jonathan might be falling in love and whether that might compromise his loyalty. And we agreed it wouldn't. Why? Because he knew right from wrong. That simple. And it's the same with Orlov. If he's concealing anything, it'll be something goofy, something to do with Vera Gruchov probably."

"I very much doubt whether we'll hear from that young lady again," Ruby Parker said. "You don't tend to get second chances in Russian politics."

"What about those ten guys who were captured on their way abroad?" Bronstein said. "They coughed anything up yet?"

"No, and I don't expect them to. In many ways, I wish we'd left them alone. We don't even know what to charge them with yet. I never thought I'd be this grateful for the 2006 Terrorism Act."

"Twenty-eight days, right?"

"And even that may not be sufficient. We've got to tread very carefully. If it really is true that they're bound by some madcap belief that they're descended from Russian noblemen, then they're more indispensable to the organisation than if they're just general dogsbodies. It's not going to just abandon them to their fate."

"What's so madcap?" Bronstein said.

"Because everyone's descended from anyone if you're ingenious enough."

"You think their organisation will make an attempt to rescue them?" Fleming said.

"Probably. And I would imagine it'll involve terrorism of some sort. This isn't over yet, believe me. Not by any means."

Bronstein looked at Fleming. Fleming shook his head.

"No further questions, your honour," Bronstein said.

Downstairs, in an office some corridors away from where Bronstein and Fleming worked, a late middle-aged man with a pencil moustache and an immaculate grey suit sat behind a desk. Marcie looked through the documents he handed her one by one: aerial photographs of cities, of mountain strongholds, account books detailing drugs for weapons, movements of suspects between the UK and Pakistan, ordnance survey maps. He was talking as she browsed them.

"… If possible, you notify your contact, who'll give you a time. Your job is to remove the civilians. Occasionally, if the opportunity arises, you might prefer to take some of these chaps out yourself, although only in very rare cases when the risk to your cover is negligible.

"I understand your Pashto is already pretty impressive. You'll be posing as a widow originally from Takhar, related by marriage to one of our operatives and his wife, native Balochistanis. They'll put you up and you'll hone the language and help keep house. You won't do anything for six months, just sit tight and acclimatise. We'll contact you through them when we think you're ready to start, and you'll either confirm or decline. If you decline you'll get more time, no questions asked. They're already involved in the same enterprise, so they'll show you the ropes.

"You'll be working under the Blue Maiden from here on in. The long-term aim of your mission isn't to kill enemy commanders, it's to gain on-the-ground knowledge of the country and its people so you can help train another generation of operatives. We don't want Afghanistan to implode after we've left, like India did for a while. We want people to look back on our time there and think it was worth it. Both our own people and theirs. That may mean tinkering from time to time, post-withdrawal, to keep things on track.

"There are lots of things that can go wrong in an operation like this. Probably more than either of us can imagine. If at any time you feel your cover's about to be blown, get out. We'll bring you back on the next available plane and find something else for you to do. It won't be counted as failure.

"I'd advise you to read *Seven Pillars of Wisdom*. It's a sort of *vade mecum* with the more intelligent class of officers over there. It'll give you a bit of common ground. And Karen Armstrong's *Islam*. They're both in the library on the third floor. And obviously, the standard works on Afghanistan. Vishna at the desk will give you a reading list.

"Don't let anyone talk down to you, regardless of rank. You don't have to salute or call them sir. Look them in the eye at all times. Any questions?"

She shook her head.

"One last thing before you go," he said. "Miss Demure asked me to give you something. She said she'd have shown you how to use it if there had been any more time, but she's sure you'll work it out for yourself."

He put it on the table. It looked like a tiny pair of dumbbells, big enough to fit in the palm.

"What is it?" she asked.

"I believe it's called a Yawara. Japanese, used in various of their martial arts. In the right hands, it can be deadly." He smiled forbearingly. "Not something I've ever considered myself, but I promised I'd pass it on."

At two o'clock the following morning, Ruby Parker was awakened at home by a phone call from the Commissioner of the Metropolitan Police. She listened in horror to what he told her.

She rushed to Thames House in a state of anxiety. She took some letter paper from her desk and wrote on it: 'Information Request: were you in any way involved in the "execution" of ten enemy operatives by firing squad at Waterloo Bridge earlier tonight?'

She sealed it in an envelope and took it upstairs to the receptionist on duty, a sallow young woman with thin hair.

"I'd like you to see this reaches the Blue Maiden as a matter of priority, please," she told her.

Half an hour later she received a reply, bought to her in her office, as she expected, by a man she had never seen before. She tore open the envelope and read the single word, 'Affirmative'.

Chapter 32: Epilogue

In a terraced house with heavy ledges in one of the most sought-after postcodes in London, a Russian émigré sat on a wingback chair and wiped his eyes. He downed another schnapps and crossed himself. Enough time had elapsed. If they were really coming for him, he'd be on the plane back by now.

He didn't know why they weren't. Orlov must have told them by now, surely. Somehow, God willing, though he still hardly dared entertain the thought, he'd acquired a stay of execution ...

An Aeroflot Tupolev carrying five passengers landed at the Bolshoye Savino airport in Perm Krai. A man in handcuffs exited with two officials preceding him and two following, and transferred to a ZiL chauffeured by an FSB officer. Two of the officials who had flown from London sat on the back seat with him, and they drove the hundred and forty miles to Solikamsk Prison together in silence, accompanied by a pair of motorcycles.

When they arrived, the governor explained to the prisoner that he had never officially left. He reminded him of his rights and responsibilities and handed him his chess set. The prisoner removed the lid and took the pieces out, spacing them equally for a full minute until they were all accounted for. He then replaced them unhurriedly, put the box under his arm and was marched back to his cell.

In a churchyard overgrown with daisies, knapweed and hare's-tail grass, a middle-aged woman and a girl in a junior-school uniform laid a wreath on a grave still too fresh for a headstone. They sat on a bench and looked at the hills. They leant into each other and held hands - and clutched.

A US Army helicopter roared over Kandahar. A British soldier stood behind a dusty glass door with a young woman in a burqa. He nodded. She turned and saw them, the wife walking two paces behind her husband. She left the building and crossed the road with composure. The couple immediately flanked her then the man pulled ahead again. The soldier watched them disappear into the crowd.

On the top floor of Thames House, a diminutive black woman in a skirt suit waited with two men and an elderly white woman. Three fighter jets emerged from nowhere and performed a roll over the building at low altitude. The black woman said something about this feeling more like a defeat than a victory, and they returned to their desks.

Big Ben struck eleven. A flock of swans landed on the river and swam for a moment against the current. The sun broke from behind a cloud. On a patch of gravel a mile away, a man in a silver helmet screamed at a line of guards to maintain their swords. Beyond and around him, men and women shopped and pointed at monuments and walked to and from taxis, buses, underground trains. And Francis Walsingham sat on his throne and surveyed his empire.

~ THE KRAMSKI CASE ~

~ JAMES WARD ~

Books by James Ward

General Fiction
The House of Charles Swinter
The Weird Problem of Good
The Bright Fish
Hannah and Soraya's Fully Magic Generation-Y *Snowflake* Road Trip across America

The Original Tales of MI7
Our Woman in Jamaica
The Kramski Case
The Girl from Kandahar
The Vengeance of San Gennaro

The John Mordred Tales of MI7 books
The Eastern Ukraine Question
The Social Magus
Encounter with ISIS
World War O
The New Europeans
Libya Story
Little War in London
The Square Mile Murder
The Ultimate Londoner
Death in a Half Foreign Country
The BBC Hunters
The Seductive Scent of Empire
Humankind 2.0
Ruby Parker's Last Orders

Poetry
The Latest Noel
Metals of the Future

Short Stories
An Evening at the Beach

Philosophy
21st Century Philosophy
A New Theory of Justice and Other Essays

~ JAMES WARD ~

CPSIA information can be obtained
at www.ICGtesting.com
Printed in the USA
LVHW111028240721
693494LV00015BA/906/J